```
Fic                              11358
Gou   Gould, Philip
      Kitty Collins
```

$15.95

DATE		
MAY 29 1990		
JUN 14 1990		
AUG 14 1990		
SEP 22 1990		
NOV 17 1992		
OCT 21 1993		
MAY 30 '95		

11358

```
FRANKSTON DEPOT LIBRARY
TOWN SQUARE SOUTH
P O BOX 213
FRANKSTON, TX
757630000
  02/25/88         15.95

                 529569      02233
```

© THE BAKER & TAYLOR CO.

PROPERTY OF FRANKSTON DEPOT LIBRARY FRANKSTON TX

Kitty Collins

Kitty Collins

A NOVEL

by

PHILIP GOULD

Algonquin Books of Chapel Hill, 1986

Algonquin Books of Chapel Hill
Post Office Box 2225
Chapel Hill, North Carolina 27515-2225

Copyright © 1986 by Philip Gould. All rights reserved.
Printed in the United States of America

The author would like to pay special thanks to Robert Cunniff and Ernest Dyson, who gave generously of their time and vast musical knowledge and whose help and encouragement were invaluable, and to his editor, Louis D. Rubin, Jr.

Lines from "Down in the Depths" by Cole Porter: Copyright © 1936 by Chappell & Co., Inc. Copyright renewed. Assigned to Robert H. Montgomery, Jr., Trustee of the Cole Porter Musical and Literary Property Trusts. Chappell & Co., Inc., Administrator. International copyright secured. All rights reserved. Used by permission.
Lines from "Easy to Love" by Cole Porter: Copyright © 1936 by Chappell & Co., Inc. Copyright renewed. Assigned to Robert H. Montgomery, Jr., Trustee of the Cole Porter Musical and Literary Property Trusts. Chappell & Co., Inc., Administrator. International copyright secured. All rights reserved. Used by permission.
Lines from "The Lady Is a Tramp" by Richard Rodgers and Lorenz Hart: Copyright © 1937 by Chappell & Co., Inc. Copyright renewed. International copyright secured. All rights reserved. Used by permission.
Lines from "Where or When" by Richard Rodgers and Lorenz Hart: Copyright © 1937 by Chappell & Co., Inc. Copyright renewed. International copyright secured. All rights reserved. Used by permission.
Lines from "Georgia on My Mind" by Hoagy Carmichael and Stuart Gorrell: Copyright © 1930 by Peer International Corporation. Copyright renewed by Peer International Corporation. All rights reserved. Used by permission.
Lines from "I'm Old Fashioned" written by Jerome Kern and Johnny Mercer: Copyright © 1942 by T. B. Harms Company. Copyright renewed. (C/o The Welk Music Group, Santa Monica, California 90401.) International copyright secured. All rights reserved. Used by permission.
Lines from "You're the Top" by Cole Porter: Copyright © 1934 (renewed) by Warner Bros. Inc. All rights reserved. Used by permission.
Lines from "Can't You Do a Friend a Favor" by Richard Rodgers and Lorenz Hart: Copyright © 1943 (renewed) by Warner Bros. Inc. All rights reserved. Used by permission.
Lines from "Isn't It a Pity" by George and Ira Gershwin: Copyright © 1932 (renewed) Warner Bros. Inc. All rights reserved. Used by permission.
Lines from "This Time the Dream's on You" by Harold Arlen and Johnny Mercer: Copyright © 1941 (renewed) Warner Bros. Inc. All rights reserved. Used by permission.

ISBN 0-912697-31-8

To Molly

PART I

1

At twenty minutes past three in the afternoon of May 23, 1940, Kitty Collins, who had just turned fourteen, left St. Margaret's parochial school on the North Side of Chicago, where she was in the eighth grade, with two friends named Fran and Alice.

The three girls skipped until they were walking in step. Had they not been carrying textbooks and notebooks they might have linked arms. They began singing in unison, lines and refrains from various popular songs. Kitty, whose command of the melodies and lyrics was greater and whose voice was more confident, led the pace:

> *You're an O'Neill drama*
> *You're Whistler's mama*
> *You're Camembert...*

They walked rapidly, successfully avoiding or deflecting groups of boys and other obstacles until most of the onrush of escaping schoolchildren had dispersed up and down the four directions of the intersection.

At a point when the pavement was otherwise empty and seemed about to stay that way a few minutes, the girl called Fran ran ahead a couple of yards, carrying the Brownie box camera she had been given for her birthday earlier that week, and without needing to be told to wait, Kitty and Alice stopped in their tracks, prepared to pose.

In the focus of the camera, squinting a little in the sunlight and turning on a wide, self-conscious, closemouthed smile, Kitty clutched a looseleaf notebook and four dog-eared textbooks against her narrow chest. A slender girl, a little taller than average, with rather striking long-lashed gray-green eyes and other pretty, assimilated Irish-American features formed from who knows what admixtures of Celtic, Iberian, Norman, Anglo-Saxon, Germanic strains. Long, straight brown hair held back at the part with a small, red velvet bow. Brown and white scuffed saddle shoes, white socks, straight legs. The hem of her serge uniform skirt needed a stitch on one side; the tail of her white middy blouse needed tucking in.

Fran and Alice gone their separate ways, Kitty crossed a vacant lot on a diagonal toward the six-story apartment hotel where she lived with her mother.

A warm, quiet day, a little windy, a little dusty. An "Elevated" train rumbled over the viaduct one block west.

The apartment elevator was out of order. A dangling sign bore that announcement. Kitty climbed the stairs to the fourth floor, not losing much breath, regaining it quickly. No one answered the doorbell, but her mother frequently forgot to latch the door, never set the double lock, if then, until late at night. Kitty simply turned the knob and went inside.

It was one of the second smallest of the furnished "efficiency" apartments. Small living room with a sofa-bed, small bedroom, bathroom, kitchenette in an unscreened alcove. One could see virtually everything at a glance if the bedroom and bathroom doors happened to be open, as they were. Kitty's mother was not there as she sometimes was at this hour. But often she would be at the beauty parlor, occasionally at the racetrack, frequently at the movies. She didn't usually go to Fossbinder's bar and grill until five or later.

Madge Collins never wrote letters (and never received any), rarely left notes. When she did they would be two or three words long: "Buy hamburger." "Call Eileen." "Back at 6."

along the length of the bar past the usual patrons, and into the small area of leatherette-upholstered booths and small tables surrounding a low platform, a stage for Roberta seated at her baby grand.

Roberta was playing slower numbers, "Dancing on the Ceiling" at the moment. Later she would pick up the tempo, still later lower it again until it came time for some rousing finale. Also, she was not expending her resources on any singing yet for such a small crowd. She finished the number, continued with bridges, runs, and flourishes, eyes lowered to the keyboard in deep concentration, eyes raised, too, to look over the audience, see who had just come in the door.

Kitty came up and stood there, out of place in such a setting on the face of it, yet looking as though she belonged.

"Where's your mother, baby?"

"She's sick." Low voice, slightly husky.

"Sick? How sick?"

"I don't know. I mean, you know, stomach, headache."

"She send you out for something?"

"Oh, yeah. To get some aspirin. I just came in to say hello."

"Well, now, don't you think you'd better go get that medicine?"

"Yeah. OK, goodbye."

"Kitty?"

"Um?"

"You sure there's nothing else wrong?"

"Oh, sure. Well goodbye."

"Did you practice any today?"

"At lunchtime."

"Keep at it. Afternoons, too. Next week I want to hear it all the way through."

"OK. Well, g'bye."

As Kitty went out, Roberta was playing "My Romance," one of Kitty's favorites, but then anything Roberta played was one of Kitty's favorites, what she had come to hear, which buoyed her up now, as she walked slowly back to the apartment in the dark. She knew all the words, even of the introductory verse, and sang them to herself on the stairs, in the empty living room, as she opened cans for her dinner.

She found recorded band music on the radio, Artie Shaw, Tommy Dorsey, then managed to do her homework, which happened to be neither difficult nor lengthy that particular day. It helped, too, to know that Roberta was close by. She was used enough to being home alone, that wasn't the problem. Her mind darted from image to image, from one thought to another, never resting, never focusing on any one thing for very long. She had no visible nervous habits. She was neither a nail biter nor a knee jiggler. But several times that evening she sat for a few moments, rather preternaturally still.

At eleven she pulled down and made up the sofa bed as usual, got into pajamas, and fell asleep with the lights and the radio on, and woke at 2 A.M., frightened. The radio hummed faintly; the station had gone off the air. Kitty stiffened and hung on, an ache in her throat, after a while drifted off again, and woke in time for school.

That same afternoon after classes she began to look for a job, began by canvassing every store in the neighborhood that might hire a responsible fourteen-year-old part-time—grocery stores, drug stores, bakeries, cleaners, tailors ...

Initial response was discouraging. If storekeepers wanted anyone they wanted a boy. Still, she could call on only so many people a day after school, and many possibilities were left. Devon Avenue and Sheridan Road north were almost solid storefronts for miles. Broadway, Clark Street the same.

At school, no one suspected anything. Kitty might have seemed a bit subdued, irritable, preoccupied, but it was easy enough to attribute such moods to spring fever, perhaps that time of the month, any number of unremarkable causes.

More than usual, Kitty sometimes found the talk, the concerns, the pranks of her classmates a little silly and childish, but need for companionship drew her into the circle even so. Because she gave the impression of being self-possessed, older, knowing, because she seemed to have no fear of any of the nuns—even though that was partly a front, a protective defense developed piecemeal over the years—she got credit for toughness, sophistication, and was allowed to detach herself from the crowd from time to time, free of criticism or mockery. She was an A-student and was never really disciplined for anything very serious, but she did not parade her grades or suck up to any of the sisters, and it never occurred to anyone to accuse her of being a grind or a goody-goody.

This was a settled neighborhood. All but one of Kitty's classmates had been together since the first or second grade. The other exception had simply arrived a few years before from a neighborhood only a parish away. Kitty alone had come from somewhere else about three years before, had a mysterious past since she was vague about it and told different stories to different people. That, plus certain innuendos overheard from parents about Kitty's mother, set her apart. Had she been homely, unpopular, in any way otherwise strange, she would have suffered for this, might still if she displayed any weakness, vulnerability, but she was street-smart as well as book-smart, and since fourteen-year-old girls usually fought each other not with fists but with words, Kitty could hold her own with any of her peers, had an edge even.

One girl, Rita Curry, had hinted around one day a few months earlier, just to be nasty, while others were listening.

"What does your mother do, Kitty? Tell us what she does," in the insinuating voice Rita had put on, and while the same classmates listened, Kitty had met this challenge head-on with a cold, knowledgeable voice: "I'd keep my mouth shut if I were you, Rita. Just because Eddie Brown's in high school do you think people don't know what you do down in Eddie Brown's basement?"

That Rita Curry, prematurely developed and probably destined to have a messy life, played strip poker and other games with older boys was no big secret, and Rita was bold as brass and a braggart, but not everybody knew, and some only half knew and some only suspected, and Rita retained a certain fear of what her father or other adults might do. And what Kitty had said had never been said on the playground before in front of certain pious, prissy prudes. Rita's hatred for Kitty was boundless, but even though she was bigger, heavier, she was afraid of Kitty now, and Kitty was almost sorry for her, and felt a little mean herself, walked away from the group to get away from that feeling, not really realizing that by walking away like that, by apparently not being interested in staying around to gloat or exchange any more words with Rita, she was dismissing Rita Curry and the incident as being of no real importance, thereby gaining an even more decisive advantage.

But though Kitty was not conscious of the effect she had created by walking away, the gesture of indifference was only a variant of something else she had learned gradually, by accident at first, by observation later, that silence could sometimes be even more effective than a few well-chosen words in maintaining the upper hand. So many people who were unsure of themselves talked too much, too long, and so revealed their insecurity, talked themselves into a hole. They needed either the last word, or some kind of reassurance from the person they were confronting, and that was a mistake. No matter how scared you were, you had to keep your mouth shut, stand straight with your head up, and maintain a level gaze without expression. And Kitty's face could be mobile. As often as not it exploded into animation, into a variety of expressions to illustrate a range of attitudes and emotions. She had been selected to play the lead in the spring play that year partly on the strength of that. So that when she froze her expression it seemed a conscious act of intimidation to those who knew her, yet an affront that being silent and expressionless could not be pinned down and denounced, though angered nuns on rare occasions (not recently) had ordered her to lower her eyes.

It was all in self-defense. Kitty had no lust for power. She simply had more to hide and more to protect than most of her contemporaries, and envied every one of them.

Five days passed. Kitty climbed the stairs to the apartment at six in the evening after still another fruitless search for work. It was the twenty-eighth of May.

Someone struck the door knocker three times.

Kitty remained perfectly still, her heart pounding in her ears.

The knocker banged twice again.

"Kitty, I know you're in there. Open up."

It was Mrs. Pomeroy, the landlady.

Kitty was in her stocking feet. Swiftly she tiptoed into the bathroom and flushed the john. Then she crossed the living room and opened the door.

"Oh, hello, Mrs. Pomeroy. Sorry. I was in the bathroom."

"Where's your mother? I haven't seen her in days."

"She's away on a trip. Her best friend is very sick."

"Where's that?"

"Wisconsin. Milwaukee."

"She shouldn't leave a young girl alone like this. I've half a notion to tell the police."

"I couldn't go with her because of school," Kitty said quickly. "But she'll be back day after tomorrow. She just telephoned about an hour ago."

"I hope she remembers the rent's due on Saturday. She don't always."

"Oh, she does. I've got it now if you need it."

"That suits me," Mrs. Pomeroy said, and set her mouth.

Mrs. Pomeroy came inside a few steps while Kitty went to the sugar bowl. Mrs. Pomeroy brought with her an odor of perspiration, disinfectant, and something else Kitty couldn't identify. She had very white blue-veined legs and wore silk stockings rolled down to her ankles and splayed high-heeled shoes. She removed a receipt book and the stub of a pencil from the pocket of her housedress and wet the pencil lead on her tongue.

Kitty handed over three ten-dollar bills. Mrs. Pomeroy wrote out the receipt and tore it off the pad.

"Be sure and double-lock your door at night until your mother gets back," Mrs. Pomeroy said. She turned and went down the stairs, and Kitty slowly closed the door behind her.

Now she had eighteen dollars left, enough for about two weeks. She had spent seven dollars on food in the past five days.

For five days, Kitty had lived from day to day, hopeful she could find some job that would keep her going, and had shoved any big thoughts about the future to the bottom of her mind. Down there, too, lay the question, would her mother realize she had made a terrible mistake and come back—without Ralph? And for five days Kitty had not cried. She had been tempted at times during her first day or so of being really alone but had stifled the urge. Now she knew that by herself she was helpless, she was too young, had too little money. She knew her mother wasn't coming back and that at fourteen she was never going to find a job.

The dam cracked. Slowly at first. Only a few tears rose and spilled over the side. Then she lost hold and slipped into the release and torment of wracking sobs that seemed to go on so long and so out of control they terrified her. She could not stop. She saw no end to weeping, no end to this darkness, this sorrow, this fear and helplessness.

But she stopped. And now it was dark. She did not turn on any lights. In the bathroom she splashed cold water on her face until it felt less puffed and inflamed. Some threatening illness drained strength from her limbs but she fought it, got out of the bathroom and got herself to the icebox. Sudden bright light when the icebox door was opened. I'm just hungry, she told herself. She ate some cookies with milk and felt better, but she still trembled slightly.

Mrs. Pomeroy couldn't be trusted not to go to the police even now, without waiting to see if Madge Collins would really show up the day after tomorrow. If they put me in some orphanage I'll run away, she told herself, but the thought of even entering through the doors of such a place was paralyzing. The apartment was in darkness, but there was enough light from the window for her to see her way to the front door without bumping into anything.

Kitty told Roberta straight off.
"Baby, you sure?"
"She took all her clothes and things and left some money. Five days ago. She never came back and she isn't going to this time."
"I thought something was wrong. I said to myself, if she doesn't come in by this weekend—you mean you've been living in that place by yourself all this time? Why didn't you tell me sooner?
Kitty shrugged. "I don't know."
She was conscious then that she was still wearing her school uniform and that her face was probably still messed up from crying. She found a comb in her pocket and ran it through her hair, untangling a snarl.

Roberta fished in her handbag, resting on the piano ledge, and came up with a handful of nickels and dimes. She went to the wall beside the bar, fed the jukebox, signaling Bernie at the same time, and spoke to him. Then, as Lionel Hampton's septet of 1937 took over "On the Sunny Side of the Street," she took Kitty by the hand and led her to a rear booth almost always reserved for Roberta's dinner setting. For half a minute or so they listened without speaking to the inspired, swinging lilt of Johnny Hodges' alto sax, the wonderful, lyrical, silvery beat of Hampton, Jess Stacy, Buster Bailey, Allan Reuss, John Kirby, and Cozy Cole behind him. It was the sound of love.

"We can eat together," Roberta said. "Can you handle the special—swiss steak and hash browns?"

"OK. I can pay for..."

"That's all taken care of," Roberta said. "You're my guest."

Erna Fossbinder brought Cokes and poured them without being asked, then sat down herself. Bernie kept glancing over at the booth, frowning, but was just busy enough at the bar not to be able to join them.

"Your mother doesn't have any brothers, sisters, nobody?" Erna asked.

"If she does I don't know where they are. I don't even know what state we came from. She wouldn't ever tell me. I don't have a birth certificate."

"You must have one somewhere," Erna said.

"I never saw one and there's nothing like that in the apartment."

"Your school must have it."

"The school wouldn't keep it," Roberta said.

"But they must have some record."

"Madge Collins could have told them anything. And not enough to be able to locate anybody after all these years. Do you remember coming to Chicago from anywhere?" Roberta asked Kitty. Kitty shook her head from side to side.

"I remember being someplace in Chicago when I was six. I started school here. I remember a few things before that, but I don't know where we were then."

"Eight years at least," Roberta said. "We'd be wasting our time trying to find anybody."

A second bartender came on duty, and Bernie Fossbinder was able to spring himself loose to join the group.

"We've got to report this to the police, let them handle it," he said, sending a thrill of panic through Kitty's heart. She got set to go to the ladies room and then sneak out through the kitchen door. She knew where it was. And then run.

"Why?" Roberta asked. "They won't find her mother, and what if they did?"

"They got homes," Bernie said.

"Listen, I know something about those 'homes.' My ex-husband was stuck in one as a kid. Believe me, they're not homes. She can stay with me, at least for the time being." A moment before she had not been aware she was going to say this, but the more she thought about it the more it seemed a foreordained thing that she was going to do.

Kitty looked at Roberta as though she might be looking at something miraculous. She didn't know what to say.

"I've got the space, lots of it," Roberta said. "She can have her own room."

Bernie Fossbinder started to say something, but held his tongue.

Customers began arriving for dinner. Installed at her piano again in her full-flaired black taffeta skirt and white, rather frilly blouse, Roberta Wilkins warmed her hands together, flexed her fingers. It was a time for swinging songs, "Thou Swell," "This Can't Be Love," "Between the Devil and the Deep Blue Sea," in her rich, cultivated Negro voice, amplified a bit.

Kitty sat and listened, as she always listened to Roberta Wilkins, with rapt, trained attention and the deepest pleasure, but now with a tremendous, exotic new prospect before her. Living with Roberta. Something that had never occurred to her as a possibility. Never.

Many an evening for almost three years, mostly on weekends but on weekday evenings, too, Kitty had sat in the same corner and listened, more than listened—empathized—imagined herself in Roberta's place—while her mother sat at the bar, drinking with one man or another. Between sessions, Roberta would retire to the booth where Kitty was, to refresh herself with a bottle of Bud, give Kitty a hug once in a while. When Kitty was still eleven, Roberta had come to the conclusion the child might well be the most knowledgeable and appreciative member of her audience. Roberta had talked Bernie Fossbinder into including a number of good jazz recordings, and the best vocalists singing the songs of the best composers, among the jukebox selections, but she did not have complete control, and hack work new and old had slipped in, too. What Roberta noticed was that Kitty unerringly responded lovingly to the finest, wrinkled her nose at the second-rate, and identified the good and the weak elements of the music in between.

Kitty had begged Roberta to teach her to play. Just after Kitty's twelfth birthday, and after a certain amount of haggling with Bernie Fossbinder and Madge Collins—both of whom had balked at first—Roberta had arranged for Kitty to take one lesson every Wednesday from 3:45 to 4:45, just before Fossbinder's reopened for business after the post-lunch closure. Roberta didn't charge anything. That sold Madge Collins, along with the possibility Kitty would be learning what could be a marketable skill sometime in the future. Bernie just had to be sweet-talked a little.

"I don't want to hear no kid bangin' on the piano," he had said. "That's out."

"Believe me, she won't bang, she'll play real nice," Roberta had said. "But you won't have to listen to her at all if you do what Erna keeps after you to do—go upstairs and take a nap in the afternoons. One hour a week, Bernie. Just think. Some day when she's famous you can tell everybody where she got started."

There was no piano in the Collins apartment, but there was one in the school auditorium Kitty was allowed to use.

And so Roberta had begun and had seen at once that Kitty not only had the musical sense but also the talent and the drive. She had worked hard from the first day and had made steady progress. In less than a year she was playing well enough to please Bernie Fossbinder who never got around to taking naps after all. What he usually didn't have to hear were the Czerny, Hanon, Clementi, and Cramer scales and exercises Kitty labored over on the school piano, the classical discipline Roberta herself had been taught by her mother, a church organist and piano teacher in Kankakee, Illinois.

Between sets, for its own sake and to keep her occupied, Roberta let Kitty select the jukebox recordings, unless some customer beat her to it, and Kitty ordered up Benny Moten . . . the Rollini brothers . . . a record Roberta had found with a talented young pianist named Pete Weathersby . . . Bunny Berigan . . . Jack Teagarden . . . Kitty had seen a photograph of Jack Teagarden's big, sleepy-eyed clown face, and to her the lustrous sonority of his trombone solos and his relaxed and plain-hearted shout sounded the way he looked—

like some favorite uncle who shows up unexpectedly every now and then, bearing gifts from far away.

Somewhere around midnight, exhausted, Kitty fell asleep, her legs folded beneath her, her long hair turned sideways against the back of the booth, like a moth against a lampshade.

Roberta returned to the piano and launched into her last set of the evening, a dozen songs in about forty minutes, starting with "Them There Eyes," "Liza," "I Know That You Know," played lickety-split, continuing with swingy, medium-tempo numbers—"Blue Skies," "Love Me or Leave Me," "Lullaby of Broadway," "If I Could Be with You"—songs a little slower yet, "Exactly Like You" and "I Found a Million Dollar Baby," still slower, "Don't Blame Me," slower still, "She's Funny That Way," and to close, picked up the tempo again as she segued into "Down in the Depths on the 90th Floor," a favorite of many regular customers. She had sung four of the other songs and she sang this one:

> ... *What's the good of swank*
> *Or cash in the bank galore?*
> *Why even my janitor's wife*
> *Has a perfectly good sex life,*
> *And here I am, facing tomorrow ...*

Kitty awakened long enough for Roberta to lead her to a waiting taxi.

"My stuff," Kitty murmured.

"We'll pick it up tomorrow," Roberta said.

Kitty fell asleep again on the long ride, out of this orbit into the orbit where Roberta Wilkins lived.

2

It seemed to Kitty she had awakened into an enchanted cave. Her own room, in a wide, comfortable bed. Roberta making breakfast in the walk-in kitchen, calling:

"How you want your eggs, baby?"

"Any way you're having them, thank you."

A neat living room reposing quietly in filtered sunlight. Nice furniture, lamps, pictures—Roberta's own, Kitty could tell immediately—framed photographs, upright piano. She fell in love with what was a small, two-bedroom apartment in a large building one block from Wilson Avenue.

And that was the catch.

When they had eaten and Roberta had poured coffee, Roberta said, "Now we've got to have a talk. First off, nobody in this building is going to care that I'm black and you're white and we're living in the same place—like they would in most white neighborhoods. But they're going to notice and what they're mainly going to notice is you. I think you're going to be tall but you don't have much of a bosom yet, especially in that uniform. I don't mean to hurt your feelings—you'll have one all in good time—but for now it's just as well. But that doesn't leave you safe from all the animals in the jungle out there. This is a bad neighborhood, baby, a dirty, dangerous, mean, bad neighborhood, and the reason I'm here is because the landlords around here will rent to anybody—Negro people, red Indians, Chinese, Arabs, Gypsies, hillbillies, anybody, and some of them would hurt you if they could and some wouldn't, but who I'm thinking about, whatever their color, are people with police records and other scum and riffraff. I'm going to take care of you as best I can but I'm going to have to be strict about what I let you do, and you have to help by really following the rules. It just wouldn't be safe otherwise. Do you understand?"

"Yes. I'll do whatever you tell me to do, Roberta. Honest."

"How much more school do you have this year?"

"Three weeks."

"Well, until school is out, starting today, I'll walk with you every morning to the El station. Once you've paid your fare you'll be with a lot of other passengers and El conductors and you'll be all right. Then in the afternoons I'll meet you at Bernie's and you'll have to stay there until I'm through playing and we can come back here by cab. In the summer it'll be easier but we'll have to go everyplace together. I can't let you go anywhere around here by yourself. If you want to spend the day with your friends I can walk you to the El and then we can meet as usual in the afternoon."

That first morning, Kitty saw for herself what Wilson Avenue was like. Run-down buildings, dingy stores. Trash and garbage on the sidewalks, in the gutters and alleys. Derelicts sleeping over hot-air grates or slumped in doorways taking their first—or their tenth—drink of the day. These poor souls were harmless enough, in Roberta's opinion, but not so the sharp-eyed or blank-eyed young men and not-so-young men who lounged along the street, or sat in the bars that opened at 6 A.M. after having closed only a sweeping-out hour earlier. Only the half-dozen strip joints that attracted similar parasites, and others perhaps even more to be avoided, were closed until midafternoon and temporarily not a problem.

On weekdays, most of the El passengers crowded the opposite platform, waiting for trains to their jobs in the Loop, but there were always a fair number of people going in Kitty's direction, north to Rogers Park and the prosperous suburbs of Evanston and Wilmette, Negro women mostly, going to work as cleaning women and maids in the houses of the North Shore.

That afternoon, Roberta wrote a note to Mrs. Pomeroy, and Bernie and Erna Fossbinder, Bernie grumbling every inch of the way, put the note in Mrs. Pomeroy's mailbox and helped Kitty move her things out of the apartment.

The note read:

Dear Mrs. Pomeroy,
Mrs. Collins telephoned from Milwaukee today to ask me to take care of Kitty while she's away since it appears her friend's illness will keep her in Milwaukee longer than expected. After that a new position she has been offered will mean she will have to move to another part of the city so will be giving up the apartment here. Since the rent is paid for the month of June that should be sufficient notice. Mrs. Collins asked my husband and me to help her move, which we did today, and left the apartment in a neat condition.

Roberta almost signed her real name, then remembered it was rather prominently displayed in Fossbinder's window, and wrote instead:

Yours truly,
   Mrs. Wilma Roberts.

Now, Kitty ate her lunch at a drugstore near the school—a sandwich and a drink at the soda fountain—and in the afternoons after classes, and after piano practice, would go straight to Fossbinder's to do her homework in a back booth, with Bernie's reluctant approval, and wait for Roberta to arrive.

On Saturdays and Sundays during the day Roberta could give Kitty lessons on the piano in her apartment; Kitty was free to practice there, and when the summer vacation began had all morning and most of the afternoon to work at her music. Roberta sometimes had to remind her to take a break.

When Kitty wasn't concentrating on music she looked around and thought about where she was, how she felt about being where she was. Welcome, at home, a new feeling. Glad, but strange, still somewhat bewildered. It was one thing to know a Negro person and see them outside, it was another to enter the mysterious places where they lived, still another to live there with them. In the movies about the South there would be scenes of children with Negro servants, usually in the kitchen, but that was very different; it would be the children's home. This wasn't the South, Roberta was no servant, and this was her home, these nice things were her things.

Roberta had pretty clothes, style. Kitty liked to look at the dresses and suits and gowns in Roberta's closet, touch them as she might browse along the rack in a department store. Roberta didn't seem to mind. Roberta sometimes wore serious expressions but she was never gloomy or angry, she spoke calmly, smiled and laughed a lot, too. She was fun to be around. It was as though they were on a kind of long vacation together.

She can stay with me, at least for the time being, Roberta had said. She never said how long that would be—maybe she didn't know herself—and Kitty didn't want to ask, didn't want to think about it.

There were other things she didn't want to think about, but sometimes she couldn't help it. Seeing Roberta's dressing table and mirror, Roberta making up. When she was six and seven she had loved to watch her mother dress, put on makeup and jewelry. She had thought her mother so beautiful she had wanted to hug her, but her mother would say, "Don't wrinkle my dress... Don't muss my hair... Don't smear my lipstick." It wasn't that her mother was never affectionate, just not very often, then it would be some surprising, spur of the moment thing. When Kitty was about to be seven her mother had suddenly gotten it into her head to give Kitty an elaborate birthday party, maybe to make up for having forgotten the occasion entirely the year before. But all the little girls made too much noise, wouldn't play some of the games Madge Collins had lined up, made a mess, and Kitty ate too much cake and ice cream and got sick to her stomach, threw up. Her mother ended up mad at Kitty, mad at everybody and everything.

Roberta thought, you'd think I'd know more about Madge Collins after working only a few feet away from her night after night for three years, and on top of that Madge had a voice that carried and was always complaining about something. But Roberta had had neither the time nor permission to stand at the bar listening to conversations, and when she played she could hear nothing above the music but random laughter, a hum of talk, and when she took her breaks she sat in a booth alone or with Kitty or with others, by choice not with Madge Collins, who would be busy hustling somebody anyway. And Bernie and Erna Fossbinder seldom discussed their customers with her.

Roberta was only guessing but she thought Madge Collins had been a farm girl. There was something about her, about the way she talked that reminded Roberta of certain white people she had known in and around Kankakee, Illinois, as a young girl herself. You could see them today as you drove along the highways on Sunday afternoons, young girls in feedbag-cotton dresses sitting alone on the steps of farm houses or leaning against the gate posts, suffering from terminal boredom, watching the cars and trucks go past and waiting, waiting for the chance to leave forever. Wherever it was, central Illinois, Iowa, Missouri, Kansas ... there wasn't much difference—endless farmland, endless plains, horizons never reached ...

Madge was still a very good-looking woman at about thirty-three when she had disappeared. She would have been pretty at eighteen in 1925 and would have wanted something in exchange for that—a good-looking man, or a man with money, a combination of both if possible, but at least the latter, but she would not have been able to be too choosy sitting out on that farm, getting into town only once a week or so, at a disadvantage competing against the town girls. She wouldn't have been able to wait forever for the banker's son. Did she just get pregnant from Jack Collins, who was probably good-looking and personable even if he didn't have a dime? Or only a smalltown job that would never lead anywhere?

Roberta did remember something. When Roberta was on her breaks, Madge Collins played the jukebox at Fossbinder's as some people play the radio all day long—to have any kind of noise for company. She didn't care what it was. She would insert a quarter and punch any five buttons at random, whatever the selections were, quality things or junk, then when the machine started to play she would return to her place at the bar and resume her conversation, seeming not to listen, not even to hear. But Roberta had a recollection of seeing Madge once respond to a late 1920s Frankie Trumbauer recording—speakeasy music—its inclusion somewhat unusual in itself because most of the selections were from the later thirties. Before returning to the bar, Madge had done a little dance, just a few steps of the "Black Bottom" all by herself.

Kitty didn't remember coming to Chicago from anywhere, but she remembered being there at six and probably earlier, Roberta thought. If she hadn't been born in Chicago in 1926 she had been brought there as a baby or very small child, in the late twenties, 1930 or '31 at the latest. But 1930 was the first year of the Depression and it was as bad in Chicago as anywhere. Worse. No, earlier than that when there were still jobs for enterprising young men who would need to hustle to bring in enough to suit Madge Collins, who would be dazzled by the big, wild city, by the beautiful clothes in the stores, the beautiful women and handsome men on Michigan Avenue, the shiny cars, the houses and apartments on Lake Shore Drive, the "real" life in the speakeasies she got into once in a while, but never often enough for her, the fantasy life in the movies she spent half her life going to see. Not enough money and Kitty is a burden, a drag, an anchor holding her back. She yells at her young husband to get a better job so he can bring her the things she wants. She is so beautiful he is still crazy about her but he hates it when she yells at him. And then he is killed in some accident. What did young men die of back then? Roberta asked herself. Wars, revolutions, car crashes ... holdups, gangland shootouts—even as innocent bystanders, which sometimes happened in those lawless days. Or did Madge shoot him?

"I'll bet he was smart," Roberta said to Kitty. "You got your brains from somebody, your looks from your mama, maybe him, too, and your brains from him. I think he saw an ad in the paper, maybe for people to go to South America to make good money—something to do with mining. He'd have a skill they could use. If he could just go for a few years and come back with some money ... Anyway, he couldn't take a family down there, couldn't take care of you by himself anywhere, a man can't do that, he had to leave you with your mother."

"Then what happened?"

"Somehow he had an accident, probably in the mines."

"Anyway, you made it up."

"I made it up but why couldn't it be true? Might be as true as any other reason. Why did I think of it and not something else? Ask yourself that. Maybe I got a sign."

But even though Kitty knew Roberta had made up the story it came after a while to seem real to her.

Madge Collins had long since started going out with other men. She was pretty enough; she could afford to be choosy now. Her boyfriends paid for everything, but some of them bored her after a while, some didn't have enough money to be interesting. There's a rich guy out there somewhere, why not hold out for him? She said it aloud often enough. Kitty watched her mother dress, brush her hair, put on makeup, and thought she was beautiful, and believed her stories that some day they'd have everything they wanted. In time Kitty learned her mother couldn't be believed, couldn't be relied on. But Kitty kept hoping things would get better. Her mother lied so much, maybe she had lied about him, too. Maybe he wasn't dead and one day he would suddenly reappear with enough money and they'd all be together and happy. That was what she used to think. She didn't think that way anymore but she remembered those earlier hopes.

Where did she run off to with that bum, Ralph? Roberta wondered. Would her photograph appear in the paper some day after she and Ralph had been killed in a bank holdup? Or would they find her shot to death in a tourist cabin? Nothing but a bad end of one kind or another seemed possible.

Some things you couldn't do for yourself. Some things you had to have other people for. And there were some things people didn't do, they just didn't do them, but they did them anyway and you could never forget that, never forgive it. You forgave everything else but not that. But you felt guilty, too, as though maybe you had done something wrong to deserve it, or hadn't done something you should have done, even though Roberta said there was no reason in the world to think that, to feel guilty, no reason in the world. Then why? Why did she do it? Crazy, Roberta said. Don't think about it anymore.

Roberta would sometimes say, "Come on, baby, let's take a holiday. All work and no play ... "—or words to that effect. Then they would get on the El and go shopping in the Loop, at Marshall Fields or at one of the other stores, have lunch at Hardings, or another cafeteria, and sometimes visit the Art Institute or the Field Museum. Bernie closed Sundays and several Sunday evenings that summer of 1940 Roberta took Kitty to free concerts at Grant Park along the lakefront where they sat on the grass, ate their supper from a picnic basket, and listened to music that ranged from Sousa to Verdi to Wagner. Once, a soloist played Rachmaninoff's "Rhapsody on a Theme by Paganini," composed only a few years earlier, and Kitty was enthralled and ecstatic.

"Would you like to be able to play that some day?" Roberta asked.

"Yes! Oh, I don't know, Roberta, I want to play jazz, too, just as much. Can you do both?"

"Well, Hazel Scott does, and yours truly does, too, after a fashion. But don't try to decide now. Try everything first. Keep your mind open. Listen to everything."

Roberta kept family photographs on shelves, little tables, the piano top. Kitty wanted to know who the people were.

"Daddy was a carpenter," Roberta explained. "He didn't have as much education as Mama, but she looked up to him. We all did. Oh, they were strict, but we had a happy childhood."

There was even a small framed snapshot of Roberta's ex-husband, Rex, a dapper, once well-known trumpeter with a thin mustache.

"Did you have any children?" Kitty asked.

"Never did," Roberta said.

The hours jazz musicians had to work, the frequent traveling, would have made parenthood difficult to impossible for Rex and Roberta Wilkins unless Roberta stayed home. Which she had been willing to do for a few years. But Rex had not wanted children. Kids made him nervous. So that was that. Now here I am with a half-grown white child, Roberta thought. But if anybody wants to know, I wouldn't have it otherwise. This child has been my friend for a long time, when she plays she's an extension of me, and if she needs a spot of mothering for a while, so do I need to give it.

There were other photographs in albums. Small Negro orchestras, Roberta standing, or seated at the piano in some, considerably slimmer in a low-necked, low-waisted, low-hemline 1920s gown, Rex out in front in a tux, holding his cornet or trumpet bell downwards as he sat and posed formally or leaned, informally, against the piano. Dated 1928, 1932, '33. One photo, 1935, showed Rex and Roberta seated at a sidewalk table in Paris, at Fouquet's on the Champs Elysées.

In 1919, at eighteen, Roberta and her twin sister, Paulette, had moved up to Chicago to attend junior college. They lived with an uncle and aunt. In 1921, Paulette got a teaching job, Roberta went on to the Chicago Musical College for another two years, then studied with a Pole in the Kimball Building. By this time, New Orleans jazz was flourishing south of the Loop in the Negro district.

"Paulette and I—escorted by Uncle Herbert at first, then some young men we met—used to hear King Oliver and the Original Creole Band at the Lincoln Gardens Cafe, the old Royal Garden, even before Louis Armstrong came up from New Orleans to join them. Uncle Herbert made us swear we'd never tell Mama or she'd have his head. Mama was against jazz. She didn't believe it was the work of the devil as some folks said, but it was definitely not respectable. Back home I had learned some of Scott Joplin's rags from sheet music and Mama sniffed at those, but playing ragtime for fun in the parlor and hearing jazz in Chicago were two different things." Adding explanations for Kitty when necessary, Roberta continued: "She knew where jazz was played—in bawdy houses or right alongside them—and that was every bit as true in Chicago in the twenties as it had been in New Orleans before the war—and who patronized such places—gangsters, sportin' house women, pimps, gamblers, cardsharps, cutthroats, hustlers, roughnecks, perfectly decent people, too, who just wanted to hear the music, but Mama wasn't prepared to have her daughters be among them, no indeed."

Chicago in the twenties was the jazz center of the world but not all the jazz musicians had come from New Orleans or were

Chicagoans. Rex Wilkins had arrived from St. Louis. He had played in Robert Dupree's band and Percy Clark's orchestra, then formed a band of his own. Roberta gave piano lessons, played in silent-movie theaters, at "rent parties," met Rex in 1925 and married him a year later. The Wilkins Five—trumpet, clarinet, trombone, piano, drums, with Rex on trumpet and Roberta on piano—played at Buddy Hudson's Rendezvous Cafe, The Paradise Club, The Tropic Gardens, and when they weren't playing they were listening to the others, often all night long, going to the Dreamland, The Nest, Elite #2, the Vendome theater, the Savoy Ballroom, and a dozen other places on South State Street or around 35th and Calumet, to hear Louis and Lil Hardin Armstrong, Jimmy Noone, Johnny and Baby Dodds, Kid Ory, Sidney Bechet, Barney Bigard, Earl Hines, Jelly Roll Morton, and so many others—white musicians, too, who came to the Sunset Cafe after playing all evening at some place on Cottage Grove, to sit in with or listen to Louis—Bud Freeman, Jimmy MacPartland, Frank Teschmaker, Benny Goodman, and sometimes Bix.

(Roberta had showed Kitty the corner of Wilson and Magnolia where Tesch had died in an auto crash on his way to a gig one evening in 1932.)

Roberta's playing had been strongly influenced by the seminal "trumpet" style of Earl Hines, but later, in the thirties, when the gravitational center of jazz shifted from Chicago and Kansas City to New York and she and Rex had made the musical migration eastward, she had fallen under the spells of Teddy Wilson and Art Tatum, though Tatum's virtuosity was so uniquely phenomenal it defied imitation.

"That man," Roberta said, playing Tatum's recording of "Mop Mop" for Kitty. "You know he's practically blind, but for him that seems to be an advantage. Listen to him. Sounds as if he had four hands going at once."

Tatum's musical powers were awesome, but like Roberta before her (and even Tatum, too) Kitty thought Wilson could teach her something, loved the lighter tracery and lyrical emotion of Wilson's improvisations as he played "Body and Soul" or "The Man I Love" with the Benny Goodman Trio or when he and Goodman and Lester Young backed up Billie Holiday singing "Easy Living" and "If You Were Mine."

Listening to these recordings—Roberta had a disc library surveying the evolution of jazz from the "Red Onion Jazz Babies" and the Armstrong "Hot Five" and "Hot Seven" sides of the mid-1920s to 1940—was as important to Kitty's training as her daily work on the piano, and in the warm afternoons that summer, she spent hours lying on the rug in front of the Victrola listening to Bessie Smith and Billie Holiday; to Bechet and Benny Carter, and how Lester Young's legato on tenor sax was so different from Coleman Hawkins' rhythmic arpeggios on the same instrument; to Armstrong and Beiderbecke, and to Rex Wilkins' golden horn playing things like "All of Me" and "I'm in the Mood for Love," with a sweetness that didn't sound quite like anyone else—oh, those thrilling, downward tumbling trills!—and to Hines, James P. Johnson, Fats Waller, Jess Stacy, Tatum and Wilson, Mary Lou Williams, Count Basie, and Pete Weathersby, and tried to reproduce some of Wilson's or Basie's deceptively simple phrases on Roberta's piano.

Roberta would play recordings, purposely hiding the labels from Kitty, and ask her to identify the soloists and sometimes say things like "This isn't who it sounds like, but who does it sound like?"

"Beiderbecke?"

"OK, who is it really?"

"I can't guess."

"Rex. But that's a tough one. That's a really old record when Rex was still taking ideas straight from Bix, before his own style evolved from that.

"Now Frankie Trumbauer's 'Singin the Blues' I just played a few minutes ago. Forget the old-timey flavor and the scratches. Who does Trumbauer's sax make you think of? Somebody later."

"Well not Coleman Hawkins. Or Benny Carter. Johnny Hodges? No. Lester Young?"

"Right on the button, baby."

And Kitty came to recognize other pairings, other influences.

"I remember seeing Muggsy Spanier hanging around the Lincoln Gardens when he was just a little peewee of a white kid your age, learning how to play trumpet from Joe Oliver. The King gave him one of his mutes. Baby Dodds taught Krupa by going outside during breaks and playing paradiddles on the dashboard of Krupa's car. I never actually saw that, but we heard about it. So many stories..."

"Then when did you come back to Chicago?" Kitty asked.

"In '36. During Prohibition there was work for everybody. When the speakeasies went out of business a lot of musicians lost their jobs. The Depression and the movies made it worse. Seemed like the only spots were in the big-name bands, mostly sweet, where you worked for nothing and couldn't play what you wanted to. Rex's band broke up, and so did we, just about that time. Chicago was home so I came back here and was lucky enough to get a job with Bernie and hang on to it all this time. Except for a few like Louis and Goodman, it's never been easy to make a living playing jazz."

"Where does Rex play now?"

"Nowhere that I know of. I haven't heard anything about him in more than three years."

Teddy Wilson's influence on Roberta—though she had been put off somewhat at first by his youth; she was eleven years older—was especially important for her because of his strong melodic line, his eagerness to play the best theater and pop songs of the era and his willingness to retain their melodies as well as improvise around them; and because of Roberta's particular handicaps. Starting with the handicaps—as a woman and a Negro, Roberta knew she was not likely to find work as a big-band pianist. Goodman had been the first white leader to employ Negro musicians; few of the other white bands did. And there were few women in the field, period. Despite Lil Hardin's early example, who was there? Lottie Taylor had disappeared into obscurity. Mary Lou Williams, the greatest of them all. The talented young Hazel Scott. And that was about it. The melodic line; long before Roberta had heard any jazz, she had learned melodies at her mother's knee—hymns, traditional songs, art songs, operatic adaptations, theater songs and popular songs of the era. She had been familiar with the works of Kern and Berlin and many others starting a decade before she and Paulette had gone up to Chicago to discover the music of King Oliver and Louis Armstrong. And great songs continued to get written. They found a welcome home in Roberta's repertoire.

* * *

At her piano, Kitty Collins sits under an imaginary spotlight, chin up, concentrating on the sheets of music, her fingers transmitting its signals to the keys below. It is Sunday afternoon, and she still wears the short-sleeved dotted swiss dress (blue dots on white) she had worn at her graduation from grammar school the month before and in which she has attended Mass that morning, and pedals with bare feet. Her legs, arms, hands, her face, are browned by the summer sun, her gray-green eyes brighter in contrast, their brows and lashes darker than her hair. In concentration and repose, her lips pout naturally, deceptively, open smiling spontaneously, when she turns her head to greet Roberta who has entered the apartment bringing vanilla ice cream and root beer from the drugstore. Kitty closes the dustcover on the keyboard, rises, walks slowly, lightly, skirt billowing from its belted waist, to curl in a corner of the couch. Windows are open but the curtains are still. Roberta sets a tray on the coffee table and fans herself with a magazine. Kitty blows a puff of air over her glistening upper lip and with fingertips wipes the perspiration from her lower eyelids.

"Hot," she says.

The radio is on. They sip black cows and listen to Vladimir Horowitz with the NBC Symphony, Toscanini conducting, playing the Brahms Second Piano Concerto—romantic, heroic, triumphant.

Every so often, friends of Roberta's from the old days would drop in or be invited from the South Side, one or two couples, and Kitty would be asked to show what she had learned.

"Roberta, she does you proud," they'd say, or something similar, and then, being a fairly normal fourteen-year-old in some respects, Kitty would drift off to her room, preferring a book or a magazine or her own thoughts to grown-up talk, with its references to people she had never met and to events she had neither witnessed nor experienced, and she did not get to know these people very well.

Bert Harper was different. He came for Sunday dinner every week or so and would still be there when Kitty went off to bed. Bert lived in the neighborhood, too, and played piano in a Wilson Avenue bar.

"Why don't we go hear him sometime?" Kitty asked.

"It's not a nice place," Roberta said. "I won't go in there myself."

But Bert would sometimes play stride piano and boogie-woogie in Roberta's living room, and taught Kitty the rudiments of these honky-tonk, barrelhouse styles with their old-timey piano-roll flavor, the strong, steady, bouncing and rolling left-hand patterns, the big chords, the glissandos and tremolos. Bert was a big man with huge hands who could play all those tenths with ease, but he maintained the size of a player's hands wasn't all that important.

"It's what you feel in here and have up here," he said, patting his heart and head.

Bert was chocolate-toned to Roberta's mahogany, both very pleasing. Kitty really couldn't see what was supposed to be so wonderful about white skin, especially when you looked at some of the people on Wilson Avenue—sickly pale or sallow or too red or blotchy. And look at all those people on the beach, lying there by the hour *trying* to get dark.

"I like Bert even if his jokes are awful," Kitty said. "Why don't you marry him, Roberta?"

Roberta laughed. "I like him, too, baby, but I don't expect to think about marriage again for quite a while."

But then Bert changed jobs, which meant moving back to the South Side, and he was able to come to Sunday dinner much less often.

At the beach near St. Margaret's one day, a boy Kitty had known in the eighth grade, Danny Egan, asked her, "Hey, Kitty, who's that nigger I see you with on Granville? You rich enough to have a maid now?"

"Don't ever use that word with me," she said, and made a fist—not a girl's fist with the thumb tucked inside, a good way to break it—but a real fist, and hit him as hard as she could on his nose, giving him a nosebleed. It was probably unfair because he couldn't hit her back, not in front of people, and he was so stupid, he kept asking, "What word, what'd I say, what'd I say?" He really didn't know, and she didn't tell him. She walked away, suddenly worried about calling any more attention to Roberta and herself, but no one besides her and Danny Egan had really heard the entire exchange, and the other kids thought he had probably said eff you or something like that. After the few days Kitty stayed away from the beach, the incident seemed to have fuzzed, blown over. Everybody ought to know by this time you had to be careful what you said to Kitty Collins.

But now she was conscious of the precariousness of her life with Roberta. No one in authority would allow it if they knew about it. And as Danny Egan had unknowingly warned her, anyone could find out by accident at any time. Even now, Danny Egan might be spreading some kind of story.

In the meantime, there was no word from or about Madge Collins, no sign of her at all. Not that Kitty expected any, but you could never tell. After three months had passed, the possibility of her mother's return still hung about like corner shadows, once in a while to surface, unbidden, in Kitty's thoughts. And Kitty did not know how she would feel if it actually happened. While she could not forgive her mother for leaving, neither did she really want her to come back or in any way deflect her life from the new direction it had taken.

3

Roberta said, "We've got to start thinking about getting you some winter clothes. I don't think anything you have's going to fit."

And Roberta had more than clothes on her mind when she and Kitty made the rounds of the Loop department stores. Where Roberta had to live was no place to bring up a maturing girl, and a pretty one at that. What was needed was what was lacking—men in the family, a husband, a father, an uncle, older brothers. Without their protection, real or implied, Kitty was too vulnerable, and the approaching autumn would only see the beginning of the problem. Through the eighth grade, like all her girl classmates, Kitty had tended to look childish and awkward in her singularly unattractive parochial school fall-winter uniform—a navy blue serge dress with beige poplin cuffs and collars—designed by the nuns first of all to be modest but also to eliminate evidence of social and economic distinctions among the school population, especially in the Depression years when such distinctions were glaring. The high school uniform wasn't much of an improvement—a shapeless jumper over a white shirtwaist. But it didn't hide a pretty face and pretty hair, and any man or boy with eyes in his head could see the rose growing under the burlap sack. And on weekends? In sweaters?

There were times when Roberta thought she might be better off in some established middle-class Negro neighborhood on the South Side, but bringing a white child to such a place would create its own set of probably insoluble problems, the impractical commuting distance being only one, and gigs elsewhere would not be easy to find. But for the moment Roberta did nothing, said nothing.

At her piano, Roberta Wilkins sits under an actual spotlight, playing "I Surrender Dear" and more good songs of the 1920s and '30s, her nilotic profile and the set of her lips intelligent, impressive, a face on some ancient Egyptian bas-relief. It is the Saturday of the Labor Day weekend, the end of a lovely summer. Roberta finishes a set and joins Kitty. Erna Fossbinder brings a small round cake with one lighted candle. Roberta's thirty-ninth birthday.

It had never been the custom of the order of nuns who ran both St. Margaret's grade school and the adjoining high school for girls to confer with parents about the education of their children, only if there was some disciplinary problem, as long as the tuition was paid. Kitty began high school inconspicuously, one among many. The autumn brought no new problems, only opportunities. Two weeks after the term began, Kitty showed up at Bernie's even more high spirited than usual.

"I'm in the glee club and choir," she told Roberta.

"That's fine. I approve one hundred percent."

"But Roberta, there's something else, and I don't know what to do. Sister Edmund, who directs the choir, gives advanced piano lessons to a few people who've had training—there isn't any charge—and she happened to hear me fooling around on the piano one day, and, well, now she wants to teach me and two other girls. But I'm doing fine with you, Roberta."

"First of all, do you think she's good?"

"I think so. I've heard her play. Yes, she's good. And the choir gets nice write-ups in the papers."

"Then she can probably teach you far more classical music than I can. You shouldn't turn down the chance to learn. We can still work together, after all."

"I don't want to get mixed up."

"You won't. I—uh—wouldn't play jazz around her, though. Just a hunch I have. No, you have my blessings, baby. Absolutely."

Kitty hugged Roberta, then went to the rear booth where she plugged in a small gooseneck lamp Bernie had dug up for her, opened a textbook under the bright, hooded light, and brushed her long hair away from her forehead.

In early October one day, Kitty heard Bernie say, "Another dishwasher quit on me."

"Look, why not? Why couldn't I do it?" Kitty protested. "I know Dillard is grumpy, but I could get along with him. And I'm here every night anyway. Come on, Bernie, please."

And Bernie, and Dillard, the Negro cook, still dubious, agreed to give her a chance.

Kitty scrubbed, rinsed, peeled with enthusiasm, singing to herself, stayed out of Dillard's way unless he grumbled at her to do something, and flourished in the steam, the heat, and the knowledge that she was strong enough to do this job as well as anybody and that she was really earning money to help pay her way. Twenty cents an hour added up. Sometimes she was a little sleepy in school, and the ninth-grade nun spoke to her about getting her proper rest. Then Kitty was more careful to suppress her yawns and learned to take little catnaps in a broken-down easy chair in Fossbinder's storeroom between 10 P.M. and midnight when the work was over in the kitchen and before she and Roberta left by cab for home.

Kitty's last class before lunchtime one day in October. Art. Sister Lawrence was giving a quiz. The door opened and Kitty looked up at the sound, looked down at her paper again; just another nun wanting Sister Lawrence for something. Sister Lawrence left the room for a minute or two, almost closing the door behind her, and came back in again. When Kitty had answered the last question she brought her paper up to the front desk. Sister Lawrence frowned at her.

In a low voice she said, "Kitty, please stay behind and see me before you go to lunch."

"Yes, Sister."

What's up, Kitty wondered? And had ten more minutes to speculate before the bell rang.

All the other girls filed out, leaving Kitty and Sister Lawrence alone.

"Kitty, I have instructions from Reverend Mother. You're to go home immediately and return as soon as possible with your mother. Go directly to Reverend Mother's office."

Panic, with its icy hands, clutched at Kitty.

"What's happened, what's it about?" Kitty had barely enough breath or saliva to get the words out.

"I have no idea. I have simply been asked to give you this message."

Kitty walked out of the classroom on legs of water. With sickening suddenness, for which she was unprepared, her life was threatened, her life with Roberta. What she had feared all along, exposure, seemed unavoidable now. She couldn't possibly bring Roberta. But if she couldn't bring Roberta, who could she bring? Erna Fossbinder was the only possibility, but Erna didn't look the part and probably wouldn't do it anyway. She was trapped. Why? For smoking in the alley? Kitty wracked her now muddled brain and could not think of any other reason to be summoned to Reverend Mother's office like this.

Outside in the schoolyard, there were just a few stragglers about who hadn't yet gone home to lunch. Kitty stood still, unable to decide where to go or what to do. If they find out where I'm living they'll send me to some home. She was hungry but didn't want to eat. She wouldn't be able to get anything down.

There was only one thing to do. She turned, went back into the school building, and slowly climbed the stairs to Reverend Mother's office.

It was locked. Reverend Mother had gone to lunch. But Kitty stayed, leaning against the wall. There was no place to sit down.

It wasn't boring or tedious standing there waiting. Kitty was too baffled and fearful for that. Half an hour passed. And then Reverend Mother startled her by rounding the corner, keys and beads jangling.

"My instructions were that you were to bring your mother," the nun said, and threw open the door to her office.

Her voice shaking, Kitty said, "My mother is away on a trip. I'm staying with a friend. But I don't know why you want to see me,

Reverend Mother. If it's for smoking, I'm sorry and I won't do it again. I didn't like it."

"It is not for smoking." Reverend Mother was behind her desk now and Kitty was standing before it. The nun wore rimless glasses and had a slight mustache. There seemed to be little stitches in her narrow lips.

"Then what did I do?"

"We have discovered certain ... photographs. Does that ring any kind of bell with you?"

"Photographs? Photographs of who? I don't know about any photographs."

"Sit down," Reverend Mother said. It was a command, not an invitation. Kitty sank to a hard wooden chair facing at a forty-five-degree angle to Reverend Mother's desk, and had to turn to the right.

Reverend Mother linked thin fingers on her desk and slowly rotated her thumbs. A quarter inch or so of off-white long underwear sleeve was visible around one wrist.

"An older boy, not from this parish but from this vicinity, recently brought a roll of film to a photo shop some distance from here. The boy foolishly did not count on the proprietor having a sense of civic responsibility. The film was developed into ... unimaginably shocking photographs. Of girls. I shall not describe them but they were ... nude. The owner of the shop went to the police. An officer recognized one girl's face. A girl from this parish. *This school!* The officer took the photographs to Father Coffey who notified me immediately. I interviewed the girl and her parents late yesterday. She admitted the photographs had been taken in the apartment of a second girl during one lunch period when the second girl's father was at work and the girl's mother was downtown shopping. The second girl has also confessed. Both have said that you, too, were present."

Slowly, then more rapidly, Kitty began shaking her head from side to side. "No. No. No, no, no, no, no! Nobody has ever taken a picture of me like that and nobody ever will! I wasn't there and I don't know anything about it! Who said I was!?"

"Do you go home for lunch?"

"No. I eat at the drugstore. Then I practice piano in the auditorium."

"Every day?"

"Almost every day."

"Then you can account for your whereabouts on the day in question and perhaps people would remember seeing you there?"

"I don't know. People in the drugstore are busy. They don't have time to keep track of everybody and I'm not the only one. There's nobody in the auditorium except Emil, the janitor, sometimes walking around, but he never pays any attention to me ... The boy! Whoever he is, he knows I wasn't there!"

"The boy has run away. When he returned to pick up the photographs, he panicked when the owner went to make a telephone call."

Kitty was suddenly angry, and the anger got into her voice, though not loudly.

"Who said I was?" It was a demand, and the omission of comma "Reverend Mother" was as obvious as a slap. "I want to know."

"Rita Curry and Rose Mulvaney."

"Rita Curry! God!"

"You will not take the Lord's name in vain!"

"I don't *speak* to Rita Curry, Sister. Everybody knows that. Ask anybody. I wouldn't cross the street with her! We had a fight a year ago, but I *never* had anything to do with her. Rose Mulvaney is a sap. She's practically a cretin. She'll say yes or no to anything you ask her. Rita Curry has been fooling around with older boys for years. Everybody knows that. She's a liar. She lies about everything. Everybody knows that, too ..."

"You're dismissed!" Reverend Mother said abruptly, the adult who cannot quite allow herself to be bested and told off by a child.

"You mean I can go?" Kitty asked. Her voice had changed. She was just fourteen again and conscious of the light through the office window. The tree outside. "This is all over?"

The nun filled her lungs with air.

"I am sorry to have put you through this ordeal. You handle yourself very well. I say that as a compliment. There are too many girls for me to get to know all of you as well as I should. Say nothing of this to anyone. I add to your ordeal the burden of silence, but I'm confident you're capable of bearing that. Rumor, scandal, these things are ruinous. With God's help perhaps these girls can be rehabilitated..." She didn't sound convinced. "Now we must pity them."

She got to her feet suddenly and came around her desk. Sometime while they had been talking Kitty had been conscious of hearing the ringing of bells signaling the start of afternoon classes.

"I've kept you a bit late," Reverend Mother said. "Why don't I assign you to do some work for me in the library the rest of the afternoon. Let me show you what I'd like done..."

Rita Curry and Rose Mulvaney were expelled from school. Rumors abounded but they were far from the truth. The Currys moved to another part of the city and were not seen again. Rose Mulvaney surfaced from time to time in various places, but few people remembered her for long.

Kitty got over it in time, but she knew she had gone through an experience she would recall with a shiver, and a sigh of relief, as long as she lived.

Later that fall, the father of one of Sister Edmund's other piano students, who rented a box at Orchestra Hall, made it available to Sister Edmund and her class of three advanced pupils, one memorable, glamorous Sunday afternoon. Kitty's first look at a concert hall, luxurious gilt and carpets and paneled wood, at crowds of sophisticated adults, European-looking people, a new and elegant world. From a box like kings and queens! You entered through a little door and sat on separate, upholstered chairs and could see everything perfectly. The audience on the main floor and in the other boxes, the grand piano on the stage, the very tall, strange-looking man with his closely cropped head, craggy face, huge hands, emerging from the wings in a dark suit, stiff high collar and tie—the great Rachmaninoff himself!—to a swell of applause. And the sounds he could produce from that piano. Rich and powerful haunting sounds that rose in sonorous, thunderous waves.

Kitty and Roberta had a small, good Christmas. Roberta sat in the back row of the high school auditorium the evening of the Christmas choir concert, wearing the very plain dress and rather old-fashioned hat with veil she had carefully selected for the occasion, and the few parents who noticed her believed her to be someone's maid. The school was patronized by many rich Catholic families of the North Shore. The veil obscured her features, if not her color, from anyone who had ever spent an evening at Bernie Fossbinder's. Roberta did not allow herself to be demeaned by this assumed role. If she lived and worked in a world populated largely by fools that was their problem as well as hers. She was here because she chose to be, because she was proud of Kitty whose voice up there was part of that joyous, collective choral sound.

In February, 1941, Roberta came down with bronchitis, fought it for a week, then finally admitted she would have to take to her bed.

"I'll be all right," Kitty said, and came and went to and from school and the drug and grocery stores without incident, cooked creditable meals for Roberta and herself, and took care of Roberta as best she could.

"You're a good nurse, baby," Roberta said hoarsely, but her wracking cough persisted. Kitty phoned a physician, recommended by the pharmacy, who came, grudgingly, wrote a prescription, and ordered Roberta to remain in bed at least another week.

On Monday, Kitty came home from school as usual, arriving at four in the afternoon. As usual, the building brooded upon itself, on its long, shabby, empty corridors, weakly lit. A dark-haired, wiry boy of eighteen or nineteen came out of a doorway.

"Hey, what d'you say?"

"Hello," Kitty said, and continued walking, her heartbeat suddenly accelerated.

"Hey, she's friendly, that's nice," the boy said, and walked beside her. He had a sour smell.

Kitty looked straight ahead and walked more quickly.

"What're you in such a hurry about?" the boy said.

"I'm very busy," Kitty said. "I have to take care of someone who's sick."

"Yeah, I know. Hey, you've gotten to be a big girl."

They were only halfway to Roberta's door, at a stairwell and another corridor going off at right angles. The boy was a little ahead now and had blocked the way. "Yeah, you've really grown up, haven't you?"

"No, I haven't, I'm just a kid," Kitty said, raising her voice, but it sounded small in her own ears. "Now excuse me, I have to go."

"Don't be in such a big hurry," the boy said. "Come on, I'll buy you a Coke. Then we can talk."

"No. I don't care for a Coke," Kitty said. "Now, why don't you go, please?"

"I don't want to go, I like you." He smiled and spread his hands. "See? I don't wanta hurt you. I can show you a good time."

But he wouldn't let her pass.

If she had a Coke with him would he let her alone?

No, it was two flights down and then half a city block to the street entrance and another block after that to any place where Coke was sold.

No.

"Let me past," she said, frightened but charged with adrenaline, poised to defend herself. Roberta's door was twenty-five yards away. She tried to run past him but he grabbed her wrist and stopped her cold. Her school books slipped and scattered to the carpet runner.

"You wanta stay male one minute longer, you creep, you let me go!" Kitty shouted, but he held on and laughed at her. She kicked out and missed and he laughed at her again, got a grip on the side of her leg, and his hand groped toward her crotch. With all her strength she twisted away from him and kicked again, kicked and kicked, and the toe of one loafer caught the hard bone below one knee. He howled and she caught him again in the same place and he released her long enough for her to break free.

She ran, and halfway to Roberta's door began yelling Roberta's name over and over at the top of her lungs. Oh, if only she isn't asleep, if only she left the door unlocked!

Enraged, the boy hobbled after her. She was faster now, but blocked by the locked door to the apartment she lost her lead. She screamed and pounded on the door with her fists just before the boy got to her again and clutched at her hair. She spit at him, bit his other hand, and the door fell away behind her. The boy saw Roberta, a bottle hanging from her right hand like a club and let Kitty go.

"You bitch!" the boy screamed. "I'll kill you. That nigger bitch won't help you!"

But he knew he was defeated, temporarily, spat, and limped down the stairs at the end of the corridor.

Still clutching her robe at her throat, her face burning with fury, Roberta slammed and bolted the door behind them.

"Did he touch you? Did he hurt you, baby?" Roberta rasped.

"No. My wrist is a little sore." She massaged it back and forth. The roots of her hair hurt where he had pulled, but that pain was fast subsiding. "He tried to touch me but he didn't, just here," and she patted her own flank. "I can take care of myself. I didn't even have to kick him where it really hurts." But her panting voice shook and Roberta could hear the sound of bravado.

"No you can't, and I can't either, not in this stinking place! That hoodlum was right. I can't help you enough."

Kitty kissed Roberta on the cheek. "Yes you can. That was a terrible thing he said to you. Anyway, it's all over. I'm all right and you'll be well in a few days."

"You're going to stay here until I am," Roberta said. "Some of the stores deliver. I'll call the school, say you have a cold. You haven't been absent a single day this year."

"All right I will. Now you should go back to bed."

"Where are your books?"

"Oh." Kitty looked down at her empty hands. "He made me drop them."

"We've got to get them," Roberta said. She picked up the bottle again and unbolted the door, looked carefully up and down the hall. "I'll go."

"I'm coming, too," Kitty said, and found a bottle for herself.

But they retrieved her scattered books without encountering anyone.

"Would you like some soup?" Kitty asked.

I'm all right, I'm all right, she told herself as she heated it up. But it was awhile before the chills and the shaking stopped, and it seemed to her the sour smell of the boy in the corridor was still in her nostrils; and for a couple of nights he burglarized himself into her dreams.

Recovered, with Kitty back in school, Roberta watched and waited. Twice that Saturday when she and Kitty went to the stores together, they passed the boy near the entrance to the building. He was with two other boys, as big as men. All three stared, unsmiling, at the Negro woman and the white girl, and Roberta knew she could expect no help from anyone if there was trouble. Monday she telephoned Sister Edmund at St. Margaret's High School and asked for an appointment in connection with the welfare of Kitty Collins. There was an interruption to get Kitty's folder from the file.

"Mrs. Collins?"

"No. My name is Wilkins."

"I don't quite understand," said Sister Edmund.

Roberta said, "If I could have an appointment to see you, Sister, that would make it so much easier to explain the problem."

"Yes, well, of course."

"Tomorrow? It has to be during school hours, and preferably in the early afternoon."

"I can see you at 1:45," said Sister Edmund. "Would that suit?"

For the interview Roberta wore a dark green wool suit, stylish but conservative, a simple white blouse, a gold pin on the suit, no other jewelry except her two rings, black pumps, her black cloth coat with the fur collar, a small hat, leather gloves, galoshes. There was snow on the ground and more of it threatening in a low, leaden sky.

A small nun with a gray, pinched face—not Sister Edmund—opened the large, heavy door of the convent after a wait of almost a minute. The nun's ankle-length black habit whispered and the rosary beads dangling from her waist clicked as she moved along the bare corridor, as if on wheels, slightly ahead of Roberta Wilkins.

"Wait in here, please."

A small, square, stuffy sitting room, windowless, with one cushioned chair and two uncushioned, a two-seat wooden bench, a votive candle burning low in a red glass shield before a small plaster statue of the Virgin, a painting of the Sacred Heart on one wall, a formal, color-tinted photographic portrait of Pius XII on another, and a second door, which was closed. After removing her overcoat and silk scarf, Roberta sat on the bench and pulled off her galoshes. She left her hat on and folded her hands in her lap. Ten minutes passed. It was like waiting in a doctor's office, she the only patient. Her pulse was regular, but she could hear her heartbeat in her ears.

The inner door opened. The nun standing in the doorway said, "Mrs. Wilkins? I am Sister Edmund."

Roberta estimated the nun to be about her own age, give or take a year. Thirty-eight maybe. She might have been called pretty, classically pretty, if she did not have such an intensely severe expression, such pallor. She remained standing, fingering the beads at her waist.

Roberta told the story briefly, stuck to the basic facts.

Sister Edmund responded dramatically.

"I must confess a great deal of shock," she said, "to learn that Kitty has been a party to a most unusual deception."

"It was either that or become a ward of the city. I decided to try to provide some sort of home for her instead. But now the situation has changed. Can she stay here, Sister? There's no point beating around the bush. That's what I've come to ask you."

As though Roberta had passed some kind of test, Sister Edmund said, "Mrs. Wilkins, let us go next door where you can be more comfortable."

They entered a large sitting room with cushioned chairs, a grand piano, windows on the street. At one time the convent had been a private home, a many-roomed mansion.

"Kitty is a splendid child," Sister Edmund said. "Intelligent, gifted ... with what seems ... a generosity of spirit. How she has managed to be these things and not some subnormal, even criminal creature, after the atrocious childhood you've painted, may always be a great mystery which can only be explained by God's grace."

"Then can we really put her in some public institution?" Roberta asked. "She's fourteen now, going on fifteen. In a few years she'll be able to take care of herself. Now, we both need your help. I can still pay for her room and board."

Sister Edmund clasped her hands together.

"We have no *provision* for boarding any child! A great, a very great exception would have to be made, and I have no authority to grant such an exception. Reverend Mother would have to make the decision and I do not know if she can be persuaded."

"But you'll try?" Roberta asked.

"Yes, I'll try. I'll go speak to her now."

It took an hour. Roberta had nothing to read except religious magazines and newspapers and a day-old *Chicago Tribune* with news of the war in Europe, the advance of the Nazi war machine, not her business. She stared out the darkening windows, looked at her watch, knowing that Kitty's last class of the day would soon be over, wondering how she was going to tell her. She had her back to the door when she heard Sister Edmund rustling, saying in an intense, low voice, "It can be arranged!" The nun was smiling faintly when Roberta turned.

"Subject to the legal question of custody, which should be no problem. The order retains a skilled attorney, and Reverend Mother has spoken with him already by phone—Kitty can stay with us as long as necessary until we can find a suitable private family willing to take her in."

Sister Edmund sat on the edge of a chair and put the tips of her long, pale fingers over her closed eyes, a gesture that struck Roberta as overdone.

"I am exhausted," the nun said. "Emotionally wrung out."

"I *will* be," Roberta said. "Thank you for what you've done."

"We have only just begun," Sister Edmund said. "Mrs. Wilkins, this ... *bar* ... where you work. You tell me Kitty spends every evening there? Unbelievable. Thank God that state of affairs will end."

"It hasn't been as bad as all that for her, Sister. Bernie Fossbinder runs a decent place. People behave or out they go. He doesn't put up with bad language or fighting."

Sister Edmund said, "And I realize you must earn a living. But it can hardly be called the proper environment for a young girl! I'm appalled. By the grace of God Kitty seems to have survived it ... You must forgive me, Mrs. Wilkins. I'm putting things badly. I have no experience with such places—with any situation like this. You taught her to play, then? Of course. How stupid of me not to have put two and two together sooner. You taught her well. She has good musical sense, great promise ... Will you play something for me, Mrs. Wilkins?"

Roberta sat up in surprise. "If you'd like." A tape of song titles ran through her mind, double-speed, and one by one she rejected them as inappropriate for the place, the occasion, or the audience. She thought of spirituals, hymns, traditional songs, even Mozart. Then she ran the tape again, backwards and forwards, stopped it. She sat at the piano, said, " 'Willow Weep for Me,' " and began playing soft, dense chords, little runs, her own version of Ann Ronell's song, a note-crowded exploration that involved more embellishment of its solid structure than improvisation—short, skittery flights around the almost-blues of its melodic lament, but never very far away from it. After two choruses she ended it. There were five seconds of silence.

"You have great skill," Sister Edmund said carefully. "You almost seem to be composing the song as you go along. Thank you for playing for me."

"I have to go," Roberta said. "I have a lot to do, none of which I look forward to."

"Mrs. Wilkins, you spoke of paying for Kitty's room and board. I have discussed this matter with Reverend Mother, and it will not be necessary."

"But I want to do it. That way I won't feel so cut off."

"But it won't be necessary. We are a well-endowed order. It would be wasted."

Roberta's eyes glistened. "I'd better go," she said. "When do you want me to bring her?"

"Tomorrow? Goodbye, Mrs. Wilkins."

"Will she be allowed to visit me?"

"Where, Mrs. Wilkins? Where you live is not safe. Where you work is not suitable. And here—we have no facilities . . . But I can't deny you this. You've done a fine thing. We'll try to arrange something every so often."

The next morning, Kitty learned why Roberta had been so subdued the evening before, learned what perhaps she had always known deep in her bones, that she could not take anything for granted.

"But I don't want to live in a convent! I don't want to be a nun! Oh, Roberta, why did you have to do this? I'd be all right here!"

"You know how I feel, baby. And I'm right. I've lived a long time in a lot of places and I know what I know. But the convent is only for now. Until they can find a family for you to live with. You need that, baby."

"People I wouldn't know? People who might not care anything about music? I need to stay here! I love it here! But you've made up your mind, haven't you? All right, I'll go. I have to, don't I? I'm not going to run away or do anything foolish. Not yet. But she can't stop me from coming to see you when I want to . . . if you want to see me."

"You don't have to ask that question, Kitty. I love you like my own child. But we both have to be realistic. She can stop you—only she says she won't. But she doesn't want you going into Bernie's. She thinks it must be some den of iniquity. We'll have to meet somewhere else. I have a feeling she'll let me come around once in a while to take you to a concert, or shopping, or something. Don't fight her. Go along with her, at least for a while. Then we'll see. And you'll see, baby. It's going to be for the best. I really believe that. You have to, too."

Roberta opened a drawer of her desk.

"Now let me show you something. For washing dishes and helping in the kitchen, Bernie paid you twenty cents an hour at first, then he raised it to thirty so you were making a dollar, then a dollar fifty every evening six days a week for five months. I know how badly you wanted to help, baby, and I let you, but I put half of that money in a savings account for you—here, you can see when I opened the account, October 5, 1940, at the bank just up the street from Bernie's. So there was eighty-eight plus a little interest, and just yesterday afternoon I added a little going-away present so you have a hundred and twenty-five of your own. It's no fortune but it'll buy a few things when you need them. It's yours and nobody's business but yours. You don't have to tell Sister Edmund anything about it if you don't want to, though she isn't likely to take it away from you. I'd save it, or most of it, if I were you. As long as it sits in there it's earning money for you. I think Sister Edmund is the kind of woman who realizes a girl needs a little money now and then for the movies or a soda or a magazine or cosmetics, so she'll probably give it to you; but if she doesn't, when you really want something, well you know you have your savings. But just don't fritter it all away in bits and dribbles."

Roberta was helping Kitty to pack now, and it was best to keep talking.

Appalled at the thought of living with nuns in a convent, a kind of prison, choked with grief over the end of this happy life with Roberta, over the loss of the only room of her own she could ever remember having, the loss of this familiar, comforting apartment with its pictures, piano, music, everything in it, and so aching with loneliness the state seemed incurable, Kitty looked at what Roberta was showing her, heard what Roberta was saying, was grateful for the money Roberta had saved for her, but was angry, frightened, inconsolable.

PART II

4

In bed at night, Kitty sometimes imagined herself in a small boat, a frail craft of vague design, borne along on the crests of waves. In the morning, sitting on its edge, bare feet exploring the floor of her room, she had landed somewhere.

The room was in a corner of the second floor of the convent, with windows overlooking Sheridan Road and a side garden, and the views they afforded, of large trees and interesting traffic—double-decker busses, chauffeur-driven town cars sometimes, besides the usual sedans and taxis—compensated somewhat for the basic austerity of the room itself. Sister Edmund had said Kitty could hang any pictures she liked, but the fact was Kitty had none. She had loved her room at Roberta's the way she had found it and had not added anything except a stuffed animal on her bed, a simulated spaniel that had moved with her to the convent. Sister Edmund had foraged here and there, and from Sister Clothilde, the instructress in French, had gotten large travel posters of Mont-Saint-Michel, Chartres, and, on the secular, romantic side, the château of Chenonceaux. From Sister Lawrence, the instructress in art, she had obtained somewhat smaller-sized reproductions of Monet's "The Artist's Garden at Vetheuil" (a garden of children and flowers) and Mary Cassatt's "Children Playing on the Beach," which now covered most of the available wall space. These were extremely pleasant scenes Kitty appreciated, but the room was too large to be cozy, and the posters and reproductions were probably not what a young girl would have chosen for herself.

And she didn't want to be there. Well, you knew all along living with Roberta was temporary. This place is temporary, too, everybody says. Everything is temporary. Every goddamn thing.

Still, it was not a bad room, not really a sad one; its smell was waxed and grandmotherly, but not unpleasant; the floor was worn smooth and polished, cool-warm under bare feet, and little by little, because there was nothing else to do, Kitty got used to it. If she sometimes felt lonely there, it was a loneliness she could control, dispel, forget. In truth, the nuns had been very kind from the beginning of her stay with them, and the room was comfortably cut off from their quarters by an unused room and a back staircase from the kitchen. No one hovered, she could more or less relax there, be by herself, though she was always conscious this was a convent and she was among nuns within these walls. Sister Edmund studiously avoided contact except during class hours. It was also the rule of the order that its members took their meals together, unobserved by outsiders, and Kitty dined alone, a great relief for her.

But she quickly became a kind of pet and would find little gifts, fruit, candy, mysteriously left on dishes in her room. Sister Martin, who did most of the cooking, did her best to stuff Kitty with the Germanic fare that was her specialty—taught her recipes and let her help prepare them—and Kitty gained two pounds the first couple of weeks. She said, "I'm getting fat," which wasn't true, but she learned the necessity of firmly refusing the third if not the second helping.

Kitty had volunteered to help Sister Martin in the kitchen as a regular job, but Sister Edmund had shaken her head.

"It is part of the discipline of the order that we clean our own quarters and take our turn in the kitchen. Keep your own room neat, dear, and that will be enough."

When you saw them only in school, nuns were like creatures from another planet. They looked different, they sounded and acted differently, they *were* different from other people because they were nuns. And they were still different inside the convent, but more human, too. They sometimes wore work habits of light blue material, veils tied back, with slightly shorter skirts, and rolled up their sleeves to scrub floors, wash windows, peel potatoes. Kitty caught glimpses of some without their wimples, with their close-cropped hair, though that was accidental. They weren't all alike. Kitty was conscious enough of this in class, but living with them reinforced the impression. There were sour faces and merry ones, guarded, scholarly faces and simple open ones like Sister Martin's. Some were shy, some self-assured. Those who were probably in their twenties were not yet like those two, three, or four decades older. Sister Clothilde was emotional, especially when she spoke of her native France, Sister Lawrence vague and forgetful, Reverend Mother dry and practical, Sister Edmund theatrical, sometimes moody. Fourteen in all ran the two schools with the assistance of an equal number of lay teachers.

Kitty's rapport with Sister Edmund was in the realm of music. Beyond that, Kitty didn't know what the nun was really like. She was strict, yet praised and encouraged more often than she criticized and chided, but kept her distance. And disappeared until the next lesson.

In the morning, bare feet on the floor of the room, Kitty had landed somewhere, and the French railway posters welcomed her.

It wasn't really a home, but it wasn't a prison; it was just something temporary. And another world from the two little apartments she could remember.

Busses swished past in the rush-hour rain.

A little bathroom with a shower stall, no tub, was located between her room and the unused room, and she had it to herself. As her room seemed to Kitty new and strange and temporary, so seemed her own reflection viewed here in the bathroom mirror. Every day she created new instant self-portraits as she scrubbed her face with a washcloth or combed her hair or simply studied herself for a few moments before she left her floor of the convent. She was never completely satisfied with what she saw in the glass. She wiggled her nose. Too ... something, she thought. Her eyes were her best feature, but she considered the brows too thick. She could never decide about her mouth. Too wide, probably. Scowly when she didn't feel scowly at all. But when she turned up the corners she thought: now I look like a simp. She crossed her eyes and gave herself the giggles for a moment. But then asked herself, Who am I? Kitty. But who's that?

Sister Edmund exacted a promise from Kitty that she would not set foot in Bernie Fossbinder's bar and grill.

"Of course you'll want to visit Mrs. Wilkins once in a while, but frankly, for obvious reasons, that does present problems. We will have to see."

Kitty was angry with Sister Edmund and with herself. It wasn't fair to make her promise not to go back to Bernie's. She couldn't break a promise. But if Sister Edmund had just forbidden her to go there, she would have been able to defy the order.

Shortly thereafter, Kitty took a long walk, alone, north along Sheridan Road to where this major north-south artery became commercial for the last several miles before it reached the city limits. On the second floor of a commercial building above a row of stores, Kitty found the North Shore Studios of Music and the Dance, which she remembered from a previous walk. She entered and climbed the steep staircase, somewhat hesitantly. It was four in the afternoon and the clashing notes of several pianos, one violin, and a dancing teacher's measured counting cascaded from half a dozen studios grouped around a central waiting room where several mothers sat. There was no reception desk. Kitty sat and waited until a pupil left the piano studio of "Harriet Palmer Rubin" and was not replaced. Kitty knocked, and entered, resolutely. A plump little woman with reddish ringlets, violet eyes, and many rings sat doing her nails.

"Ma'am, could I ask a question? You see I'm getting free piano lessons at school but I don't have any place to practice (*It's true*, Kitty thought. *Not jazz*.) and I wondered if maybe on weekends, on Saturdays, if you didn't give any lessons that day, I could rent your piano for a couple of hours."

Harriet Palmer Rubin stared.

"Play something," she commanded.

Kitty ran through some scales, then played a few bars of "Summertime," rich, two-handed chords.

"Well, you're not bad from what I can see," said Harriet Palmer Rubin. "What school did you say you attended?"

"St. Margaret's," Kitty said, her heart pounding.

"I don't know it," Mrs. Rubin said.

Harriet Palmer Rubin was pleased at the possibility of a small windfall involving no effort on her part. Her husband earned a very modest salary for his work in the second-violin section of the Chicago Symphony, and that plus fees from her piano lessons barely kept them and one sickly child out of middle-class penury.

"I'll tell you what," she said. "I don't give lessons Saturday afternoons, but there's a dance class up here so the building'll be open. I can let you use the room and the piano from two to four for a dollar fifty. You can get the key from Madame Zubritszka. Come along, I'll introduce you."

"OK, I guess I can pay that. Can I start this week?"

Kitty went to a nearby drugstore to telephone Roberta. There was an unfamiliar dial tone, then a voice: "That number has been disconnected."

Kitty's legs quivered for a few seconds as she stood in the stuffy phone booth, the receiver hung up just above her eyes. A prop had been knocked out from under her. She walked back to the convent quickly through the slush, sick at heart. There was a message in her room: "Mrs. Wilkins phoned while you were out. She will call again at seven." Kitty normally had her dinner at six. She picked at it, alarming Sister Martin, who felt her forehead for fever.

Roberta phoned at seven. "Kitty? I didn't want you to worry, baby, if you called and didn't find me there. I moved out of the apartment. I didn't want to stay there anymore. I was scared. That white boy who molested you threatened me. So I came to this hotel for a few days. Then I'm going to stay with my sister in Kankakee for a while."

"How are you going to *play*?" Kitty demanded.

"Oh, Paulette has a piano and there may be work around there. I'll do all right."

"All because of me."

"What's all because of you?"

"Moving out. Quitting Bernie's. Roberta, I feel awful!"

"Baby, one thing leads to another, that's life. Look, I wish I could see you before I go but I'm taking the train tomorrow, early. But I'll keep in touch. You, too. You have a pencil? Here's Paulette's address."

Safely in her room, Kitty wept, and fell asleep. She awakened around midnight and the room seemed too hot. She opened a window wide and buried herself in blankets. Her resistance lowered, she caught the flu by morning and was in bed for seven days.

Playing jazz on Harriet Palmer Rubin's Knabe was keeping faith with Roberta, and this became Kitty's secret life for two hours every Saturday. Sister Edmund had said Kitty was free to do as she liked Saturdays and Sundays so long as she left word where she was going and was back at a given hour. It was easy enough to cover her whereabouts by spending part of Saturday with one friend or another. With a friend she would often be out of doors or browsing at the magazine rack or cosmetic counter of some drugstore, or going to a movie, and temporarily out of contact anyway. No direct deception was necessary, and from the revealed inspiration of classical music, under the intent, watchful gaze of Sister Edmund, to the inspired surprises of jazz, Kitty moved between the two musical worlds and each, she believed, complemented the other, though Sister Edmund would not have agreed.

Kitty withdrew more of her savings to invest in the least expensive portable phonograph and then spent many contented Saturday mornings in record stores listening to every fifty-cent Wilson, Tatum, Hines, Stacy, Bushkin, Weathersby, Waller, Sullivan, Basie or Mary Lou Williams recording she could find, and many others, and buying at least one a week.

Kitty determined correctly that Sister Edmund could not possibly object to Kitty having her own bank account, told her early on, and, indeed, Sister Edmund praised Roberta Wilkins' foresight.

"And you must not only keep it, dear, you must try to add to it," Sister Edmund said. "Reverend Mother has decided we will give you a weekly allowance of one dollar and we urge you to set aside part of that to put in your account."

"A dollar? That's a lot, Sister! Thank you very much."

But Sister Edmund, making one of her rare appearances at Kitty's door, having been told of a large package Kitty had brought in, frowned at the purchase of a phonograph.

"As you know, there is a perfectly good phonograph in the music room with records to match, and you are perfectly free to use it."

"I know, Sister, and I do use it to play concertos and Chopin and things, but, well, to play some of the records I buy I thought I ought to have my own phonograph in my room. So I wouldn't bother anybody."

"Records you buy such as what? Please be so kind as to play one for me."

Nervously, Kitty flipped through her small collection, and decided on the Goodman Trio playing "Memories of You."

"This is really good, Sister. I think you'll like it. It's not too loud or anything."

"Loudness, per se, is neither a defect nor a virtue," Sister Edmund said. "I think what you mean is this is not, in your opinion, raucous, caterwauling?"

"I guess so," Kitty said. "Anyway, this is the Benny Goodman Trio—clarinet, piano, and drums. Teddy Wilson is on piano. He's great. Well, so is Benny Goodman." Kitty took a deep breath. "I don't think any symphony clarinetist could play any better."

"A bold statement, indeed," said Sister Edmund. "And since when is one 'on' piano? What kind of language is that? Jazz jargon, no doubt. Well, put it on."

The clear, always exciting line of Goodman's clarinet pierced the corners of the room with a flowing, nineteen-note introduction to the melody, and then Wilson came comping in behind it with imaginative, lyrical right-hand notes woven seamlessly into light, emotional tenths in his left, and then his brief, tantalizing-satisfying soloing balanced pure clarinet refrains, and all the while Kitty kept perfect time with one small, scuffed, saddle-shoed toe, along with Krupa's (this time) self-effacing drums. It was all over in about three minutes and was followed by silence.

"Mr. Goodman has great control over his instrument," Sister Edmund said at last. "Mr. Wilson gives evidence of similar talent, though it is difficult to determine his real capabilities from this abbreviated and slight example. He plays with a certain delicacy I found quite surprising, even original. The song itself? Pleasant enough, facile—and shallow. It strikes me as too bad Mr. Goodman and Mr. Wilson have wasted their talents on it . . . Now don't look so downcast. Perhaps it was unfair of me to criticize the song itself for not being sublime when it was never intended to be. It is really quite pretty and well made. We must get the sheet music so you can learn it." She picked up the record, peered at the label and repeated aloud "Blake-Razaf . . . As a change of pace, a form of musical relaxation, I see no reason why you shouldn't listen to and play this kind of music occasionally—so long as it doesn't interfere with your training in the music I consider far more important."

One afternoon that spring, following many days of practice, Kitty played the Chopin Etude in F Major without a mistake.

"Bravo," cried Sister Edmund, clapping her hands once. "You got off to a late start but you've made remarkable progress. I think you'll be ready to give your first recital at the Christmas concert. And ready to perform a recital-length Mozart work—the C-major Sonata. We must begin to work on it immediately."

Now that she could play popular music in the convent, Kitty considered dropping her arrangement with Harriet Palmer Rubin, but decided to hang on to it a while longer—for good luck, and to have more hours of jazz than Sister Edmund would probably allow.

Kitty and Roberta exchanged a letter apiece, but each seemed to find writing difficult. Sadly, it seemed, they could only really communicate face to face, sound to ear. It was not until late spring that they wrote again, and their second attempts were no less clumsy than the first. Roberta was still resting, looking around, not yet playing professionally again. Roberta sent her photograph, a copy of one of the two in the window at Bernie Fossbinder's, and Kitty bought a leather frame with a stand and propped up the photo on the top of her chest of drawers.

Kitty's closest school friends numbered three—Eileen Byrne, Fran Abbott, Alice Hanrahan. Of these, Kitty saw Eileen most often. Eileen looked up to Kitty, though not literally since Eileen was taller, the tallest girl in the class. Eileen came to Kitty for advice on practically everything; she believed Kitty was a superior being who was going to be a famous musician, maybe a famous Hollywood star some day. Kitty was flattered by Eileen's devotion but sometimes found her naivete a little wearying.

Fran and Alice had had slumber parties for the four of them that spring. Eileen's parents had vetoed Eileen's turn on the grounds the Byrne apartment was too small, but said Eileen could invite Kitty alone. After the 8:30 double feature one Saturday evening at the Granada, which let out at twenty to twelve, Kitty and Eileen walked to Eileen's place, and in their pajamas made themselves grilled cheese sandwiches and cocoa in the kitchen. Mrs. Byrne wished them goodnight and went off to join her husband, already asleep. Younger sisters were asleep in another room. Eileen and Kitty were going to spend the night on the back porch off the kitchen, a retreat for the Byrne family on hot summer nights. Eileen tuned in some dance music on the radio, Irving Bennett from the Lake Shore Hotel.

"He's terrible, Eileen," Kitty said. "Can't you find anything else?"

Other stations had more of the same, sweet bands. Eileen fiddled with the dial and found a station playing a recording of the Goodman Sextet's "I Found a New Baby."

"Leave that on, leave that on!" Kitty said. "God, this is great. It's new. I heard it in the store but I didn't have enough money with me. I've got to get it!"

Brief, memorable solos by Goodman's clarinet, Cootie Williams' muted trumpet and Georgie Auld's tenor sax, one of Count Basie's look-how-easy-it-is (but just try it) right-hand piano solos up there in the quicksilver treble keys, a sensational electric guitar improvisation by young Charlie Christian—"God, do you hear that, Eileen?"—and a fine, old-fashioned rideout, with drummer Jo Jones and bassist Artie Bernstein at the controls, which flew in six different directions at once and still hung together beautifully to the end.

Eileen nodded, though she wasn't sure she appreciated the performance the way Kitty had, and wished Kitty wouldn't say "God" so often, her mother might hear. The recording was the final selection of the program. Eileen had to switch back to some sweet band, and Kitty sighed and put up with it.

Eileen plugged the radio into an outlet on the porch, turned it very low, and she and Kitty climbed into cots at right angles to each other.

They had talked about the movies they had seen, so that subject was pretty well exhausted, but Eileen was going to want to talk about something.

"Do you think Kevin Clohessy is cute?" Eileen asked.

"Do you?"

"Sort of."

"Maybe he'll ask you out."

"Oh," Eileen said, and Kitty could almost see her redden in the dark. "I've never even talked to him."

"Well, say hello to him. You see him at church. You see him at the drugstore. He probably goes to the tea dances. Let him see what a pretty girl you are."

"I'm too tall."

"Not for him."

"I'd die."

"No you wouldn't. You've got to get over being so shy, Eileen. Look. I'll get somebody I know to introduce him to me, and then later I'll introduce him to you."

"He'd probably want to go out with you, then."

"I'm not really interested, and anyway I'm sure the nuns wouldn't let me date."

"My mother and father think I'm too young, too. They say fifteen, even sixteen is time enough."

"Well it won't hurt you to get to *know* some boys."

"You'd probably prefer to go with older boys."

"Why do you say that? I've never had a real date. I've just been to parties."

"I just think the boys our age are too young for you."

"Well, I liked one once but he never got the message."

"Who?"

"Jimmy Williams."

"He was probably too shy like me."

"Maybe. Anyway, he moved away."

"Kitty?"

"What?"

"Never mind."

"Don't do that, Eileen. If you want to ask a question, ask it."

"Have you ever seen a boy—you know—down there? I mean without any clothes on?"

"I've seen men. Same thing."

"Kitty!"

"Well, you asked. I lived in a dinky apartment. I slept on the sofa bed in the living room. There were different men around. I mean, they didn't parade around or anything. I just happened to see a couple of times. Eileen, do you *know* what boys look like?"

"I saw a drawing in a medical book."

"Well, that's close enough. Let's go to sleep."

"Kitty? It's none of my business and you don't have to tell me, but why did your mother leave?"

"She ran off with one of her boyfriends."

"I'm sorry."

"That's OK."

But it wasn't OK. Damn you, Eileen, did you have to remind me?

Little by little tears came, silently, not so Eileen could hear. But it wasn't her mother she missed, whose loss she mourned, it was Roberta.

On the last early evenings of spring, the first summer nights, Kitty leaned out of her open window. Along Sheridan Road, convertibles, tops down, drove past carrying young people to proms and parties, their hair blowing. Boys strolled with girls along the sidewalk, holding hands. "Stardust" played on her phonograph. And she wondered who she was and what would happen to her, who the nuns would find for her to live with and if she would like them, or if they would find anyone at all.

She had been kissed only a couple of times during games of post office and spin the bottle at eighth-grade parties, by clumsy, hard-lipped boys who meant nothing to her, and no boy she had liked had ever even held her hand. What she longed for now was tenderness and romance, mistily envisaged, that would dissipate forever the memory of the one boy who had ever touched her, the boy in the corridor who had defiled her with his sour smell and dirty hands and had tried to take by force what was only hers to give with love, who had made her for a while hate all boys and men because of their greater strength and the one thing on their minds most of the time. She still had nightmares about him. In one terrible dream, he and those two other boys he hung around with had gotten into Roberta's apartment somehow. Roberta was tied to a chair and her mouth was sealed shut with adhesive tape. Kitty herself was on the bed and they were holding her down, tearing her clothes off and laughing at her and she was powerless and terrified . . .

"They're hoodlums, criminals," Roberta had said. "You mustn't ever think all men are like that."

And now she didn't. She despised only that one boy, and most of the time she was able to forget him.

5

Sister Edmund usually spent at least part of the summer vacation with her parents, in past years traveling in Europe and Asia or at their fifteen-room "cottage" in Bar Harbor, Maine. In 1938, a disastrous fire had destroyed the cottage and a number of neighboring houses, and for the third year in a row now Sister Edmund's parents planned to remain at their home in Lake Forest, an enclave of the very rich some twenty-five miles north of downtown Chicago along the lake. Sister Edmund invited Kitty to join her there from late June until the Labor Day weekend so that Kitty's piano instruction would not be interrupted, an invitation that had the effect of a command since Kitty did not see how she could comfortably decline, and anyway the prospect intrigued, even excited her.

On June 20, a friend of the convent, a Mrs. Barry, drove them to the Rogers Park station of the Chicago & Northwestern Railroad where Kitty and Sister Edmund boarded a suburban train for the one-hour journey, including stops at the half-dozen affluent suburbs strung along the lake between Chicago and Lake Forest.

As the train slowed to enter their station at half past three in the afternoon, Sister Edmund said, "My father will meet us. His name is Franklin O'Donnell, which means you now know what my family name was before I entered the order. That fact is not one I expect you ever to discuss with any of your classmates. May I have your promise?"

"Sure, Sister. Don't worry. I'll never say anything."

"Good. Now, as I told you, we will be guests of my parents. I expect my brother, Charles, to visit from New York later on. Kitty, my mother and father, my mother especially, can appear rather formidable at first. They are used to giving orders and having their own way. But you're not to be frightened of them. Their bark is often worse than their bite. I want you to enjoy yourself here. This should be a vacation for you, too. I think we should maintain a schedule of three one-hour lessons weekly, and two hours daily practice, but the rest of the time you'll be free to relax—on the beach, reading, whatever you choose. Well, here we are."

The sixtyish man who waited for them on the platform was neither unusually tall nor heavy, but he gave an impression of size, presence, power. White-haired, tanned, neatly dressed in the casual clothes of the era—light-blue Palm Beach jacket, white shirt, blue-and-white polka-dot bow tie, white slacks, brown-and-white wing-tip shoes. He carried a malacca walking stick and removed a cream-colored panama hat when he caught sight of Sister Edmund.

"Mary, my dear," he murmured as he embraced his daughter, another mystery solved. Nuns were so secretive about their personal lives, Kitty thought, as though they had none and lived only on some spiritual plane, hiding their real names as they hid themselves, under yards of black cloth, under veils and wimples.

Kitty was introduced, but Franklin O'Donnell acknowledged Kitty's "How do you do, sir?" by looking through her as though she were a pane of glass. What also went through Kitty was the chill of unfriendliness of this man who felt no obligation not to be rude.

Feeling lonely, out of place, angry—and the visit had hardly even begun!—Kitty said to herself, *Some vacation. And her mother is supposed to be the scarier of the two. Why did she bring me here? I could have stayed on the Granville beach with my friends.*

They left the station in a 1934 Packard touring car with a canvas top and an adjustable, chrome-bound glass partition between the front and back seats. Franklin O'Donnell drove—his driver had taken Mrs. O'Donnell somewhere, though she was expected to be on hand to greet them at the house. Sister Edmund sat beside him. Kitty had the back seat to herself.

It was a fine day, warm in the sun but cool as they drove through tree tunnels past the entrances to private estates.

The house, at the end of a long, private drive, remained entirely hidden in its acres of forest until the car entered a cobblestone motor court.

Wow, Kitty said to herself. It's a castle.

It was, more accurately, a copy of a sixteenth-century Norman manor house, built in the 1920s, but its lofty massiveness and fine proportions, its many high-pitched tiled roofs and projecting round and polygonal towers, and its four multi-flued brick chimneys did suggest the grandeur of medieval fortifications.

It was an impressive house and Kitty was afraid of it, or of the people in it. A tall woman in a white linen dress, with Sister Edmund's face framed by silver hair, stood in the open doorway clasping opposite elbows with her hands. A pale pink cardigan sweater was draped around her shoulders. Two Irish setters bounded back and forth, frantic to be noticed.

Mother and daughter embraced, and Kitty was ignored again, but then Sister Edmund remembered her and said, "Come in, dear. Come inside. I'll show you to your room. It has a view of the lake."

A young Irish maid, wearing a uniform and speaking with a brogue, came out to take the luggage, and while Kitty was noticing her, Franklin O'Donnell and his wife managed to disappear.

Inside, from the two-story-high entrance hall surrounded on three sides by a balconied mezzanine, and the mounted heads of deer, elk, moose, and other horned creatures, the house seemed to go on and on in three directions.

"How many rooms does it have?" Kitty asked as they crossed the black-and-white checkerboard tiles of the hall.

"Twenty, twenty-five or so," Sister Edmund said. "It depends on what you count."

The room Kitty was to occupy for the next two months was at the side and back of the house at the end of one wing on the ground floor. Sun streamed through wide windows onto a double bed with a bright patchwork quilt, on blue-cushioned white wicker chairs, blue flowered wallpaper, and a white dressing table with a mirror.

"Closet. Bath," said Sister Edmund, opening two inside doors.

"It's so pretty," Kitty said, her spirits rising.

Beyond the window, an arcade, the corner of a low-walled formal garden broken by the entrance to a stone staircase going down to the beach, the sparkling lake beyond.

Sister Edmund stepped into the corridor, which doglegged to the right.

"You can go to the beach whenever you want through this door. The kitchen is down that way. Are you hungry? Would you like something to eat?"

"No, thank you, Sister. I'm fine."

"Then I will leave you for a while. You must not mind my parents too much, Kitty. They don't know how to talk to young people. Children, yes, young people, no. I don't think they're conscious of being deliberately rude. Some people mellow as they grow older. I thought they might. Perhaps they will. Others become even more set in their ways. You must not mind and let that spoil your time here."

The nun was not looking at Kitty as she spoke.

"Yes, Sister," Kitty said in a low voice, and then asked, "Sister, where can I play the piano so I won't bother anyone?"

Sister Edmund brightened, seemingly glad of the opportunity to change the subject.

"Well now. There's a Steinway in the music room, which is just to the right of the entrance hall as you face the front door. Unless it's been moved, there is also an upright piano in the gazebo, the summer house in the garden—a little, round, open pavilion—you'll find it easily—but that may not be in tune. Try it and let me know.

"Mealtimes are always rather informal here, and one eats more or less when one wishes to. When you're hungry just let Mrs. Cassidy in the kitchen know what you'd like. Of course I must take my food alone, and I think you'd prefer to do that, too, am I right?"

"Oh, yes, Sister."

"Enjoy yourself, dear."

She left, and Kitty unpacked her suitcase and began putting her things in the chest of drawers. It was a pleasant room. But she knew where she was—in the servant's quarters.

* * *

Sister Edmund, dressed now in a white summer habit of lightweight material, sat with her mother on an outside terrace.

"Well, what are your plans for this child aside from a career on the concert stage?" the older woman asked in the hoarse voice of the older rich. "You try to mold people. I know you, Mary."

"And you don't, Mother?"

The older woman declined to answer.

"I'm a teacher," Sister Edmund said. "Kitty is unusual and lives with us in the convent, so naturally I am devoting more time to her than might otherwise be the case."

"This is more than teaching, this is shaping—an attempt to create someone. I don't believe it will work. May I remind you Pygmalion is fiction?"

"Mother, this is much more a question of exposure, of experience, than shaping or molding. In her own way, Kitty has already shaped herself, surviving an abominable childhood to become what she is today—an attractive, highly intelligent, very gifted young girl who can become anything she wants, given the opportunities."

"Become what she is, or what you think she is? You're an incurable romantic, Mary. Oh, she's a pretty little thing, I won't deny that. And well spoken, your father says. I had expected someone much more common. But do you imagine for a minute she would ever be accepted in our circle? Knowing who the mother was, not knowing who or what the father was, could you seriously attempt, say, to marry her off in a few years to any young man we know? Do you know anything about retrogressive genes? Then why did you bring her here? It was unkind! It can only give her notions, raise her expectations, which can only bring disillusionment. Breeding takes generations!"

"I used to believe that, Mother, and still do to a degree, but what you're talking about is social snobbery, a sin I, too, must confess to. Your grandfather—no, let me claim him—my great-grandfather, arrived here from Ireland a penniless immigrant."

"He was a pioneer! Men like him built this country! Save your lectures for your pupils!"

They had arrived on a Friday. Sister Edmund scheduled a lesson for the following Monday afternoon, but said that if Kitty felt like trying out the piano before then she should feel free to do so.

Over the weekend, Kitty stuck to her end of the rambling house, shy about wandering too far away from it. She explored the formal garden with its maze of hedges, beds of flowers, urns and statuary, played with the setters, found the little summer house with its piano, tested it briefly. It was in tune. Two men were working in the garden, an older man clipping hedges, a younger man hauling dirt in a wheelbarrow. She had the beach to herself, though in either direction, on the beaches of adjoining houses, she could see an occasional standing or seated figure. She swam and read and worked on her tan. When she returned she ran into Sister Edmund in the garden who chatted with her for a few moments and departed.

Mrs. Cassidy, the cook, was friendly and talkative and served Kitty in a sunny little breakfast room, light luxury fare at lunch and dinner, fresh salmon, trout, lamb chops. Kitty had never eaten trout before and found it delicious. There was a screened porch with the latest magazines and a radio; she had use of another radio in her room. For a day or so this was all the space she needed.

Monday morning at breakfast, Mrs. Cassidy said, "Take a look at the rest of the place, dearie. No need to stay cooped up back here. You'll have it to yourself for a while. Mr. O'Donnell has gone to his office and Mrs. O never comes downstairs before eleven. Sister Edmund usually stays in her room most of the morning, too."

Feeling bolder, Kitty began to explore the rooms and porches of the lower floor. What she saw dazzled her. She had never seen pieces of furniture, rugs, things like these. Things. A vast profusion of things—and each one must have cost a great deal of money.

There was too much to take in. Even after half an hour of wandering she had hardly begun to look.

One room was a kind of museum crowded with fearsome masks, spears, daggers with jeweled handles, war clubs, idols, a variety of headdress, feathered capes, and pieces of ivory—or maybe whalebone—painted with little scenes of ships and towns. In one connecting corridor were marble statues and suits of armor. Three walls of the paneled library were lined with leather-bound books, colors kept together, a row of green, a shelf of cherry red, a row of black... the complete works of Trollope, Thackeray, Washington Irving, other authors she had never heard of. The books didn't look as though anyone had ever read them. The large, formal dining room (there was a smaller one, too) and four sitting rooms were stuffed with carved and gilded tables, and cabinets full of porcelain cherubim, cupids, goddesses, shepherdesses, enameled and gilded urns, ewers, candelabras, clocks, and other objects in the form of real and mythical creatures—Kitty was particularly fascinated by a pair of winged dragons—whose purposes were obscure.

"Well, did you see anything interesting?" asked Mrs. Cassidy when Kitty returned to the kitchen.

"Everything," Kitty marveled. "Some of those china things are really wild."

"Ain't they gorgeous? Mrs O collects it and Mr. O buys it for her. Some of them pieces was made for royalty, believe that or not. Cost a fortune," she whispered loudly. "Only Maureen, my daughter-in-law, is allowed to dust it all."

At 11:30 there was still no sign of either Sister Edmund or Mrs. O'Donnell. Kitty was drawn to the music room, to the Steinway grand. Double glass doors from the music room opened to a solarium where a little fountain gurgled from the mouth of a green bronze dolphin, a green mermaid riding sidesaddle.

Kitty began playing Hanon doubled thirds and two-handed arpeggios. After a while she began Chopin's Etude in G-flat Major, fifty-two seconds of scampering charm and humor and an ideal encore for the Christmas recital. When she had zipped through it, the voice of Mrs. O'Donnell said, "I see what Sister Edmund means. You're very good, indeed."

Kitty turned her head. Mrs. O'Donnell was seated across the room. Kitty had not heard anyone enter.

"Thank you," Kitty said. "It seemed late enough. I hope I'm not disturbing anyone."

"Not at all. Will you play a request? Sister Edmund tells me you've mastered 'Für Elise.' I'm fond of that."

Kitty began the pristine little Beethoven piece, its notes clear water over polished pebbles. At its conclusion she heard the clapping of hands, but when she turned, flattered, she saw that it was Sister Edmund, having joined her mother, who was applauding.

"So you want to be a concert performer," Mrs. O'Donnell said. "My mother heard the great Anton Rubinstein during his American tour in 1873, the year I was born ... My daughter tells me you sing well, too. Have you considered a career in opera? Of one thing we can be certain. No man sings the role of Mimi or Tosca or any of the others written for women. Women and men are equal in opera. That's the nature of the art. Well, I shan't keep you."

She rose and left the room without a further word or backward glance. Sister Edmund rolled her eyes heavenward. Kitty said, "I'm getting hungry. I think I'll stop awhile."

And she said to herself, I never said I wanted to be a concert performer. Sister Edmund did. I'm not sure. But what do I want to be?

6

The summer days lazed on toward July. The brush of a cool-warm breeze through the windows of her room in the early morning, the not unpleasant burn of a little too much sun in the late afternoon, the good feeling of nakedness under a clean sheet, a light blanket, at night, and again in the early morning.

Sister Edmund told Kitty that if she wished to walk beyond the limits of the O'Donnells' beach, she could do so without trespassing on other private property simply by walking below the highwater mark, which was the property of the state. Then, when Kitty tired of swimming or sunning or the magazine she had brought, she strolled along the shore, a mile or more in either direction. Once in a while other people did the same, and if she happened to be seated on her towel or lying on one side facing the shore, she might look up.

Twice she had passed the boy on her walks, and twice he had walked slowly past her along the water line of the O'Donnells' beach. She remembered him from the first time and thought about him a little in between. The fifth time she saw him approaching from a distance. She did not stare at him or follow him with her eyes but put her magazine down and kept her face raised looking out over the lake. And what she wanted to happen, happened. Their eyes met, they both smiled tentatively at the same instant, he said, "Hi," and she returned the greeting. Kitty got to her feet and walked slowly toward the surf, her eyes lowered, convinced he wanted her to come forward, and afraid if she didn't he might walk on. But before she reached him she sat again, to let him come to her. And he sat on his heels beside her.

His name was Tom Webster. He was staying next door with his paternal grandmother.

"Are you related to the O'Donnell's?" he asked.

"No, I'm just visiting with Sister Edmund."

"Does that mean you're going to become some kind of nun?"

"No," Kitty said, trying not to sound panicky (No, no! she said to herself), "I never would. I don't have a vocation."

"My parents and grandmother know the O'Donnell's, I guess, but I don't think they see each other. We're not Catholic. I guess that makes a difference to some people. It doesn't to me. Would you like to take a walk?"

When she stood he was only about two inches taller. But he had good posture and was compactly built, with swimmer's muscles. She put on shorts and a blouse over her one-piece wool bathing suit. She glanced at him a little as they strolled over hard-packed sand near the water's edge. He had a nice face, she thought, even though his expression was quite serious and determined. Brown curly hair that didn't look as though it would ever need much combing.

"Are your parents away?" Kitty asked, looking up at the tile roofs and stucco walls of his grandmother's sprawling Spanish-style house on a bluff above the beach.

"They're on a cruise to British Columbia and Alaska," Tom said. "Ever been on a cruise?"

"No. Not yet."

"I went on one with them last summer to Australia and New Zealand and some of the Pacific islands. It's boring. All you do is lie around and eat and get dressed up. So this year they said I could stay with my grandmother and go to camp in northern Michigan."

"When do you go to camp?"

"Week and a half from now."

Kitty's heart dropped a little.

"How long is it?"

"Six weeks. Then I'll come back here. What about your parents?"

"They're dead," Kitty said. "My father was killed in a mining accident in Bolivia. He was an engineer. My mother died of TB. She was a harpist in the Chicago Symphony."

"I think I saw her," Tom said. "When did she die?"

"A year ago."

"Well, I went to the Symphony a year ago last Christmas. So I probably did. I'm sorry. Then where do you live?"

"In the convent where Sister Edmund lives. It's just temporary until I go to college. She's my music teacher. She was a friend of my mother."

"Don't you have any relatives?"

"Well, of course. But they're in California. I didn't want to stop studying with Sister Edmund."

"Would you like to have lunch?" Tom asked. "The cook can fix us something. My grandmother's not there. She's playing bridge. She goes to bridge luncheons practically every day, or has her friends to the house for the same thing."

"If you're sure it's all right. Where do you go to school? Up here?"

"I start at Amherst this fall."

"Oh, sure." Kitty pretended to know where it was.

They climbed a stone staircase. The house was cool and dim behind shuttered windows. There were old Spanish chests and chairs but mostly the rooms were Santa Fe and California modern, spacious and comfortable, and instantly Kitty liked them better than the cluttered, ornate salons of the O'Donnells' castle.

Tom led Kitty to a screened porch overlooking the beach.

"Wait here," he said. "I'll get us something to eat."

Surrounding a glass-top table were wrought-iron chairs with leather cushions, and there were a lot of hanging and standing plants. Rush matting and Navaho rugs covered the floor. Kitty sat on a leather hassock, legs together and folded to one side, fingers linked, and waited. Tom returned followed by a large black woman carrying a tray.

"This is Kitty, Clydell," Tom said.

"How you do, honey?" Clydell said.

"Fine. Pleased to meet you," Kitty said.

Clydell laid out cups of cold vichyssoise, plates of cold cuts, cheese, pickles, salad ingredients, and bread, and tall glasses of iced tea.

"Need anything else, just give a yell," Clydell said.

Tom pulled a chair out for Kitty and she sat, and then he sat across from her.

"This is nice," Kitty said.

She was dubious about the soup, but when the first cold, creamy, leeky flavor surprised her taste buds she sighed a little and finished her cup off as though she had been enjoying vichyssoise all her life. She didn't ask what it was until she got back to the O'Donnells' and could describe it to Mrs. Cassidy.

They met again the following day and every day after that for a week until he left for camp—almost as children do who hit it off, the new child on the block investigated and accepted as a friend by the kid next door even before the movers have finished unloading. They lunched again on the porch and picnicked on the beach, pooling sandwiches from Clydell's and Mrs. Cassidy's kitchens. They swam together off his grandmother's beach and lay side by side, prone or supine, stretched in the sun. All this in the afternoons, and Kitty did not mention any of it to Sister Edmund. In the late mornings she practiced or had a lesson. In the early evenings after dinner Sister Edmund would come by to read or listen to the radio for a while on the porch next to Kitty's room. The nun believed she was keeping Kitty company, but in reality now she was keeping Kitty from meeting Tom, and Kitty sat with Sister Edmund and longed to get away. Then one afternoon Tom left for camp, by car and train.

One hot morning, Kitty was in the gazebo playing "I Married an Angel," singing the lyrics to herself. The gazebo upright had been kept on hand for large outdoor parties when the O'Donnells would hire a dance band, something they had not done for a number of years. The Cassidy men brought it into a storeroom in the winter but out again in the summer in the event someone, Sister Edmund most likely, should want to use it. Kitty used it to play jazz and popular music, reserving the Steinway in the music room for classical.

A black-haired, red-faced man of about thirty, slightly overweight in white duck slacks and an open-collared blue sport shirt, crossed the lawn from the house, folded his arms on the railing of the gazebo and rested his chin on them. Kitty stopped singing but continued playing.

"You're good, you know that?" Charlie said after introducing himself. "You're good enough to perform at the Ruban Bleu or the Versailles."

"Are they New York nightclubs?"

"Nightclubs, supper clubs."

"What're they like?"

"Well, let me describe them this way. A friend of mine is a newspaper reporter, and once I went along with him to the Versailles after lunch. It's not open during the day, but he was doing a feature interview with the owner. In the daylight it looked sort of forlorn and shabby. But at night it glitters. There's electricity in the air. The performers make it come alive. The performers and all the people watching and applauding and enjoying themselves."

Charlie came around and made himself more comfortable, sitting on the steps of the gazebo.

"Play some more. Do you know any boogie-woogie?"

"A little."

Kitty launched into "Honky-Tonk Train Blues," her left hand rocking the repetitive eight-to-the-bar framework for her charging right hand. Charlie smiled broadly and kept time with bobbing head and drumming fingers. It was limited music, Kitty knew, but also original and fun to play, and she kept at it until Sister Edmund rushed up, white and wrathful, to put a stop to it all.

"None of that, none of that here!" she cried. "At least you had the decency to play those dreadful sounds outside and not in the house! Do you have any idea where that so-called music originated? In brothels! You're not too young to know what they are! Abominable places where women sell themselves!"

Too late, Sister Edmund suddenly remembered Kitty's mother and put a hand to her mouth for a moment.

"Now Mary, calm down," Charlie said. "Blame me if you have to blame anybody. It's all my fault. I asked for it. Hey, listen, those musicians had to work somewhere and might have preferred more genteel surroundings themselves. Anyway, I question whether there can be anything wicked in a piece of music without lyrics."

"Don't presume to instruct me about music, Charles. I won't have it! I'd like to speak to you privately ... Kitty, I'm not angry with you. You couldn't have known. But I think I would like you to work on your Mozart in the music room now. Or perhaps your Debussy Arabesques."

Sister Edmund closed her eyes and wiped perspiration from her brow with a large handkerchief she pulled from her sleeve.

Sensing Kitty's restlessness without knowing its origin, Sister Edmund brought books from her personal library and suggested Kitty might like to ride along with one or another of the Cassidys occasionally when they drove to the village on errands. Across from the railroad station were a few shops, a drugstore, a small movie theater. Kitty was glad enough to go. A few early evenings she saw things like *The Road to Zanzibar* and *I Wanted Wings*. The O'Donnells had tennis courts, and Charlie, perhaps prompted, said, "I would dearly love a partner. Why don't I give you some lessons?"

Only rarely did Kitty catch even distant glimpses of Franklin O'Donnell. A few times she accidentally encountered Mrs. O'Donnell in some room or hall but only long enough for a shy greeting from Kitty and a nod, or a vague "Yes," from Sister Edmund's mother.

In the afternoons Kitty lay and walked on the beach and swam alone, counting off the days, and daydreamed about living in a house like Mrs. Webster's and taking cruises to far-off places.

Tom's parents lived in Chicago, in an apartment off Lincoln Park. His grandfather lived alone down there, too, somewhere. His other grandmother, a widow, lived in Connecticut. Tom's older sister, his only sibling, was spending most of the summer with friends in Maine and was due to arrive at the house sometime after Tom returned from camp. A few of Tom's friends would be at the camp in Michigan; the rest, former classmates from the Deerfield Academy in Massachusetts, were scattered in a number of states.

In Kitty's imagination she could begin to people his world and imagine herself a part of it. It had never even occurred to her before coming to Lake Forest to look for a rich boy, and she didn't think of Tom as rich now, though she knew his grandmother was and thought his parents must be, too, to be able to take cruises every year. But Tom was just Tom as far as she was concerned. And so the weeks passed while she waited for his return.

On a Sunday afternoon Tom reappeared on the beach, and they walked slowly towards each other, smiling hesitantly. Neither of them could take up exactly where they had left off. They circled each other tentatively, to get reacquainted.

"I'm hot. Let's swim," Kitty said, and they ran together into the cold water of the lake, dived below the surface, and came up a few yards apart. Tom swam over to her. Kitty was treading water, her face glistening, her hair plastered against her head.

"Did you have a good time?" she asked.

"It was OK. I'm glad to be back."

She plunged toward the shore and he followed, and they walked, dripping and shivering, toward their towels.

Kitty was suddenly inspired to do a series of long-legged cartwheels across the sand. Tom did backflips and handstands. Then they sat on Kitty's blanket facing each other.

"You have gray eyes," Tom said.

"Green."

"Both."

"You have longer lashes than I do," Kitty said, leaning close to his face and squinting. "Hold still." She reached up and brushed sand from his eyebrows with the tips of her fingers, then continued to hold her hands in the air as though she might be drying them or perhaps about to conduct an orchestra.

Tom looked from her narrow nose and generous mouth, which he had been studying, to her rather long tanned fingers and asked, "Do you have to have different hands to play the piano?"

"I don't think so. They're just hands. You have to use them a lot. Practice, I mean. Two hours a day at least. Four is better if you're really going to be a professional. Even more."

She dropped them into her lap.

"Are you?" he asked.

"I don't know."

"I've got some pretty good records," Tom said. "Why don't we go up to the house and listen to them?"

"Sure."

She stood and put on a cotton dress over her head, shook her hair and combed it. They walked barefoot in a slightly zigzag, up-and-down pattern across the hot, dry low dunes of the upper beach. Tom reached out and took her hand as they climbed the steps.

He led her through the silent, restful house to a long verandah where there were chairs, couches, tables, a phonograph.

"I'll get some cola," Tom said and went away for a while. Kitty looked at magazine covers, then through his record collection. Dance bands—Glen Gray, Skinnay Ennis, Jan Garber—not great but OK—and Tom returned with tall, tinkling glasses.

Kitty had scarcely danced at all before, but lightly held by Tom, the steps—barefoot on the verandah, circling, dipping, swaying to phonograph music—came to her as easily as walking. When their dancing slowed to a gentle rocking, barely keeping time, Kitty sang "There's a Small Hotel" just above a whisper and Tom looked at her in surprise.

"You have a very nice voice."

"Choir, glee club," Kitty said.

"Better than that. You don't sound like most kids."

"Thank you. But I wish I could sing like Ella Fitzgerald or Lee Wiley or Mildred Bailey. I'm sure I never will. Mrs. O'Donnell thinks I ought to try opera. Ah ah ah ah ah ah ah ah ah," she mimicked, going up and down the scale.

"Would you like that?"

"Not if I'd have to get fat."

"I don't care for a lot of opera."

"It takes getting used to. Some of it's lovely. Who knows, maybe I will."

A woman in her sixties wearing a pink dress, gloves, a wide-brimmed hat, and pink high-heeled shoes, stepped onto the verandah, stumbled slightly, and caught herself. Tom stopped dancing, but continued to hold Kitty's hand.

"This is my grandmother, Kitty. Nana, this is Kitty Collins. She's spending the summer with the O'Donnells."

"How do you do, Mrs. Webster," Kitty said.

"Hello," Mrs. Webster said. "You're not one of Joanna's daughters, are you?"

"No, ma'am."

"I didn't think so. That would have been a surprise."

"Kitty is one of Sister Edmund's pupils," Tom said. "She plays the piano."

"Well, I wish you could play for me," said Mrs. Webster. "But we have no piano. No one in this family is musical. No one in this family has one iota of artistic ability. I would have guessed you were a dancer. You move like a dancer. You have a dancer's face. I hope you don't mind my saying so."

"No, ma'am."

A few of the old woman's words had come out thickly, a little slurred.

"Well, make yourself at home," she said, and went out.

"Who is Joanna?" Kitty asked.

"One of the O'Donnells, I think. I'll find out. What time do you have dinner?"

"About six."

"Well its still light until seven-thirty or eight. Can you come out afterwards? We could take a walk. It's nice then."

"I'll try."

Sister Edmund dropped by as usual after Kitty's supper.

"It's so hot," Kitty said. "It got up to a hundred today, the radio said. I thought I'd take a walk on the beach."

"As you wish," Sister Edmund said. "Perhaps, then, I'll do my father the honor of playing chess with him."

Kitty felt suddenly light and free. The last hours of daylight were a prize, a delicious gift. She sang to herself going down to the beach. Tom was waiting by the steps to the Webster house and smiled when he saw her.

"I asked my grandmother," Tom said. "Joanna is Sister Edmund's older sister. She got married outside the Catholic Church a long time ago and hasn't been back here since."

Far beyond his grandmother's house they linked hands and swung them slowly between them, absorbed in the moment. The sun began to set over the houses above. The lake lapped coldly against the shore. The lights of an ore boat appeared far out along the dark horizon. There were only three and a half weeks left to the summer, and a faint coolness could be felt in the evening air.

They had met before only in the daytime. They had never "dated," never been alone together in the dark. Despite athletic skills and a certain well-trained self-assurance in social relationships, Tom had areas of shyness and diffidence, and Kitty's precociousness had developed in other directions, from other roots. They had never kissed each other, and when they did now in the dark, in the shadows of his grandmother's garden, they clung together, holding each other, knowing there was nothing sweeter in life.

Before night fell completely, Kitty said, "I've got to get back. I don't want her to come looking for me."

"Five more minutes."

"She doesn't know about you. I'm scared she might try to keep me from seeing you. I'll see you tomorrow."

Kitty broke away from him, then came back, kissed him again, and began running down the stairs.

Late in August, Tom's sister, Caroline, arrived from Maine with a quartet of friends and from then on the Websters' house was filled with guests and visitors, Caroline's college crowd. Their manner seemed to Kitty either distant or condescending and she and Tom avoided them, which restricted their access to the beach and the house. But they were invited to a large beach party scheduled for the Thursday evening before Labor Day.

From far below the porch of Sister Edmund's bedroom came the faint sounds of beery laughter, and the bonfires on the neighboring beach seemed to her the signal lights of some late summer pagan ritual. It was past midnight, but she was still in her white habit. Restless, she put down the book she had been trying to read and went down to the kitchen, intending to heat herself a cup of milk. The door to the garden was open into the night. The Cassidys were noteworthy for their meticulousness; leaving a door open was completely unlike them. Sister Edmund opened the door to Kitty's room. The bed was made up, empty. Swiftly, Sister Edmund crossed the garden, descended the staircase but never reached the bottom step. For several moments she remained rooted to the last landing from the bottom from where she could see the complete expanse of beach and the water line under the moon. Lying close together on the sand were Kitty and Tom Webster in swimming clothes, locked in embrace.

Climbing two steps at a time, Sister Edmund reached the house and then went up the stairs to Charlie's room. There was a light under his door. Barefoot but dressed in slacks and a T-shirt and holding a glass of beer, Charlie answered her knock.

"Charles, Kitty isn't in her room and the door to the garden is open. I'm terribly concerned about her!"

"Why, she probably just went to look at the Websters' beach party," Charlie said.

"At this hour? She's a child! She has no business there! Will you look for her?"

"Well, of course, but I really wouldn't worry, Mary. After all, this is private property. Did you warn her about not swimming alone at night?"

"Yes, I did. Now hurry!"

To his surprise, and amusement, Charlie O'Donnell found Kitty and Tom, arms around each other, standing at the water's edge. Kitty had put on a cotton dress but was still barefoot. Charlie started whistling "I Married an Angel," and they broke apart.

"Kitty, I hate to be a wet blanket, but Sister Edmund is worried about you being missing. Maybe you'd better come back up to the house now."

"Let me do all the talking," Charlie said as they climbed the stairs. He stopped. "Let me look at you first." He handed her a comb from his back pocket. "You might use this a bit."

Combing her hair quickly, Kitty felt at once panicky and defiant. Sister Edmund was waiting in the garden near the gazebo.

"Well, Mary, as I said before, nothing to be alarmed about. Kitty saw the lights, wondered what they were, and decided to investigate."

"Thank you, Charles. It's late. We should all be asleep. But I wish to speak to Kitty for a few moments."

God, disaster, Kitty thought.

Charlie O'Donnell went into the house.

"Behind my back!" Sister Edmund whisper-cried with her theatrical intensity. "Consorting with this boy—this non-Catholic boy—behind my back! Is this how you repay my hospitality?"

Kitty held back her anger but there was an edge to her voice.

"I don't know what consorting means, Sister, but I haven't done anything wrong. I had all day, and nights, too, to be alone, and you let me sit on the beach and walk on the beach as much as I wanted to. You didn't say what I was supposed to do there, and you didn't ask me what I did. Well, I made friends with Tom and I have a right to friends, to my private life."

"I saw you! I went down to the beach before I sent Charles! Sent him to spare you my discovery!"

"Saw me what? Kissing Tom?"

"I won't describe it, but it was not just kissing. There are chaste kisses and there are unchaste kisses. You are too young for this! You are not ready for this, for relationships that should lead, if they lead anywhere, to the holy sacrament of matrimony! He is a boy of college age, a non-Catholic boy with different notions of right and wrong!"

Kitty had no more answers ready at hand, but she held her head up, not freezing her expression but not lowering her eyes either. Instead, she directed her gaze just over Sister Edmund's left shoulder. The nun sighed heavily.

"We'll discuss this further in the morning!" she whispered, a rasp. "Now, go to sleep."

She whirled away and went into the house.

Alone in her room, Kitty pulled the damp dress over her head and got out of her two-piece bathing suit. She wanted a bath and late as it was turned on the tap. Her skin was taut and dry and still a little sandy. She sat on the edge of the tub and then in it and waited for it to fill up enough. Because Mrs. Webster had been friendly—hadn't she?—and she had never met Tom's parents, Kitty could imagine them on her side. But Tom's sister wasn't. That shouldn't count as much but somehow it did. Kitty soaped and rinsed and scrubbed the tub as the water ran out, climbed out and towled herself dry and put on cotton pajamas hanging behind the door. All lights off, she stood by one bedroom window looking through the shutters at the night, at gleams of moonlight on the lake, remembering him. Where his hands had been on the top of her bathing suit, she now put her hands over her breasts.

After breakfast Sister Edmund took Kitty's hand and, as if she were guiding a child, led her outside to the sunny garden. The nun's anger of the night before had fizzled out, and she now assumed one of her other roles.

"If I've misjudged you ... forgive me," she said. "But you have your whole life ahead of you. Don't rush it! When we get back to Chicago—not now—we must have a serious discussion about your future."

Kitty abruptly blurted out what had been on her mind for weeks: "Sister, I love classical music and I hope you'll still teach me, but I don't think I can be a concert pianist. I listen to records of the really great people and I know I'll never be that good. They gave their first concerts at my age or even way younger. You said yourself I got off to a late start ..."

"You're overwrought," Sister Edmund interrupted. "This is an entirely premature notion. I won't consider it now! I said when we return to Chicago."

Sister Edmund and Charlie sat with their mother in the solarium.

"Mary, what was all that commotion about last night?"

"Commotion?"

"Do you and your brother both take me for an idiot? It woke me and I met Charles here in the hall who didn't want to tell me anything either, but I managed to squeeze out of him that Miss Collins, it seems, had taken a little excursion, unauthorized no doubt, it being the middle of the night. Charles said this was all of no consequence, yet you were concerned enough to dispatch him to look for her."

"It's all over, mother. It's all taken care of."

"Mary, may I remind you this is my house? I intend to know what goes on in it. And on my property. Does it have something to do with the Webster boy? I've seen her walking on the beach with him."

"Mother, if you had told me this sooner, I might have been able to prevent... No, the matter is closed. There is no need to discuss it further."

"Mary, you are transparent beyond belief. Has she had an affair with him?"

"No! If you mean a sexual liaison! It was a summer romance that went too far, that's all. But the summer is over. We're leaving, and the boy is leaving."

"Don't be naive. This is the modern age. He'll be back here at Thanksgiving, Christmas. He has a car of his own, money of his own—though by no means all he can expect to get in a few years if he behaves himself. That's something he may need to be reminded of. You let me take care of this. I don't suppose I've spoken two words to Eleanora Webster in the past dozen years, but I know my neighborly duty."

"Duty to whom?" Sister Edmund asked.

"To the Websters, of course! They need to know who the girl is, what her background is."

"That's going a bit far, don't you think, Mother?" Charlie said.

"Charles be quiet! This is no concern of yours."

"Mother, I can't permit this!" Sister Edmund said. "To tell anyone about that child's past would be a cruel sin against charity. It is *my* duty to tell you that. May I have your solemn promise not to carry this further?"

"How dare you lecture me again about morality! I'll do what I see fit! And never bring that girl here again."

Shortly after noon, Labor Day, Kitty and Sister Edmund left the O'Donnells' house for Chicago. Sister Edmund had said her goodbyes in private; the O'Donnells were not at the door. Mr. Cassidy drove them to the station. Tom Webster had not been on the beach, neither Friday, Saturday nor Sunday nor that Monday morning, and had not tried to see her.

"Did you tell him about me?" Kitty asked in the flat voice of someone who has just regained consciousness after a catastrophe.

"Oh, my dear, no," Sister Edmund said, and there were tears in her eyes. "But my mother spoke to his grandmother in spite of all my protests."

"It doesn't matter," Kitty said. "I lied to him about my mother and father. He would have found out sooner or later. And I guess that matters to him."

"Then I think he must be a great coward or a fool," Sister Edmund said, thinking, I will never come here again.

Would it have made any difference if she hadn't lied? Kitty didn't think so. Her anguish began as a physical thing, an actual pain in her throat that widened and deepened in her chest. But worse than that was the sense of loss, not so much of Tom Webster but of confidence in herself.

7

Kitty's first instinct was to flee, to run away, to try to find Roberta. But running away was for little kids who wouldn't get very far, or dumb kids her age who would not solve their problems but only get themselves into worse kinds of trouble.

The new school year demanded intense concentration on her studies—Latin, French, English literature, religion, art—and maybe there were keys there, too—to security, to freedom, to the future itself. But most of all she had her music. Without it she would not be the kind of person she was. It was her refuge and her strength.

A week after their return, Sister Edmund knocked and was let into Kitty's room. The nun lowered herself to Kitty's desk chair and fingered her beads. Kitty hesitated, then sat on the arm of her easy chair, knees tightly together.

"Kitty, as you've known from the outset," Sister Edmund said gently, "I have a mandate—an order—from Reverend Mother to find a suitable Catholic home for you. I have been given no time limit and we will not settle for second-best. It must be a family that not only has room for you and adequate resources, but one that can also help you develop your capabilities to the fullest." She smiled thinly. "In that respect, you may eventually find yourself more fortunate than some of your classmates.

"But no such ideal family is yet in sight," the nun went on. "For one thing, it is simply a fact that not enough people know you. So one of the first, practical steps I believe we should take is to add a feature to your December recital. I think we should begin now to work on a medley of popular American music—to show what you can do along those lines—in advance of the holiday party season. A number of the parents of our girls, who are well off, entertain frequently for their children when the girls become seniors or come home from college, especially during the Christmas season."

Sister Edmund paused.

"Look at me, dear." Kitty had been listening with downcast eyes. She looked up. Sister Edmund placed the palms of her hands together in a gesture that was similar to but not quite prayerful—part prayerful, perhaps, part professorial, part theatrical.

"If you can play at these parties and dances, you'll find this a valuable social, even financial asset. If you can play for an evening with professional skill, you can charge a professional fee as a performer.

"But I have in mind not merely opportunities to perform and be paid for it, but opportunities for you to be introduced to society. You are, in my view, still too young to date members of the opposite sex—but not too young to meet fine Catholic young men, at surpervised dances and parties. I am not quite the fuddy-duddy you may think me. Such encounters—in moderate doses—can be an important part of your social education."

Sister Edmund paused again, breathed deeply, rose to her feet.

"I don't . . . trespass on your room—your privacy—lightly," she said. "Or often, as you know. Only when I feel it's my duty. I may make mistakes sometimes." She smiled. "You seemed so young when you arrived here. Now, well—you're growing up. Kitty, I know you received a small package from Mrs. Wilkins one day before we went to Lake Forest. That only registered later and when we returned from our trip I checked your school records. Lo and behold, we seem to have neglected a most important occasion. A bit late, Reverend Mother and the other sisters and I would like you to have this." From the folds of her habit, she produced a small, square package wrapped in gift paper, and placed it on the desk.

"Thank you, Sister. You didn't really have to. I never got used to birthdays much."

She had said what she had said quite factually and unsentimentally, but Sister Edmund found it necessary, even so, to exit rather hurriedly then, after saying, "Nonetheless, many happy returns of the day!"

The gift was a diary with a key, bound in green leather.

Kitty told no one of Tom Webster's betrayal, and so there was no one to remind her except herself—and Sister Edmund, who never mentioned it again. The weeks passed into a limbo of half-forgetfulness. These things could be recalled. But they could also be buried—under the passage of time, in the changing air and colors of autumn. With her friends she scuffed penny loafers and saddle shoes through fallen leaves, babushka scarves tied around their hair. She went to St. Margaret's autumn tea dance (where no tea was ever served), and boys she knew and newer, older boys singled her out of the crowd and took her around the gymnasium floor half a dozen times during the afternoon. None of them happened to interest her very much but they were the kind of boys she was used to—Irish Catholic, or Irish-German Catholic, or a stray Italian Catholic or two—and she felt comfortable with them. She was Eileen Byrne's guest at the Byrnes' Thanksgiving dinner. The following weekend she began Christmas shopping for Eileen, Fran, Alice, Roberta, and the nuns.

Watching and listening from the podium, from the wings, sometimes from a side seat in the front row of the audience, Sister Edmund evaluated the Christmas season concert-recital and believed it to be a qualified success, if by unqualified one means great performances before an appreciative audience. The choral numbers were well done and genuinely popular she felt—who can resist those sweet, pure young voices caroling?—and there was no lack of applause after the piano renditions by her three prize pupils, but in truth, as she was well aware, not all the parents really enjoyed solo piano works from the classical repertoire, and the performances of Kitty's two colleagues, while competent and correct, were somewhat less than truly inspired. Kitty, herself a bit nervous, played the Mozart C-Major Sonata a shade too rapidly in places, but she played with a recognizable fervor the other girls lacked. She received the loudest and longest round of applause, but Sister Edmund knew a measure of this enthusiasm could be attributed to the fact that Kitty was, by far, the best-looking of the three girls, with the prettiest dress, which she had bought herself. What can have possessed the mothers of the others, the nun asked herself? The first girl, skinny, solemn, damp, with unfortunate sausage curls, wore a lace dress of pale peach, a color suitable only for mothers of grooms. The second, pasty and dumpy, wore an equally unbecoming dress of red velvet much too young for her. Had this pair been carefully selected to set off Kitty's even but interesting features under straight, brushed hair, her trim, small-breasted figure in a simple navy blue frock, the nun thought, the job could not have been better done.

But Kitty received the biggest round of applause yet for her final selection, a second encore in effect, following the cheeky little Chopin piece, a medley of fifteen lushly romantic hits of the twenties and thirties, drawn heavily from the works of Jerome Kern, songs of the caliber of "All the Things You Are" and "Smoke Gets in Your Eyes."

They were all songs of high quality, melodious, easy to remember, but, most important, in the eyes of Sister Edmund, danceable.

A reception—cookies and soft drinks in the auditorium after several rows of rear chairs had been quickly folded by the ushers and stacked against the walls—followed the concert, and when Kitty emerged from the stage door, flushed and pretty, Sister Edmund—saying, "Bravo! Congratulations!"—led her proudly through the crowd to the reception area where she was introduced to several sets of parents and left for ten minutes or so.

"You were terrific," said one father. "Would you consider playing at a party I'm giving for Mary Ann Christmas week?" (Who Mary Ann was Kitty had no idea.)

"OK. Sure. Yes, sir, I would."

He seemed genuinely enthusiastic, but it was too easy somehow, and Kitty suspected the fine, Irish hand of Sister Edmund.

"Only one?" The nun asked afterwards. "I had expected two or more. Well, no matter. Word will get around."

Roberta sent a Christmas card from Cleveland. She was working as a pianist in the cocktail lounge of a downtown hotel.

Julio, the convent's devout, devoted Filipino handyman, was given the job of escorting Kitty, by bus, to the Lake Shore Drive apartment where she was to play, the evening of December 27. Julio then, by prearrangement, donned a white jacket and assisted the resident serving staff the rest of the evening.

It was a large apartment, ten rooms, not including the kitchen, pantry, and baths, a dozen floors above the Drive, with superb views of the Gold Coast, the towers of the Loop, and the lake. The public rooms—living room, drawing room furnished with period French pieces, ornate and not especially comfortable, dining room, library—were still empty when Julio and Kitty arrived. A maid in a black uniform trimmed with white took Kitty's coat. No one else appeared, and Kitty sat at the piano in the drawing room with second thoughts about this job. These trappings of luxury, of money, reminded her too sharply of Lake Forest and put her on her guard. But she began playing softly. Worked out informally beforehand between Sister Edmund, Kitty, and Kitty's employer, Kitty's job was to play sophisticated background music for talking and listening earlier in the evening, and danceable music more or less all along, though recorded dance music would also be provided. She was playing when the first guests arrived and was never really mistaken for a guest, at least not for long, since all the guests knew one another and they did not know anyone who could play a piano that well. Kitty wore her blue recital dress and in the eyes of the girls who had attended the recital, that marked her, set her apart, because they would never wear the same dress twice in a row. But not everyone at the party had attended the recital. For some, Kitty was a new and interesting face and presence, guest or not—for several young men, especially, who were either alone, bored with their dates, or easily distracted by a new face. For a while, though, their interest was not apparent. It would be awhile before anyone would pay much attention to the piano or its player. First guests and later arrivals were too busy talking to each other—mostly about the outbreak of war and what it might mean for them—getting drinks (beer or soft drinks exclusively), lighting cigarettes, or nibbling at food. Still, when a few couples began dancing, it became evident the music was being heard by some and that the tempo was stimulating.

Kitty had known for some time not only how to sight-read and play popular songs only seconds after she had looked at them for the first time, but was also able to play by ear in any key, or transpose from one key to another, with the same apparent lack of effort. She did more, though, than follow the melody with simple chord progressions; by now she knew dozens of songs and had practiced them so she could shape, embellish, and refine them according to her own style and digital skill, leaving room for later inspiration that would lead her to improvise new little melodies from the harmonic base of a song. At her best, and more and more she did not have to settle for less than that, there was already a professional polish to her work, a sureness, an ease. In any case, she was more than good enough for this crowd, and those who truly listened knew it, even though they might not be watching her at that particular moment. As the evening skimmed along over the surface of things, and the beer flowed, more and more people did watch and were pleased by what they heard, and, if they were boys, were drawn by what they saw.

Kitty was conscious now that quite a few people were around the piano. Some faces changed but some stayed the same. One boy, especially, seemed to have installed himself for the duration of the evening and she wished he would go away. Tall with blond hair falling over his forehead, one cigarette after another—big, big deal—bow tie, and she hated bow ties on men, and that smile as though he owned the world. Look at him. He thinks he's so damn handsome. God's gift to women.

"Take a break, Kitty," said the mother of the hostess. "Get yourself something to eat."

After the young man had looked at Kitty for the first time, looked again, looked some more, and felt a bit self-conscious about doing this, he went away for a while, curiously buoyant, the way he felt after lift-off from the airfield; but he came back and was definitely, positively smitten, no doubt about that, within the hour. Oh, this had happened before, but not this way. In his mind he lined up all the girls he had known since the age of twelve and Kitty glowed like the star of some review picked out by spotlight at center stage while the rest of the cast fades into the background. What a tremendous lift she gave him! All just by being there in the same room with him. He crossed his fingers, almost held his breath, watched—after all, she was the entertainer; he had the perfect excuse—and waited. When the lady of the house spoke to her and the girl stopped playing and got up, he followed her across the hall into the crowded dining room.

In the dining room, around the buffet, Kitty did not get an overwhelming amount of attention, but it might be said—and there were some girls who certainly thought so—that she got as much or almost as much attention as any girl there, though this was mostly an eighteen-to-twenty-one crowd.

"Where did you learn to play like that?"

"Oh, different places," Kitty said.

"Do you know 'Deep Purple'?"

"Would you do 'I Concentrate on You'?"

Kitty arranged herself a small plate of sliced filet mignon, hot rolls, and salad, and drifted with it, conscious that she did not belong and did not want to belong. She did not really like these people and was accepted only as the girl who played the piano, the paid entertainer. That part she liked, the knowledge that she could do something really well, something that people liked, better than anyone else.

The tall, blond boy was in her path, deliberately, cigarette in hand.

"Why so solemn?" he asked.

"Oh, get another line," she said, and went past him quickly back to the piano, and didn't see the surprised, hurt look on his face. She didn't see him again as a matter of fact.

Kitty played on, and people began singing the lyrics to the songs. She took another break and was invited by a college girl with a snobby voice to play at a New Year's Eve party four days hence. Half-flattered, half-reluctant, Kitty provisionally accepted, leaving the decision to Sister Edmund.

Her contract was to play from seven until midnight. At 12:10 she played her last number, "Two Sleepy People." No one near her sang the lyrics, so Kitty did, softly, a little under the sound of the piano.

When she walked away from the piano she received some applause (there had been intermittent applause all evening) and several voices said, "Play some more. Don't stop now." As she left the apartment with Julio, she heard the sound of a phonograph starting up. The envelope the host had discreetly handed to her at her departure contained fifteen dollars, a fortune!

"I hear very fine reports!" said Sister Edmund the following day. She was willing to let Kitty play again New Year's Eve and spend the night at that house, as invited, since the party would not get under way until 10 P.M. and would go on (well chaperoned, Sister Edmund had determined) until the wee hours.

On December 31 a chauffeur-driven car called for Kitty at 9:15 in the evening and drove her to a large, lakefront house in Evanston. Once again, servants greeted her, took her things, brought her a glass of ginger ale, and left her sitting alone in the living room near the piano, on the edge of a chair, waiting for the guests to arrive.

The young hostess and her mother descended the staircase. The older woman wore a practiced smile; the girl didn't bother. They came across to Kitty, the older woman making last-minute, unnecessary adjustments to ashtrays, book matches, and other objects en route, the girl making unnecessary adjustments to the back of her hair. It was 9:50.

"Let's hear you," the older woman said (leaving Kitty with the distinct impression of having heard "Snap to!"). "I think it's nice to have music playing when people come in the door."

Kitty began "I Can't Get Started." The woman listened a moment, seemed satisfied, and moved off. Guests began arriving, and many of the faces were now familiar. It seemed as though the previous party had simply shut down for a brief rest and had started up again.

Among the crowd was the blond boy she had brushed off. She caught sight of him a couple of times, but he didn't hang around the piano or even stay very long in the same room with it. Later on he seemed to be alone and if anything looked rather lost. Kitty felt mean and was sorry she had been bitchy and had snapped at him. She took a short break and found him half in and half out of some conversation. If he saw her he didn't let on, but when she spoke to him he turned to look down at her.

"Um, excuse me," Kitty said. "The other night I was very rude. I'm sorry."

Kitty could swear he actually started to blush. Anyway, he beamed at her a surprised and appealingly self-conscious smile.

"Oh, well, don't worry about it," he said. He had a naturally slow voice that cracked humorously, almost a drawl. "It's nice of you to say so, though. I'm Graham Allen. And you're Kitty Collins. I asked. I don't know much about music but you sure know how to play it. May I make a request? Uh, 'Nola.' If you know it?"

"Oh? OK, sure," Kitty said. "I'd be glad to. It's been a long time, though. Give me a few minutes to work on it. I have to start again. Talk to you later."

"Graham? I've been looking all over for you," a girl intruded and dragged him off.

He's not remotely arrogant, Kitty thought. He's as friendly as a puppy.

"Nola." That had been one of the first pieces Roberta had taught her, a simplified, slow-tempo version to give her the satisfaction of playing a recognizable tune, not just scales and exercises. It couldn't be turned into jazz, there were no lyrics to it, and it would take a fast, bouncy fox-trot to dance to, if you could dance to it at all. It was a performer's novelty tune, an old-fashioned crowd-pleaser Roberta had grown up with. Kitty hadn't played it since she was eleven or twelve, but she had heard Vincent Lopez play it on the radio often enough since. It always made her think of background music for some prancing cartoon pony: Hippity-hop-de-hop-de-hop ... Graham asking for it seemed sort of sweet and old-fashioned and unsophisticated in itself. It was probably one of the few tunes he had learned to care about. But that was all right. Maybe she could educate him. The thought pleased her. He pleased her. I wonder how old he is? I wonder how old he think I am?

Back at the piano she selected a key and worked out the melody of "Nola" with barely struck right-hand notes, filled in some left-hand chords more audibly, went over it once more, and it came back to her. But because he wasn't in the room now she set it aside and began "Three Little Words," which she followed up with "Back Home Again in Indiana" and "I Would Do Most Anything for You." When he still didn't reappear, she thought, that girl won't let him, and began playing "Nola" at a medium clip, still feeling her way into it. Still no sign of him after two choruses and the waltz-me-around-again bridge, so she transposed keys and began playing a double-time reprise. That got him. He had to bring the girl with him, but he came back. Standing a fraction behind the girl's line of vision he made a bull's-eye circle of approval with thumb and forefinger and winked at Kitty, who pretended not to notice. Before the other girl could drag him off again Kitty skipped into "Them There Eyes," which drew a round of applause soon after she started on it, as fast, bravura pieces usually did. She could see Graham applauding, but then he had to leave again.

At 11:45, the younger hostess leaned over and said "I want you to stop for a while now. We want to listen to the New Year's Eve stuff on the radio. Get yourself some supper. Then about 12:15 start playing again."

From the radio, volume turned up, horns blared, a chorus of unsynchronized voices loudly welcomed in the New Year, 1942, and Kitty tried to ignore all the embracing couples around her. She particularly didn't want to see Graham Allen at that moment, and didn't. But a complete stranger surprised her with a kiss in passing. She returned to the piano, and when some orchestra on the radio finished "Auld Lang Syne" and all the guests finished singing it, she waited for someone to turn off the radio, and began playing again. She sang now for the first time that evening—"Thanks for the Memory," consciously imitating Shirley Ross.

Kitty lowered her eyes to the keyboard, lost track of time, of the number of songs she played and sang. She *believed* in the lyrics of the good songs—and there were so many good songs then—and she sang with the fervor of a girl who believed because she wanted to believe, and because the words were sometimes true.

> *... Some things that happened for the first time*
> *Seem to be happening again ...*

"Hey, I think you need a rest," Graham Allen said. He was alone. The other girl was nowhere in sight. Nor was either hostess. He set a record spinning on the Victrola alongside the piano, the first one he picked up, without looking at it, and lowered the needle onto the Goodman Orchestra's version of Ellington's "I Let a Song Go Out of My Heart."

"D'you like to dance?" he asked.

"Well . . . I guess it'd be all right."

No one else was near the piano. The crowd had thinned out considerably. There was room to move, even more on a side porch.

"What time is it anyway?" Kitty asked.

"I don't know. One-thirty, two, something like that. Is it true you live in a convent?"

"Temporarily."

"How old are you, anyway?"

"Sixteen. Almost."

"I would have said seventeen, eighteen. Doesn't matter."

"How old are *you*?"

"Twenty."

Twenty!

He was a junior at Northwestern and had wanted to be a commercial pilot. He had a small-plane license already But now he was going into the army air corps, having enlisted on December 8.

When they had danced through four records, Kitty said, "Maybe I'd better play some more."

"You've played about four hours already. Don't go."

"Don't you have a date?"

"Had one. Seems to have left."

"I bet if you look you'll find her."

"No, honest. She really left, went home with some people. I guess she's a little mad at me. Tant pis. How's your French?"

"I know what that means. But maybe you'd better make up with her."

"Too late now."

"Tomorrow then. I really have to go. I'm supposed to be working."

"How can I see you again?"

"Maybe you shouldn't see me. You've got a girl."

"I'm not engaged. And never was."

"She's pinned, I'll bet."

"Not any more. Voilà." He scooped in one pocket of his jacket and came up with a small red-and-gold pin in the shape of a shield. "I got it handed back this very evening."

Kitty's heart was thumping. Everything was going so fast.

"I don't know how I can see you. I'm not allowed to date."

"But they don't keep you locked up in that convent, or they wouldn't have let you come here. We could meet somewhere."

"You're going in the air corps."

"Not until March."

"Why do people always have to go away?" Kitty asked, not Graham especially, but the world at large. She was looking down. Then she looked at Graham's face. "Do you know Nelson and Bailey's drugstore on Sheridan Road? I usually go there every Saturday about three."

He kissed her only once and only very briefly, holding her face lightly with one hand, brushing her lips with his. The gesture—it was scarcely more than that in execution—took no more than five seconds, and perhaps it was only half-spontaneously natural, half-remembered from the movies (Gary Cooper?)—but the effect on both of them was visible from twenty feet away. The gesture *and* the effect were visible. And seen.

"Bye," Kitty said, touching his hand, and half-floated back to the piano. The world had changed.

The younger hostess was standing there. Kitty was startled to look at an ormolu clock on the mantlepiece and see that it was 2:30. Her eyes were gritty. The Victrola was still playing. A few couples were dancing.

"Do you want me to play anymore?"

"No. You seem to have stopped. You might as well stay stopped. Let's see, you're supposed to sleep here, aren't you? Do you know where your room is?"

"Yes. Down the hall. The maid put my things there."

"Did she? How nice. Well you trot on down there. But don't go to sleep just yet. There's something I want to say to you."

Kitty was sitting on the edge of the bed, still dressed, waiting, when the older girl came in and shut the door behind her.

"Is that what you wear to bed?"

"No. You wanted to tell me something."

"Yes. It's this. Listen, dear, you were hired to play the piano, not to make out with the guests."

Kitty went pale.

"That's not fair. I didn't ask that boy to kiss me at midnight. I didn't even know who he was."

"Oh? Something else. Isn't that interesting? You do get around. But I'm not talking about that at all, and you know it. I'm talking about trying to make out with Graham Allen. He and Dee Dee had a big fight about you, you know. At *my* party. Well I don't like that. That's not what we're paying you for."

"It wasn't my fault. He hung around the piano all evening, at that party the other night, and I didn't even like him. Tonight he asked for a request, and then he asked me to dance. What was I supposed to do?"

"Not dance with him. Especially not neck with him."

"I didn't neck with him! He kissed me once! And I didn't dance with him until way after he had his fight."

"You didn't have to encourage him."

Kitty supposed that was true. Her throat filled up. She just couldn't stop it, couldn't squeeze the tears back, couldn't quite shut off the sounds she started to make. She was too tired and mixed up, and sometime during the past few minutes she had thought of Tom as well as of Graham and of people and places and events long before them.

"Oh, look, come on, stop it," the older girl said, suddenly concerned. "Come on, now, stop it. Don't worry, I'm not going to say anything to Sister Edmund. Go to sleep."

The girl kept her word. She said nothing to Sister Edmund. But she talked to other people and in due course, in a matter of days, in fact, exaggerated and distorted in the telling, the story got back to Sister Edmund, through a grapevine too convoluted to trace.

"Oh, Kitty, how could you disappoint me so?"

"I didn't *do* anything," Kitty managed to interject in a pale, uncertain voice. "I—"

"Go to your room!" the nun said. "I must confer with Reverend Mother!"

Kitty went upstairs. It was a cold afternoon in January. She did not want to stand, sit, read, sleep, listen to jazz on her phonograph, do anything except blot out the present. But the room was cold and she was cold. She lay on the bedspread, pulled an extra blanket around her, and closed her eyes. In a few minutes she got up again, put on a sweater, and went down along silent, empty corridors to the music room and turned on lamps. Baldwin piano, large console phonograph, a cabinet stacked with recordings and music scores. She took out the score of Schumann's "Kinderszenen"—Scenes of Childhood, eighteen short pieces for piano—and opened it on the piano music stand at numbers eight and nine—"By the Fireside" and "Knight of the Hobby Horse"—which she loved for their charm and jazzy qualities, and which were very tricky to play. Her fingers were stiff and she misstruck a few keys, but she persisted and began to get a better hold over the difficulties. After a while she turned back a page to the slower number seven—"Träumerei"—and carefully, lovingly, laid out that familiar melody. She wished she could go back a hundred years and be one of Schumann's daughters.

Sister Edmund appeared silently in the doorway and stood listening, tears in her eyes, her efforts rewarded by this talent, but all her plans defeated. For several months the order had known of a musical family willing to take Kitty in, but Sister Edmund had opposed the move because the Barrys had only boys and four of them at that. But Edward J. Barry and Margaret (Peg) Barry were prominent Catholics, prosperous, with a house big enough to accommodate two or three Kittys in addition to the existing family, and had the reputation of being splendid parents. That afternoon, faced with the unfortunate turn of events reported by Sister Edmund, and with no other prospects in sight, Reverend Mother had decreed that further delay was unjustified and could bring the risk of scandal into the convent. Calmed down, Sister Edmund had argued that they should not act on the basis of gossip, that Kitty had denied any wrongdoing, and that she, Sister Edmund, was prepared to give Kitty the benefit of the doubt. Perhaps, Reverend

Mother had said. But something had happened, and what might happen next?

"That was lovely, dear," the nun said with a gentle voice, and Kitty knew she was off the hook. "You've made so much progress. But now I have something to tell you."

PART III

8

"I've seen her several times, unbeknownst to her," Peg Barry told her husband and sons. "Seen her, heard her play, heard her talk, and I know all about her background, which I'll tell you about in a minute. And she's a doll. So now listen to me, boys," Peg said, aligning herself alongside Edward J. Barry and addressing herself exclusively to Joe, nineteen, Jim, eighteen, Ted, seventeen, and Matt, sixteen. "Kitty is going to be your *sister* and don't ever forget it. I suppose it's too much to demand chastity outside this house from them who no longer possess it, in spite of all the prayers and teaching—if the shoe fits, put it on, and if it doesn't, thank God—but inside this house I expect decent behavior. And with a girl in the house for the first time, a lot more modesty is called for than is generally the rule around here. Be advised. Wipe those smirks off your faces. I'm serious. And another thing. Watch your language."

"How does she play?" Matt asked.

"Rings around you," Peg Barry said.

"Good. Then she can play piano and I can concentrate on bass and electric guitar. If I had an electric guitar, that is."

"Save your money."

It went on that way, bantering-serious. They were all keyed up, each in their own way, to one degree or another, over Kitty's pending arrival. All looked forward to it. There were no dissenters.

It was scheduled five days hence. Peg Barry had asked Sister Edmund for time enough to fix up Kitty's room. Peg knew exactly how she wanted that room to look. She had known for years.

"All kidding aside," said Edward J. Barry, the second voice of authority, "making this move is bound to be a traumatic experience for the girl. Let's everybody start thinking about her as a human being who needs a warm welcome, privacy, time, all the rest of it—and no teasing until you get to know each other better. I'm not sure exactly how we ought to go about it the day she arrives. I welcome ideas."

"What day is it?" Joe, the oldest, asked.

"Sunday."

"Can she come home after church?" Matt, the youngest, asked.

"I like the way you put that," his father said. "Yes. If we can avoid it, let's not make the poor kid sit around all day getting more and more nervous waiting for us."

"Straight back to the house for a big breakfast," Peg said. "But all of us together? Maybe we'd better not overwhelm her."

"There's six of us, Ma," Joe said. "How're we not gonna overwhelm her, one way or the other?"

"I'm thinking one or two of us at a time and we might not seem like so many."

"Your mother has a point," Edward J. said. "Think of the car going back—three in front, four in the back. If Kitty rides up front she has to sit there knowing you guys are all boring holes in the back of her head, and if she sits in the back she's crammed in too close too soon. There's also the matter of her luggage. I think what we'd better do is this. Joe and Jim, you two take the coupé, and I'll arrange with Sister Edmund to have you pick up her things at the convent. Leave church a few minutes early, swing by the convent, then go straight to the house with the suitcases. The rest of us will meet her outside the church. Peg, I think you and Matt might sit in back with Kitty, with you in the middle, Peg, while Ted rides up in front with me."

"Then after breakfast," Peg said, "I think the logical thing would be to just get out the instruments and play a few things to break the ice. Later on you'll all be listening to the game and Kitty can help me with the dinner. Sister Edmund tells me she's a good cook."

"Kitty, how exciting," Eileen said. "A rendezvous, a tryst!"
"It's just at the drugstore, Eileen. Don't exaggerate," Kitty said. But her stomach had been upset since the day before just thinking about it. Part of the problem, of course, was caused by the upcoming move to the Barrys. Too much was happening at once.
"I hope he hasn't forgotten all about it," Kitty said. "He was a little tight when he asked me to meet him."
"If only there was some way to remind him," Eileen said. "Let him see you or something."
"I don't know where he lives. His name isn't in the phone book. He's probably in a dorm, or rooms with some other guys."
But Eileen looked at Kitty and couldn't imagine any boy would forget her even if he was twenty. Twenty!
"A pilot!" she breathed. "A pilot already! I love the air corps uniforms, the way they take that metal thing out of their caps so the top is sort of soft and rumply."
Kitty couldn't argue with that. She was proud of what he was, what he was going to be. Ever since she had started counting the minutes toward her "rendezvous," her "tryst" with Graham Allen— ever since she had met him—her mood had fluctuated between pride and apprehension that he would forget, or go back to his old girl, or just remember how much younger she was, or think that since he had to leave for the air corps so soon maybe it would be better not to . . .
"So what time are you supposed to meet him?" Eileen asked.
"Three, tomorrow, Kitty said, and her upset stomach was worth the thrill of anticipation that went along with it.

Kitty waited expectantly at Nelson and Bailey's soda fountain, nursing a cherry coke through a straw, swiveling from side to side on the stool between sips, trying to stay calm, appear casual. It helped to be wearing a winter coat with a big collar over sweater and skirt. She could hide inside it a little, not give herself away. She looked at everyone who came in through the door as though by some act of will she could metamorphose any of the strangers or familiar neighborhood people into the boy she was waiting for. She was intensely curious to see what he would look like again, what clothes he would be wearing.

Then looking for him and not seeing him made her so nervous she bought a fashion magazine, and back at her counter perch, paged through it slowly.

A man in a pharmacist's smock came up to her.

"Young lady, is your name Kitty Collins?"

"Yes." Startled.

"You have a telephone call."

Kitty followed him back through the store, puzzled and apprehensive, and went behind the drug counter to the phone dangling off its hook.

"We don't normally provide this kind of service," the druggist said sternly.

"Hello?" Kitty said.

"Kitty? This is Graham Allen. I feel really bad about this, but I just won't be able to meet you this afternoon. I have to take the train to Minneapolis half an hour from now. When I said I'd meet you I forgot I was expected at this big family gathering tonight and tomorrow. I didn't want to call the convent or come around to your school and maybe get you into trouble, and I just didn't know how to get in touch with you otherwise."

"I'm not going to be staying in the convent anymore. I'm moving in with a family named Barry," Kitty said, thinking it probably wouldn't make any difference.

"What's their phone number?"

"I don't know!" Kitty mourned. "I don't have it yet."

"Well, what's the address? I can look it up."

"Sixty-three ten Glenaire," Kitty said quickly.

"OK. I really have to run. Sorry again, I really am. Bye."

"Oh that's OK," Kitty said, trying to sound offhand, though in her own ears not succeeding, and the connection was broken a fraction of a section before she had finished speaking.

He'll never call, Kitty told herself with a sinking heart. He's thought it over and he thinks I'm too young for him, and he's leaving in two months. No, why should I think that? It's probably just like he said. Not his fault. What else could he do? But her joy had been flattened, everything around her suddenly seemed wrong, asymmetrical, ugly, every face unfriendly, every sound off-key.

Sorrowing and desperate, she went to a public phone booth in the back of the store and called Eileen.

"Tell me!" Eileen said. "I can't wait!"

Kitty told her.

"Kitty, you're being silly!" Eileen said. "I've never heard you talk like this. I'm sure everything is all right. People do have to go to family things sometimes" (and Kitty had to admit to herself this was one area in which Eileen had more experience). "If he'd changed his mind, if he didn't want to see you anymore," Eileen went on, "he wouldn't have called at all, he'd have just stood you up."

"No, he's just too nice to do that."

"Kitty, he asked you for your phone number! Just because you didn't know it wasn't his fault, for Lord's sake. He'll find it. He has your new address. He'll call. I know he will! Everything's going to be fine! I'm sure of it!"

"Then why do I feel so awful!?"

"Because it was a big disappointment not to be able to see him. It's all in your mind. Listen, come on over. Do you want to have dinner with us and spend the night?" Eileen crossed fore and middle fingers on her free hand. "I'm sure my mother will say OK, and she can call Sister Edmund."

"Yes," said Kitty miserably. "Thanks Eileen."

Dressed for church, for departure, for any number of occasions—in low pumps, stockings, wool skirt, pullover sweater, cloth coat, wool scarf—Kitty saw Sister Edmund climbing the church steps with six people who could only be the Barrys, and her heart began pounding. But the meeting was to be delayed; they were gone when she reached the vestibule. She blessed herself with holy water, cold on her forehead, from a marble font, joined other parishioners opening the hydraulically controlled glass doors and moving into the body of the church, and positioned herself in a rear pew a dozen rows behind and across the center aisle from the black-shawled head of Sister Edmund. When the Barrys turned their heads occasionally, she could see them. They looked familiar, which is to say they resembled other Irish-American Catholics, but for Kitty this was by no means necessarily comforting. Irish-American Catholic though she was herself, she had never, as many of that race did, thought of herself as clannishly set apart from (i.e., superior to) non-Irish-American Catholics. Edward J. Barry had the thin lips, in the curve of jutting nose and chin, and the tight, transparent skin of some Irishmen, pink and white, flush and pallor, not altogether a healthy look, though he might well have three or four decades left; now he was forty-four. Peg Barry, only three-fourths Irish, modified by an Irish–North German mother, was darker, rounder, two years younger than her husband, and with stronger genes; her dark-haired, broad-shouldered sons tended to resemble her.

Peg left the pew, genuflected, and walked briskly to the rear of the church and upstairs to the choir loft.

Kitty stared at the Barry men, apprehensive and hopeful, and scarcely heard a word of what the priest in the pulpit, Father Kane, was saying. Her stomach was empty from fasting for communion, and she felt a little light-headed. Returning, head bowed, from the communion rail, the host stuck to the roof of her mouth as usual, hearing Peg Barry's solo contralto singing "Panis Angelicus," she knew at least six pairs of eyes were upon her, but she had the sensation that hundreds, the entire congregation, watched her until she could lower herself, half out of sight, to the kneeler in the pew.

"Ite, Missa est," intoned the celebrant. "Go, the Mass is ended," but before they could go, there were final prayers, in English, the priest kneeling on the altar steps, asking God's help for the president (a president still hated by many in the congregation) and the nation's other leaders guiding the country in the war against the dark forces of Nazi Germany and militarist Japan. (And hate Roosevelt or not, only a few diehard isolationists were now left in this former isolationist stronghold who denied the necessity of battle.)

The final hymn—"Holy God We Praise Thy Name," all the stops open on the organ, everyone joining in—raised their spirits and turned the Barrys' attention to Kitty, pointed out now by Peg, as they filed out down the crowded aisle and out into the cold, onto the steps where the pastor, Father Coffey, in cassock and biretta, was shaking hands with parishioners.

Pillar to post, poor kid, thought Edward J. Barry. *But she's lovely. She'll do all right.*

When Kitty came up to them, pale, smiling faintly, Edward J. resisted the impulse to put one arm around her shoulders—*might embarrass her*—and, instead, for a moment or two made a sandwich of her proffered mittened hand between his gloves. Then, patting his hands rather woodenly, he let brasher Peg give her a one-armed hug.

"We met once before," Peg said. "Remember I drove you to the train one day last summer?"

"Yes, Ma'am."

Matt and Ted grinned, said, "Hi." Matt entertained some brief, normal, carnal speculation—*cute face, does she have a cute build?*—and Ted promptly looked stricken with love.

"See you Monday!" Sister Edmund cried, and left with her escort, Sister Clothilde.

Peg Barry kept up an easy flow of chatter on the ride to the house, and Kitty began to enjoy herself, if not to relax. Inside her coat she trembled slightly as though she might be coming down with the flu, but she was certain she did not have the flu.

Joe and Jim were at the house already, and Kitty's luggage—two medium-sized suitcases, one portable phonograph, one box of records—was stacked in a roomy entrance hall.

Blur. Activity. Talk. Her room. Beautiful. Partial tour of the big, rambling house. Sausage and bacon, fried eggs, toast, jam, milk, and coffee. The multisections of two Sunday newspapers strewn all around a long living room on tables and slipcovered chairs and couches. The Barrys, senior, smoking with-coffee cigarettes. On the piano—trumpet, tenor sax, clarinet. Ted setting up the drums and cymbals, Matt bringing in a bass fiddle. Edward J. stubbed his cigarette, picked up the sax, noodled a few notes, charged suddenly into "I Found a New Baby," Joe's trumpet taking the lead, and Jim's clarinet quickly catching up and hanging on for the ride, bass and drums slamming behind him. Kitty, delighted, seated beside Peg Barry on one of the couches, applauded vigorously when they finished and was still clapping when they launched into "Sweet Lorraine." Edward J. played, briefly, one-handed, and looking at Kitty pointed to the empty piano bench. She went over to it, a little hesitantly, sat for a few moments, listening, then picked up the melody. When they came to the release, Kitty found herself playing solo, just a light brushing of drums and thumping bass to back her up; then they all came in on the main theme again.

They played solidly for almost forty-five minutes, though Edward J.—who nowadays performed only rarely, at home or at fraternal organization gatherings, if strongly urged—bowed out after "Sweet Lorraine." He was beginning to squeak and fluff, and the faces of his wife and sons were wincing with theatrical exaggeration. Joe took over as leader and introduced part of the band's through-the-years routine, speaking into an imaginary microphone before each number. "Nineteen oh six, 'Chinatown' . . . Nineteen eleven, 'Melancholy Baby' . . . Nineteen eighteen, 'After You've Gone' . . ."

On her tour of the house, Kitty had paused in Edward J.'s study to examine three of the framed autographed photographs on one wall—of the Austin High School Gang-Blue Friars and the Wolverines of the early 1920s and the McKenzie-Condon Chicagoans later in that decade.

"These are the people we try to play like," Joe said.

"Roberta had some of their records," Kitty said. "I love the old two-beat jazz."

In the middle of the routine there was a one-line gag, Joe announcing the title of a comic song of the early twentieth century: "And now we're gonna play 'Who Ate Napoleons with Bonaparte When Josephine Was Away'?" Jim, playing sax now, responded with a derisive musical raspberry while Matt and Ted groaned. "Nineteen nineteen," Joe said, not pausing to collect any laughs, though he got one from Kitty, " 'Alice Blue Gown' (and they gave this gentle old number Muggsy Spanier's punchy, double-time treatment) . . . Nineteen twenty . . . Nineteen twenty-one . . ."

Kitty knew them all, and if she had never seen the sheet music for some, she played by ear, and Joe concluded the set by jumping a decade to 1932 and giving as big and stirring an Armstrong sound as he could manage to "When It's Sleepytime Down South."

"Well, you're in the band, kid, if you wanta be," Joe said.

"I'd love to be in it," Kitty said. "Where do you play? How often?"

"Schools mostly, sometimes other gigs. K of C dances. Afternoons, weekends. Can you sing, by any chance? We've been charging twenty bucks, five bucks apiece. With five of us we'll have to make that twenty-five, and maybe we'll have to offer an added attraction."

"Well ... yes," Kitty said. "I mean I think I can."

"You name it," Joe said.

" 'Embraceable You'?"

"Why not? You want to play, too, or stand up?"

"I've always played. Lemme do that at least for now."

"OK. Pick up the vocal at the second chorus."

But when she had gotten out the title line she shook her head and stopped. "No, it's not right. Maybe I'm not ready for that yet. Can you try 'Georgia On My Mind'? And look, I might as well stand. I've got to learn sometime."

She stood self-consciously, a bit pigeon-toed, in front of and a little to the right of the band, clasping her hands together because she didn't know what else to do with them, and her voice shook a little, but even this nervous delivery had a disarming charm—she was on key, her timing was right, and the quality was there in the timbre she produced from her diaphragm and throat.

" 'Georgia, Georgia,' " Kitty sang, shaking her head slightly to get the sound out better, bending that sunny, lyrical name into a sound uniquely sweet, something of her own she could share with anyone lucky enough to hear.

" 'The whole day through ...' "

She kept going and gained better control with a restrained fervor that sent a thrill through Ted's chest and, indeed, touched everyone there to one degree or another. Peg reached over and held her husband's hand.

> *Georgia*
> *Georgia*
> *No peace I find ...*

Somewhere in the back of Kitty's consciousness sounded a note of revelation. It was one of those moments when everything comes together, like some design of nature.

9

Graham Allen telephoned on Monday, early, too, before eight o'clock in the evening, when Kitty had barely finished helping with the dishes. By joking a little about something with Peg Barry, she had managed to suspend for a few minutes the agonizing waiting that had begun about five that afternoon; so the ringing surprised her, went right up her spine—and then the mere sound of his voice dissolved all her troubles as though they had never existed.

A movie on Saturday, some place afterwards, it didn't matter.

"Yes, I'd love to," Kitty said.

Graham didn't linger long on the telephone, and in a way Kitty was glad. Both of them seemed overcome by shyness, and Kitty needed to be alone to savor her relief and happiness.

But she wanted to share some of it, too. She told the Barrys senior, who were alone in the living room, the boys having scattered toward various pursuits.

"We're going to a movie in the Loop and then someplace called Riccardo's for a late supper."

"Riccardo's!" Peg Barry exclaimed cheerfully. "Too *bad*! When was the last time *I* was taken to Riccardo's?"

Edward J. put his arm around her waist and gave her a squeeze. The Barrys seemed to Kitty quite affectionate around the house and even out in public, talking to friends after church, for example.

"Is it nice?" Kitty asked.

"It's very nice," said Edward J. "We've been there a number of times, in spite of what you've just heard."

"What's his name again?" Peg asked.

"Graham Allen."

"Well, he has good taste," Peg said.

Kitty's weekend was one of the main topics of discussion at the dinner table the following week, besides the war and which branch of the service each son favored.

"Out to dinner on the first date," Joe said. "He must be loaded. Hang on to him."

Kitty blushed. "What should I order?"

"It's famous for chicken tetrazzini," Peg said. "Do you like mushrooms?"

"I love them."

"Then you'll like the tetrazzini."

"Too bad Riccardo can't serve you wine to go with it," Joe said.

"I should think not," Peg said.

"You'd let her have it around here," Joe said.

"On special occasions, Christmas, New Year's, that's different. And since when can you order alcohol in public places?"

"Ma," Joe said, grinning with friendly exasperation at her naiveté. "I look older. I move with an older crowd. Anyway, I can see this guy's off to a good start," Joe said. "Riccardo's is my kind of place."

"It's really ideal for young people," Peg said. "Some places are too fancy when you're first going out. Inhibiting. Riccardo's is very casual, but it's got class. Wouldn't you call it one of the most sophisticated places in town, Ed?"

"Oh, certainly. Big names go there. It's in the columns all the time. Riccardo is one of the great publicans. He makes every woman feel beautiful and every man distinguished."

"You'll see some very elegant people," Peg said. "What did you think you'd wear?"

"I don't know. I can't decide."

"Maybe something new is in order," said Edward J.

"That's a thought," said Peg. "Come right home from school tomorrow," she said to Kitty. "We'll run up to Evanston and look around."

"I'll—uh—have to go to the bank first," Kitty said.

Peg patted Kitty's hand. "No, no, luv, this'll be our present," she said.

Kitty enjoyed these dinner-table sessions. Peg and Edward J. made an occasion of them. The boys were expected to wear ties like their father (jackets, too, if there was company), to hold knives and forks properly, not to slouch, and not to wolf their food. No one ate before Edward J. said grace. Yet the atmosphere was relaxed, convivial, festive, especially after Kitty came there. Arguments and somber or unpleasant topics were banned. Also, the food was particularly good—Peg had the touch—and there was plenty of it, including two or three vegetables, bread, and invariably some kind of dessert.

The Barrys senior presided, but in a sense Joe, at once crown prince and jester, was the natural host. Kitty liked all the boys but liked Joe the best. He was the friendliest, the funniest. Even his parents were genuinely tickled by some of the lines he could get off. Which he enjoyed as much as anyone.

"Hey Dad, you ever hear this one?" Joe asked. "I was talking to some of the guys at the Cafe Royale on Rush Street last weekend. This trumpet player and band leader, a big organizer, was a really heavy drinker and his wife nagged him about it all the time, and one day she ticked off all the musicians they knew who'd kicked off because of booze—'J. T. Brown,' the sax man, 'Sonny Smith,' the trombonist, 'Buddy Jones' on bass, and so on. The trumpet guy listened, nodding his head, and when she'd finished he thought a minute and then he said, 'They need a drummer.'"

Joe seemed to have lots of girls on the string and a somewhat spotty academic record in college. Matt was her age, still a kid, still more interested in his bass fiddle, basketball, and the gang he ran with than girls, or any one girl, though he was beginning to appreciate their interest in him—he was good-looking and had charm, a light heart. Jim was the quiet, studious one and had been going steady with a senior in Kitty's school almost a year. Ted was the only problem. He was the pessimist, the one with the temper, and his grades were not encouraging. Ted tried to hide it, but he stared at Kitty. He seemed to manage to pop up in just the parts of the house where she happened to be, more so than the others. He was too anxious to pass her things at the table, help her with the dishes. It was painfully obvious she gave him the pitty pats, as the expression went, and she did not know how to discourage him without being unfriendly, which she wasn't inclined to be. She liked him; she thought he was sweet in his stubborn, touchy way; and she didn't want to hurt his feelings. But now she was much too excited about Graham to worry about Ted.

Graham's own Chevy was in the shop. He had borrowed a roommate's 1931 Duesenburg Model J coupé, a gorgeous classic from the golden age of the American automobile, silvery gray with red wire wheels, chrome-encased extra wheels set into the front fenders, rakish, serrated vents along the long low hood, a gleaming vertical louvered grill, two pairs of headlights, and a pair of horn bells in front looking like silver herald's trumpets. It was now about a mile away from the Barry's house, cruising slowly, growling as richly as a power boat. Graham didn't want to be too early.

On the second-floor landing of the house stood Kitty, Peg, and Joe, Peg making a last-minute adjustment to the small sash at the back of Kitty's dress, Joe admiring Kitty as he leaned against the doorjamb to his room, hands in his pockets, ankles crossed.

"You look gorgeous," he said. "That dress is a knockout."

Kitty beamed and lit up the space around her.

"He's due any minute," Peg said. "I'd better join your father in the living room."

Joe strolled over to the window overlooking the front lawn and the street.

"Somebody's here now," he said, and produced a low whistle. "Holy cow, a Duesenberg, a real, honest-to-God Duesy! What'd you say this guy's name was? Boy, you're really going places."

Joe turned and contracted his thick black eyebrows into a point over his nose, his Bela Lugosi–Dracula routine.

"As I have pointed out," he said sepulchrally. "Rich! Fabulously rich!" He rubbed his palms together and chuckled diabolically. "Enjoy yourself, my dear. We will have our little fun—later, eh? Ha, ha, ha!"

Kitty giggled appreciatively, but Peg said, "Joe Barry, cut out that clowning right this minute and make yourself scarce."

"This happens to be the second floor, Ma," Joe said in his normal voice. "I'm already scarce. Have a great time," he said to Kitty with a ring of sincerity, and below, the front doorbell rang.

Peg and Edward J. had to be introduced—that was an absolute social requirement—and Kitty did not make her entrance until Graham had removed his topcoat and was seated in the living room; but the Barrys were relaxed and cordial and Graham came across as poised and friendly, too. The introductions really went very well, and soon Kitty's dress and overall appearance were being admired anew by Edward J., ... then Kitty was coated and gloved and crossing the walk toward the beautiful car. When she had settled into the soft leather of the front seat, Graham pulled away quickly and headed for Sheridan Road, and a different world seemed to be unfolding through the windshield.

"Let me get it all straight," Graham began asking in a chatty, let's-start-a-conversation way, "how long did you have to stay in that convent?" And Kitty knew she would have to make the decision she'd been dreading. Because one question would surely lead to another. Oh, not dreading. Not on a night like this. Not since she had met him. She wanted to believe he was different. She swallowed once over a little ache in her throat and told the truth, watched him, and waited.

When she had finished he said, "Now I know why I thought you were older."

He had never heard of Roberta Wilkins, or of Rex either, but when he realized Roberta was Negro he simply said, "It was swell of her to take care of you so long. I mean I never heard of anything like that happening. Is that why it wasn't safe? Where did you have to live—on the South Side?"

"No. We lived in a mostly white neighborhood. Off Wilson Avenue."

"Oh, geez. No wonder. What happened?"

She told him that, too.

"The sonovabitch!" he said, steering with his left hand and clenching his right fist for a moment. Then he unclenched it and held her hand.

"You're some girl," he said. "I didn't mean to pry so much, but I'm glad I know."

"The Barrys seem like real nice people," he went on. "Maybe your luck is changing."

"I think so," Kitty said.

The movie was Billy Wilder and Charles Brackett's *Hold Back the Dawn* with Charles Boyer and Olivia de Havilland, a story of a Romanian ladies' man who marries an American schoolteacher just to enter the United States, and then falls in love with her. It was romantic, charming, funny, and poignant, and for a few moments after they emerged from the darkness of the theater into the bright lights of the lobby Kitty's eyes glistened, which did no damage at all to her appearance. Then Graham smiled at her and she laughed at herself, and he took her gloved hand and held it as they walked toward the parking lot.

Riccardo was a broad-shouldered, dark-haired, handsome, middle-aged Italian with a bow tie and a dashing mustache, the perfect host who did, indeed, make Kitty feel she was the most beautiful and fascinating girl who had ever crossed his threshold. His tetrazzini was delicious—spaghetti thick with velouté sauce, chicken, cheese, and mushrooms. Their waiter brought it, but Riccardo served them himself with a flourish, as though they were celebrities.

His restaurant was very crowded. People waited in line for tables, but Graham had a reservation. Paintings on the walls. A pleasing blend of older patrons and college-age dating couples, the former predominating. Inviting aromas of cooking food from passing trays and from the kitchen itself when the doors swung open. The din of animated talk, the great changes pending in the lives of so many there that night. Life had suddenly speeded up for everyone, and Kitty could feel it, too. Already she could visualize Graham in uniform and how handsome he would look, but she didn't want to think about him leaving; she wanted to luxuriate in the state of being with him now, here where she was.

Kitty looked across the table at him. He was wearing a regular four-in-hand tie, not a bow tie, and looked better for it, but she thought for once she wouldn't even mind a bow. His hair was carefully combed away from his forehead. For some reason she found this endearing. He was so easy to talk to, to just be with. She didn't feel shy or awkward or tongue-tied or nervous with him at all, only high and elated.

"Have you lived in Minneapolis all your life?" she asked.

"Well mostly, except for the first five years in St. Cloud which I don't remember. I was born there. Why didn't I go to the University of Minnesota?"

"I don't know. Why?"

"Everyone always asks me that. I mean it's a fine school right there in Minneapolis. My parents weren't too happy about it but I thought it would be a good idea to get away from home. Northwestern seemed about the right distance—five hours each way by train. I can go up there weekends if I have to, but it's too far to go very often."

"Do you have any brothers and sisters?"

"An older sister. She's married, but she lives just over in St. Paul."

He was studying accounting and business administration. "But," he said, "I love flying so much I can't make up my mind what I want to do after the war, maybe fly for an airline. I know where I want to go, though. West. Way out west. Have some kind of ranch some day. I spent two summers in Colorado and Wyoming and I've never forgotten it. It's really beautiful out there. The only place to really feel free. Snow on the mountains and green valleys where you don't see anybody else for miles, and lakes and streams full of fish. Have you ever been horseback riding?"

"No."

"Would you like to go some time? I know a good stable out west of Evanston. I'll teach you. You'll get the hang of it right away."

"Yes, I'd love to."

"I want to travel, too." he said. "To Africa, Tibet, Tasmania..."

His face reddened a little. He seemed a bit embarrassed.

"I get all wound up about it sometimes," he said.

"Why shouldn't you? It sounds so wonderful. Where will you go in the air corps?"

"Oh all over, practically anywhere. Maxwell Field, Alabama, at first. Then Texas or California maybe. Lot of air bases out there. Then I hope they send me to China. Things look pretty bad now. The Japs have taken one place after another. We were caught off base. But we'll stop them."

Too many places to think about. Too much to think about. It was better now to come back to this intimate little table at Riccardo's in Chicago. Their waiter was spooning something airy and creamy and wine-flavored called zabaglione over a compote of pears and then dribbling melted chocolate over that, and Kitty sighed contentedly.

A glorious winter night. Dry cold, windless, snow still clean, reflecting lights from street lamps, stars strewn across the sky. The fabulous Duesenberg was parked on a side street near the restaurant. In the front seat they couldn't wait to put their arms around each other. Graham actually moved first, but Kitty responded so quickly it was virtually simultaneous. She had never kissed anyone like this before, not even Tom on the beach at Lake Forest. There are chaste kisses and there are unchaste kisses, Sister Edmund had said. This was somewhere in between and it was lovely; it went on and on and curled her toes. But while sensations electrified her that were clearly physical, and might be described as verging on the unchaste, something else was going on, too, in uncharted regions of her heart, the best thing of all, which she would be able to carry with her wherever she went when he was gone. She came up for air.

"I have to breathe."

With the tips of her fingers she studied the topography of his face, smoothed his hair.

Startled, she asked, "What time is it?"

"Twelve-fifteen."

"I have to be home at one."

He started the powerful engine of the car. "Don't worry, we'll make it. I'm not about to get off on the wrong foot with the Barrys."

She leaned against his shoulder and found, like some good omen, the sound of superb jazz on the radio, Coleman Hawkins's "Body and Soul" of 1939 followed by another hauntingly beautiful classic of that year, "That's All I Ask of You," with Chu Berry, more probing, sinewy, heartfelt tenor sax this time playing behind Billie Holiday. The tail end of a program, followed by symphonic music, Beethoven's Seventh, which carried her all the way back along snow-glistening boulevards.

On the Barrys' front porch Graham said, "Why don't I give you your first riding lesson tomorrow? Would you like that? I'll still have the car."

"I don't have any riding clothes."

"All you need are slacks and a couple of sweaters. Borrow a pair of dungarees from Matt. He's about your size."

Eileen Byrne, of course, wanted to know every detail of Kitty's weekend. What she got was Kitty's accurate but edited version, though Kitty wanted to be obliging. Eileen deserved a good account in exchange for the moral support she had given in general, but particularly the weekend before when it had really been needed.

"Twice in one weekend! Kitty, I told you he liked you! When are you going to see him again?"

"Friday, after the band date. Something Saturday, too. He goes in the army air corps in March. We have less than six weeks."

"It's all so romantic I can't stand it!" Eileen said. "It's like a movie but it's real."

Eileen hinted, tried to work the conversation around so that Kitty would declare herself, but Kitty could see through these stratagems and wouldn't be drawn down that path. Graham was "good looking... very nice... fun to be with" and she "liked him a lot" and it was obvious she was going to see as much of him as she could, and she didn't deny that he had kissed her more than once, but beyond that—no, she wouldn't say more.

10

Scene: a high school gymnasium immediately following a Friday evening basketball game. The home team has been victorious, and the spectators—almost all of them home-team fans—are jubilant and noisy. At the far end of the shiny hardwood floor, a small stage, about two-and-a-half feet high, draped with the school colors, blue and red. On the stage, the Barry boys have quickly set up music stands and chairs in front of a set of drums and alongside an upright piano, and have installed themselves, with Kitty Collins at the keyboard. Joe Barry, trumpet in left hand, gives the downbeat with his right hand, brings hands together into playing position, and trumpet notes signal the Barrys' theme song: "Once upon a Time," inspired by an early Teddy Wilson recording—an obscure tune but a nice, slow sweet-sad one that must have sounded like nostalgia itself the day it was written. Because it was obscure, never heard anywhere else, it made an ideal theme and a good song to get people dancing slowly.

            di
          da   *di*
        da   *da da*   *da*
La   *da*   *da*
                      La

Kitty misstruck a few notes in the opening bars. No one in the audience seemed to notice but Joe Barry did and glanced at her quizzically. During a couple of other numbers her playing was a bit ragged, too. When they took a break, Joe didn't say anything, but Kitty said, "Joe, I'm sorry. I know I haven't practiced enough lately and it shows. It always does."

Joe smiled at her and raised her chin slightly with a forefinger in his best avuncular manner.

"You're head over heels, kid. It's harder to play that way."

"You should be bawling me out, not being nice to me," Kitty said.

"Well, now it's time for you to sing, and I know Ma hasn't let you skip any lessons. So show me what you can do."

Kitty did three vocals before the dance ended at midnight (Matt Barry set aside his bass to take over the piano then), and for those in the audience with discerning ears, for those who appreciated melodies full of sentiment but not sentimentality, who admired wry, intelligent lyrics and clear, beautiful diction to do them justice, certain lines and phrases were the high point of the evening.

> *So worth the yearning for*
> *So swell to keep every home fire burning for . . .*

Graham Allen arrived in time to hear her last two songs. He wore neither overcoat nor hat in spite of the cold, only a wool scarf tucked into a gray tweed jacket, which he kept on as he waited for Kitty off to one side of the dance floor, holding a cigarette, standing casually at ease.

Joe Barry, trumpet silent for a few bars, waved a cordial greeting at which signal Ted Barry caught sight of Graham and burned with jealousy and unrequited love, even more fiercely as he watched Kitty putting on her coat, tying a wool scarf around her hair, glowing as if she was already outside, walking in the cold. As shortly she was, turning her face to look up at Graham.

They stopped at an all-night restaurant for chopped steak sandwiches—Kitty was always ravenous after a performance—and smiled at each other across the table, gazing at each other's faces.

"What's it like in Minneapolis?" she asked.

"Cold. Colder than Chicago even. A good place for ice skating."

"That's something I've been doing since the fifth grade."
"Great. Then let's go tomorrow night."
It seemed to Kitty time to ask.
"What are your parents like? Do you have any pictures?"

Graham withdrew a snapshot from his wallet—a middle-aged couple posing stiffly on the lawn of a large, early twentieth-century house. They looked prosperous and rather forbidding.

"What are they like?" Graham said. "Proper pillars of the Lutheran Church. 'Active in civic affairs' as the newspapers say. My father's in insurance."

"What would they say about me?"

Graham looked as though he wished the subject hadn't come up. He sighed and put his hands over hers.

"Well, to tell the truth I don't think they'd know what to make of you," he said, smiling a little sadly. "I guess my father must run across people in his business who happen to be Catholic, but my mother and father together don't have anything to do with Catholics. I don't think they even know any ... I don't agree with them about a lot of things, I want you to know that. I believe in God and the Ten Commandments and things like St. Paul's Epistle to the Corinthians—some of it anyway. But all those religions fighting and killing each other for hundreds of years, each of them claiming to be *the* one and only right one, makes me wonder whether any of them are ... My parents would be, well to be honest, pretty upset to hear I was dating a Catholic girl but that's just something I'll have to live with. I've gone my own way for at least a couple of years and I'm not going to go backwards now ..."

He squared himself, and Kitty thought later it must have cost him a great effort to decide suddenly that now—now, not later in the dark at some moment of mutual ardor when it would be easier—was the time to say it:

"Kitty, I *love* you. I want to tell you that when we're just sitting here like this, when I'm not even kissing you, just sitting here talking. I love you. I love you very much."

Kitty didn't make a sound. She didn't need to.

"You kids care for anything else?" asked the stocky waitress. "Besides each other, I mean."

They didn't mind her little joke at all.

* * *

The porch light was on, one lamp in the front hall was still lit. Peg Barry appeared at the top of the stairs in her nightgown and waved. She came down a few steps.

"If you're hungry, there's cold roast beef in the icebox," she whispered loudly.

"No thanks. We ate something at the Crosstown Grill."

"How late do you want to sleep?"

"I'll set an alarm for eight. I have tons of homework."

"Well, goodnight, then, luv. Don't forget to turn off the porch light."

Peg Barry did not mention Graham Allen when she talked to Kitty, and though her manner when she greeted Graham at the door, or in the living room if someone else had let him in, could not be faulted for politeness, behind it was a reserve.

"I withhold judgment," Peg had told Edward J. "Lord knows he has good manners. Obviously intelligent. A girl like Kitty is going to be attracted to older and more sophisticated boys just as she attracts them. That's inevitable. But she *is* less than sixteen and he's twenty. And not a Catholic. Neither are half our oldest and dearest friends, I well know, but that doesn't create any problems for us. It does for Kitty."

"I like him," said Edward J. "He's solid. I think he's crazy about her, and she's safe with him. He's going in the air corps soon, and the future is a long way off. Let them enjoy themselves."

"Oh I agree on that score," Peg said. "I don't think he'll take advantage of her . . . But are they matched? Impossible to tell when they're that young."

"That young and that little age difference was commonplace even in your mother's day, and I don't see much evidence couples nowadays are any wiser or more successful. If anything, less."

"Yes, these days mismatched couples get divorced. In my mother's day they suffered and endured. Mostly the women, I might add . . . Of course Kitty can't see any of this for the stars in her eyes. She adores him. He *is* good-looking, I'll say that for him. And can charm a bird out of a tree—which always makes me wonder. What's behind the charm, I ask myself? Don't you find him a little domineering at times?

"No, not a bit," said Edward J. "Protective, yes. He's older, maybe no smarter but more experienced. And Kitty does daydream and forget things once in a while. It's a kind of ritual act they put on. They both love it. They're devoted to each other."

"And I know. That just tickles your sweet, romantic soul. I still wish she'd start dating other boys, too, so she can make comparisons. Maybe she will after he leaves for the air corps."

"I wouldn't count on it. But in the long run that wouldn't matter a whit to you. No boy she brings home is ever going to be quite good enough for her in your eyes."

Peg snorted briefly and changed position in her chair, unwilling to be labeled a stereotype. She picked up a section of the newspaper on the floor beside her and put it between herself and Edward J. for a few minutes. But she didn't deny his accusation.

As an adopted "daughter-sister," Kitty might, over a long stretch of time, display a certain normal lack of modesty in the Barry household in front of Edward J. and the boys, but she had lived with them less than two months and had never appeared outside her room other than fully dressed, either in street clothes or a neck-to-ankle-length robe. This night, the upper hall dark—everyone seemed to be home and asleep—Kitty, as she sometimes did under those circumstances, visited one of the two bathrooms in her slip. Emerging, teeth brushed, face scrubbed, she saw that Ted's doorway, which she had to pass on her way to her room, was open and lit up. Ted, in his pajamas, said, "I can't sleep."

In her slip she was actually more covered up than she would have been in a bathing suit, but one is dressed in a bathing suit, undressed in a slip.

"Just lemme get my robe," Kitty said, and went on, barefoot to her room where she swiftly got out of everything and into pajamas. They seemed enough, and she didn't want to bother with the robe. The house was quite warm.

Kitty was almost sure that by now Ted realized he was hopelessly too young for her, and that in any case she had no intention of getting romantically involved with any of her surrogate brothers.

"You have anything to read?" Kitty said in a low voice. "If you can't sleep, you might as well read."

Ted was standing, looking at the floor.

"You're the reason I can't sleep," he blurted out, and looked up at her.

"Oh, *Ted*," Kitty said. "You shouldn't say things like that. I like you very much, you know that, but I'm in love with someone else."

As she said this, she realized it was the first time she had said it aloud to anyone. The joy it gave her to say it, startled her—and gave her a feeling of guilt, too, because Ted was anything but joyful, and she was the cause of that. She was suddenly conscious of her own nakedness under pajamas that were not transparent but thin and to a degree clinging, and of Ted in his pajamas. It could only be cruel, not kind to him to stay any longer.

"Goodnight, Ted."

"You haven't known him any longer than you've known me," Ted said. "And you haven't seen him as often."

"Length of time isn't important. Ted, listen. You're a good-looking guy. You're smart. You've got personality and talent. There are lots of cute girls, nice girls around, if you'd open your eyes. Honest."

"I'm not interested in anybody else," he said miserably. "I don't want to be."

"I know you don't want to be, but you have to be. If I'm going to live in the same house with you, we've got to agree just to be friends. Otherwise it won't be nice for either of us, don't you see? If you like me you wouldn't want me to be uncomfortable living here, would you?"

Ted didn't answer.

"Please, Ted. Now don't think about anything. Play some music. And then try to sleep."

She left before he could say anything else.

For a long time, like Ted in the adjoining room, Kitty lay awake in the dark, dazzled over Graham, frowning over Ted. Even if from now on Ted pretended to be just a friend, how he really felt was out in the open, a problem for both of them that wouldn't go away until he fell for another girl, which might take years.

But Ted, Kitty had discovered after a few weeks, was not the only problem of living with the Barrys. The simple truth was she was too old to be adopted. It was too late for her to become a daughter to Peg and Edward J. Barry who had longed for one for years, too late to become a sister to the Barry boys. The circumstances of Kitty's new life were hardly unpleasant. Her room was cheerful, very comfortable, with its own sun porch. The food was generally excellent. For Kitty, life with the Barrys was a little like living in some expensive, interesting resort hotel she sometimes saw in movies, where anything might happen. But it was not home. Not her home, wherever that might be. The Barrys senior were kind, indulgent, generous, often amusing. But Edward J., for all his Irish charm and gallant gestures, was uncertain how to behave with this young girl he had taken into his home. Afraid to intrude on her privacy or embarrass her in any way, he avoided contact, appeared startled and awkward when encountered unexpectedly in hallways, and overly polite in the much-used communal rooms of his house.

But Peg? Peg was everywhere, always there. Of course it was her house, so why shouldn't she be? And she had work to do, beds to make, furniture to dust, food to cook, doors and phones to answer, telephone calls to make, bills to pay, letters to write, people to entertain, voice lessons to give Kitty, lessons Kitty valued highly. But only late at night, with lights turned off, could Kitty be sure of being alone when she needed to be alone. Even late at night, she could often expect last-minute visits from Peg, friendly visits to check into supplies of underwear, socks, and blouses, to confirm following-day schedules and the like, or just to chat. It was all normal, natural, to be expected, and often enough Kitty appreciated Peg's company. There was just—sometimes—too much of it. It sometimes seemed that Kitty could not enter an empty room without Peg entering a few minutes later. To say that Peg snooped or pried would be unfair. Hovered would not be accurate, either. But in her house she was a felt and dominant presence, and some afternoons when Kitty would have preferred staying inside to read but did not want to appear standoffish by shutting herself in her room, she would take unnecessary walks to the drugstore, hands stuffed deeply into the pockets of her winter coat, to be by herself for a while.

11

Kitty's senses were open like a shutter in a timed exposure to every nuance of light, sound, and touch. She noticed the shape of clouds, the outline of towers against the sky, and was acutely aware of even slight changes in the density and direction of the air across her face and hands. An empty room became a spacious one; the gray day wasn't gloomy but had the beauty of classic black-and-white photographs and motion pictures; the damp cold meant she would soon be dry and warm; people on the street seemed no longer indifferent but to rejoice with her that she was hurrying toward some exciting rendezvous, some marvelous destination.

They had a month left, a month in which to compress what might have taken them half a year in peacetime. They met every day at least for a little while after classes and were together throughout the weekends. Peg Barry frowned but saw the end of it clearly ahead and made no attempt to curtail Kitty's activities.

But when Kitty was with Graham and when she had to be away from him she lived on air, she didn't eat enough, was often hollow-eyed from lack of sleep, and her schoolwork suffered and so did her music. Then she would furiously practice extra hours on week nights to make up for it and so exhaust herself even more.

They went to dances and parties at Northwestern, to a performance of *La Bohême* at the Civic Opera House, to plays at the Goodman Theater. He took her dancing at the Camellia House at the Drake, to the Pump Room and The Buttery at the Ambassador East and West, and to dinner at Irelands and Jacques. They went skating at an outdoor rink along the lake and sledding in a forest preserve west of the city where there were a few little hills, and walked on paths and pavements in freshly fallen snow.

One Sunday afternoon he took her flying in a Piper Cub from the small airfield twenty-five miles into the countryside where he had learned to solo. Kitty had never been aloft before. It was a clear, not too cold, sunny day with snow on the ground. With Graham at the controls in the instructor's seat behind her they sped down a short concrete runway, left the earth, and soared blissfully into space, toward a cloudless sky of cerulean blue. For Kitty the sensation was marvelous. Graham banked, and flat Illinois farmland under snow stretched for endless miles. She hung suspended and buoyed in a state of exhilaration that was absolutely new, yet flying, she thought, was almost like singing.

Graham let her take the controls and keep the little craft straight and level for a bit; then he took over again.

"Kitty?" he called over the engine noise.

"What?"

"Will you marry me? I love you more than anything. Even more than flying."

No answer, and he could only see the back of her head and shoulders. If she said no, he thought he would want to die.

She turned her face toward him as far as she could.

"When!?"

"When my training is over. When I get my wings in the fall."

"Hold on!" he shouted, and the world spun and whirled.

He did a barrel roll to the left, then one to the right. He looped the loop. Right side up again, Kitty's heart returned to where it belonged, but her soul seemed to be in a new place.

Back on the ground Kitty threw her arms around his neck, and he lifted her off the ground. Then in her flannel slacks, loafers, and houndstooth-checked sport jacket over a green pullover sweater, she posed for a photograph beside the little yellow plane.

The flight had lasted only thirty minutes. It took longer to drive back to Lake Michigan. Now it was almost five in the afternoon, growing dark, and a fog had rolled in under the sun.

At Wilmette, Graham turned into the lakeside park, past ghostly tennis courts toward the empty yacht harbor. The lake was still partly frozen over along the shoreline into jagged miniature massifs, and cold waves dashed over them against the breakwater. Nothing moved along the horizon.

He was suddenly trembling almost uncontrollably, as though he might have a chill, and it was she who held him and whispered, "Stop it, stop it, you'll be all right, I'll keep you warm," and found a cigarette in a pack on the seat and lit it for him because she thought it would calm him down.

"At sixteen you can get a marriage license," Graham said. "But only with the Barrys' permission. What do you think they'll say?"

"I don't know. I think Mr. Barry might be on our side, but I don't know about her."

"What about being married in your church?"

"I don't know about that either."

"If it's important to you we can be married by a priest. I don't care one way or the other if I'm married by a Lutheran minister or not."

"Graham, what about your parents. Have you talked to them about us, and what did they say?"

"Yes," he sighed. "I warned you about them before, and they haven't changed. They won't accept you. I told you before that won't stop me."

"What about the Barrys?" Kitty asked, herself as much as Graham. "Should we tell them now, should I tell them, get them used to the idea?"

"Maybe not yet," Graham said. "I don't want to be sneaky about it, but some things are our business. We've got to wait eight or nine months anyway. At least wait until after you're sixteen in May. I didn't plan to ask you so soon even though that's all I wanted to do. Ever since that night at the party in Evanston I knew you were the only girl I was ever going to want from then on."

"And I'd been so awful at that other party. It's a wonder you didn't bop me one and tell me to get lost."

"But today, up in the air with you," Graham said, "I just couldn't wait, I had to ask."

She threw her arms around him again and buried her face under his ear. After a while, with the engine off, the car grew cold, and Graham started it and began driving away from the lake. He turned down his street and parked in front of the six-flat building where he shared an apartment with two other students.

"You've never met Rick," Graham said. "Brian'll be up there, too, studying. To be honest, I have to go to the john."

Kitty had never been in his apartment. Graham said it was messy, and she didn't particularly like Brian. They climbed to the second floor, and Graham unlocked the door with his key. There was only one lamp lit in the inside hall.

"Are you guys decent?" he called. "Kitty's with me."

They weren't there. There was a note. They had gone to a party somebody had decided to throw at the last minute. There was a name and address. Graham and Kitty were welcome to come, too.

"Excuse the mess," Graham said and went down the hall. Kitty remained standing, not moving. Graham entered the dark room again. Unsmiling, he put his arms around her and drew her to him. As always when they danced, when they embraced, they seemed to fit together perfectly, and she responded to him with weightless grace. But now everything was different. She wanted to be with him alone in this apartment. The wanting was scary but so powerful something happened to her just thinking about it and she shivered, and as at all such moments it seemed to her she couldn't think straight, couldn't see straight; but now she had to. She knew very well they had entered a zone of danger that threatened not just her virginity—that by itself seemed the least important thing (when she lost it, it would only be to Graham) and what her mother had been had nothing to do with it either; she would never feel like a whore making love to Graham Allen—but rather it threatened the strength of their beliefs and the subtle fabric of their relationship. This place was wrong, the time was wrong, the circumstances were wrong. And afterwards, when it was too late, Graham would be the first to realize it, and nothing might be quite as good again. She had to help them live up to their own acceptance of the double standard, though its inconsistency sometimes puzzled them, for it assumed he might find girls to seduce before he married but that his wife would be a virgin.

Kitty got the palms of her hands around on his chest and pushed herself a little away from him as gently as she could.

"Darling, we shouldn't stay up here any more," she said in a very low voice.

He didn't want to let her go.

"I love you, I'm crazy about you, I'm leaving soon, and now I think I'm going absolutely crazy."

"I love you, but don't you see, it would spoil things not to wait."

"I don't know whether I believe that any more."

"I believe it. And you do, too. I've heard you on the subject . . . Oh, I don't want you to be frustrated . . ."

He dropped his arms, took a deep breath and let it out.

"Let's drive out to the White Horse and see who's around," he said. "I don't want to go to this party, do you?"

"No."

"We can play the jukebox and after a while get a steak. And get you home early for a change. Me too. We could both use a little sleep."

Kitty took a comb from her shoulder-strap bag and smoothed back a lock of hair from his forehead. He submitted to this grooming patiently. The gesture seemed touching to him, and he smiled at her a little and looked, it seemed to Kitty, perhaps as relieved as she was.

But the night of his last full day in Chicago, past midnight, standing in the darkness of the Barrys' living room, for the first time he reached under her sweater, up the warm, taut smoothness of her back, fumbled with the clasp there and absolutely could not unhook it.

"*Wait.*" Kitty whispered, and did it for him in a moment.

The warmth of his hands on her breasts was heavenly.

"*Oh, Kitty, you are so beautiful, so lovely,*" he whispered with gratefulness that was profound.

"*I'm too small.*"

"*No. Perfect. Perfect, perfect, perfect.*"

"*Do you want me to touch you?*" Kitty asked.

"Yes—no, we have to wait!

"We're almost married, we don't have to wait for everything. Then just hold me close!"

It was she who pulled him to her until he was hard against her, and his brief convulsion of ecstasy happened so soon afterward she was quite astonished.

Unplanned, overwhelming, it had just happened, and now Kitty was scared he would feel guilty and worry. It hadn't been his fault—she was to blame if anybody was to blame; boys can't help it, can't help themselves.

Even in the dark he could see her smile of reassurance.

"It's all right," she whispered. "Now we can wait for the rest."

Early in March, Graham Allen went home to Minneapolis to say goodbye to his parents and his older, married sister, and returned to Chicago only long enough to change trains for Maxwell Field, Alabama.

Escorted by Joe Barry (the time was nine in the evening) who stayed discreetly out of the way at a lower-level lunch counter, Kitty met Graham in the station concourse. Streams of people arriving and departing, crowds of people waiting in the vast, vaulted marble hall, echoing with amplified announcements. Many uniforms—army, navy, marine—and many young men who would soon be wearing one.

"Kitty!" Graham called, and Kitty caught sight of him.

Twenty minutes left and a good eight minutes of that would see Graham alone beyond the gate, finding his car somewhere down the long, cold platform, and climbing aboard in time.

They walked up and down, arms linked, and then there was only a minute left.

"Do you have everything?" Kitty asked protectively. "Have you had anything to eat? Do you have enough cigarettes? I know why you have to go but why do you have to go? Write to me."

And he was gone.

Driving back with Joe, Kitty said, "I want to marry him. I know you think I'm too young."

"I've never said that," Joe said. "When have I ever discouraged you?"

"No, I know you haven't. I just get that feeling sometimes. Don't tell your mother and father what I just said."

"I won't. Listen, it's your business, your life—I really mean that. You don't need anybody to tell you what to do. Don't let anybody tell you. 'You're the Top' as the song goes, and you're going to stay right up there whatever you do."

Kitty smiled at him gratefully. She found music on the radio and after a while was inspired to sing along with an instrumental version of Irving Berlin's "Isn't This a Lovely Day," and in a lovely little display of effortless melismatics, got five separate notes out of one five-letter word alone.

"You know me," Joe said. "I throw a lot of compliments around because I like to hear myself talk, but I really mean it, no flattery, when I say I'd rather listen to you than Forrest or Bailey or Ward or Wiley, and as much as Stafford or Whiting. You have a unique, beautiful *sound*. It's a gift. And your pipes aren't even fully developed yet. Take horn playing. Louis is Louis, Bix was Bix. They couldn't be anyone else. Sometimes you guess wrong about the other guys but mostly they sound just like themselves, too. That's why they're as good as they are. Whereas I can only imitate. Try to. Hackett or Butterfield or Berigan. That's the big difference."

"Joe, you're a *good* trumpet player," Kitty said. "I love to hear you play. You've got a *cheery* sound. That's your sound."

"No. I know better. But you've got it. You're a natural. I'm gonna be proud to say I knew you when. I mean if you stay with it."

"I'm going to stay with it," Kitty said, though she didn't sound entirely certain.

"Well," said Joe, changing the subject, "Now it's my turn." He had just enlisted in the navy.

A mile to the south of the Barrys' house another parish began, and a mile and a half away stood that parish church where Kitty never went and where she was unknown. Saturday afternoon the following week, the hour of confessions. She stood at the end of the shortest line. The priest's name would be on the door under the little green light that announced his presence, but she didn't look to see what it was, and then she was alone in the darkened booth waiting for the little screened window to slide open at face level where she knelt.

Open. The side of the priest's face barely visible.

"Bless me, Father, for I have sinned. I confess..."

"Who is this boy?" The tone was demanding, harsh.

Frightened, she hadn't expected this, Kitty said, "He's not from around here, Father."

"You must promise never to see him again, or I cannot give absolution."

What?

The window still open on her, Kitty got to her feet, pushed open the door, and as quickly as was seemly in church walked to the rear entrance, terrified. She thought she heard the priest's door opening and almost expected to suddenly feel his cold hand on the back of her collar, but she escaped and fled this strange neighborhood and didn't stop until she reached St. Margaret's where she should have gone in the first place. Father Shea was old and not unkind and probably didn't know her from Adam anyway and wouldn't try to recognize her voice.

In the dim, quiet, familiar church, cold winter light in the stained glass windows high above, short lines of standing penitants shuffling forward every few minutes on either side of three functioning confessionals.

Her turn to enter, to wait for him to finish with the person in the opposite booth. Then his old, bent, white head, visible only as a shadow.

"... against the sixth commandment," Kitty said.

"What form did this take?" he asked, matter of factly.

"Petting to a climax." For him, she thought, almost regretfully.

"He's not married?"

"No, Father. I'm going to marry him."

"When will that be?"

"Soon. This year."

"Is he going into the service?"

"He's in service. He's away now."

"That may be the best thing." He sighed. "Being young is very difficult. Try to avoid these occasions. For your penance say ten Our Father's and ten Hail Mary's..."

He pronounced the absolution, the window slid closed, and she went out.

Shrived, Kitty left the church, and walking away felt sorry for people like Eileen Byrne who hadn't started any of this yet but would, sooner rather than later, and who would probably not get married for years and so over and over again would try to eat their cake and have it, too. As Father Shea had said, it wasn't easy to be young.

But who was that other, awful man?

12

Kitty had thought of it for a long time but had hesitated to ask Edward J., not because she was afraid to ask but because she was afraid to find out. But now she had to know. And for the first time she knew someone who was important enough, and rich enough, and who knew other important people, maybe to be able to get the answer.

"Mr. Barry, can you help me find out who my father was, how he was killed?"

They were alone in Edward J.'s study. He did not appear surprised at her question, but then his mouth and eyebrows assumed the shape of a thoughtful frown.

"It's a natural thing for you to wonder about, of course, but why now?"

"Because if I marry (she almost said Graham but at the last moment substituted "someday") I want to know if I should have children."

"Of course you should have children. Someday. You're a bright, healthy girl. Presumably you'll marry someone equally bright and healthy. But that's way off... First of all, I don't know if I can find out. I'll try, but there's very little to go on. It might take weeks, even months. We can only guess what year he died. We don't know where. Or if the accident was reported. If it was an accident. If your mother was telling the truth. I don't think a few hours running down obits in some newspaper morgue is going to do it. I'm sure I'd have to hire a private detective."

"I can pay—well, I can help pay for that."

"No, I'll take care of it. You save your money. But completely aside from the time and difficulties involved, is it wise to dig into the past like this? I don't know. I'm not sure."

"Don't I have a right to know?"

"Of course. Yes. It's entirely up to you. I'm only suggesting you don't necessarily have to know, and it might be better if you didn't."

"Mr. Barry, I know what you're thinking—that he might turn out to be some terrible person—a crook, or worse. Well, my mother was a prostitute—" The sound of the word visibly jarred Edward J. His expression didn't change but he sat up straighter for a moment—"and I've lived with that for a long time. I can live with whatever you find out about my father. If he turns out to be not so bad, well, then I'll be better off. I just don't want to guess about him anymore, if I don't have to. But Mr. Barry, if you do this for me, you have to promise to tell me the truth."

"If I find it, I'll show you the evidence," Edward J. said.

Though Joe Barry had enlisted, he wouldn't leave until after he had completed his sophomore year in college that June. That didn't mean the breakup of the band, not yet, though who would replace him? But by fall when Jim would probably be in service, too? In the meantime, the band was busier than ever and would be until the end of the school year.

Graham wrote once or twice a week and Kitty replied as often. And one day she wrote excitedly:

Darling, I've got some real news! I've been discovered! A week ago at the St. Stephen's high school gym during a break, a man came up to me and introduced himself as Herman Miller, an "Artist's Agent" who represents the Irving Bennett orchestra at the Lake Shore Hotel. To make a long story short, Mr. Barry checked into him right away and Mr. Miller really does. Anyway, he said somebody he knew had happened to hear me—I'm not sure where, it doesn't matter—so he had come around to hear me himself, and was very impressed and would I be interested in singing with Irving Bennett. I don't understand why since Laurie Lee Hill is still with him. Maybe she's leaving, I don't know. I know it sounds like a great opportunity—I'd be on radio, too, all the time—but Graham, I don't *want* to sing with Irving Bennett. I don't think he's any good! Maybe some people play with him because they need the work, but I hate that Businessman's Bounce style, the silly tunes they always play, and what they do to good songs, and that dumb clowning around.

And besides, of course, the Barrys think I'm too young, and I didn't argue with them. But if it had been Benny Goodman! Or Artie Shaw. Or the Dorseys.

Anyway, when he came around again I said no thanks and Mr. Miller said if I ever change my mind to let him know. But I was flattered anyway. I don't like the way Laurie Lee Hill sings, or those corny "cute" songs they dig up for her, but she's on key and her timing is professional.

Joe Barry had no special girl. He dated four, tried to make out with all of them, succeeded all the way with one, in varying degrees with the others. Some nights he preferred drifting with friends, looking for new girls. Often enough he would take Kitty someplace after a band date. "So I won't get too lonesome," she wrote Graham. She wrote that Joe had taken her to the Panther Room to hear Krupa and to hear Bob Crosby at the Blackhawk. Joe never tried to make a pass at her, but in public, especially after a few beers, he was able to carry off a kind of brotherly affection—one arm around the shoulder hugs, brief hair mussings—which Kitty accepted gracefully. They kidded around a lot, harmlessly, as she did to a lesser degree with Jim and Matt, and tried to do with Ted, though Ted, sullen and sulking, would have none of it.

When Ted was out of earshot once, Joe said, "Sorry he's such a pain in the butt. He won't take no for an answer. He won't listen to me, he won't listen to anybody. Just ignore him."

"I can't do that," Kitty said. "I don't want to do that. I like him." She sighed.

"Drastic measures may be the only cure for a stubborn, lovesick Barry," Joe said.

Joe suddenly flared his nostrils, leered, and danced Kitty the length of the living room, doing a very good Groucho Marx burlesque of a tango glide.

"We've got to quit meeting like this, Raoul," Kitty said.

Joe partied his way through the last few weeks of college and civilian life.

"Well, I'm going to look at the bright side," Peg Barry commented to her husband. "You might say he's often sober, too."

In whatever condition, his trumpet playing, if anything, seemed to improve. Perhaps he played with more fervor and inspired his brothers and Kitty to do the same. They all felt a heightening of life. It was in the air, it was part of the time in which they lived.

Not having any one girl, Joe did not spend any last evening with any of them—though several wanted him to—and, in fact, to please his mother, who worried about the state of his soul, stayed away from all of them the very last week.

He was scheduled to leave by train for the Great Lakes Naval Training Center Friday evening. There was a farewell party Thursday evening at the home of a friend to which all the younger Barrys, and Kitty, were invited. Joe drank a lot of beer and had a great time. Jim, who had a test the following morning, left early, and Ted and Matt went with him. Neither Ted nor Matt were allowed by the Barrys to drink beer yet (Jim had permission but hadn't as yet taken much advantage of it), and parties given by people Joe's age where Ted and Matt had no choice but soft drinks that cloyed after a couple, and where the older girls paid no attention to them, tended to make them restless.

At midnight, Kitty said, "Come on, Joe, you'd better get some sleep."

"Got my whole life to sleep "

"Not in the navy."

"Thaas true, oh thaas very true, I hear. OK," he said cheerfully, "les go home. G'bye everybody."

Peg Barry did not wait up for Kitty when Kitty was with Joe. Kitty guided Joe up the stairs holding one elbow. At the top of the stairs he held her chin with one hand and kissed her on the lips.

"Now Joe," she whispered with mild reproof when he began sliding his hands around the small of her back and shoulders. But she let him kiss her again for a few seconds before she pushed him gently away. He didn't try a third time.

"G'night, Joe," Kitty said. "Go to sleep now. Don't go getting any more beer, and take some aspirin, eat a piece of bread, drink a glass of milk."

She was getting undressed, smiling at her smeared lipstick in her closet mirror, thinking to herself, half-amused at the thought, if it wasn't for Graham . . . when she heard low voices and more than one person moving around in the hall, steps going down the stairs. But when she opened the door a crack, no one was in sight.

Who was with him, she wondered? Well, someone was. But she wasn't going to chase after him to prevent him from giving himself an even worse hangover. She closed her door again and got into bed but she was wide awake, her ears tuned. Was Mrs. Barry or his father bawling him out down there? She hoped not.

But something was going on, and it seemed to be outside now.

A street lamp illuminated the garden below her window. Joe, and his brother, Ted, were out there in their shirt sleeves, circling each other, their fists raised. Joe had greater bulk and strength—he weighed about 175—but Ted was taller with a longer reach and only five pounds lighter. Neither had their full growth yet, but they were stronger than most grown men.

For a few seconds Kitty could not imagine why she was seeing what she was seeing. Then it struck her. Ted must have seen Joe kissing her and had reacted in a rage of jealousy. He caught Joe on the cheek with a left fist, and Joe swung a left to Ted's ribs and a roundhouse right that glanced off Ted's temple. Then they were both swinging, missing, connecting.

They'll kill each other, Kitty thought, and grabbed a raincoat from her closet to fling over her pajamas, ran downstairs and out the back door through the kitchen.

They weren't making much noise on the grass, not enough to wake anybody who was deeply asleep. The only sounds were grunts and the crack of bone on bone. Joe went down.

"Stop it, Ted, you fool, stop it!" Kitty cried.

"Stay out of it, Kitty!" Joe rasped as he crawled to his knees.

"I won't stay out of it!" she said, and planted herself between Ted and the fallen Joe.

"You better stay out of it," Joe mumbled, getting to his feet. "I needa teacha l'll bassard a lesson!"

"Stop it! You'll both kill each other. Or hurt each other badly. For what?"

"I hate him!" Ted said, tears of hatred running down his cheeks. "He did this to me before. He had all the girls he wanted, but he had to take my girl away from me just to see if he could do it, the dirty, lousy cocksucker!" He was sobbing.

"Ted, I'm not your girl!" Kitty said.

"Get outa the way, Kitty," Joe warned.

She didn't move but Ted stepped around her to go after Joe, and both flailed at each other with murderous, sickening punches. Blood ran from Ted's nose, from Joe's left eye.

"Oh God, please stop, please stop, please stop!" Kitty cried, but the only thing they heeded was their own exhaustion—and the sight of their father storming out of the house, the force of him coming between them.

"What in the name of God is going on here! Are you crazy, both of you? Get in the house! Get in the house! Do you want the police here? Do you want to kill your mother?"

Before he went inside, Edward J. Barry looked at Kitty as though he didn't recognize her or didn't see her. Or was he silently accusing her of being responsible for this savage rending of the Barry family solidarity? She didn't know, but she knew that she had been the cause of it and that she could not stay in this house very much longer. Where will I go now, she wondered? and shivered in the night air.

Kitty tossed in her bed for more than an hour, saddened, brooding, apprehensive, then fell into a shallow, troubled sleep, and slept through breakfast. At ten when she descended, the house was quiet. Jim was in the living room, reading, and greeted her in a normal voice; then Matt came in through the kitchen door after depositing empty trash cans outside and behaved normally, too. but neither Ted, Joe, Edward J., nor Peg Barry seemed to be anywhere about, and Kitty didn't inquire. Change was in the air. After breakfasting on milk and a roll, she went outside, intending to walk to the lake, but halfway down the block she spied the Barrys' car, Peg at the wheel, alone, and retraced her steps. Peg parked in the driveway. Several bags of groceries were stacked in the back seat.

"I'll help with those," Kitty said.

"Get the boys," Peg said.

"I can handle this."

Peg looked sleepless and withdrawn.

"Mrs. Barry," Kitty said as they moved toward the back door with a sack apiece, "why don't you leave dinner to me today? You'll be seeing Joe off."

"It won't be necessary. We're just going to have a pickup meal. Jim! Matt!" she bellowed. "Get the rest of the groceries!"

Kitty rehearsed in her mind "I blame myself for what happened last night. I told Ted I couldn't be his girl but he wouldn't listen, and I suppose I shouldn't have let Joe kiss me but he was tight and it was just an innocent smootch..." No, no matter what she said, it wouldn't sound right, it would leave the wrong impression, it would only make matters worse. She didn't know what Peg Barry even knew, what Edward J. knew. Edward J. hadn't been outside when Ted had said why he was enraged at Joe, and maybe afterwards Joe and Ted had refused to say what the fight was about. Even if either of them had brought her into it, maybe they had done so only in some general way. If Ted had disclosed his jealousy, Joe would have stoutly, with truthful conviction, denied Ted had any reason to be jealous of him, Joe, anyway. Maybe nobody, aside from Ted, blamed her for anything. And why should they? But even if nobody blamed her, she had been the cause of the fight— there was no getting around that. She had no power to resolve this family crisis; she could only impede its resolution. Though Joe was leaving, Ted was not. How could she live with that situation? Maybe she should pack and leave this very day, but go where? She didn't have enough money to pay for a room anywhere very long.

"If it's OK I think I'll go over to Eileen's this afternoon," she murmured to Peg Barry.

"Don't you want lunch?"

"Well, I had a late breakfast."

Peg didn't reply. When the groceries were stashed and the kitchen was neat, Peg drifted upstairs and Kitty left the house again. She didn't go to Eileen Byrne's apartment, but at the drugstore she telephoned Eileen and arranged to go to the 8 P.M. showing of *How Green Was My Valley* with Walter Pidgeon and Maureen O'Hara playing at the Devon Theater. Then she just walked.

At 3:30 when she returned, she entered through the kitchen. There were voices in other rooms, Peg's, Edward J.'s, one or another of the boys'—who she couldn't be sure. Joe, one sounded like, but at a distance Joe sounded much like Jim. To get to her room she would have to enter the front of the house, and she didn't want to do that now. The kitchen was in good order but she found chores to do. One cupboard of staples needed straightening; the vegetable bins in the refrigerator needed washing; the sink could use some whitening with bleach. A little after four, Joe came into the kitchen wearing a large patch over his left eyebrow, a smaller bandage on his right cheek. He was dressed to go out, in his best slacks, sport jacket, white shirt, tie.

"Well, goodbye, kid," he said.

"You're leaving now? I thought . . . Can't you stay for dinner?"

"I thought I'd catch an earlier train. Make sure I get there on time. I don't want to get thrown in the brig on the first day."

"Oh, Joe, take care of yourself."

She was drying her hands on a dish towel. Some tears got the better of her and escaped.

"You take care of yourself. Don't stop singing. Or the piano. Why don't you try the job with Irving Bennett for a while? I know it's a Mickey Mouse outfit, but he's popular. You'd sound good whatever you were singing, or whoever you were singing with, and a lot more people would get to hear you. It might lead to something. I'll never be a pro. None of us—the Barry brothers—will, but you will be, are already."

"Maybe. I'll see . . . I'm sorry I got you all banged up."

"Shh," he said. "It wasn't your fault."

"Do your parents think so?"

"They shouldn't. I told them exactly what happened and not to blame you, but I don't know what that little—never mind—might have said. Anyway, it'll all blow over."

Joe had to go only as far as Howard Street, a few miles north, at the city limits, to catch a North Shore Line train to Great Lakes, and Peg and Edward J., who drove him there, were back, subdued, less than an hour afterwards. While they were gone, Ted knocked on Kitty's door. His right hand was bandaged, his nose was swollen, and his lips were puffed.

"I'm sorry about last night," he said. It wasn't an apology. It was something he had been ordered to say.

"You were the one who got hurt, Ted. *I'm* sorry for that."

He waited a few seconds, not looking at her, then left without saying anything more.

The atmosphere at dinner was strained and awkward. Ted made himself a sandwich and disappeared. Everyone avoided everyone else. Kitty went off to the movies, and when she returned, the Barrys had gone to bed. Peg Barry did not wait up.

They shouldn't blame her, Joe had said, but did they at least say to themselves, if she hadn't been living here the whole thing never would have happened?

By Sunday, though Joe's absence left a noticeable gap, an air of normalcy, or perhaps it was resignation, had returned to the Barry household. The Barrys were fair and had a duty and a commitment as Kitty's guardians. But Kitty felt on trial, on borrowed time, awaiting some final judgment, for the moment suspended. On Monday, without informing the Barrys, she telephoned Herman Miller, who set up an audition with the Irving Bennett orchestra.

PART IV

PART IV

13

The Lake Shore Hotel, a vast, Florida-Spanish palace between Sheridan Road and Lake Michigan, was nearby glamour for residents, like Kitty, of Chicago's far North Side. In the dead of winter, when the lake along the shoreline often froze over, the pastel and sandstone-colored pile shivered, out of place; but now it was July, and the beach was crowded during the day under a hot summer sun. At night, guests promenaded along The Strand strung with Japanese lanterns, and the hotel could pretend again it was located in a palm grove at the edge of some tropic sea.

In a short-sleeved, boat-neck, yellow linen dress, white gloves, her small feet in brown and white spectator pumps, her straight, dark brown hair carefully brushed, her face rather remarkably radiant, Kitty crossed the marble and carpets of the spacious, elegant lobby to the silk-curtained tall glass doors to the ballroom.

The ballroom itself, sunlit, was empty. On stage, the Irving Bennett orchestra was rehearsing a number Kitty didn't recognize immediately. Saxophones bleated and burbled as though their bells might be filled with warm milk. Kitty winced, offended by this sound, but continued her progress toward Herman Miller, the agent, who waited for her, a stocky little man, his back to the band.

To one side of the orchestra, sat another girl—woman—more casually and flashily dressed than Kitty, chewing gum. Laurie Lee Hill, evidently.

"Glad you could make it, kid," Herman Miller whispered hoarsely. "Have a seat."

Kitty sank onto a gilt and satin chair beside him and peeled off her white gloves. Her hands were damp. Laurie Lee Hill removed her gum—which she folded in a small piece of paper and held in one fist—stood, and walked toward the microphone alongside Irving Bennett's waving left hand and fanny, and bald, bobbing head.

"Oh, you crazy moon," she sang with a voice like many others, not bad, not distinguished, but for Kitty that didn't matter one way or the other because in her opinion the song itself was inferior. Disheartened, Kitty waited for it to end. Well, what did you expect? she asked herself. Then it stopped and since no one else applauded, neither did she.

Laurie Lee Hill, a dyed blonde who appeared to be in her mid-thirties, looked down at Kitty, then said to the world at large, "Well, look at her! Isn't *she* pretty."

This was not said derisively, but Kitty found it disconcerting to be referred to in the third person as though she might be an object up for auction.

"Come on up here, little lady," Irving Bennett said in his well-known nasal radio voice, and Kitty, with a dry mouth, went to the side steps and climbed to the stage.

"Now just relax," Bennett said, putting his arm around Kitty's waist. His hand slid a little lower than Kitty cared for but he took it away when she stiffened.

"What I'd like for you to do," he said, "is sing a little number by yourself, and then one with Laurie Lee. OK?"

"A duet?" Kitty asked, trying not to sound as appalled as she felt.

"You got it. Little idea I have, see how it works. So first, by yourself, sweetie. 'Specially for You.' You know it? A few years back?"

"Uh, yes," Kitty said. "But I'll need to look at the lyrics."

"Right here," Irving Bennett said, handing over the sheet music. He began tapping his foot and the orchestra played a rippling intro to the theme and the lyrics, which Kitty sang as best she could, considering her indifference, even aversion, to this lightweight ditty. The best she could say about it was that it was sort of "catchy," but it wasn't her kind of song and couldn't be bent to her style. In her own ears she sounded awful, but Irving Bennett applauded when it was over and said, "We're gonna make a star outta this little lady."

For the duet, Kitty and Laurie Lee Hill were required to sing "Three Little Fishes," a dreadfully cute aberration from the otherwise generally rich soil of the 1930s. Irving Bennett had a positive genius for reviving forgettable songs of earlier eras and for spotting mediocrity destined to be popular. In her mind, even as she sang, Kitty was composing a letter to Graham Allen: "I wanted to throw up, but..."

But she was offered a job at twenty-five dollars a week, as soon as she got herself a union card, to sing duets with Laurie Lee Hill on Friday and Saturday evenings, and with great reluctance mixed with the thrill of first regular employment, she accepted.

"Does he ever play anything good?" she asked. She was sitting at a table in the hotel coffee shop with Laurie Lee and Laurie Lee's husband, Artie Rosen, Bennett's drummer, who had invited Kitty to join them after the audition.

"You mean you don't *like* this music?" Rosen asked in mock shock. He held up one forefinger. "But to answer your question—once in a while, once in a while. Of course what we do to a good song..."

"It pays the bills, honey," Laurie Lee said to Kitty. "Musicians have to eat, too, and Bennett pays as well as anyone. These aren't the best of times in this business, but Bennett hasn't missed a performance in six years. I wish we'd been lucky enough to come with him sooner. He also stays put right here. No traveling. No one-night stands in drafty gymnasiums. No busses, no fleabag hotels, no indigestion. However, while we're on the subject, there are certain drawbacks, pitfalls, things you have to put up with. Such as the fact that Irving is a fanny patter and would really like to try a little more than that, though if you want my opinion I'm not sure he's capable. I don't mean to be crude, honey, but I saw him up there trying to cop a little feel. You need to be warned, but don't let it worry you too much. Brush him off. He won't fire you. But don't accept any invitations to go to parties after the show unless Artie and I are going to be there, too. Always have one of your stepbrothers around to take you home. And by the way, honey, you're real good, you know that?"

"You should have discussed this with us first," Peg Barry said sternly, sitting beside Edward J., and Kitty knew she was being chastised. "We're your legal guardians and you're under age. We *could* forbid you to take this job but we've decided to let you do it—provisionally, this summer. The Lake Shore is a respectable place, and Irving Bennett is a fixture there. When school starts again we'll have to take another look."

Kitty said "Thank you" to that but did not add any "I'm sorrys" for anything, and the tension in the air faded only gradually.

Twenty-five dollars a week was probably enough to live on, Kitty thought, but now with Joe gone and Ted, after all, going into the service in just a few months, moving out of the Barrys' house right away no longer seemed necessary. But at least she could offer to contribute something to the household budget or buy her own clothes and necessities.

Kitty did not write to Graham about the fight—it would be too difficult to explain—which made it more difficult for him to understand why she had accepted the job in the first place when she couldn't stand Bennett's music.

He wrote back:

I'll have to go along with the Barrys on this one. I'm proud you were the girl Bennett picked out of all the singers who must have applied for the job—I can't really agree with you about Bennett's orchestra, incidentally. Most people think he's pretty good, especially to dance to, or he wouldn't have stayed at the Lake Shore and on radio so long. But I wish you'd talked it over with me first, too. It's swell of you to want to make a little money so you won't just be 'taking' from the Barrys all the time. But they don't expect you to have to work yet. They can afford to take care of you. It makes them happy to. But if they think it's OK for you to sing on weekends I guess I'll have to go along with that, too. What station are you on—WGN? Let me know so I can try to pick it up down here.

In the hot evenings of July and August, the Irving Bennett orchestra moved outside to The Strand where couples danced under the stars, and beach parties listened to the same music over radios all along the shore. Westward, away from the lake, other radios played from the open windows of apartment buildings, and thus, on weekend evenings, Kitty's voice—in duet with Laurie Lee Hill—was broadcast throughout the city. Late at night, if atmospheric conditions were favorable, the driver of a car in the Illinois countryside might hear clearly stations states away, and conversely, someone like Graham Allen in Alabama might hear a station in Chicago. And once, he wrote, he did hear music from The Strand of the Lake Shore Hotel, but on a week night, and in any case he heard no vocalist at all.

"You don't know how lucky you are," Kitty wrote. "You might have had to listen to me and Laurie Lee doing 'Praise the Lord and Pass the Ammunition.'"

And things like "I'll Never Smile Again" (a little treacly, but in wartime, not too bad) or "Chattanooga Choo Choo" (a quality song, but as usual, Bennett's watery orchestral accompaniment was deplorable.)

Now Roberta wrote from New York, her usual half-page note. She was playing with a quintet in a Harlem night club called The Carousel Lounge. On Kitty's job, she commented: "Well, it may lead to something better. At least you're learning how to stand and sit on stage, microphone technique..."

Edward J. reported that the investigation was proceeding.

Graham Allen had already flown over sixty hours in light planes before joining the air corps and had been allowed to skip the first of the three phases of flight training. In his early letters from Maxwell Field he had high hopes of becoming a fighter pilot, but as time went on he began to report, resignedly, that his instructors believed he'd be more suited to bombers.

"Just like driving a bus," he wrote.

He was scheduled to get his pilot's wings and second lieutenant's bars in early September, then would go directly into transitional training on B-17s at Hendricks Field, Sebring, Florida. Kitty was secretly relieved. Big bombing planes with other crew members alongside seemed safer to her than fighter planes.

Later that summer of 1942, Jim followed Joe into the navy, and in the fall, after his eighteenth birthday, Ted became the third Barry to join that branch of the service. The Barry brothers band was disbanded. Unexpressed was the feeling it would never be revived. As adults, the Barry boys would not consent to be the less than the top-ranking group they were willing to be as high school and college students, and each of them would be able to earn more money, a lot more money, as something other than a journeyman musician. They played for the fun of it, and they would continue, as their father did, to play occasionally for their own pleasure, but the band would be no more.

Kitty was back in school, still singing on the weekends with Irving Bennett, and in spite of her dislike of the music she was paid to perform, she had become a popular local vocalist with the mostly older, conservative couples who went dinner dancing at the Lake Shore Hotel. She began to get a trickle of fan mail, and to her great chagrin it came mostly from radio listeners who couldn't stand the jazz she loved and believed she and Irving Bennett and Laurie Lee Hill were to be applauded for performing "decent music you can dance to."

Sister Edmund grumbled about "unwanted publicity" for the school, though there was very little of it really—a couple of smallish newspaper ads with photographs of Laurie Lee Hill and Kitty Collins together that ran a few weekends, none of them mentioning St. Margaret's. But to a degree, Kitty had also been neglecting her classical piano studies, and Sister Edmund was sometimes exasperated and displeased. In the autumn cold, in the dim fall light, in the stuffy music room at the convent, Sister Edmund's face seemed to grow older, paler, more severe by the month, and Kitty, feeling guilty, would cram in a practice session or two before the lessons she had come to rather dread, so as not to disappoint Sister Edmund still further.

Letters, postcards, photographs from Joe, Jim, and Ted Barry. By

October, Joe was on sea duty in the Caribbean hunting Nazi U-boats. Jim was in California and expected to join the crew of an aircraft carrier in the Pacific by the first of the year. Ted was training at Pensacola, Florida.

Edward J. Barry did have influential friends—in the press, on the police force, in the courts—willing enough to cooperate with the private investigator he had hired, but there was no urgency to the matter, no money in it for anyone except the investigator (and no fortune for him—this was not the only case he was working on), no promotions or particular advantage for anyone doing a favor for Edward J. or the friends of Edward J. Routine requests got answered eventually but stayed for some time rising slowly from the bottoms of bureaucratic piles of paper, and the summer holidays produced inevitable, additional delays. It was not until October that Edward J. had the answer, wrapped in the nine-by-twelve manila envelope he brought home one evening. Peg Barry, though intensely curious, was not invited to join Edward J. and Kitty in the study where he closed the door.

"It isn't bad," Edward J. said. But before Kitty had a chance to breathe a sigh of relief, he added, "It isn't good, but it isn't bad." She sat absolutely still as Edward J. removed the contents of the envelope and laid them on the coffee table before the two-seat leather couch on which they sat side by side.

"He drove a truck for a bootlegger—do you know what a bootlegger is—was?"

"Yes, sir."

"He was driving a truck of bootleg liquor back from Canada when it was hijacked by a rival gang. There was shooting, he was among three dead. The year was 1929. How do they know this Jack Collins was your father and not someone else? They're ninety-five percent certain because a Madge Collins identified him, because there's a distinct family resemblance between his photograph and one of you I made available. But the final judgment is yours. You can decide. There's a photograph of her." He slid a glossy print in front of her.

She was so beautiful, Kitty thought.

"It's her," she said. "May I see his picture?"

"No."

"No?"

"I don't have it, Kitty. He was dead, you don't want to see it. You really don't. I wish there was another but there isn't ... Prohibition—telling people they couldn't drink—was a stupid law, incredibly stupid. It was such a stupid law that practically everyone defied it, broke it. I did, too. I made beer—illegal beer—in the basement of our first house. I bought illegal whiskey in drugstores and in 'blind pigs.' I drank it in speakeasies. So what your father was doing when he got killed was illegal at the time but not really so terrible. The reason there is no other photograph of him is that apparently he had no previous criminal record."

"But he worked for a gang," Kitty said evenly. "So he was a gangster."

"Sometimes, my sweet, you are too smart," Edward J. said, conscious of the fact that he had never before used such an affectionate term to Kitty. "They were very mixed-up, morally ambiguous times. Give him the benefit of the doubt. At least he was bringing in good whiskey, not the poisonous rotgut that killed so many people in those days. And driving that kind of a truck in those times—through enemy territory—took guts. Let him rest in peace."

"Does it say where he was from?" Kitty asked.

"There's only a Chicago address on the Near North Side. Do you want me to try to dig further back?"

Kitty thought a few moments, then shook her head sharply once. She had never missed grandparents, uncles, aunts, cousins. What could they do for her now except in some way limit her freedom?

"No," she said.

She didn't really know how she felt about the revelation she had sought, only that she was suddenly very, very lonely for Graham Allen.

So there it was, Edward J. thought. Just when Jack Collins was making a lot of money to buy Madge the things she craved, he let her down with a crash by getting himself killed. The other crash comes a few months later and the Depression is on. There would be over twelve million out of work within a couple of years and she was uneducated, unskilled to begin with. But Prohibition was still on, and she would know a name or two Jack had worked for and where to find them. What had killed him could keep her alive. They could get her jobs as hat-check girl, dice girl, and she could leave Kitty with neighbors or alone with the door unlocked so that neighbors could look in if the child cried. Checking hats and bar jobs, before and after Repeal, or waitressing, manicuring nails in men's barber shops, the kind of work she could get and do, would never maintain the expensive tastes she had acquired. But they would give her exposure to the public, make it easy for her to meet people, to realize she did, after all, have something more expensive to offer . . .

14

By the first of November, Kitty was counting the days, the hours, until Graham's return. After completion of his transitional training he would proceed from Florida to Rapid City, South Dakota, to form a crew, join a squadron, and conduct operational training exercises for approximately three months as part of a heavy bombardment group. After final leave, sometime in March, 1943, the group would move to an as yet unknown destination overseas, ready for combat. En route to South Dakota, he would have time to spend Thanksgiving Day with his parents in Minneapolis and the rest of the long weekend in Chicago with Kitty. Through Kitty, the Barrys invited him to stay with them.

Late Friday afternoon, she met him at the Northwestern station in Evanston, a prosaic location made glamorous by the occasion and the crowds of shoppers and students on holiday, hurrying along the streets in the dusk, the winter cold.

Kitty, even at her worst—that is to say, 'f, chameleon-like, she had become rundown, pale, drab—could still be seen to be a pretty girl; at her usual best, in good health, an exceptional one; at her best, at a moment like this, her eyes bright, her skin clear, scrubbed, glowing, she was truly beautiful.

Graham was tanned and to Kitty looked marvelous in his uniform and his tilted, visored cap.

West of the city and west of the alcohol-dry northern suburbs were strings of roadhouses, some of the more elaborate ones with floor shows, gambling, and mob connections as well as simpler places devoted to beer drinking and jukebox dancing, popular with the college crowd. Like The White Horse Tavern west of Wilmette, their destination.

Kitty had a driver's license now and had taken the Barrys' LaSalle to meet Graham. She then let him drive it.

"We've got to talk to the Barrys tonight," he said.

Kitty swallowed.

"Graham, I've got to tell you something. You know what my mother was. I just found out something about my father—Mr. Barry did. There are photographs. I saw the proof. He was killed in a gang war. He worked for a bootlegger, driving a truck. Mr. Barry says what he was doing wasn't really so bad, and maybe that's true, but if he was in a gang, what else had he done? There's no way of knowing. I want children, but what if they took after my mother? What if my father wasn't much better and they took after him?"

"Take Mr. Barry's word about your father, don't make him worse than he was. And you told me about your mother right after we met. So what? It doesn't matter. I don't believe in that kind of heredity."

"Lets go talk to them now, before we do anything else," Kitty said. "I couldn't eat a thing."

At the next crossroads, Graham turned south, toward Chicago.

In the privacy of Edward J.'s study, the Barrys listened, stunned, and Edward J. got out of his swivel chair to pace and reply.

"Graham, Kitty. Good God, we simply can't, in good conscience, give our permission to this now! Kitty is only sixteen, and in a couple of months you're going off to war, to be gone how long? Only God knows. We beg of you to wait! You're going to have to wait a long time to be together again in any case, and if you love each other, as I believe you do, you'll still love each other at the end of that time. But you'll also be older, Kitty will have finished high school at least, and with the war over, God willing, you'll both have a chance to think, to know what you want to do with your lives."

"We know now," Graham said.

"I'll never be more sure," Kitty said.

"You say that, you believe it," Peg said. "But I don't think you can know yet. Have you ever written to each other about this? I don't think so, am I right?"

"No, wrong," Kitty said. "We decided last February."

Peg Barry shifted gears. "We know how you feel, believe us. We've gone through the same thing. And for now it's all based on emotion. It seems to you that because of the war, because Graham has to leave, that everything has to be speeded up or somehow you'll lose each other. But that isn't true. Wait, kids. As Ed says, you've got to wait anyway, there's no help for that, but don't wait on a too hasty marriage."

Kitty realized arguing with them anymore now would be futile. The Barrys just didn't understand the depth of her need for him, the emotional security he offered. Without him, or someone like him, she had, in the final analysis, at sixteen, as she had had at thirteen, at ten, at seven, only herself. If Peg Barry did, instinctively, understand this, she did not want to accept it, and so did not. She and Edward J. had gone all out to take Kitty in, to provide her with a home, a refuge, a secure place to wait until she was old enough to know whom she should marry. And if that man should still be Graham Allen two or three or four years hence, she and Edward J., in spite of grave misgivings over the religious aspect, would give their blessing. Now, relying easily on conventional wisdom (not always wrong—surely, often right!) they felt it their duty to withhold that blessing.

Peg Barry left the study and climbed to the second floor of the house. Edward J. followed shortly after and went to the kitchen. Graham and Kitty got their outer coats, left the house and walked goallessly in the cold. It was snowing lightly.

"Maybe they'll change their minds," Kitty said. "But if they don't, we'll do something else. I love you. I'm going to marry you. Soon."

"Where can we go now?"

"Anywhere. It doesn't matter. A movie? Never mind what. Then maybe I'll be hungry enough to eat something. Unless you're hungry now."

"I can wait."

Their underlying self-confidence could not make Saturday something other than rather miserably deflated. They simply endured the listless hours. Saturday evening they drove to The White Horse Tavern where the bartenders weren't too fussy about ID cards and where Graham, twenty-one now, looking older than that, and in the uniform of an officer, wasn't even asked for one, nor was Kitty who could pass for eighteen, especially when the lights were low. For the first time in public she was served a beer. She had tried it once or twice in the Barrys' kitchen and didn't really like the taste of it all that much, but it was the thing to do; cola drinks were boring, and tonight especially she appreciated the pleasant effect. She sipped slowly, half as slowly as Graham, and had only two glasses before they left.

After one sip she took his hands and said, "Don't be discouraged. I'm not." She smiled, that smile he could never resist. "I'm very proud to be engaged to you."

"Oh, Kit, I love you so."

"Then be happy. There's nothing to be sad about."

Around midnight they left and drove in silence to the Barrys. No one had waited up, everyone was asleep, the house was silent.

"Graham," Kitty said. "I'll go with you. When you leave tomorrow I'm going with you. I've got money saved, and I could find a place to live in Rapid City."

"I'll be flying cross-country all the time. I'd hardly ever be at the base, and even when I was I wouldn't be able to get a pass just when I felt like it. I'd hardly ever get to see you. It'd be worse than you being here. Worse for you. You wouldn't have anything to do. And the Barrys might really write us off. We can't afford to let that happen. What would you do when I'm overseas? I don't want to leave you, but you've got to stay here for now. Besides, I want you to have a regular church wedding.

"Listen, talk to your priest, see what he says," Graham said. "If he won't marry us, then we'll figure out something else. But talk to him. The Barrys want to think of you as their daughter. They haven't had you around very long and they don't want you to go away. That's one of their big reasons. But whether you stay or go won't mean anything to the priest. He's just going to go by his rules, whatever they are."

Sick with the pain of knowing he would once again be gone in the morning, gone for another three months, and after that gone halfway around the world to fight a war for how long, how many months and years?—already America had been at war for almost a year, and in Europe it had been going on for two—she couldn't leave him now, couldn't say goodnight. Tomorrow she would talk to a priest. Tonight she would stay with Graham.

"*I'll be back,*" she whispered and in stocking feet went up to her room, undressed completely and dressed again in only skirt and pullover sweater, silently descended, went to the side sunporch where Graham waited, slumped in the dark at the end of a couch, in uniform shirtsleeves, tie loosened, a wide lock of hair over his forehead, her boy-man, the dearest human in her world besides Roberta who occupied a different plane.

She lay beside him and kissed him deeply, tongues talking a new and secret language that thrilled them through and through, and lifted her sweater so that he could see the breasts she had thought too small and he found so perfect and of which she was proud now because they pleased him, and, her chin ducked, watched him with faintly smiling curiosity cupping their buoyant weightless weight as though they were wondrous works of art, and tracing their aureoles with the tips of fingers. With her left hand she suddenly felt for him and found him through endless layers of cloth it seemed, but his hand encountered no obstacles as she guided it up to her.

"I'm already as married to you as I'll ever be," she whispered. "*I want you to make love to me now now now!*"

It was over for him in one blinding, ten-second-or-less roman-candle burst; and Kitty did not know if what she felt was what she was supposed to feel, but she knew she felt marvelously fulfilled and at peace.

Decorously clothed again, only slightly rumpled, they fell asleep sitting up, Kitty's head against Graham's shoulder, babes in the woods, and woke at 4:30 A.M., time enough to make coffee and telephone for a taxi.

Graham's train was scheduled to leave at 7 A.M. The station was not located in the safest part of downtown Chicago and Kitty had reluctantly agreed to say goodbye, a little before six, at the Barrys' door. No arrangements had been made for anyone else to get up that early to see him off. Graham held her warm, early-morning face in gloved hands, kissed her, and for a few moments, while the cab waited, engine running, at the curb, they couldn't get enough of each other. The sky was still dark, street lamps were lit, snow glistened on the roadway; a few figures hurried along the opposite sidewalk on their way to early Mass.

Both Peg and Edward J. tried to be kind. At the breakfast table following the noon Mass that day, Peg reached over and put a hand over one of Kitty's for a moment. And Edward J. preached a message of combined realism and hope by quoting from war dispatches, analyses, and editorials in the *Tribune*. The enemy was formidable and might take a long time to defeat, but Allied strength was growing, and of that Axis defeat there could be no doubt. Kitty listened politely but with detachment, dry-eyed, and the Barrys mistook her quiet determination for stoic resignation.

"Eileen Byrne and I are going to the Granada this afternoon," Kitty said to change the subject. But whatever she spoke of, permanently engraved in her mind, it seemed, was an image of Graham and herself together.

"Oh? What's playing?" Peg asked.

"*Casablanca* and *Shadow of a Doubt*."

"I wanta see them, too," Matt said.

"Not with the homework you've got piled up," Peg said. "You'd really better work on that math, buddy boy, if you ever expect to qualify for cadet school next year."

Safely off the subject, Kitty could even allow herself to bubble a little publicly, to suggest that Edward J. and Matt join her at the piano, with Edward J.'s clarinet and Matt's bass, and play a little—"My Honey's Lovin' Arms" and "I Can't Believe That You're in Love with Me," which just about exhausted Edward J.'s musical stamina for the day. And the Barrys were just as publicly pleased by Kitty's evident refusal to brood, to sulk, not that they had ever seen her sulk. If she had gone through that phase she had mercifully gone through it before reaching the Barry household. But the fire beneath the visible bubble in Kitty's spirit was the excitement born of pride in Graham, of the knowledge he wanted to marry her, of the memory of their act of love, of the awareness that she was approaching some great adventure the Barrys, in the long run, had no real power to prevent. Which produced a kind of guilt, a kind of pity, that spurred her to be kinder to them and thus to reinforce their comforting self-deception that they would be able to enjoy the company of their adopted daughter for years to come, a prospect made all the more important to them now that three sons were gone and the fourth and last was preparing himself to leave.

But she did not yet talk to a priest. Given time for reflection, she realized it was too soon. Come what may, she had three months to wait. She would still have to have another, final showdown with the Barrys, and after that how long could she stay under their roof in any kind of peace? They wouldn't throw her into the street, but staying could be just as bad. There was no one she knew who had room enough to put her up for very long. She could get a room somewhere; she could afford it now, but that would hurt them even more. There was no solution, but for the time being doing nothing, delaying the inevitable, seemed better, easier, more charitable, than taking some kind of action.

Music really was such a wonderful thing to have at a time like this. Teddy Wilson soloing on "These Foolish Things" or Armstrong's solo on "I Gotta Right to Sing the Blues" on the Victrola in her room had the timelessness to lift her out of the present to some golden moment fixed in the score of years between the wars.

In early December she had her period on schedule, which answered one question in the negative.

A short note on a Christmas card from Roberta. The quintet had moved to the Ivory Tower Club on 52nd Street, the first time Roberta had played the Street since the mid-1930s.

15

In formations of B-17s, Graham Allen was flying, as often as weather would permit, back and forth across the Great Plains of the United States between the borders of Canada and Mexico, and over the mountains to the west, landing at other bases for the night, continuing on, but which enemy he would ultimately face, German or Japanese, and where, he would not know until his commanding officer opened sealed orders on the first leg of their journey outward bound. Just before then, he would have three weeks leave. Filial duty would compel him to spend one week of that with his parents in Minnesota. Then he would have two weeks with Kitty in Chicago.

In December she had to tell him she had not yet talked to any priest, and why.

"But when?" he asked just before the subdued Christmas of 1942.

"Pretty soon," she wrote.

The third week in January, Graham's leave only a month away, she shattered the Barrys comfortable complacency.

"I've got to ask you again," she said one evening—it seemed for the Barrys out of the blue. "Will you give me your permission to marry Graham?"

Edward J. slowly drew the palm of his right hand up his forehead, over the crown of his hair to the back of his neck. Peg Barry got to her feet and walked out to the winter porch and back into the living room again to get control of herself.

"Kitty," Edward J. began, in a discouraged voice. "We thought you had ..."

"Kitty, no!" Peg Barry interrupted. "Nothing has changed in two months. We've taken the stand we're convinced is right, and we're not going to change it!"

"I'm going to marry Graham when he comes to Chicago the first of March," Kitty said, and was surprised at the calm control in her voice. "I'd like to do it with your blessing, or at least with your permission. You've been very good to me and I'll always be grateful. But if you won't give your permission, then I'll have to get married without it."

"You can't get a license from the state of Illinois *without* our permission!" Peg said.

"I can get along for a couple of years without that piece of paper. And tomorrow I'm going to talk to Father Kane."

"Do you expect him just to ignore how we feel?" Peg asked. "Do you think the Church is less strict than we are?"

"I don't know. But I have to see him and find out."

Peg left the room and climbed the stairs. She was in tears and would not stay in public in that condition. Edward J. lit a cigarette with nervous fingers.

"I'm sorry, Mr. Barry," Kitty said. "But deep inside me I know I'm old enough, and this is my life. I have to do what I'm convinced is right. If I have to, I'll elope."

She swallowed once before speaking again.

"We're already living together," she said.

"Kitty ..." He fell silent again, but the sound of her name held her there "... If Father Kane will marry you, I'll sign whatever paper is necessary."

He stood, and drew on his cigarette. "... You have no birth certificate. We'll have to draw up an affidavit attesting to our belief that you're sixteen, based on your own witness, grade in school, school records. For that matter, in my opinion you're not only as mature but rather more mature than any eighteen-year-old girl I know. I'll make note of that too. There won't be any difficulty. An assistant state's attorney is a friend of ours." His voice lowered, almost to inaudibility. "But tomorrow, as you say, you'd better talk it over with Father Kane."

Not emotionally involved, and an intellectual as well, Father Kane could remain dispassionate, objective. Thin, bespectacled, somewhat cold in manner, he sat with Kitty in the parlor of the parish rectory at 4:30 in the afternoon, listening carefully, patiently. He had some knowledge of Kitty already, of her background, her talent, and was impressed by her poise, by the way she organized her thoughts and expressed herself. But was this true maturity?

"I like them. I'm terribly fond of them," she said. "I appreciate what they've done for me. But I'm not their daughter, I didn't ask them to be my guardians, and I'm old enough now not to need guardians anymore. I'm old enough to marry the man I love."

"From the standpoint of the Church," Father Kane said dryly, "technically, you would have been old enough at fourteen. But Graham has to go overseas. Even if you married him now you would still have to return to the Barrys or live by yourself. I'm not at all convinced it would be safe for a sixteen-year-old girl to live alone these days. Quite the reverse."

Kitty listened politely, but Father Kane could see the stubborn determination in her expression.

"Kitty, you strike me as an exceptionally intelligent girl. And because you are intelligent, I know you can see why the Barrys are so concerned. Not so much over the fact of Graham's Protestantism as over the simple fact that at sixteen, no matter how intelligent you are, how mature beyond your years, you lack experience. In a real sense that means you lack freedom of choice. You haven't met and known enough boys to be able to make comparisons and form sound judgments.

"The war," he went on mechanically now, knowing she was unconvinced, "the war and the forced separations caused by war, are painful for everyone affected, but you try to cheat the war, cheat time, only at your peril."

He groped one last time for some effective argument. "Kitty, do you know any young married couples?"

"Not well. I've met a few."

"At the end of about a year, or even less, do you think any couple like that would know, or remember, the difference between fifty weeks of married life and fifty-two?"

"I don't know."

"I can't be sure either, but I don't believe they would."

"No," Kitty said, "because they've had all those other weeks. What if two weeks were all they had?"

"But, Kitty, you don't know that two weeks are all you'll have together. God willing, you'll have hundreds, even thousands!"

"Then will it matter so much to anybody else that we have two weeks now? You think if we don't have that time now we'll change our minds. People change their minds later, too. They make mistakes later, too."

The priest sighed. "Kitty, under canon law, you and Graham can be married in the Church. And I will officiate, if you request it. In any event, I urge you to defer your final decision until you've gone home and have thought for a few days about what we've talked about today. I also urge you to attend daily Mass and pray for guidance, for wisdom. But if your decision is to marry now in spite of this advice, I have no power—the bishop has no power—to prevent it."

The day was spent. The winter evening came into the room, and Father Kane went around lighting lamps.

"But there is no time to lose," the priest said. "Graham must receive instructions from a Catholic priest. In normal times, he'd receive this instruction from me. That's obviously out of the question now. So as soon as possible have him contact a priest in Rapid City. As soon as I know this man's name I'll get off a letter to him. Graham will also have to sign a paper in which he agrees to raise any children of this marriage as Roman Catholics."

She listened, she heard, but these were details. The interview was over, and like some discovered treasure, Kitty now possessed the one piece of information she needed. For the first time in her life she felt in control of events. Almost.

"Father, now will you hear my confession?"

His expression said he wished it wasn't necessary, but aloud he said, "Certainly," sighed, and went to close the door to his study.

Kitty bowed her head as she spoke in a low voice, not looking at him. "Graham and I made love all the way. It was my idea..."

As she was leaving the rectory, Father Kane said, "Kitty, you must make every effort to be as kind as possible to the Barrys, to Mrs. Barry especially. It won't be easy for anyone. If your decision to marry now is final, that's going to be a blow for them, you know that."

"I will, Father."

Edward J. and Peg were sitting in the living room with their before-dinner drinks, but they were anything but relaxed. Their faces were grim. Kitty stood in the doorway, her winter coat and gloves still on.

"We can be married by a priest," she said.

There was no reply. After a few moments of silence, Kitty said, "I'll just make myself a sandwich for dinner if that's all right."

From the drugstore, Kitty put in a long-distance telephone call to Rapid City, South Dakota. Graham was on a training mission and would not return for forty-eight hours.

In the afternoon before the evening when she would call him again, excused from classes, Kitty took the El to the Loop and met Edward J. in the Adams Street offices of a four-name firm of attorneys. She was not there long. The affidavit and his declaration giving permission for her to marry were ready for signature. With little ceremony Kitty and Edward J. sat on the edges of red leather chairs and signed the documents, which were then duly notarized and sealed. Kitty received the original copies folded into a heavy envelope, which she placed in her shoulder bag.

They stood.

"Thank you, Mr. Barry," Kitty said.

He patted her shoulder.

The call took a long time to go through many voices, many silences and delays, but finally Graham was on the line.

"*... Wait a minute, wait a minute. Of course I'm glad Mr. Barry has signed the papers. I knew you could swing it! But that other* business. I'll be glad to go and listen to what some priest has to say if it'll make Father Kane happy. I'm open-minded. I'll go into town tomorrow and send you the name right away. but signing away my rights just like that? I don't know how I'm going to feel a few years from now. For all I know I might think Catholic schools and all that were a good idea. Sometimes they're better than the public ones. But I don't want to be pinned down now without a chance to think about it . . . Anyway, give me time to talk to the priest here, and I'll get back to you. Don't worry, we're going to be married . . ."

A letter from Graham arrived with the name and address of a Catholic priest in Rapid City and the information that on their honeymoon they would have the use of an apartment on the Near North Side owned by friends of an uncle of Graham's who spent their winters in Florida.

The following day she brought the address to Father Kane, and they set a date for the wedding—March the third, a Wednesday.

Graham had also written:

We've got to think about what you'll do while I'm overseas. I think you've got to stay on with the Barrys for a while, at least until you're eighteen and finish high school. Then you could live in a dorm at Northwestern or some other college. But with the allotment from my pay you can offer to pay some kind of rent for your room and board at the Barrys'. Mr. Barry sounds pretty sympathetic even if she doesn't. I'm sure she'll come around after a while . . .

But for Kitty the prospect of spending even another month with the Barrys seemed unbearable. What would they talk about? Would they even speak to each other at all? And after the wedding? She absolutely couldn't go back to living with them. That was out. She would have to find an apartment. But singing with Irving Bennett until the war was over? Oh, no, no, no, she said aloud to herself.

She stuck it out, though, the month, making herself as invisible as possible, eating early, eating out, spending a lot of afternoon and weekend time in libraries, at the movies, taking long walks in the cold, staying overnight with Eileen. Peg Barry packed up and took the train to Moline where she planned to spend two weeks or so at the home of her sister.

* * *

In a series of letters over the next two weeks, the following dispute took place:

Graham: "*New York?!* How can you go to New York? I can't let you go there alone. You're only sixteen. I'd never forgive myself if anything happened to you. And why New York? What if I'm sent to the Far East? You'd be even further away."

Kitty: "If I'm old enough to be married, then I'm old enough to take care of myself. I've got a job now I could live on even though it's only on weekends. I can get a full-time job in New York. Darling, I wouldn't be alone. Roberta's there! We're in touch. She'll expect me. That's why I want to go to New York and not San Francisco or someplace. And you might go to Europe and then I'd be *closer*."

Graham: "I've talked to some New York friends. 133rd Street is in Harlem. You can't live there and go there by yourself. She wouldn't be able to take care of you if you got into trouble. I can't let you do this."

Kitty: "She *lives* on 133rd Street. She works on 52nd Street. I'll get to know other people, too. I'm not dumb, you know. Nobody's going to take advantage of me or hurt me just because I'm sixteen— and I'll be seventeen two months after I get there—any more than they would if I was twenty-six. I've made up my mind. I'm not going back to live with the Barrys, so what's the difference if I live in an apartment in Chicago or in New York?"

Graham: "I'm still going to worry, but there may be a solution. One New York fellow says you'd be perfectly safe living in one of the hotels for women in Manhattan—the Barbizon and a couple of others. I've sent off for brochures ... But what about school?"

Kitty: "I'll finish high school in Manhattan."

Edward J. was alone in his study. Peg was still downstate.

For the first time he looked truly stricken, though he tried to inject a matter-of-fact, even cheerful and congratulatory tone into his voice.

"Roberta is there now, of course, isn't she? I can't blame you for wanting to see her again, possibly work with her, especially now ... when Graham is going to be overseas ..."

171

We'll miss you, he thought to say, but though he still believed it he did not say it, not to punish her but to avoid punishing her—and himself.

"Well, in May you'll be seventeen," he said instead. "On your own. You'll be good at that, no question in my mind . . . The Barbizon. I've heard of it . . . It sounds to me like the ideal arrangement!"

Oh, she didn't relish any of this at all, she wished things could be different, that she didn't have to hurt anyone, but he said it for her—

"You have to follow your star, as they say. Take your talent where you can do the most with it. Chicago isn't the jazz town it was. These things move in cycles . . ."

"And the Rosens have asked me to spend the last two weeks with them in their apartment."

"Oh? Well, I guess . . . I can see . . . If there's anything we—Matt and I—can do to help . . ."

"It's going to be in the rectory at four in the afternoon," Kitty said. "I'm only going to invite you and Mrs. Barry and Matt, Eileen and the Rosens, Graham's sister and her husband. So I won't send out any invitations. I hope you can come."

It was over. Peg had lost. Edward J. had lost, too. Kitty didn't want anyone to lose, but someone always did. Highly nervous, she excused herself, went for a solitary walk in the bitter cold, wondering what was really going to happen, how everything would turn out.

Despite Kitty's new affluence as a paid vocalist, and the Barrys' generosity, she had frugally kept her wardrobe to the minimum. Travel light, she had read somewhere, and this seemed to her sound advice. The two suitcases with which she had arrived at the Barrys were still adequate, with careful packing, to hold everything she owned, aside from her portable phonograph and records.

She was awake early Saturday, alert, and knowing without a doubt that she was nearing the edge of another great and irrevocable change in her life. She got out of bed long enough to turn on the radiator, which hissed and gave a loud, metallic knock, then got under the covers again and watched the room grow gradually brighter. She was acutely conscious of herself, of the feel of her own skin over her bones, the textural contrasts between the flannel of her nightgown and the wool of the two blankets. She saw with particular clarity the pale blue walls and pale yellow furniture, the bright, primary colors of the braid rugs, the white ruffled curtains, the odds and ends, the photograph of Roberta on the bureau. Outside, cars started up and tire chains bit into the snow.

When she had dressed, Kitty sat at her desk and in a lined school notebook, in pencil, drafted a letter to the Barrys. She made a few changes and corrections and then began copying it in ink on sheets of her best stationery:

> Maybe I can somehow explain in a letter what I didn't seem to be able to explain in person. I love Graham, you know that, and you believe he loves me. Now he has to risk his life in the war. I just believe if he wants a wife he should have one—and a honeymoon before he leaves. Sometimes you just can't wait. There isn't enough time to wait. I want to be married in the Church and I'm so glad I'll be able to. But the most important thing to me is to marry Graham no matter how. I need to start my own family, but oh, if only I could make you believe that doesn't mean I'm turning you down! You were so great to have me live with you and I loved it—the Barrys, every one of them, the music, the lessons, the clothes, the presents, all the trouble Mr. Barry went to find out who my father was, the home you made for me, the laughs—and I haven't done right by you, but I just have to go with Graham. I know you think I'm making a mistake and I can't blame you for that. All you've ever done is think of what was best for me. And you didn't even know me. You just took me in out of the blue. I'll never forget that. I'll always be grateful. Please try to understand.
>
> With love,
Kitty

Edward J. wasn't in the house when Artie Rosen drove around to collect Kitty and her luggage. Matt was home and helped her carry things downstairs. Kitty left her sealed envelope addressed to Edward J. and Peg on the hall table.

"I'm sorry you have to go," Matt said. "I really am. Mom's funny. She's stubborn about some things. Once she makes up her mind you can't budge her."

Kitty kissed Matt impulsively, quickly, and left the house.

16

A week before the scheduled day of the wedding Graham telephoned from Minneapolis.

"Kitty, I've got to talk to your priest."

She didn't ask him why. He had told her once already, and now he was with his mother and father. But maybe they could work something out with Father Kane. Frightened and yet strangely calm, she said, "All right. When do you get here? I'll call and tell him."

"Tomorrow. There's a train that gets into Evanston at two. I'll meet you at school, and we can walk over from there. Then I'm going to have to go back to Minneapolis on the 7 P.M. train. My mother and father expect to see me a few more days."

"Sister Edmund wants to meet you," Kitty said.

"She does?" Graham said, a trifle nervously.

"She knows we're going to be married, and I owe her that much. And I'm proud of you. Since you're coming by the school let's get it over with now. It'll only take a few minutes, and she won't bite. I can't wait to see you."

As Graham approached St. Margaret's High School adjoining

the convent, classes ended for the day and streams of girls flowed out of the building to Sheridan Road. Graham, splendid in uniform, was admired, and Kitty was envied.

Sister Edmund received them in the music room, standing imperiously, her expression, which always gave her away, saying clearly— to Kitty at any rate: *I am impressed, but he is not a Catholic, and the Church rule permitting marriage at fourteen, fifteen, sixteen, simply recognized the reality of uneducated peasant girls in Mediterranean countries where women mature early, but Kitty, you are too young, you are rushing your life, you should be devoting yourself to your studies, your music, and you have grievously wounded Margaret Barry who has given you so much, but I am impressed, and I will be gracious.*

She held out her hand. Graham took it for a moment and said, "It's real nice of you to see us, Sister. I know how much you've done for Kitty."

"The pleasure is mine, Lieutenant," Sister Edmund said, suddenly appearing to enjoy herself. "It is very flattering of you to call on me when your time together is so short."

Sister Martin, beaming and blushing with shyness, appeared with hot tea in a fat white china pot and freshly baked sugar cookies on a plate.

"Oh, it's sweet of you to have gone to this trouble," Kitty said sincerely, including both nuns in her gratitude. She was beginning to feel quite sentimental. The nuns had been good to her and had taught her much, and this might be one of the last times she would ever see them or sit in this room.

"Sister Martin could not be restrained," Sister Edmund said jocularly, warming to her role as hostess, flattering Sister Martin who backed out of the room, vastly pleased. "Nothing, I believe, is quite so comforting as hot tea on such a cold day as this."

"I'm sure I've never had any this good before," Graham said. "Is it English?"

"Brewed in the English manner," Sister Edmund said. "The tea itself is orange pekoe from Darjeeling, in India, the gift of a missionary priest who visited us not long ago. Well, perhaps you will have an opportunity to visit Darjeeling, a lovely place. If it is not too cloudy, as it often is, the view of Kanchenjunga is magnificent. Do you have any idea where you'll be going, Lieutenant? Which theater of operations? That is, if you can say."

"Sister, we won't know until the day we leave. It might be the Pacific. It might be North Africa, or England."

"Well, I have been privileged enough to have visited all three places, several times, in fact. England remains my favorite. But everything must be so much changed since I was last there."

"When was that, Sister?" Graham asked.

"Nineteen thirty-seven? No—thirty-six." She sighed and smiled slightly. "Another world."

For a few minutes she reminisced about people and places she had known in those days, putting Graham and Kitty further at their ease, interesting and amusing them.

"Sister, I know you have a lesson at four," Kitty said, when the clear opportunity arose.

"And you must continue your holiday." The nun stood and pressed Kitty's right hand, Graham's left, simultaneously, an acknowledgement of Graham's importance Kitty found surprising and touching. "I have so enjoyed meeting you, Lieutenant. Talking to you both."

She looked at Kitty.

"Let me say this now while it is on my mind. So that you can remind her, Graham. I know that you will keep up with your music, Kitty. But you must also, somehow, keep up with your studies. Read. Don't ever stop reading."

She looked at Graham.

"Godspeed," she said. "I shall remember you both in my prayers ... Now we have something for you to take along. Our wedding gift."

A flat round package that turned into a silver tray.

The interview was formal, cold. Graham and Father Kane shook hands briefly, and that was the extent of the amenities.

"I just can't give up all my rights by signing that paper, Father," Graham said, as Kitty watched and listened.

"Then I cannot marry you," Father Kane said.

Panic swooped through Kitty and then flew out again and left only anger and a sense of inevitability behind it. Hadn't she worried all along that it would probably come to this?

"So the non-Catholic has no rights," Graham said.

"Can you divide a child in half? What of the Catholic's rights? This is simply one illustration of the difficulties of mixed marriages and why the Church opposes them in principle."

"No compromise."

"The compromise is that the Church will permit such marriages under certain conditions. Your Lutheran Church has the same right and no doubt exercises it and in that instance, should the Catholic party refuse Lutheran conditions, does your church then abrogate its responsibility as it sees it? I am the instrument of my church. I have no powers beyond its powers."

Graham shrugged. "Well," he said, smiling painfully, and stood, and Kitty stood with him.

"I'm sorry," Father Kane said. "If you would like to talk further, I'll be here."

Kitty felt sorry for the priest in a way. He'd tried to be nice; he'd done what he could.

Outside on the sidewalk Graham held Kitty's hand tightly and she returned the pressure.

"Kitty, I just couldn't do it. It isn't fair."

"You don't have to be sorry. You *shouldn't* sign if you don't feel right about it. One thing I know. I learned this much in religion class. People marry each other in the sight of God. The priest or the minister or the judge doesn't do it, they're just witnesses to make it legal. So we'll let a judge be the witness. I'm still going to be a Catholic no matter what we do or what anybody says."

"They won't excommunicate you?"

"Who's going to do it? I won't even be here. Anyway, I think you have to do something really awful, like desecrate a church. I'm not doing anything awful. Is it awful to love you, to be your wife? No, how could it be? ... OK, now stop it," she admonished herself. "Stop crying. There's nothing to cry about."

He put one arm around her shoulder and held her to him as they walked toward the bus stop.

"Tuesday afternoon, the same as before, I'll drive down with

Ruth and Perry. They're staying at the Drake. We'll all stay at the Drake. It'll be late. I won't try to see you."

"You can call, though, any time. The Rosens don't get home from work until almost two in the morning. I'll just be there babysitting."

"Then around noon we'll pick up the license at City Hall—and find someone to perform the ceremony. Perry's a lawyer, he can phone down there tomorrow and find out what the procedure is, make sure there won't be any hitches."

He grinned at her. "Better make that, make sure there *is* one."

What to do about the Barrys, Eileen? Could Mr. Barry withdraw his permission? The only way she could be sure he wouldn't—or wouldn't have to feel guilty about leaving things the way they were, was not to say anything until it was over. She had moved out, she was already on her own, she could make this decision. She had to. She had to protect herself.

Could she trust Eileen not to blab? Would Eileen think she was committing some kind of sin just by going to a civil wedding? Would her parents forbid her to go to it or even to the supper afterwards? (Should we cancel that? No. By that time we'll be legally married. Nobody can take him away from me then.) But Kitty asked herself, too, would Eileen ever forgive me if I didn't tell her, if I left without saying goodbye?

Father Kane had left things open. *If you would like to talk further, I'll be here.* She felt sure he would keep their conversation confidential, would not discuss it with the Barrys. Peg wouldn't show up at the rectory on the third, Kitty was certain of that. Edward J. and Matt might—might, that was all. Eileen certainly would. Graham's sister and her husband would have their own car, and the Rosens theirs; that was how they had planned to get from the rectory to Le Petit Paris on Michigan Avenue for the nuptial supper Artie Rosen had arranged. Then afterwards the Rosens were to drive Eileen home. They could still drive Eileen both ways if she was willing to go, if she *could* go.

Mr. Bryne was a conductor on the North Western, gone a lot, and when he was around he didn't have much to say. Mrs. Bryne was really dense about most things, nice, kind, but a dim bulb.

Neither of them seemed to know what was going on half the time, what Eileen did, and didn't really care as long as she was home on time. Eileen would simply walk to the rectory by herself just before 4 P.M. the following Wednesday. By that time the City Hall ceremony would be over. If instead Eileen just went somewhere else ... She could take the El, she took it all the time. The Rosens could meet her at the Merchandise Mart or the Randolph and Wells station so they wouldn't have to go out of their way. Eileen wouldn't give her away. She had always kept Kitty's confidences before, and the need for secrecy now would appeal to her romantic nature.

But being romantic—and naive at the same time—could be a dangerous combination. What if she spilled the beans by accident? Eileen loved to talk. Kitty couldn't risk telling her too soon. She'd wait until the day itself—afterwards—then telephone to tell her about the slight change of plans ...

Oh Lord.

Kitty wore a new wool suit, gray-blue with a little check, new white blouse, new navy blue leather pumps, a little blue cloth hat with a veil.

Ruth Allen Groff looked sad, as thought she might have been crying, but kissed Kitty and squeezed her hand. Perry Groff was comfortably neutral. None of this was his worry; he was enjoying the first of three days he was taking off work and rather looked forward to a night on the town in Chicago.

"We've heard you many times on the radio," Ruth Groff said to Laurie Lee Hill.

"That's sweet of you to say so," Laurie Lee said. She was all dolled up for the occasion, her hair newly bleached and marcelled.

"Kitty, or Katherine?" Judge Kavanaugh said, looking at his docket, then saw the title of the top document before him. "Oh, I see. Missing birth certificate."

"I've always been just Kitty, sir."

And for the first time in her life Kitty said to herself, *Maybe I was never baptized. It would have been just like my mother—and father—never to have gotten around to it.* Certainly she had never found a baptismal certificate either.

The ceremony was over almost before it began and Kitty was looking down at the thin gold band on her finger and looking up and smiling at Graham, at everyone.

Judge Kavanaugh began to disrobe even before he left his chambers.

Eileen Byrne, still stunned by the extraordinary last-minute change of plans but already awed by the glamorous surroundings of Le Petit Paris, the panels of draped silk curtains masking the street windows from the curious eyes of passersby, the soft lighting, silver champagne buckets, the pale yellow napery, and sparkling crystal goblets. She hugged Kitty unreservedly and turned as pink as the silk lampshades when Graham kissed the corner of her mouth.

"Thanks for coming, Eileen," Kitty said.

"Oh, Kitty," Eileen wept, though not loudly. "I know you'll be happy."

It was really an ill-matched little group. They had in common only their various relationships to the happy couple, but by focusing on them, on the rich food—lobster bisque, tournedos Rossini, baked alaska—and the bubbling wine, distracted, too, by the European waiters, the sophisticated clientele at the other tables, any awkwardness between individuals, between, say, Perry Groff, who even laughed off-key, and Artie Rosen, or between Eileen Byrne and practically anyone except Kitty—Eileen was not at all a bad-looking girl, but painfully conscious of her height, still very unsure of herself—any awkwardness was headed off, smoothed over. The champagne went to Eileen's head, and she said more in two hours than she usually said all week, though the next day she would not remember what she had talked about.

"Kitty's going to be famous, I just know it," Eileen said, and the thought thrilled her. *I'm one of her closest friends.* But when she remembered Kitty would soon leave for New York, she grew sad, and her eyes filled.

"Do you think I should marry Kevin?" she asked Kitty. "He hasn't asked me, though."

"No, Eileen, for heaven's sake. Not Kevin. Not anybody yet. Don't go by me. I've had to grow up faster. Wait till you're in college at least."

Artie Rosen proposed nice, conventional toasts. He had no pretence of being clever, but his sincerity was of more value to Kitty than cleverness.

"You're doing the right thing," he said to Kitty, after sitting down again. "You're not tied down to Chicago like we are with the kids and all, and any longer with Bennett won't do you any good. You've got a real chance now to make good doing exactly what you want to do—play and sing quality music exclusively, and screw the schlock. Goodman can do it, a few others, so can you. You've got the spark, kid. We'll miss you, but pay no attention to my sentimental meanderings, have some more champagne."

"I've had too much already. I'm liable to bust out crying any minute."

"Now, don't do that," said Laurie Lee. "Come on. I need company to the little girl's room."

Kitty and Graham spent the night at the Drake Hotel. The following afternoon they moved to the borrowed apartment, an expensively furnished suite of five rooms on a short street two blocks east of Michigan Avenue.

Graham had already made a reservation for Kitty at the Barbizon Hotel for women in Manhattan. The Barbizon had replied to his query first, and among the special attractions described in its brochure—pool, sundecks, lounges, library, radio in every room—were "music studios with Steinway grands." That settled it. Graham saw no reason to delay further and had mailed off a check to cover the first month's rent.

"Twelve dollars a week seems a lot for just one room," Kitty said. "Can we afford it?"

"That's reasonable when you consider the location and what you get. And the security."

He tried to sound casual and succeeded fairly well, though his voice was a bit choked from some shortness of breath. Kitty had been reading the brochure lying on her stomach across the bed, wearing nothing at all. Still reading, she had shifted position so that now she was reclining on her side and back, graceful and innocent as a dozing cat. He could not imagine any other girl could be lovelier than this, and the knowledge that this slender perfection, these dizzying delights were his to partake, that she was his girl, his wife, excited him to an absolutely remarkable degree, though the exact same thing had happened twice that day already.

The length of her, where she was concave or convex, was a paradise of smoothness, softness, a landscape of endless, fascinating interest.

"Little mouse," he said, and put one hand over the vital intersection.

"Too soon," she murmured. "Kiss me," and drew his face down to hers. "My beautiful man. Don't ever leave me."

"Wait," Kitty said, and he left off exploring while she got up, crossed the room lightly, and put a record on the turntable. She liked to have music playing. Graham didn't object. She walked back proudly, a dizzying vision—5'6", 115 lbs., 34-24-34, long brown hair falling down her back, over one shoulder—and stretched out beside him again. The rest of the Ellington orchestra behind him, Johnny Hodges' alto sax began weaving a slow, lovely, sensuous melody.

"Do you know this?" Kitty asked, and drew up her knees.

"No."

"It's called 'Warm Valley.' Roberta explained to me what that means."

"I'm there," Graham said.

"Yes, you're there. Oh yes, you're *there!*"

Moistly receiving, closing, counterthrusting, eyes shut—"I ..." she said. "I ...!" and letting go!

Even as they were luxuriating in the belief they still had another entire week to be together, the telegram was delivered. Graham's group would be moving out five days ahead of schedule. He was ordered to proceed to Scott Field, Illinois, within twenty-four hours where he would be able to hitch a ride back to Rapid City.

"Oh, *no*, they can't *do* this!" Kitty said.

"I'm afraid they can."

"Twenty-four hours," Kitty moaned, unbelieving.

Graham phoned the Barbizon immediately and arranged to advance Kitty's reservation.

"You'll go first," he said. "I want to see you safely on board that train."

Then they discovered changing a train reservation at the last minute in wartime, especially trying to advance it a few days, would be virtually impossible.

"See what Bennett can do," Artie Rosen advised by phone. "He knows a lot of big shots. The hotels, the trains, they always keep a couple of spots open for VIPs. Better you see him yourself. He can't resist you any more than anybody else. Bring your lieutenant along. Bennett likes a production, especially these days, if its patriotic."

"*I'm* no VIP," Kitty said.

"You're *our* VIP, honey," Laurie Lee said over the extension line.

Kitty had never looked prettier, and Graham, who sincerely liked to dance to Bennett's music, played his part to perfection without realizing he was playing any part at all. Bennett magnanimously telephoned somebody and talked about "a coupla wonderful American kids, a flying ace going off to fight the Japs, and his new bride, a great talent, she'll probably be off singing for the troops before long, but right now, just a kid you know, she needs a little extra protection. Rilly appreciate anything you can do." And that somebody phoned somebody else who called a third person who had a few words with a railroad executive who passed along the instructions to the operating level, and Graham picked up Kitty's new reservation at a travel agency on Michigan Avenue.

"This is Chicago," Artie Rosen said. "You can't get anywhere without a little pull."

Humming "Little White Lies" to herself, Kitty wrote a gushy thank-you letter to Irving Bennett, working in her gratitude for the "wonderful professional experience" she had had under his tutelage, delivered along with a box of his favorite Havana panatelas, and a simpler, more sincere note to the Rosens, sent with a large bouquet of flowers.

In Union Station, Kitty said, "I can't believe that train is going to leave ten minutes from now. With me on it. And you going where? I don't even know where."

"If possible, I'll try to send you a letter, or a telegram, or phone, as soon as I know. I don't think that's going to be before Sunday, maybe even later. If the message comes from somewhere on the West Coast, that's easy; you'll know we're headed for the Pacific. If you hear from me from the Northeast, like Boston, we'll be headed for England. If I'm in the Southeast, Florida probably, we're either going to North Africa or England. Via Trinidad, Recife, Brazil, Dakar, and Marrakesh. I'm not supposed to know that, but I do. Don't talk about that route to anyone. If it's Africa, I'll say something about oranges. If it's England, let's see; the English drink a lot of tea. Tea with lemon. So lemons. The first letter of each word in a sentence will spell it out if I have to write or send a telegram. Don't worry if there seem to be too many letters. Just stop when the word is spelled."

"Graham, I'm scared. Not for me—oh, a little for me—but mostly for you."

"We'll be OK. Both of us."

He seemed determined to be matter-of-fact, unemotional. The time for emotion had passed, and Kitty took her cue from him as the minutes passed. Her luggage was already on a cart, a Red Cap waiting alongside it. A blurred, amplified voice announced the departure of the New York train.

"We'd better get moving, lady," the porter said.

Graham was allowed on the platform. Kitty's compartment was in a car five down from the end. He climbed aboard with her.

"Pretty ritzy," he said.

"We probably shouldn't have spent the extra money," Kitty said.

"Oh, yes, we should have. My wife's going to ride in style. Don't forget. You should get the first allotment check from the army in about a month. If you don't, you know where to call."

"I've got my savings. I can live a long time on twelve hundred dollars."

They knew all this already. They were talking to keep talking. Everything was unreal.

A conductor came along the side corridor.

"All visitors off, please."

One last, hurried embrace, a few last inadequate words, and she was alone. The train jerked to a start, rolled forward. Through the window that wouldn't open, she saw him wave, disappear.

PART V

17

They met in one of those bustling, midtown places where fast-talking, nimble-fingered countermen swiftly turn out thick kosher sandwiches for streams of people between eleven and two. At 1:30 it wasn't quite so crowded. Kitty saw Roberta enter, looking a little grayer, a little stouter, perhaps a little sadder. But when Roberta saw Kitty, her smile could have kindled wet logs. After they had hugged each other, both found it necessary to dab at their eyes for a few seconds. They found an empty booth.

"I told you all about me," Kitty said. "Now it's your turn."

"I found Rex," Roberta said.

Restless in Kankakee in 1941, Roberta had made several trips to Chicago to stay with friends on the South Side, and it was then she had met people who had talked to other people who had claimed to have seen Rex, down and out and out of music, in various cities, one of them Cleveland, though others had heard he was dead. She was still carrying a torch for him, so she went to Cleveland, worked at a white hotel as a cocktail lounge pianist, lived in the Negro district, but never found a clue. Then someone wrote to her from Chicago. Somebody else swore that they had seen Rex working as a porter in Pittsburgh, that he even had an address. When she got there, whoever it was, Rex or not, had moved on, address unknown. And the name hadn't matched, though that didn't necessarily prove anything. Low on funds, Roberta had gone to work in a Pittsburgh bar and stayed for several months. Other letters came. Rex was reported to be in Detroit, but Roberta stayed put. Tiring of Pittsburgh, she had moved to Philadelphia and worked there, but found no trace. One day, a friend phoned from New York to say they had seen Rex, that he was working in Harlem as a dishwasher. She had taken the train the following day, and it was him.

Given comparable talents, why does one man succeed and another fail—or fail to keep going? Tough times and bad luck had started the process in Rex Wilkins, and alcohol, womanizing—the chicks had always flocked around him in every town—and indifference to punctuality had continued it until no one was willing to put up with him any longer. But the deadliest flaws of all had been the loss of belief and a failure of will.

"Oh, he was good," Roberta said. "Those few recordings you heard don't really do him justice. You never heard a purer, sweeter tone or more feeling, except maybe Louis, but there were others as good—Eldridge, Red Allen, Buck Clayton, Bobby Hackett, people at the top like that—and Rex thought he had to be the best or nothing."

Too many people had told him he was the greatest, and he believed it. When fame, the really big time, eluded him—he was known and his playing was respected in the jazz world, but he never caught the public fancy as Louis had—instead of playing the way he played best, he tried to be spectacular, to outdo the competition with sheer technique, but the effect was hollow. He'd always had chronic lip trouble, too, had always been a little strange, eccentric, self-destructive, and doing nothing but playing music, thinking about music, can be a dangerous thing. Sometimes the demon beauty got to be too much for him. He couldn't stand it. At thirty-seven, he had walked away from music into obscurity and silence.

"Some things about Rex are a mystery to me," Roberta said. "Mama once said you can live with a man all your life and not understand him completely. Well, people don't understand themselves half the time. You say 'God only knows,' usually an excuse for not thinking, or an easy way to change the subject, but in Rex's case it's the truth."

One thing Roberta knew was that she had been the one element of stability in Rex's life. He always came back from his escapades—until one day he didn't find her. She thought she had had enough. Later she felt guilty, as though she had deserted him. So now she was back, and she would stay if he would play by her rules. And play trumpet the way he played best.

"It's not depriving him of any freedom to get him out of the kitchen of a third-rate chop house," Roberta said. "I'm stronger than he is but I'm not as talented, and I need him, too. I didn't tell you sooner we were back together because nothing is final. We agreed to try it for a year, and even now we've only been at it six months. But I think it's working. He's off the hard stuff and can handle a beer once in a while."

"So he's with you at the Ivory Tower Club."

"I'm with *him*," Roberta said.

"Why didn't I read about it in the Chicago papers?"

"Even New York papers don't print much about jazz musicians." Roberta took a small clipping from a compartment in her purse and read: " 'Rex Wilkins, the jazz trumpeter, is featured in New York again after a six-year absence, nightly except Sunday at the Ivory Tower, 55 West 52nd.' That's it. Three lines."

"I'm living only a few blocks from 52nd Street!" Kitty said. "Well, about twelve. I've got to hear him tonight! Hear you again! I can't stand it!"

"Speaking of which, when can I listen to you? Good Lord, it's been more than two years. Can you get at one of those Steinways at the Barbizon this afternoon?"

Rain and colder weather had been forecast, but at three in the afternoon it was dry, and warmer than usual at this time of year—in the upper fifties—and Kitty and Roberta walked with their raincoats opened. Dodging taxis and pedestrians across Fifth, Madison, and Park down to Lexington and 63rd, the buxom black woman and the slender white girl, chatting animatedly, close friends obviously, Kitty revealing her tremendous excitement over being in New York, where she instantly belonged, both photographable, each with a distinctive style, turned heads occasionally. They were an uncommon combination, an uncommon sight.

Midafternoon found the Barbizon Steinways unused, a music studio empty. To warm up, Kitty played, without singing, a solid, rhythmic version of "Somebody Loves Me," then remembered the weather forcast, and began, a honeyed huskiness in her voice, to sing:

> I'm old fashioned.
> I love the moonlight.
> I love the old fashioned things—
> The sound of rain upon a windowpane
> The starry song that April sings . . .

Which led to "April In Paris" and "September In The Rain," and she stilled her voice, left her hands away from the keys.

"You really are my prize pupil, baby," Roberta said, smiling, a little teary. "And your singing just knocks me out. You hit those notes true, just the way they're written."

"Mrs. Barry taught me a lot."

"I wouldn't doubt it, but that sound is yours. I think you could make it big on radio—on records if this recording ban ever ends. And you're pretty enough for Hollywood."

"Oh, I don't think I'd ever want to go out there," Kitty said. "Even radio. How much corny stuff—like the kind Irving Bennett plays—would I have to do on radio? That's what you mostly hear. I really don't want to sing with a big orchestra either. I just want to play piano and sing, and I don't care where. Graham wants to move West after the war is over . . . but I'm here now and I just love New York."

"Sad thing is," Roberta said. "If you stick to just what you want that's going to limit the audience you'll have, the money you can make."

"Well, you're my inspiration."

"But I'm not really a singer," Roberta said.

"Of course you are!"

"Oh, I've always done it for my own pleasure, and maybe my singing was good enough for Fossbinder's, but even there it was an afterthought. I was hired just to play piano. Then Bernie heard me singing to myself one afternoon and asked me to add the vocals part of the time, and I did. Enjoyed it, had fun. But I don't sing on 52nd

Street, not with Billie Holiday and Mabel Mercer next door. Oh, I might even on the Street if I was playing cocktail piano. Late at night when everybody is lubricated and in a good mood and nobody gives a damn. But at the Ivory Tower Rex is the star."

"Well, I'll never agree. You're one of the best jazz singers there is," Kitty said.

Roberta laughed and gave Kitty a hug around the shoulders. "But let's get back to you. Now that you've told me how you feel, I think what you should do is get a job playing intermission piano at first, introduce the singing gradually, later. In the meantime, you can sit in with the quintet whenever we can arrange it. On piano. Singing. Friday nights are jam sessions at the Ivory Tower. That's tonight if you feel up to it. Or next week for sure. The owner won't pay you anything but..."

"Oh, that doesn't matter now. It's the experience!"

"... and the exposure. Chance to build a little reputation so when the opening comes up people will know you and you'll be ready. Also, in the meantime, you've got these Steinways to practice on. It might take a few months, but you'll be learning all that while. Of course, I'll keep my ears open and introduce you to the people I know, tell everybody I see how good you are. I wish I could just push a button and a job would pop out but..."

"Roberta, you took care of me once, I can't ask you to do it now. You've got your own life to lead, especially now that you're back with Rex. Besides, I'm a married lady myself. I've got to make my own way."

"Well, let's see. You're sixteen, going on seventeen, that's about the age of Billie Holiday when she got started. Also Ella, Lee Wiley, plenty of others. And you know, this is a good time for a girl. People are getting drafted all along the Street or volunteering, so there's apt to be openings."

Roberta returned to Harlem. Kitty napped awhile, went out into the early Manhattan evening of lights and crowds and traffic, sat through a performance of *Journey into Fear*, and found herself at a stylish, crimson-bright Longchamps restaurant at 57th and Fifth where she splurged a dollar fifty on a complete dinner featuring filet mignon and broccoli hollandaise. While she ate, she read a chapter of Jerome Weidman's *The Lights Around The Shore*.

Fifty-second Street between Fifth Avenue and Sixth and a block beyond was lined with five-story, late nineteenth-century brownstones. Jutting out from basement entrances were the shabby, tattered awnings of about two dozen nightclubs and of low-priced French and Chinese restaurants. With the exception of the spiffy and expensive 21, these places looked even sleazier than she had expected. Strippers—including "Zorita, the Snake Dancer"—were the attractions at several establishments. But 52nd Street was also a state of mind, and what names were displayed outside the jazz clubs! Billie Holiday at The Onyx, Art Tatum at The Three Deuces, Coleman Hawkins at The Downbeat, Mabel Mercer at Tony's, Red Norvo at The Famous Door, Eddie Condon, Zutty Singleton, Wild Bill Davison, and other Dixieland immortals at Jimmy Ryan's, Rex Wilkins at The Ivory Tower..."

The luridly lit sidewalks were crowded with men in uniform, enlisted men mostly, soldiers, sailors, some standing around talking and smoking, some staring at billboards, some going down basement stairs into strip joints, bars, restaurants, jazz clubs. Kitty got a lot more attention than she wanted, and one drunken soldier worried her, but she got around him and into The Ivory Tower.

A cave. Darkness. Spots of dim light here and there, one bright light, a pin spot illuminating the face and hands of an intermission pianist at work, a slight Negro with glasses. About half the tables and half the bar stools were still unoccupied, but already a pall of cigarette smoke was rising and collecting under the low ceiling.

A white manager confronted her.

"Roberta Wilkins reserved a table for me. My name is Collins."

He led her to a front table facing the still darkened little stage, and relayed her ginger ale order to a waiter in a soiled red jacket.

But not even the greedy gloom of the setting could flatten for Kitty the electric anticipation of waiting for the legendary Rex Wilkins, and Roberta, to appear.

The pin spot went off; the intermission pianist disappeared; there was a pause. Dim figures climbed to the unlit stage. Scattered applause when the lights went on—it ought to be deafening, Kitty thought! Don't they *know? She* could feel it, though not in so many words, the thrill of being in the presence of an historic figure, not just of American music but of the American experience. Instantly recognizable as the man in the photos in Roberta's apartment in Chicago, a thin man of medium height, charcoal dark with a distinguished aquiline nose, curly gray hair, thin mustache, neatly dressed in a dark blue, double-breasted, pin-striped suit, white shirt, and small-figured four-in-hand necktie.

Roberta, poised and queenly behind her piano. Harold Saunders on tenor sax and clarinet, short, round, about thirty-five. Rodney Blake, bass, tall, lean, in his early twenties. Clay Mitchell, drums, a husky middleweight, in his early twenties, too.

Fired off by bass and drums, Roberta began a sturdy, swinging introduction. Seated on a folding chair alongside Saunders, Rex Wilkins raised his trumpet from his lap, placed the mouthpiece to his lips, and took the lead to "Sweet Georgia Brown," with Saunders riding closely but loosely behind him on clarinet.

Rex Wilkins didn't try for any really high notes—he kept to the middle or upper middle register, full power leashed, at half-throttle—but his tone was round and full and as golden as his horn, and the sound filled the narrow room. Kitty was transported to some breathless uplands. Saunders took a swooping solo and the trumpet was silent, but during Roberta's solo that followed, Rex punctuated her statement with brief, haunting little commentaries, and continued these embellishments when Saunders returned, this time on sax, and then the order of precedence was reversed, and Rex led again to the finish. There was the thick applause of a small but growing, and now appreciative audience, overlapped by the beginning of the 1917 "Rose Room," still as fresh as when it was written, with its constantly shifting harmony, a new chord to inspire improvisation every measure or two.

Rex Wilkins etched this and other evergreens with even greater authority. He and Harold Saunders were standing now and this alone created greater tension and expectancy.

"Poor Butterfly" was all Rex's, a long solo that began at the first beat, a bittersweet old ballad he didn't let go of for five minutes. A moving purity of tone was Rex Wilkins's great emotional and technical virtue, never better revealed than now, and the first set ended on that lovely, nostalgic note. Kitty was standing, still applauding, when Rex, Roberta, and the others came down off the stage.

"Come on, baby, we can't stay here between sets. We're going across the street to get something to eat."

Only when they were outside on the sidewalk did Rex pause to shake Kitty's hand, say "How do you do?" with a little smile, a courtly little bow.

Saunders, Blake, and Mitchell went off to the White Rose bar, a musicians' hangout on Sixth Avenue. Rex, Roberta, and Kitty crossed 52nd Street and went down a few entrances to the Moon Palace, a Chinese place. Rex and Roberta ordered soup and two dishes. Kitty wanted only tea.

"Manny Sherman, the owner of the Ivory Tower won't allow black musicians to mix with the customers," Roberta said. "Which means we either stand outside on the sidewalk if it's warm enough, or stay in the toilets. Go to the White Rose. Eat if we haven't eaten already."

"That's terrible," Kitty said. "It's so stupid."

Rex Wilkins's expression was inward-looking. But he came back from wherever he had been and said, "Roberta says you play like a dream and sing like an angel. Will you stay through the evening? We jam with the guests during the last set. I'd be pleased to have you sit in with us, do a couple of vocals, too."

"God, I wouldn't miss it," Kitty said. "I can't tell you what a thrill it is just to hear you. To play with you! I could die happy."

The quintet devoted the second set to old blues and new, to original instrumental things composed by Rex, Harold, and Rodney, and Kitty soaked it up as one continuous wave of often inspired and sometimes sublimely inspired sound. The three of them went outside again, strolled this time in the mild evening, and as they walked under the awnings of jazz clubs and stopped to chat with other musicians spending their breaks catching a smoke on the sidewalk, as though they might be on the main street of some small town on a Friday night, though the nearby towers of Rockefeller Center said New York, New York, Kitty shivered with excitement and anticipation, and thought, I'm here, I'm here, but looked at the night sky and added, Graham, where are you now?

The time had come. The Rex Wilkins Quintet slammed out the first notes of "I Got Rhythm" and stayed with it for seven minutes, joined now by a white alto saxophonist from one of the other clubs.

Rex's gently magnificent "I Can't Get Started" went on for almost twelve with a guest tenor sax, Harold Saunders on clarinet, and a guest trombone. During the brief pause filled with applause that followed, Kitty slipped onto the piano bench vacated by Roberta, and for the next dozen minutes of "Out of Nowhere" and "Stars Fell on Alabama" gave Rex Wilkins, and what was now an octet, the kind of professional support that is heard, admired, remembered, but does not detract from the principal solos—rather, enhances them, helps define their shape—and Rex Wilkins and Harold Saunders extended themselves, released lyrical flights to the crowded room. Then Kitty saw in her mind several bars ahead what her solo on "Alabama" would sound like, and it wasn't quite like anything she remembered having done before, and it came out clean, full of unabashed lyric emotion that surprised even her, and she knew she hadn't fluffed a note, and a couple of voices in the band called out "Take another chorus. Yeah," and she played on and didn't repeat herself, and coasting lovingly through the rideout, she had the illusion of being carried along on the shoulders of the crowd.

Exchanged places with Roberta again, whispered, "I don't think I should try to sing tonight. Tonight has been too perfect. I don't want to crowd my luck."

She hadn't slept much on the train the night before. Jolts of fatigue had hit her intermittently all evening. Sitting at a table in the audience again, she felt the adrenaline that had been keeping her going run out. During a brief pause between numbers, her chin dropped to her collar bone and she jerked her head back awake out of a ten-second sleep, her heart pounding, got up and waved to Roberta, left, and hailed a cruising taxi to get her through the gauntlet of soldiers and sailors.

She slept thirteen hours, until one o'clock Saturday afternoon. Once she was awakened just after dawn by a sound she couldn't identify that seemed to come from far below—THOK KLUMP—but she was too sleepy to investigate, and sank again, far below the level of consciousness.

Wide awake at one, she raised the window high enough to lean out, see sky, the long canyon of Lexington Avenue to the left and right of 63rd Street ten stories below. Manhattan towers soared up and beyond, at once a promise and a fulfillment. It seemed an achievement just to *be* here!

Down to the street by elevator, and out for a leisurely brunch at a Lexington Avenue drugstore where she felt like a New Yorker. She walked in Central Park, browsed in the splendor of the Plaza Hotel lobby and boutiques. When she returned to the Barbizon, there was a telegram.

ARRIVED FLORIDA SOONER THAN EXPECTED AND YOU WERE OUT WHEN I TELEPHONED STOP AU REVOIR DARLING STOP LOVE EVERY MOMENT OUR NEW LIFE STOP

GRAHAM

AFSTEAYWOWITARDLEMONL

"Don't worry if there seem to be too many letters," he had said. *"Just stop when the word is spelled."*

Nothing made sense until she became conscious of the odd ring of the last sentence:

> LOVE EVERY MOMENT OUR NEW LIFE
> LEMONL. Strike out the final L.
> Lemon. Florida and lemons.
> England.

18

Kitty would never remember those first days of those first weeks in New York as single drops of time, but as a tide that swept her up and down the streets of Manhattan from the Battery to Central Park. Marking time, waiting to hear from Graham, she explored—sometimes with Roberta—the department stores, the shops, the art galleries and museums, the glamorous midtown hotels—the Plaza, the Ritz-Carlton, the Waldorf. She loved the theater district at night, and Fifth Avenue at any hour but especially at dusk when she and the great swelling crowds seemed to find it the magnetic center of the universe where no one could be unhappy or unlucky or unexcited.

The sound of Manhattan that year was a cab's wheels jiggling manhole covers on Lexington Avenue in the early morning—THOK KLUMP. It was all those great names on 52nd Street and more to follow later in the year—Count Basie, Roy Eldridge, Lionel Hampton, Bobby Hackett, Ella Fitzgerald, John Kirby, Ben Webster, Cab Calloway, Woodie Herman, Charlie Shavers, Helen Humes. It was Mildred Bailey, Teddy Wilson, Mary Lou Williams, Hazel Scott, and Eddie Heywood at Cafe Society Uptown and Down; Fats Waller at the Greenwich Village Inn, Benny Goodman and

Jess Stacy on stage at the Paramount Theater, Harry James at the Astor Roof, Frank Sinatra at the Riobamba, Jimmy Dorsey at the Pennsylvania Hotel, Duke Ellington at the Hurricane, Charlie Barnet on the Capitol stage, Dick Haymes at La Martinique, Maxine Sullivan at Le Ruban Bleu, and Dizzy Gillespie, Charlie Parker, Thelonious Monk, and Kenny Clark up at Minton's and Monroe's in Harlem inventing modern jazz. It was *Oklahoma* just opened, and Rodgers' *By Jupiter* still running, Ethel Merman singing Porter's "Something for the Boys," Gertrude Lawrence projecting Weil-Gershwin as the "Lady in the Dark." It was Toscanini at NBC—and Reiner, Mitropoulos, Kurtz, and visitors Ormandy and Koussevitsky; Hofmann, Rubinstein, Horowitz, Arrau; Milstein and Szigeti, at Carnegie Hall. It was Martinelli, Warren, Tibbett, Milanov, Albanese, and Sayao, and seventeen-year-old Patrice Munsel at the Met.

And it was then, too, in the spring of 1943, the *Daily News* and *Herald Tribune* and *Times* raised to her eyes, that Kitty finally began to confront the reality of Graham Allen's war—and decided the only way she could survive it was to tune it out.

Crushing Air Drive On Nazis Forecast
U.S. Fliers To Play A Major Role

London—Signs are multiplying that the great Anglo-American bombing offensive against Germany that was promised last summer soon will become a reality ... Day and night attacks on a devastating scale by the Eighth Airforce of the United States and the R.A.F. are expected to reach proportions unprecedented in air warfare before the summer is over ...

A review of last week's air warfare in the European Theater showed that the Allied Air Forces lost 72 planes ...

... five failed to return.

Reports from a bomber base said two Fortresses crashed about five miles apart in the North Sea and sank.

It wasn't possible to ignore headlines entirely, not in nine daily newspapers stacked on the dozens of newsstands she passed on her daily midtown rounds, and behind endless cups of coffee in the counter and booth restaurants where she breakfasted and lunched, and held up by all the people occupying the lounge chairs in the hotel lobbies through which she passed on her way to shops where she liked to browse, and abandoned on benches and stuffed into trash baskets in Central Park. Especially not screaming from the front pages of three daily tabloids, wide, black, and up to two inches high, usually covering half the page, and sometimes falling all the way to the bottom border. But she soon learned that if she saw a Russian or a North African, Italian or Asian placename or RAF or LIBERATOR she didn't have to think about it, and not all B-17s, Flying Fortresses, Fortresses, and Forts flew out of England over France and Germany. "8th" was always something that needed forgetting, but if she didn't read the story she could put it out of her mind. She was young and Graham was young, and the young know they are immortal.

She liked the *Herald Tribune* and *The Sun* the best, the *Trib* in the morning and the *Sun* in the afternoon, and she opened them from the back to miss the headlines and get at the entertainment columnists and the theater, movie, book, and music reviewers—Robert Dana, Harold Barnes, Ward Morehouse, Malcolm Johnson ...

The woman behind the front desk at the Barbizon smiled and said, "I think I have a letter you've been waiting for."

They had a brief reprieve. He was still in transitional training and would be until about the middle of April. His home was a cramped, uncomfortable Nissen hut, still cold in the wet, muddy spring since coal was scarce and the stove didn't work very well anyway. But he didn't mean to complain. The base was located near a village he wasn't permitted to name. It had a quaint pub that tended to get overcrowded because of the swollen population. For other entertainment—reading, card playing, crap shooting, ping pong, volleyball, listening to Armed Forces Radio.

"When I heard an Irving Bennett recording I wished you were back with him so that maybe I could hear your voice again ..."

At her second Friday jam session, she sang. Rex began playing the lovely melody to "If I Had You," a song Kitty considered particularly "hers," and when Rex saw her stand he gave her the nod and she climbed the four steps to the stage and joined in at the next chorus with her fresh, fervent voice, lovely decoration by Rex and Roberta behind her. The applause was loud, but it was late, the audience was applauding loudly for everyone, exhilarating even so, and when Rex began "I Only Have Eyes for You" she was ready for this test of her ability to perform without warning or rehearsal, on the spur of the moment. And was there something else in the ovation now, some extra measure of acclaim, some higher intensity of enthusiasm? In the glare of the stage lights she could not see the faces in the audience that might have given her the answer, only, as she left the platform, the approval in the eyes of Rex and Roberta Wilkins, and of Harold Saunders. Behind the drums and bass, behind their dark glasses, the faces of Clay Mitchell and Rodney Blake were blank, expressionless.

Kitty faithfully practiced three or four hours daily on one of the Barbizon's Steinways, but after two weeks or so in New York, the amount of free time she still had on her hands left her feeling restless and a little guilty. It seemed too late in the winter-spring to consider going back to school. That could wait until the fall. But she began to think about getting some kind of job even if it wasn't in music right away. Scanned the want ads at breakfast. There seemed to be regular openings for telephone operators and waitresses. The first didn't appeal at all. And eight or nine hours of waitressing might leave her too tired to keep up with her music. All the other positions for "Girls" or "Young Women" either required specialized skills, suggested assembly-line tedium, or demanded applicants be eighteen or older.

Then one morning "Usherettes Wanted" leaped out of the page at her, and an hour later she was waiting in a West 46th Street employment agency while a hugely fat man flipped banana fingers through card files. She hoped, briefly, for *Oklahoma* or one of the other musicals, but that same evening went to work at the Empire Theater where *Life with Father*, then in its fourth year, had taken root.

In the meantime, having brought her junior year high school

textbooks with her, she continued to study them on her own, read other books, mostly novels, from the Fifth Avenue public library, and thought that just living in New York was an education in itself.

Kitty had often made the eight-mile trip to Chicago's Loop and other downtown areas of the city from the North Side where she had lived—with Roberta, Graham, Joe, other Barrys, Eileen, the Rosens, even Sister Edmund—but that was it, always with someone, and she had never lived downtown. Only during her ten days with Graham in that posh apartment on the Near North Side did she get a taste of the kind of life she now had in Manhattan, and even on the Near North Side they had had to bus or cab it to the Loop; it was really too far to walk. And so though she had (as far as she knew) spent all the first sixteen and three-quarters years of her life in Chicago she had never once been to the South or West Sides, and the Loop, Michigan Avenue, no matter how often she saw them, seemed to her somehow alien and overpowering, exciting in their way but threatening at times, and never intimate. Her New York, the East Side and some of the West Side of midtown Manhattan, was intimate in spite of soaring towers, noise, crowds of strangers, traffic congestion, or perhaps partly because of the crowds and congestion and partly because she walked everywhere and because of narrow streets often strangely quiet, peaceful, even in midday, along their brownstone, beaux-arts elegance, punctuated here and there by canopied entrances to small, intimate clubs and restaurants; and though New York was even tougher and more demanding and challenging and could be, she sensed, she knew, even more heartless and unforgiving than Chicago and she was alone, but partly too because she was alone and on her own, and even though there were myriad corners yet to explore and some she might not get to for years but partly because they were still to be discovered, she felt more excited and yet at home here than in any place she had ever lived. To her, this great vertical city was lighter, livelier, zestier, faster, more graceful, less somber than Chicago even in the dim-outs of wartime, oh infinitely so, always new, and the center of everything, aside from Graham, important to her, the great magnet for people like herself, a city unmatched by any other in America. And, in wartime, the world.

* * *

Joe Barry wrote from the Atlantic Fleet Sound School in Key West where he was undergoing additional training to become a SONAR operator, a letter inside a package containing a wedding gift, an early nineteenth-century silver serving spoon he had found in Charleston, South Carolina.

Congratulatings, kid, best wishes and all that! I was really flattered by your long letter. I'd already heard you were married, of course, from my mother—who hereafter will be referred to as Peg, which sounds more objective coming from me... I don't know exactly what you wrote in the letter you left for them, but if I answer your question honestly I have to say it wasn't enough for Peg and I'm afraid I don't think another letter now would make much difference. They feel you let them down—I'm pretty sure it's mostly Peg feeling this—and that Graham was selfish and irresponsible to let you defy them—and the Church—for the sake of one week or so with him, and then let you make your way alone at sixteen— excuse me, seventeen, in a city like New York. God, I hate to have to be that brutal but you wouldn't want me to hand you any soft soap. But I'm done with the brutal stuff. How do *I* feel? I think you know me well enough to know if I agreed with them 100 percent or even 51 percent, I'd say so. But I don't. You had a terribly tough decision to make and you did what you thought you had to do. Graham is risking his life over there and has a right to a wife who loves him, a time together, however short—you can live a lifetime in a week—and a wife to come home to... Sure, Peg is disappointed, bitter. She wanted a daughter so badly, and she was so proud of you, but she doesn't hate you and she hasn't used the word betray, and they say time heals everything, most things anyway. I think it probably does. If you want my advice, wait a while. Maybe another year. You're going to make good, I know that, and then you can tell her about it... Keep me posted. And keep your chin up.

Matt, who got her address from Joe, sent her a wedding present too, a silver candle snuffer from Marshall Field, but "Things are pretty much the same around here" was all the news he had to offer on the card inside the box. Nothing came from any other Barry.

Graham wrote about once a week, but he who could talk to her so effortlessly in person seemed to find it difficult to express himself adequately once the excitement and novelty of his first few missions—when he had been too inexperienced and busy to be afraid—

had settled into the deadly routine of constant combat on longer and longer missions, alternating with the restless boredom of waiting on the ground to go up again. His letters were always at least two weeks old, and since he told her only about himself and never or hardly ever commented on what she was doing, their communication had a disjointed quality. Kitty herself was not the greatest letter writer, either. As eagerly as she reached for a pen to talk to him in the only way she could, or tore open a letter from him when one finally arrived, she felt they were at opposite ends of the earth and insuperable barriers lay between them. They were not meant to live apart like this.

But new days dawned and weeks passed; the spring came on and New York continued to grow on her. Chicago faded. She found it difficult to imagine going back there to live. It was easier to imagine living someday in Denver or San Francisco, about which she knew nothing, because Graham loved the West.

Kitty became friendly with another usherette at the Empire, Danielle, who aspired to be a dancer, a pale, willowy girl of seventeen who wore her long black hair tied up in a great bun at the back of her delicate head. Danielle came from Philadelphia and lived at the Midston House hotel for women.

Sometimes the two of them went to Saturday matinees at other theaters together or to operas and ballets at the Met. Kitty was dazzled by the Edwardian splendor of the opera house on Broadway, the gorgeous riot of sculptured gold plaster around three sides of the great proscenium arch and up the tiers of boxes and balconies to the fabulous ceiling. But she felt at home. In this theater, among this cosmopolitan crowd, she seemed to find her natural milieu.

Kitty knew she was living in an age of giants, of great composers, conductors, virtuosos, dancers, choreographers, painters, singers, writers, actors—an age as glittering as any preceding it. Massine, the original choreographer of *The Three-Cornered Hat*, who had danced the role of the miller in the original 1919 production, recreated the role again, then went on to perform the role of the tragic puppet in *Petroushka*. Kitty was awed by the presence of Stravinsky himself on the podium and Massine on stage, by the dancing, the

Picasso sets, but most of all overjoyed by the music that held it all together, that caught her in its whirl. De Falla's rich, rhythmic sonorities, the orchestra playing in unison as one gigantic guitar, created an instant Andalusia and swept her off to a mythic Spain. Darker, deeper, original, inventive, and complex enough to escape banality for at least a century or two, perhaps forever, was *Petroushka*, a dream of marvels, of mystery and surprise. Rumblings and chirpings, woodland whispers, bird songs, strange underground mutterings and sawings, subterranean detonations, shiverings, shudderings, shimmerings, spritely melody breaking through, lovely, plaintive flute refrain; glissandos, crescendos, piano as another orchestral instrument; noble melody, drum rolls, calls of dissonant trumpets, splashy colors painted by clashing instruments; sinister bassoon heralding explosions; circus trumpet, carnival hurdy-gurdy; shimmering tension, frantic strings, sweeping, soaring, leaping orchestral effects; haunting melody; mocking trumpet, derisive echo; three bass strums—exciting footsteps, waves of applause.

Matinee symphony concerts at Carnegie Hall, and sometimes tea and blinis afterwards at The Russian Tea Room next door, Kitty at once drained and exhilarated beyond measure at what she had heard, delighted now by the soft, red leather of the cozy curved banquette, the mirrors and marble and polished brass, the faces and laughter and talk around her. (Once, the widower Stravinsky entered with his pretty second wife, spied Arthur Rubinstein and his pretty wife. With glad cries the Stravinskys and Rubinsteins embraced one another.) Even outside on the sidewalk, itinerant violinists played for coins.

With Danielle, Kitty went one weeknight after their theater closed to Barney Josephson's Cafe Society Uptown on East 58th Street to catch the twelve o'clock performance. Roberta had recommended it as an eminently respectable supper club where young people, non-drinkers, could go safely and not be hustled, and as the first club in town where both the performers and the audience were racially integrated.

Kitty and Danielle were surprised at the size of the place. It could accommodate an audience of 350 at descending ranks of banquettes and tables on either side of a dance floor facing the stage and at tables on a rear balcony. There was room for the girls in the balcony.

"Look at those crazy murals," Danielle said, after they had both ordered the creamed chicken supper and ginger ale.

"I think that's surrealism," Kitty said. "Boy, what a difference between this place and most of the 52nd Street clubs. *Clean* for one thing." She laughed to herself. "She'd never come here—it's probably against the rules ever to go to a nightclub—but I'll bet the nun who taught me classical piano would like it here. I went with her once to Orchestra Hall in Chicago to hear Rachmaninoff. Well, this is like a concert hall, too, like a nice little theater. The only difference is you can eat and drink at the same time."

While they supped, the Ellis Larkins Trio played for dancing and listening.

"I've never heard of him before, but *he* is good, you know," Kitty said. "He's got his own style, and that's not easy to work out. I don't have one yet."

Danielle was most interested in seeing the dancers to come, Beatrice and Evelyne Kraft, and Kitty waited with fine anticipation to hear Mildred Bailey in person for the first time, but most of all Teddy Wilson (and his sextet) whom she had never seen either but whose recordings had inspired her as he had inspired Roberta before her more than any other jazz pianist. The time came, and from their good vantage point above and facing the stage they watched intently. In the bright lights of the stage Wilson appeared seated erect as a sergeant major at the visible keyboard of his concert grand, black tie and tux, short hair, light skin, Spanish grandee nose, whippet-thin as Astaire. And those long, flat, marvelously accomplished fingers shooting out from starched white cuffs flashed with apparent effortlessness, with classical precision, a touch his own, lyrical, troutstream clear, through the particular arpeggios, octaves, chords, and single-note runs, the original, ever surprising, beautifully balanced combination of sounds that were his unmistakable signature.

"I could listen to him all day long," Kitty murmured.

"When am I going to get to hear you, Kitty?" Danielle asked.

"Oh, any time. Come over to the Barbizon tomorrow afternoon.

Don't expect me to be anywhere *that* good, though. He's my idol."

Wilson's orchestra backed up all but one of the other acts, too. Danielle confirmed Kitty's impression that the Kraft sisters were first-rate, and the Golden Gate Quartet harmonized bass-treble stories about Job and Jonah and Gabriel and ringing those golden bells, and Bailey, plump and sequined, warbled "Rockin Chair" and "More Than You Know" and "Someday Sweetheart" and two other standards in her wise, sweet, little-girl voice that no little-girl could keep under such swinging control, and Teddy Wilson soloed on medleys of Gershwin, Youmans, McHugh, and Johnny Green with Sid Catlett, Bill Coleman, Edmond Hall, Benny Morton, and John Williams, all of them virtuosos in their own right, giving him exemplary support. In Coleman's trumpet Kitty seemed to hear some of the just-born lyricism of Buck Clayton combined with almost the dazzle and drive of Roy Eldridge into a sound his own.

"People don't know him as well as they should," Roberta had said. "Moves around too much. Before the war, Paris one day, Egypt the next. Now you turn around and he's off to the Coast or someplace. Catch him while you can."

And then the Ellis Larkins Trio was playing again.

Another time they took in a midnight performance at Cafe Society's Greenwich Village older sister on Sheridan Square. It was a major thrill for Danielle, especially, to see the superb black dancer Pearl Primus, and a rocking pleasure for Kitty to hear the boogie-woogie pioneers Albert Ammons and Pete Johnson and Frankie Newton's trumpet-led band. Kitty thought she might have learned something about phrasing and projection from Georgia Gibbs who sang things like "Ballin' the Jack" and an unfamiliar and lovely late-twenties Berlin ballad "How about Me?" in a big, throbbing voice.

Five o'clock every Sunday afternoon at Jimmy Ryan's on 52nd Street (another rare fully integrated occasion) where for one dollar and no need to buy a drink underage people like Kitty and Danielle got folding chairs to sit on to hear a three-hour jam session organized by Milt Gabler of Commodore Records. No more exciting improvisations were being played anywhere else in America by the greatest names in jazz.

And all the other wonders. Two dozen legitimate theaters. So many good restaurants you could eat out every night for years and never repeat yourself. New York was under the Christmas tree, a cornucopia, a prize package, at reasonable prices, and sometimes free.

19

The break came in mid-May.

The Basin St. Bar-B-Que on 52nd Street served neither barbecued nor Creole food; nor was the music New Orleans Dixieland. Ribs and Dixieland had been the format of the two bankrupt former owners when they had opened in 1938, but the formula had not worked for them. They had underpaid a succession of cooks, and the food had been poor and overpriced; people didn't go to a nightclub to eat anyway. And the Dixieland played at Ryan's by the top names of that genre seemed to attract all the traffic the Street could bear. The second-rate journeymen this pair hired could not compete. Without bothering to change the name—a new sign would have been costly—the original owners introduced variety acts—a standup comic whose material was just blue enough to be titilating rather than really dirty, an "exotic dancer" who didn't display much more than what one could see on the beach at Coney Island, and, to fill out the rest of the bill, a juggler, a harmonica player, a sing-along accordionist, a tap dancer who also sang, and a magician who also told jokes. Before the war, backup music had been provided by a small "German" band. The same group was still there, minus lederhosen and tuba and otherwise deteutonized, but still replete with funny hats, whistles, flatulent reports, and other comic tricks. It was a show designed to appeal to amateur night-outers—tourists from small towns, unsophisticated couples celebrating birthdays, anniversaries, New Year's Eve, and nowadays callow servicemen from everywhere.

The place had been profitable enough. The former owners had been in serious difficulties because of gambling debts and bad investments elsewhere. A man named Harry Field, who had been in and out of the 52nd Street scene for years and who was still part owner of successful clubs in Atlantic City and on Long Island, had bailed them out.

"This is the poor man's Leon and Eddie's," Field often said. He was thoroughly bored with it, but now, in the late spring of 1943, what he also had to contend with was the fact that two of the acts were about to be drafted, and what he had to take advantage of was that the contracts of the others were running out. Business was off. The servicemen nursed their beer, were not big spenders. And seven acts plus a band were getting to be prohibitively expensive.

Fifty-second Street, was, after all, known as the street of jazz, in spite of the exceptions. A small, if possible draft-proof, combo would make more sense these days and would give him more personal satisfaction. The Basin St. Bar-B-Que had been a business investment pure and simple. Now that its profitability was on the decline he could justify changing to a format that would allow him to present artists worthy of the name he'd enjoy listening to himself. And changing the name of the place to Harry's.

Though they had never been friends and never would be, Harry Field knew Manny Sherman, owner of the Ivory Tower, knew something about him, what sort of man he was, who he had been associated with, his habits, his practices. He also happened to know the Rex Wilkins Quintet was unhappy in Sherman's employ and how much Sherman was paying them. Field was prepared to offer more. He knew, too, that Roberta Wilkins handled business arrangements for the group.

"The pay is acceptable," Roberta said. "But working conditions are important, too. Where do we spend our breaks?"

"You're welcome to sit with customers if they invite you, to sit at a table if there's an empty one. At the bar. But like you see, this place is no bigger than most of the other clubs. I got no lounge to offer you. I'd put easy chairs backstage but there's no space."

"I can see that," Roberta said. "As long as we can stay inside, especially when it's cold, that's reasonable. Now. You're going to need an intermission pianist. I know just the girl for you."

"Girl?"

"She sings, too. As well as anyone around, and I'm thinking of the big names. Two talents for the price of one, and she won't be drafted. Don't take my word for it. Come around to the Friday jam session this week and hear for yourself."

Field was impressed, but he was thorough.

"I heard you play with a group, sing with a group, and you're very, very good, but now I think I oughta hear you play and sing by yourself," he said to Kitty.

They were seated at a minuscule table at the Basin St. Bar-B-Que in midafternoon. Field was a natty little man with a close-mouthed V-shaped smile that seemed more or less permanently stamped between nose and chin. A white handkerchief was in full sail out of the breast pocket of his blazer.

"Your husband in the service?" Field asked.

Startled, Kitty stiffened her hand, and she looked for the gold band as if she expected not to find it.

"Yes," she said. "In England. He's a bomber pilot."

"Well, I got to hand it to you kids. One over there fighting the Nazis, one back here starting a career." He pronounced Nazi with a flat A, and without the T-sound. "This is Mrs. Field," he said, introducing a fortyish woman who had come up and said, "Pleased to meet you."

Kitty sat at the piano in this drab, faded, ghostly place, slowly stacked up several layers of velvet chords to see where they might lead, and found herself dealing out a careful but easygoing version of "Ghost of a Chance," a random choice. Then she played and sang "This Is New" from *Lady in the Dark*, an urbane little song without rhythmic beat that gave her an opportunity to project her voice, expand it, use it very professionally. And Harry Field said, "Well, *I'm* convinced. That was a very classy performance. Can you start July 15, same time as the Wilkins quintet?"

"Mr Field, I'm speechless! I can't believe it."

"This is how things happen. You gotta be on the spot, make your own luck."

"Roberta, if it wasn't for you. And Rex ..."

Roberta shook her head. "You had to do it yourself, baby. All we did was maybe speed things up a bit."

20

Almost summer now. Warm May days and nights and Kitty felt cramped in her little room at the Barbizon. She scanned the classified ads, half-looking for an apartment, but automatically rejecting those located very far from midtown and finding nearby locations too expensive. Then one morning she saw "33 West 52nd St. Furnished, two rms, $15 wk." It seemed like an omen. Well, why not? Above the nightclubs and restaurants, she had noticed curtained windows, signs that people lived on the Street, too. By 9 A.M. she was at the address, above the Restaurant Concarneau, ringing a bell, climbing stairs behind a dark-haired woman with a drawn, indifferent face, and securing the fourth-floor flat by paying two weeks in advance. By noon she had moved and was writing Graham:

I have to pinch myself. It's perfect! Please don't disapprove. I just needed more room and a place of my own. It costs three dollars a week more than the Barbizon but I can make that up easily just from what I'll save fixing breakfast at home. The furniture is old but not too bad and the bed is comfortable. It needs a couple more lamps and could use some pictures but I should be able to find things in secondhand stores. The front room, a sitting room, overlooks the street. The bedroom overlooks the garden of a French restaurant on the ground floor. The restaurant serves out there in the warm weather. The striped umbrellas on the tables look cheerful from up here. In a little curtained alcove is a tiny kitchen, the smallest refrigerator I've ever seen, a hot plate, and a cupboard. But what I really love is a bath of my own! The plaster is cracked on the walls, the tub is one of those ancient ones with claw feet, and the water starts off rusty, but it's good and hot and just fine. I'll have to give up the Steinways at the Barbizon but Mr. Field says I can practice at the Basin St. Bar-B-Que ("Harry's" as soon as the new sign is delivered) every afternoon when he's there doing his bookkeeping and ordering. And it's really safer for me than the Barbizon because I'll be so much closer to my job—just down the street.

Late at night, Kitty could hear the sounds of jazz through her open windows as doors were opened, or left open because of the heat, all along the street. She went to the Downbeat to hear the rhapsodic flights of the incomparable Coleman Hawkins. To the Three Deuces to reaffirm her belief that it was impossible for Art Tatum to play as much piano as he did. To Tony's, still another former speakeasy, to sit at the feet of the goddess Mabel Mercer in order to learn how the words of any song should really be sung. What presence! Radiating calm, creating an aura of peace with magic at the center of it, she sat on a stool, back straight, and the audience, all those Algonquin Hotel sophisticates, sat in the palm of her hand. A lady of a certain age who has seen everything but has learned how to be at peace with herself. Black dress, ample figure, sculpted face beneath the spotlight, eyes closed, hands folded, modest piano accompaniment behind her: "It's De-lovely"..."Just One of Those Things"... And to the Onyx to hear what feeling Billie Holiday could put into "I Cover the Waterfront" and "I Must Have That Man." Regal in a white dress that set off her gold-brown skin, a white gardenia in her hair, masterfully backed up by Cozy Cole's drums, Johnny Guarnieri's piano, and Hank D'Amico's clarinet, she sang a little behind the beat, a slight swaying motion of her body, the provocative snapping fingers of her right hand marking the tempo of the song; and that small voice of hers with not much range, sometimes harsh, sometimes shrill, always vulnerable, took deadly aim at the spinal column, the shiver traveling swiftly to the back of the neck where it raised the short hairs there. But everywhere, Kitty looked around and lamented that jazz had to be played in such places. The stage of a big theater wasn't right either; it wasn't intimate enough, but there must be better places than these airless, sleazy little shoeboxes—and there were—the two Cafe Societies, The Blue Angel, Gabriel's in the Village, a few others. All too few. Jazz was an art, so much worthier than its places of origin and usual habitation. Musicians, Kitty among them, didn't notice, didn't care when they were playing. They were happy to have a place to play at all. But sitting in the audience you really noticed what crummy, shabby joints these mostly were.

"Yeah, you can walk up and down this street," Harry Field said, "and hear the whole history of jazz in one evening. But the Street is slipping. I don't know how long it can last. You read *Downbeat*? You read what they said a few months ago? 'Swing Street has become Sucker Street.' Well, it ain't that bad. Yet. People blame the strip joints on the boys in uniform that flock down here but strippers have been part of the scene from the beginning. Not as many, I admit. And the first years, maybe they were the best."

"Definitely," said Mrs. Field.

" '35, '36. Billie was already here. Teddy Wilson. Tatum. It really took off in '38 with Basie, Lester Young, you name them. There's still a lot of talent around, a lot of the big names like before, but the war and all has changed the audiences. The Street used to be like a village. Everybody knew everybody else and got along. Not any more. Now you gotta watch your step. Not all the GIs and sailors who come to the street are bad kids. Some of them really love jazz. But places like these are bound to get the troublemakers, too. They come to the Street for the skin shows and the pickups and get drunk and get into fights. I'll be glad when the war's over and they go back to the farm or wherever."

A letter from Graham that, still unsealed, hot in her hands just out of the mailbox, made her heart jump more than usual.

... I don't really understand what you're doing or why you're doing it. You can't expect me to be very happy about you not only working on 52nd Street but *living* there, too. The whole point about the Barbizon was that while you were inside there you were safe. This is an order. Take care of yourself! Don't take any chances late at night! I'll really be glad when you start school in the Fall...

The tone of his letter seemed to Kitty more puzzled than angry, as though he was too preoccupied and too tired, seized as he was with overwhelming concerns, to be able to focus on her life. Most of his somewhat rambling letter was about his missions. But it was deflating. She wished she could make him understand, but he was too far away, fighting a war that just went on and on.

Jazz groups and individual performers moved from club to club on 52nd Street with confusing regularity, even more often than the clubs themselves changed names, owners, and format. No one was very surprised to find the Rex Wilkins Quintet, in mid-July, at a different address only a few doors away from the Ivory Tower, at Harry's. The engagement was for three months, with an option to renew if mutually agreeable. Of the variety acts left, Harry Field retained only the standup comic who functioned now as a kind of wise-cracking M.C. Miss Kitty Collins was intermission pianist, playing three forty-five minute breaks nightly, starting at 8:15, 10:15, and 12:15.

Thus, with almost unbearable pride in the knowledge she was now a true professional, Kitty became again in public an exponent of America's two original and closely linked musical forms—jazz and the popular songs of Broadway and Tin Pan Alley. She would be paid and applauded to do what she loved to do.

She also enrolled in a public high school in the West 40s, to begin classes in September.

21

In America, in the dark, hot city nights, hatred bloomed.

"Some kinda trouble up in Harlem," Harry Field murmured to Kitty about 10 P.M. on the evening of August 1. He had been talking to a cop on the steaming sidewalk. Inside it was stifling. Everyone perspired even with the fans going. The memory of a race riot in Detroit earlier that summer was still in everybody's mind. Twenty-nine had died.

"What happened?" Kitty asked.

"Not clear yet. Somebody shot, or so they say, and gangs of kids are breaking into stores."

Roberta and the quintet had heard, too. Kitty could see it in their faces.

Harry had a radio in his tiny office. Sometime after midnight he reported, "They got soldiers up there now besides all the cops in town, evidently. Kids throwing stones and bottles. Looting. Maybe twenty-five in the hospital so far. The mayor's going on the air at one."

Just before one, Harry brought the radio out to the bar and plugged it in there. The quintet finished a number and climbed off the stage to listen along with the dozen or so customers left, the bartenders, the waiters, the Fields, Kitty.

This is Mayor LaGuardia talking," said the chatty, familiar voice. "I am sorry if I am interrupting any programs ... there seems to have been interference with the arrest and a soldier attacked the officer, the arresting officer. Whereupon the officer pulled his gun and wounded the soldier. The soldier is not seriously injured, fortunately. The police officer is also in the hospital. A crowd gathered first at this hotel, then at the front of the Twenty-eighth Police Precinct post ... Now my purpose in speaking at this time is to ask all of the people in the neighborhood involved to please get off the streets and go home and go to bed. Unless you do that we may have serious trouble ..."

The mayor introduced two black leaders, Dr. Max Yergen and Ferdinand Smith, who also went on the air to support LaGuardia's appeal for calm.

"Roberta, you can't go back up there tonight," Kitty said. "It's too dangerous. Please stay at my place so I'll know you're safe. You can all stay. I'll find room."

"We'll see, baby. Another hour to go here."

At about 2 A.M. Harry Field said, "The cops and army troops got a big area cordoned off. All traffic diverted from 110th to 155th streets and from Fifth to Eighth avenues."

"That does it," Kitty said. "You've got to stay. Your apartment's in there. And just thinking of you on the subway ..."

Rex and Roberta and Harold accepted. Rodney and Clay didn't reply. When they left Harry's, Rodney and Clay walked off in another direction. Kitty looked after them for a moment, shrugged, and led the way to her building.

She gave Rex and Roberta the bedroom, and though he protested she should have it, put Harold on the sofa. She curled up in two old overstuffed chairs pushed together.

"I'll be fine here. I could sleep standing up," she said.

She slept but woke from time to time trying to twist herself into a more comfortable position, thinking of the violence that seemed everywhere in the world and of the frail power of music to prevent it.

Just before first light, the street bell sounded. Kitty was on her feet in a few seconds, slipped on loafers, and went quickly down the stairs. It was Rodney.

"Where's Clay?" Kitty asked.

"No Clay."

Rodney had had more gin. He stumbled noisily going up the wooden stairs—they were uncarpeted; there were only rubber mats on the treads—and bumped against the wall.

"Would you sleep with me?" he asked challengingly.

"*Rodney,*" she said, exasperated with him. "I'm married."

"Don't give me that married shit. You think that white fly boy of yours don't have some limey piece over there? You wouldn't because I'm black."

"You picked the wrong person to accuse of that."

"You mean because you lived with Roberta one time? You didn't have no choice. You would've starved."

"Rod, I don't want to argue with you. Your color doesn't have anything to do with it. You're a good looking guy and you know it. If you want to stay here you can stay here."

Kitty turned and walked into her apartment leaving the door open, started heating water for coffee in the alcove. Rodney followed.

"Where'm I supposed to sleep?"

He could see Harold under a blanket on the couch.

"One of these chairs, or the rug, that's the best I can offer you."

"I ain't sleeping on no floor for no ofay broad! That's what you'd like to see, wouldn't it?"

Harold woke up. "Goddamnit, Rodney, zipper up your mouth and let me sleep. What you expect from Kitty, the Waldorf? She's givin you the best she's got."

Rodney laughed and laughed at that, without mirth, waking Roberta.

"They steal you blind and then give nothin back. They steal your music and give you the floor."

Roberta came out from the bedroom in her slip, holding her dress up for cover. "It's not worth talking to you now, Rodney, drunk as you are, but I'll say this. Kitty didn't *steal your* music. Now sit down or lie down and keep quiet or take your leave."

Exhausted, Kitty curled up on the rug below the front windows. When she awoke two hours later, stiff and sore, Rodney was slumped in a chair, asleep. Kitty tried dozing for another hour or so without much success. At 9 A.M. she washed her face, combed her hair and went out to buy rolls, extra milk, and the *Herald Tribune*. She read the story standing on the sidewalk.

The most violent disturbances in Harlem's history. Five killed, four hundred wounded or injured ... hundreds of stores wrecked and looted ... property damage estimated at five million dollars ... Not a race riot as in Detroit since the only whites involved were police trying to maintain order, and some storekeepers ... gangs of zoot-suiters ... outside agitators ... tensions exacerbated by overcrowding, bitterness over discrimination in the armed services and war industries, the greater number of white policemen than black ... Mayor La Guardia praised by both Negro and white leaders for his tireless, round-the-clock efforts still continuing, though the situation appeared under control. Five thousand police and squads of soldiers maintaining order with help from Harlem neighborhood groups.

When Kitty returned to her building the landlady met her on the stairs.

"Get those people out of here," the woman said.

"What?"

"You heard what I said. Get them out of here. Raising the roof in the middle of the night."

"It was an emergency. It was dangerous for them to go home," Kitty said.

"That's none of my business. I'm not running a free hotel."

The woman went into her apartment and slammed the door.

Furious, shaking, Kitty continued climbing, then composed herself. They don't need to know about this.

They were all up, disheveled, trying to make themselves presentable.

"Rolls. Milk. Dig in," Kitty said. "I think there's plenty of coffee and tea. I'm sorry, I only have two extra towels but help yourselves. There's a bunch of washcloths." She opened the closet door where they were.

Roberta took the paper and read the story aloud.

When she had finished and Harold was reading the story to himself with Rodney looking over his shoulder, Roberta said, "We've got to be going along. See what we find."

"It didn't say anything about houses being damaged," Kitty said.

They ate, washed up, Kitty nervous the landlady might *do* something, barge in, make a scene. She avoided looking at Rodney, who was absolutely silent. Ready to leave, Roberta hugged Kitty briefly.

"Thanks for everything, baby," Roberta said. "You've been a big help."

"Indispensable is the word," Harold Saunders said. "Thank you, Kitty. Nice to know where your friends are."

Rex squeezed her hands between both of his.

Kitty blushed an embarrassed little smile, shrugged, made self-deprecating gestures with her hands.

From the front windows she watched them walk toward the Sixth Avenue subway station.

A short while later the landlady knocked, and Kitty faced her through the doorway.

"You're paid up through Thursday," the woman said. "I want you to leave by Friday noon."

"Don't worry, I'll be out of this place before that," Kitty said with a steely steadiness that seemed to take the woman aback for a moment. "And if you'll take your foot out of the door I'll close it."

The main streets of Harlem—Seventh Avenue, Lenox Avenue, 125th Street—looked as though a hurricane had hit them. Broken store windows, broken glass everywhere, clothing store dummies and other objects of no interest to looters, debris of all kinds littered the sidewalks. Kitty saw some of this in newspaper photos; Roberta, Rex, Harold, and Rodney looked at it in person. But where they lived was untouched, and they slept through the afternoon until it was time to go back downtown again. Rodney and Clay—where Clay had spent the night he didn't say and no one asked—met Rex and Roberta at the subway entrance, and Roberta said, "Sit with me, Rodney."

In the car she sat with him a little removed from the others, who cooperated in this arrangement, and Roberta asked, "You remember any of the things you said last night?"

"You gon preach to me?"

"No, I'm not going to preach to you. I'm just talking to you. I'd like to see you quit hassling Kitty just because she's white and happens to be handy. She offered you shelter and you threw it back in her face. She's my friend. She's like my own flesh and blood. She can't change the color of her skin any more than you can. She makes less money than you do and a lot less than Ella or Billie or Maxine Sullivan, to name three, and if she keeps on doing only what she wants to do she'll never get rich."

Roberta reached over and briefly patted the back of his hand, and they rode the rest of the way in silence.

Kitty spent the rest of the morning reading the want ads, but it wasn't really necessary because in the afternoon what she was looking for, an "apartment for rent" sign, she saw in the window of a brownstone further down the street. No one answered the bell for a while but she had it lined up before the end of the afternoon. The rent was five dollars more a week, but the furniture was a little nicer. She told the Fields what had happened.

She was packing up a little after six-thirty when the doorbell rang. It was Rodney Blake.

"You need any help movin'?" he asked.

22

Heavy rains, gales, and high tides battered the Atlantic coast of America. High winds swept rain down the streets of Manhattan. Going anywhere was an adventure for pedestrians. Watching Kitty ducking in and out of doorways, struggling with her umbrella, back to the wind, whipping raincoat sculpting her body, several men passing by half fell in love with her.

The Rex Wilkins Quintet, Rex's trumpet leading the rideout, finished a stirring version of "Beyond the Blue Horizon," the final number of the first set of the evening. The members of the quintet, shadowy outlines now, climbed down off the darkened little stage, and a pin spot went on, directed at the keyboard of a baby grand at floor level, which lit up in the dark like a very wide, toothy grin.

Wearing a black, off-the-shoulder cocktail dress, her long hair pinned attractively back behind her ears and away from a generous forehead, Kitty Collins came into view, a tall girl relatively speaking, not Texas tall, but up there, and looking seventeen but a very special seventeen. The assured way she carried herself had something to do with that. But having extremely pretty features, even her ears, and a lovely figure, as good a one as she would ever have in her life, made age irrelevant.

Kitty's fingers began working the center of the keyboard with economy of motion—scintillated suddenly in both directions and were off and running.

She had bounced into "A Shanty in Old Shanty Town" and that familiar melody from the early years of the Depression remained clearly in the foreground, a farmhouse-parlor, summer-at-the-lake kind of song, but the way she set it swinging was something else entirely, a joyous, professional sort of thing.

In a little under three minutes, Kitty segued right through scattered applause into her next number. She couldn't see anyone clearly beyond the first ring of tables, but sitting out there herself, at a table against the wall when the quintet was on, she could size up an audience, and this one was typical. Servicemen mostly and some of them didn't know why they were there. They were there because 52nd Street was supposed to be one of the places to go for a good time. Some people didn't listen, went right on talking, laughing at jokes during a performance, maybe applauded, maybe didn't. Total losses. Some customers paid attention to the main attraction but figured the intermission pianist was just there to provide background music for their conversation. But there were people who listened, even if it was for the first time, and they weren't sure what they were supposed to be listening for. You could spot them and you liked them and tried to think of things they might appreciate. Like the naval officer at one of the ringside tables who had spent the entire previous evening near the piano and was back again, who hadn't requested anything but who so obviously appreciated everything she did. And then there were the few who knew, who understood, who cared, who loved what you were doing. You could always recognize them, the intent way they sat, kept time, closed their eyes sometimes, smiled to themselves. As though, at least for the moment, nothing else was more important for them. They knew when she was improvising on the harmonic chords of a song, composing new melodies as lovely as the original song itself and more surprising, but even she didn't know exactly how she did this. Where did inspiration come from? Like the song—out of nowhere.

"Sometimes I get so discouraged," Kitty said. "Some nights there doesn't seem to be anybody out there who's really *listening*."

"Oh, baby, you're just beginning to learn one of the things you have to learn," Roberta said. "Being a performer can be a lonely business. So often you end up playing for yourself or other musicians. Always been that way and always will be. Don't expect miracles. Only a few people will ever really appreciate what you're doing. Big bands pull in big crowds sometimes and a few know how to turn that into big money while the rest of us just eke out a living. But don't be fooled. Most of those people in the crowds aren't listening either. In one ear and out the other. They're there because it's the thing to do, the place to be. And don't expect any sympathy from them. 'Who asked you to be a musician? Not me.' So why do we do it? Because we want to. Because we have to even if it doesn't make us rich or happy all the time or solve anything. Just don't stop. And get yourself on records for people to hear a hundred years from now."

Roberta paused a few moments, said, "Listen, baby, you are appreciated, don't ever think you aren't. By a few out there in the audience and by musicians on the Street. I wouldn't want you to get a swelled head or anything, but word gets around and Rex and I hear it. Guys come in from the other clubs, and when you're working you don't always know they're there, but we hear them, and you're one of us now, part of a great tradition ..."

Ever since she had left Chicago Kitty had exchanged occasional postcards, once in a while letters, with Joe, Jim, and Matt Barry. (She sent a few postcards to Ted, but he never replied and she finally dropped him from her list.) The Barry boys' correspondence was simply a reflection of their personalities. Jim, the quiet one, wasn't much of a correspondent. Joe had always talked the most and now wrote the longest letters and somewhat more frequently. Matt was a breezy, chatty in-between.

Joe wrote:

Your publicity photos from "Harry's" have honored places on my locker and inspire as many appreciative whistles as any pinup. The guy in the bunk above me has a crush on you and is pitiful to behold ...

I hate to disillusion you—I loved it too—but the place I'm at at the moment isn't much like a certain movie. You would hunt in vain for "Rick's." However, after weeks at sea, the white city is a welcome sight rising off the rocky coast, and not a bad town. Great French restaurants. I never realized fish and seafood could taste so good...

But in the snapshot of himself Joe included there was a French policeman in the background wearing a kepi just like Claude Rains.

At the end of the evening—2 A.M. the following morning, actually—Rodney and Clay would be the first out the door, on their way to Minton's or Clark Monroe's in Harlem to listen until dawn to the new jazz being developed there, and sometimes to sit in. Rodney was twenty-three, Clay twenty-five. Harold, at thirty-five, had more conservative musical tastes but was just young enough to wonder if the new music might not be the wave of the future and maybe he had better get a handle on it. Rex, at forty-three, from the generation of 1900 rejected it out of hand. Roberta tried to be objective. She was a product of the old school, too, but said, "Music has to evolve. Just don't throw out the baby with the bath water."

Kitty was very curious to hear it, and Roberta said, "Pick a night. We'll all go up after work, and then you can sleep over at our place."

Released from work, from maintaining the beat of music they considered old-fashioned, that didn't give them enough scope, and still lubricated with the evening's gin, Clay Mitchell and Rodney Blake, sprawled, relaxed, on the lengthwise seat of the speeding, Harlem-bound subway car, across the aisle from Rex, Roberta, Harold, and Kitty. The train was noisy and not all of Clay's and Rodney's talk was audible, but what came across clearly in every third sentence or so was the Oedipal obscenity most urban Americans take to be a Negro invention. Used as a noun, as an adjective, as an insult, as a nondescriptive label attached randomly to things and people they were indifferent to, or even liked, it was all-purpose, poverty-stricken, wearisome, its shock value or originality long since dissipated by incessant overuse. It was not the first time Kitty had heard it, and she knew, sadly, it would not be the last.

At Clark Monroe's Uptown House, an after-hours incubator of the new jazz that didn't get going until 4 A.M., Kitty listened for the first time to Dizzy Gillespie and Charlie Parker, and thought their trumpet–alto sax ensembles and solos some of the most exciting music she had ever heard. Their technical skill, the dazzling number of clearly defined notes they could crowd into a single bar, was undeniable. And she had learned enough harmony to know that intricate harmonic changes were as important to this new jazz as technique. It was musicians' music, to listen to, and she wondered how popular it would ever be. It was too soon to tell, but there didn't seem to be much in it for a singer, and maybe you could dance to it, but would enough people want to? She could see the appeal for Clay Mitchell and Rodney Blake; there seemed to be more for drummers and bassists to do. Thelonious Monk's piano accompaniment fascinated and tantalized her, but he didn't solo much while she was there and she wasn't able to isolate what he was doing.

Roberta didn't want Rex to get overtired. They left after an hour, cabbed it to Rex and Roberta's apartment, a neat, two-bedroom arrangement on the second floor of an old building.

"I'm old hat to these young cats," Rex said. "A 'mouldy fig.' Well, they're going to outsmart themselves right out of sight with that Chinese music."

Kitty, with a foot in both worlds, couldn't be sure she agreed and didn't comment.

After Rex had gone to bed, and while Roberta and Kitty were still unwinding in the kitchen with hot tea and cinnamon toast, a kind of first breakfast, Roberta said, "Just like old times."

"Um huh. Roberta, I thought I'd been getting along with Rodney and Clay lately. Better anyway. But tonight they seemed uptight around me again."

Roberta sighed. "You're up in their territory, baby, digging their new music."

"Tell them not to worry. I think it's interesting but I'm not going to copy it. I don't see me doing it."

"Oh, they know that, more or less, but with them this new music is a revolutionary kind of thing. They're hoping it's too tricky for whites to learn, something 'Charley can't steal' is the way they put it. They're kidding themselves. Three or four white musicians sitting in already up at Minton's.

"But like I've said, black musicians are bitter and they have reasons to be. White musicians still have the top jobs in radio and Hollywood, the best places to make a good steady living. There's as much discrimination in this business as in any other."

"I thought things were getting a little better? The radio networks started hiring blacks."

"About three so far and one got fired already. I thought things might be improving, too. The Street isn't as Jim Crow as it was in the thirties. But after the riot in Harlem some ballrooms around the country stopped booking black orchestras. Said it was too risky."

"I get so mad and feel so ashamed when I see it and hear about it," Kitty said. "I feel so helpless."

"Well, you're not helpless, baby. Every time a bunch of those white kids in uniform come to Harry's and see you playing with us and knowing us the way you do, maybe a few of them with good instincts will get a different idea of the way things should be and take it back home with them. Just be yourself, baby. We know. Even Rodney and Clay. It's just going to take them a little longer to admit it."

On October 14, Flying Fortresses again attacked the Nazi ball-bearing plant at Schweinfurt, and sixty of the American bombers failed to return. The price of success was too high. But Graham Allen, one of the lucky ones, completed twenty-five missions that day and was given three weeks of rest-leave in the States to begin November 13; then he would return to an assignment on the ground as an intelligence briefing officer with the rank of first lieutenant.

And Kitty said aloud to herself, "Oh, my God, he made it, he made it, he made it!"

23

As overjoyed as Kitty was over the prospect of Graham's return, she was equally nervous about it. They had been apart so long and so much had happened to both of them and she wanted everything to be right, for Graham to be pleased with her and proud of her. He had never been to New York, had never seen 52nd Street, which could look pretty ratty, especially on a cold, gray day in the fall, if you weren't used to it, if you didn't see it in context, which takes time, and he hadn't wanted her to move there in the first place. Well, she would just have to redeem at least one little spot on the Street with her piano and songs and just the fact that she was there herself. She had half won him over once before at that party on Lake Shore Drive, and now she was better, a true professional.

One thing worried her, though. He didn't know that she had dropped out of high school after a few weeks. It was just too heavy a load to carry, working, practicing, and attending classes all day. She was looking into correspondence schools but hadn't taken any action yet. Now she would have to sign up before he got back. But he still wouldn't be pleased with her about that.

He had written that he would arrive somewhere in New England. Because of security considerations he couldn't be more specific.

"Why don't you meet him on Nantucket?" Miriam Field suggested. "Have a second honeymoon. You'll love it up there, both of you. We always did. You say he likes wide open spaces. There's plenty of those even though it's just a little island."

"Where would we stay?" Kitty asked. "Are there hotels?"

"None that I know of," said Harry Field. "They wouldn't be open in November anyway. But I'm sure you'd find a cottage to rent. Let's look at the *Times*."

In the Sunday edition they found several offerings, one listed with a Manhattan telephone number.

The woman who answered the phone had a hearty, fashionable voice as though she might be speaking through closed teeth.

"There's electricity but no central heating, you realize. Do you know how to light a fire?"

"Yes."

There had been fireplaces at the convent and at the Barrys' house.

A week's rent was reasonable, and so it was arranged.

Kitty immediately felt a wave of love, a thrill, though she still couldn't truly relax, and was tense at work.

"I just *played* that," she snapped at a perfectly nice young soldier who had asked for "Someone to Watch over Me," and was sorry for her bitchy behavior shortly afterwards, but though she eventually played the boy's request, she had spoiled his evening, and she brooded about the delicate edges on which everyone seemed to live.

The quintet finished the second set at Harry's and climbed down off the stage. Kitty got up from her table, and Roberta gave her hand a motherly squeeze as she went by. She and Rex and Harold Saunders left for a walk. Rodney Blake and Clay Mitchell took over Kitty's table, got drinks, and for a few minutes Kitty could be seen chatting with them, laughing at something Clay had said.

She sat at the piano, adjusted the mike.

"Hey!" said the sailor at the bar loudly. "Play 'The Beer Barrel Polka'!" He began bellowing the words but heard no piano accompaniment, and stopped.

229

"Come on, play it!" the sailor demanded.

"Sorry, I don't play that," Kitty said, and began "Tea for Two."

"Sure you play it, everybody knows that!" the sailor said over the music, and began shouting the words again but trailed off when the piano stopped, and Kitty folded her hands in her lap and stared into the middle distance. Rodney Blake rose from the table. He was taller than the sailor, though not as broad. Clay Mitchell got up, too.

"Didn't you hear the lady?" Rodney said. "She don't play that. And you're disturbin' the other customers who want to hear what she does play."

"You talkin' to me, nigger?" He turned to Kitty. "You like black stuff, huh, you whore? I saw you makin' up to this nigger."

Rodney didn't wait to talk. He had one of the sailor's arms twisted back and up in less than five seconds. Speechless pain contorted the man's face, turned it gray and sweaty. Clay Mitchell had opened the front door.

"Walk," Rodney ordered, and the sailor walked, doll-like, through the doorway, up the steps to the sidewalk. Rodney returned alone. Kitty was playing "Can't We Be Friends?" trying to reestablish the atmosphere the other customers had presumably come to Harry's for. She smiled wanly at Rodney Blake when he passed her line of vision on his way back to his table, but his face was expressionless. The sailor had been the only navy man; maybe that's why the incident had the outcome it did. A tableful of soldiers hadn't made a move. They were fresh-faced boys who seemed to enjoy the music. Harry Field and his wife watched this scene, tense and pale, but did not interfere, let it take its inevitable, justified course, but Harry went outside for a few minutes after Rodney had returned from his mission. When Field returned, he shook his head briefly, shrugged, which Kitty interpreted to mean: "He's gone. I don't know where."

Rex and Roberta and Harold Saunders came in from their break, and Kitty concluded with "Fine and Dandy," bowed to applause, and got herself a glass of tonic water. She was tired. She really wanted to go back to her apartment now, but because of what had happened didn't feel she could just leave now. She wanted to show solidarity. The evening had been irremediably soured, and she would be glad when she could get back to her oasis above the Street and listen to something symphonic and cleansing.

The last set ended finally. On the darkened little stage, the members of the quintet packed up their instruments, talked among themselves, came down off the stage through the stale, smoky air, grim-faced. Kitty had her coat on, went outside with them.

"I don't like you going home by yourself this late," Roberta said. "No need to sit around waiting for us. Rodney, see Kitty to her door. We'll start walking."

"It's not necessary," Kitty protested, knowing she was causing another problem. "It's less than a block."

"Then it won't take long," Roberta said.

Kitty walked quickly away in the opposite direction, trying to keep up with Rodney Blake's long-legged stride. Under canopies, around parked cars, across the empty street. She had her keys out and ran up the steps to the outside door, turned when the door was open.

"I'm OK now, Rod. I'm sorry that awful sailor had to ruin the evening. It's the war. Those dumb Southerners don't belong up here."

But he was already walking away. Kitty watched him recrossing the street, and unexpectedly stopping in the middle. No cars moved in the roadway. No pedestrians on the sidewalks. Rodney reached in his hip pocket suddenly and whipped something out. Then he began loping up the street and on to the opposite pavement. Full of fear, Kitty looked ahead of him and under a street lamp near the corner saw Roberta, Rex, and Harold, three white sailors surrounding them.

"Oh God!" Kitty said aloud, ran into her hallway and up the stairs two at a time, her apartment door key in hand. Her phone was in the bedroom. The police emergency number rang only once. Sergeant somebody.

"Hurry! Please hurry, they might be killed!" she yelled into the phone, repeated the address, and hung up. Looked for some kind of weapon but nothing likely struck her eye.

Kitchen. Where she grabbed an empty milk bottle from the floor and raced down the stairs. She had left the street door open and left it open still behind her. Ran down the sidewalk on her side of the street, not seeing anything yet, her view blocked by parked cars, but she could hear Roberta screaming, male voices shouting. When she crossed the street she could see everything, Rex Wilkins slumped to the sidewalk, Harold Saunders sitting there. Roberta was on her knees beside Rex. A few paces further down, the three sailors circled Rodney who held them at bay with the thin-bladed knife in his hand. Clay was nowhere in sight.

Two of the sailors grinned slyly, evilly, sniggered.

"Give us that knife, nigger, then we gonna whup you good!"

"Maybe we just gonna carve you up with it!"

The sailor who had been at Harry's wasn't smiling, and his face was pop-eyed and murderous.

Kitty heard herself yelling for help at the top of her voice, saw the red lights whirling down toward them from Sixth Avenue, the sailor who had been heading for her changing directions, looking for a place to hide, saw the police car and the shore patrol car right behind, pulling up quickly, sirens trailing off, men jumping out...

Neither Rex nor Harold was badly hurt, though they suffered painful bruises from being punched to the pavement and kicked.

"The main thing was the fright!" Roberta said over the phone the following afternoon. "Rex is unnerved!"

The worst of the nightmare had ended on the sidewalk, but everyone, Kitty included, had also to endure another hour or so in the police precinct station, answering questions, making statements, doing a lot of sitting on hard benches, waiting, feeling imprisoned themselves, before Rex and Harold could get some perfunctory first aid at the station and they could all go home.

Rex would not come to work either Friday or Saturday. Roberta stayed with him and phoned Harry Field to say she would be in on Monday to discuss the situation. Harold and Rodney, Harold bandaged, showed up on time Friday evening. Surprisingly, Clay did not, and Harold and Rodney disclaimed any knowledge of his whereabouts. Kitty filled in, formed a trio with Harold and Rodney, and played through the weekend.

Early Monday evening, Kitty brewed coffee on her tiny stove and carried cups to Roberta seated on the couch behind the coffee table. Streets lights were on, lamps were lit.

"Rex won't come back here," Roberta said. "He wants to go to California. He thinks the grass is greener out there and I can't talk him out of it. 'Hate California, it's cold and it's damp' but I'm committed to him. I've got to go along."

"My fault again."

"Don't talk silly. You responsible for some peckerwood sailor making trouble?"

"If I'd humored him, hadn't let Rodney get dragged into it . . ."

"Rodney's a big boy. He wasn't doing it all for you."

"Then if I hadn't stayed so late . . ."

"Baby, with Rex, if it wasn't this it'd be something else. He's always wanted to move on, move somewhere else. As far back as 1926 just before we got married. He wanted to go to China with Jack Carter's band. I said, well, you can go without me, and he stayed. Maybe lived to regret it. Later on, in the thirties, he wanted to go to Europe and we went. France was one place he didn't want to leave, at least not when we did, after a year. We didn't have to. We could have gotten new bookings. I just thought, well, we've had our trip, now it's time to go back to our own country. Of course, we would have had to go anyway when the war broke out. At least get out of France. But we might be in London now—playing for your husband when he came to town."

"But I probably never would have met him if I hadn't met you first, and if you were in England I wouldn't have met you."

"Oh, I'm just dreaming out loud. But if this war ever ends, maybe we should try to go back there, stay there . . . Being a jazz musician is a hard life. All the ones that died so young just from moving around too much—black and white. Bessie Smith, Teschmaker, Chu Berry, all in car crashes. Beiderbecke and Berigan and Charlie Christian of just getting sick . . ."

"Oh, I wish I had a place of my own," Kitty said. "I mean a club, a really nice club, clean and comfortable with good light and good air, where we could all play and be safe. But I'd probably mess things up for everybody."

"Baby, you're a pretty girl. An automatic catalytic agent. Accept it. And are black and white people not supposed to have anything to do with each other because some racist might make trouble about it? That's going to improve things? You do what you think is right, and sometimes that has consequences you can't foresee. But even then you don't know what the final result's going to be. Look what happened when you came to live with me. That hoodlum kid in the building forced both of us to leave. That seemed too bad at the time but look what happened afterwards. Like you said, would you have met Graham if it hadn't been for living with me and then at that convent? Would you have learned as much piano, how to sing? Would I have tried to find Rex if I hadn't been in Kankakee with not enough to do? And the story isn't over yet. Won't be until all of us check out for good."

"Is Harold going with you? Are Clay and Rod?"

"Harold is. Clay's flown the coop. He doesn't have a draft card and's afraid this trouble might bring the police around here. Rodney has a deferment as the sole support of an invalid mother. He's going to look for another job in New York. We've found another drummer in Chicago from the old days. He's been driving a cab, and he'd like to try L.A., too. We'll see about picking up another bassist or maybe some other instrument out there."

"How soon?"

"If Harry Field will agree—" She looked at her wristwatch. "I'd better think about going down there; it's after seven—Harold and Rodney and I will stay on to November first . . . Come on, baby, don't look so sad. We'll all get together again sooner or later like everybody does in this business . . ."

It doesn't take long to say goodbye or fade out of sight. Snap your fingers, done in a trice. What takes longer is getting over it.

Kitty saw them off at Grand Central Station. There was a certain amount of fussing over baggage, tickets, newspapers. That passed the time, covered things up. Off to one side, Roberta said, "Baby, I'd so much rather stay here!"

Kitty kissed them all, spun around, and walked off alone, hands in her pockets.

PART VI

24

Kitty took an early morning train to Boston, then a bus to Falmouth–Woods Hole, which reached the little port in time to catch the afternoon ferry to Nantucket. The Sound was rough and the boat mostly empty; she felt like the last dried bean in a barrel. Gray skies to an indistinct horizon. Out of sight of Martha's Vineyard and for two hours only rolling, open sea surrounded her.

The low line of houses, steeples, a faint etching growing gradually more distinct, had a reassuring look of permanence, and the boat entered the harbor into a haven of protection and repose.

It isn't America at all, Kitty thought. I love it.

A Chevrolet taxi, circa 1925, brought her to a grocery store where she bought supplies from a list the woman in New York had drawn up—staples, and enough food to last a week. By four in the afternoon, in fading light, the old car was laboring along narrow streets of ancient, lovely houses to the edge of town and out the one east-west road across the treeless moors.

The driver was an old man, taciturn, but glad enough to have the unexpected business, and not unfriendly.

" 'Sconset's quiet if that's what you're looking for. Not many stay there year round."

"My husband's meeting me there tomorrow. If you meet the boat at three o'clock he'll be on it."

The house was on a cliff overlooking the sea, on the outer edge of Siasconset, a tiny village nine miles from the town, bravely breasting the Atlantic at the end of America, or perhaps it was the end of the world, beyond which a terrifying escarpment would drop off into boundless space.

Each key on the ring had been identified with ink-marked strips of adhesive tape. Front door opened, the driver departed, she found the shed, wood, kindling, soon had a fire going after two false starts.

Dating from the early eighteenth century, the house was tiny, as though it might have shrunk little by little as it aged.

"A captain built it for his retirement but was lost at sea before he could move in," its owner had said. "I'm not sure if he'd be permitted to haunt the place under those circumstances. In any case, we've never seen his ghost which is rather a disappointment."

A parlor, open deck beyond it—a modern addition—a little dining room with slanting floor, kitchen, two bedrooms. Old furniture, a few solid Victorian pieces, the rest of no great value, worn throw rugs, unmatching odds and ends of china, silver plate and stainless steel in the corner cupboard, watercolors of local scenes askew on the walls, a map of the Cape and the islands. Triangular Nantucket with trailing fins—needle sharp northern cape and string of southern islets—resembled a scup or sea bream diving southeast into the Atlantic with 'Sconset in its mouth.

Kitty put away the groceries, unpacked, found sheets, blankets, pillow cases in a locked cedar chest, and made up the bed in the front bedroom. Exhaustion overcame her. She fell asleep with the lights on, woke around midnight to the sound of breaking surf, ate a cold sandwich with milk, undressed, and fell asleep again.

Getting through the night was to have been the difficult part, but fatigue and a long sleep had blessed her, made it easy. Now, in such a setting, waiting the few remaining hours was a positive pleasure. One savors anticipation, even the fear of unforeseen delay, if it may not be too long and some great prize lies at the end of it.

From the open deck of the house she was in possession of a

universe of ocean, sky, vast banks of clouds, the long, wide beach far below. A flight of wooden steps with a series of landings led down to it. Clouds curtained the sun, leaving only brush strokes of pale light, and the air was cold. Kitty went inside to look for a book. Everything she could do to make the house ready was done, and it was noon. She went for a walk through the almost deserted village and out for a way along the road.

At 2:30 she took a bath. Dried, she put on only a skirt, a Fair Isle pullover sweater Graham had sent her for her birthday, rough and soft against her skin. Put Ravel and Mendelssohn on the Victrola with the automatic changer. Trembled, waited. Heard at last the old car on the road. Saw him through the window! Paying the old man, the car moving away.

Names cried happily once above the music and after their standing, whirling, her-feet-off-the floor embrace, hand in hand they sped to bed.

He slept. He had slept little in the past thirty-six hours. In sleep his face seemed boyish and peaceful but he had seen too much and been through too much not to have changed. Kitty sat and watched him, fulfilled but wanting him again.

It was seven o'clock in the evening. If she let him sleep through, he might wake in the night and be hungry. For a while she read (*H. M. Pulham, Esquire*) and then went in and sat beside Graham on the bed and brushed back a lock of hair from his forehead. He stirred and twitched once but didn't wake, and she took one hand in hers. His eyes opened, then closed again, but he drew her hands to his face.

"Would you like something to eat?" Kitty asked. "You slept almost four hours."

He was still not fully awake, but he said, "Guess I should."

He stumbled into the bathroom to wash his face. When he came out she had a cold beer for him. She was proud of herself for having been able to buy it without anyone questioning her age.

Sweatered, hair behind her ears, eyes shining, tip of her tongue curled up over her upper lip in concentration, Kitty grilled their steaks under the kitchen broiler. Graham stood in the doorway, sipped occasionally from a cold bottle of beer and watched her with half-unseeing eyes, part of him still somewhere in sleep or somewhere in the sky. He yawned deeply.

"Sorry," he said after a while. "I'll wake up eventually. Tomorrow. I hardly know where I am. I've never been in this part of the world before."

"Look and see," Kitty said, pointing with her turning prongs, and Graham crossed to the dining room wall. He studied the map for several minutes.

"We're halfway out into the ocean," he said. "Are you sure this is part of the U.S.? What's beyond?"

"Atlantis," Kitty said.

"Well, I hope the anchor holds."

Something new seemed to occur to him as he looked at the blackout curtains on the windows, and the tone of his voice changed. "I wonder how many U-boats are cruising along out there?"

Kitty had set up a table for two in the little dining room. As a centerpiece were sprigs of yellow broom she had picked during her walk along the moors that morning, arranged in a china vase she had found in the dining room cupboard. She brought in the salad, lit candles, and said, "Now sit down so I can serve you."

With steak, medium rare the way he liked it, baked potato, salad, on plates that even matched.

When she brought in her own plate he started to get up to hold her chair for her, but she said, "No, don't get up. This is the first time I've ever had a chance to be a real wife to you. I want to wait on you hand and foot ..."

"And say grace and toast each other."

He seemed willing enough to let her play this role and went along with these rituals, and then they supped.

"I just can't believe you're here," Kitty said. "If only you could stay now, really stay, not just three weeks—two with me. But at least it's over. When I read those awful headlines I'll know it can't be you."

"It's not over yet."

"I know. But I mean you're safe on the ground. And we're winning, aren't we?"

"We started winning a few months after we came in, but that was almost two years ago. Nobody knows how long it will take."

"You're safe. That's all I care about now."

By the time Kitty had cleaned up it was past ten. When she went out to the parlor, even though the Schumann piano concerto played rather loudly Graham was in a chair asleep sitting up.

"Graham? Graham?" she murmured, shaking his shoulders, then took his hand. "Let's get you to bed."

He woke enough to get to his feet and let her lead him to the bedroom.

"Sorry," he muttered. "D'nt mean to . . ." He never finished.

He undressed to his shorts and got under the covers. She kissed him goodnight, kissing his cheek, a kiss he did not return; he was asleep already. Kitty got into a flannel nightgown and climbed in beside him, lay awake for a while hearing a little wind around the house, the measured far-off sound of crashing surf, felt the warmth of his body against hers, was at peace, content and drowsy, and fell asleep herself.

At six it was light. The air was cold but she was warm under the covers, in the sheets. With one hand she groped on the floor for woolen knee socks, found them, pulled them on under the covers, braced herself, then slipped out of bed and hurried to the fireplace in the parlor next door to start a fire. When it was blazing nicely she stood and let it warm her, waited to make sure the logs had really caught the flame and would hold the fire, looked out through the windows and door, which rattled a little, to the deck and a wide band of sky scumbled with clouds. Moving closer she could see the edge of the beach at the shoreline, sea, a far horizon.

She went back to the bedroom and Graham was awake, his hands clasped behind his head, smiling at her.

Neither spoke. She stood at the foot of the bed, slipped off her nightgown over her head, but left her knee socks on.

"Oh, God, you're beautiful," he said.

"I'm glad you think so . . . But I'm freezing!"

She chuckled and climbed in beside him. They pulled the covers up and the bedspread over their heads, and on their sides facing each other they were in a kind of tent through which the early morning light filtered faintly over their skin.

He was still wearing his shorts but was bursting out of them.

"Why don't you take those silly things off," Kitty said.

She did this for him and then began to stroke him everywhere, still a little surprised at the shape and size of him, as he was immeasurably fascinated by her exact curvilinear shapes and dimensions, textures and warmths (which he could never recall, exactly, the minute she was gone.)

"Some places you're as smooth as a baby," she said.

"When you were a little kid did you ever have show parties with the little boy next door?" he asked.

"Vaguely remember one time," Kitty said.

"As the little boy with the little girl I was caught and punished," Graham said.

"You were only being naturally curious."

"As I told you, my parents and I didn't always agree on everything."

"What about later on?" Kitty asked.

"What, later on?"

"Show parties with little girls. Or not so little girls."

"Who? Me?"

"I never expected you to be innocent, or a virgin," Kitty said. "I won't ask any more questions. But now I think I want you to kiss me some more right now, and do that too, right now, right now..."

Spent, Kitty lay back and recited:

> Here's to the happiest couple in town
> Ten toes up and ten toes down.
> First a moment of sheer delight,
> Then it's fanny to fanny
> The rest of the night!

Graham laughed.

"I never heard that before. Where do you pick these things up?"

"Some girl in school."

They assumed the spoons position, drawn-up knees fitting snugly into the backs of drawn-up knees, Graham in front, and dozed off until 9 A.M.

In the bright daylight, for the first time Kitty noticed the indented scars and slightly raised cicatrices along his left side below his arm, half a dozen of them.

"What are these from?" she asked, suddenly serious.

"Oh. Flak. They weren't all that serious."

"Why didn't you tell me before?"

"I didn't want to worry you. I was out of the infirmary in less than a week."

But his voice and face had turned serious, too, and for a few minutes they were silent as they dressed.

"I'm starving," Kitty said finally. "I could eat a horse. Let's get some breakfast."

They walked along the beach. A convivial Labrador retriever appeared from somewhere and joined them, his long tail sweeping ceaselessly. Graham threw a few pieces of driftwood for the dog to fetch, then seemed to tire of that.

"Who belongs to you?" Kitty asked the dog.

Guess, said the dog, looking at her, then loped on ahead of them.

Graham seemed to Kitty to be a kind of convalescent. Not all of his happy-go-lucky manner of before had gone; his face was the same, his ambling way of walking hadn't changed, but he was different. She could see the difference in the expression of his mouth, which seemed at the same time to reflect new assurance and new doubts. How could it be otherwise? He wasn't some automaton. He had seen men die and had escaped death himself. He had carried death into the enemy country and had seen things she hoped she would never see.

He stooped to pick up a knarled twist of driftwood. Tensed, alert, overjoyed, the retriever dashed unerringly after it when Graham flung it like a boomerang in a low, slightly curving arc.

They made love in every room of the house, even the kitchen, on the beds, on the couch, on the rug, and once, convinced no one could see them, on the open deck.

Wrapped in themselves, in each other, even so the world was in sharpened focus. Everything stood out with particular clarity, the contours of the island earth and shore, the colors of foliage, the light above. They wondered if this was the first time they had ever really seen the sky. For Kitty it truly was the first time she had taken in the green immensity of the sea.

They made love, slept long, walked for hours on the empty

beach, along the road, across the heath, and saw no one, built fires, cooked, ate, drank beer, lay in each others arms while the Victrola played the records Kitty had brought, seized the moment, and did not talk about the war.

And then the week was up.

25

"I love this house," Kitty said. "I'll remember it as long as I live."

The old man with the old car came for them and brought them to the afternoon boat, and both Kitty and Graham were conscious of his uniform, his ribbons, his military greatcoat, his cap.

"We've hardly looked at the town and it's so beautiful," Kitty said.

But Graham was looking ahead of him. The boat rumbled and shuddered, began moving, and the wharves and sheds, masts, houses, steeples pulled back, slipped away, and soon were gone. They held mittened hands and watched the gulls and the gray-green swells for a while until they were uncomfortably cold and went inside where they stayed till they reached the mainland.

Neither the bus to Boston nor the train to New York was conducive to much conversation; it was enough for them to be together, look at each other, memorizing. Then it was 10:30 and the train was pulling into Grand Central Station and they were getting her suitcase and his carryall down from the overhead rack, and Kitty began to think apprehensively of the scene ahead when he saw her apartment for the first time.

"It's going to need dusting after a week, and there won't be anything to eat for breakfast," she said, "but we have to eat out mostly anyway—I just have a hot plate—and nothing to drink either because I'm still not old enough to buy it, but you can do that—I have an icebox. I hope you like it anyway. It's not fancy, but it's my little place."

In the taxi she sat close to him, turned toward him. The expression on his mouth seemed almost forbidding, and she tried to kiss it away, with only partial success. Graham didn't like displays of affection in public, but the cabbie was paying attention to the traffic and didn't notice.

Fifty-second Street was thronged with soldiers, sailors, civilians. Friday night at eleven. Kitty ran up the steps of her brownstone to unlock the door while Graham was settling with the driver. When he came up to the doorway his expression was furious.

"What's the matter?" Kitty asked, alarmed.

"I'll tell you when we get upstairs."

The apartment smelled stuffy. Kitty opened a front window, and the noise of the street came up.

"What happened? Why are you so mad?"

"Do any other girls, women, live in this building?"

"I don't know. No, only some old people I hardly ever see. Why?"

"Some godamned sailor down there saw you and said, 'Hey, Lieutenant, how long do you have to stand in line for that?' He was in a cab and was gone before I could kick his teeth in. Kitty, of all the streets in this city to live on, why in God's name did you have to pick 52nd Street!? Strip joints, gin mills, drugs, prostitution obviously. What else? The Mafia?"

"It's those sailors and soldiers, some of them anyway, that're spoiling everything," Kitty said. "I've never seen a prostitute, at least I don't think I have. I don't know, I wasn't looking for them. They don't come in where I'm working. Harry Field, the owner would kick them out." Her voice was shaking. "I wrote you why I came here to live. To learn what I could and get a chance to play and sing myself. The music is what matters."

Her apartment, which had seemed so cozy to her before, now seemed shabby, inadequate, something to be ashamed of.

Graham still had his coat on.

"I don't want my wife living and working in an atmosphere like this! Where you're automatically insulted by some sailor! I don't want you associated with people with reputations like Billie Holiday's. A guy in the squadron has friends in show business who know about her."

"I don't know anything about her private life, but she's a great singer!"

"How can you say that?" he scoffed. "A 'great' singer? For God's sake. A whorehouse singer." His slow, drawling voice that cracked occasionally on a note still had the power to amuse, to charm, but now it was saying harsh and ignorant things.

"What do you know about it? Do I tell you how to fly airplanes?"

"She worked in one! She's on drugs. You should hear some of the stories."

"God, you're beginning to sound like Sister Edmund. Maybe you think I worked in one, too. Maybe you think I'm a whore now. Like that sailor does!"

"Shut up, Kitty! I never said that or implied it, and you know it! I said I don't want you working in an atmosphere like this!"

"You shut up! Don't shout at me in my own house."

"I didn't mean to shout, and I'm sorry I said shut up. This street has a bad reputation. Don't you know that? I'm not making it up. You must know Gene Krupa is in jail for possession of narcotics."

"That was in California."

"Other characters have been arrested around here. Somebody else was picked up on a Mann Act charge."

"I don't know what that means."

"Transporting girls across a state line for immoral purposes."

"Where do you read these things? Do they sell all the American papers in that little English village?"

"People send me clippings."

"People? Who? Your mother and father?"

He was silent. So that was how it was going.

"Making sure you hear all the dirt so you'll think the worst of me. The big Minneapolis music lovers!"

"These things happened, didn't they? *They* didn't write the stories. They just read them and thought I should know what's going on, too. I didn't realize it was this bad."

He walked over to the front window and looked down. He swept his hand from left to right.

"All you have to do is look at the place. Cheap, sleazy dives."

"Not all of them." She was angry. "There's some beautiful music down there. Do you know who's down there right now? Art Tatum, one of the world's greatest pianists. Rachmaninoff admired him. People like Vladimir Horowitz come to hear him!"

But he was obviously unimpresseed.

"If they're so great, why don't they get out of these joints? Play in theaters, on the radio?"

"A lot of them can't get hired because they're Negroes."

"Now wait a minute, Louis Armstrong. Duke Ellington . . ." He was ticking off his fingers. "If they're really good . . ."

"There are a lot of great musicians who just aren't famous enough yet who can't . . . oh, I don't want to argue any more. Why are we doing this? Tearing each other up like this? This was supposed to be a homecoming. Christmas in November . . . Great!"

They had both gone too far but maybe not so far they couldn't go back—not to where they had been but at least to where they could live. Graham took off his coat now, his jacket, loosened his tie, ran one hand through his hair.

"No, you're right. Right. We shouldn't argue." His voice had flattened.

He's humoring me, Kitty thought suddenly.

"That sailor made me see red," he went on, "but I shouldn't take that out on you. Anyway, here we are. Is it still early enough to get something to eat? That sandwich on the train didn't stay with me."

"The Concarneau's open. Just below us."

"Fine!" His voice was forced.

A shiver zig-zagged through her like a little silent bolt of lightening. The fight, Graham's still uneducated attitude about music and musicians, had caused it, but in the back of her mind a voice had also been asking, *How do you know Harry Field would kick them out? What if Bernie Fossbinder had kicked my mother out?*

She kissed him on the mouth as he stood with his hands at his sides.

"I need you so much," she said in a low voice, then louder, "Come on, you must be starving."

The Concarneau's chef-owner, a favorite of Kitty's and an admirer—she practiced her French with him—was able to come up with mushroom omelettes, and he and his wife, madame behind the reception desk—she, suspicious, grasping, often bad-tempered, but now putting on her most charming manner—were introduced to the returning hero, the husband they had heard about, and these civilities, satisfaction of simple hunger, the relaxing effect of a bottle of 1939 *Quincy* (compliments of the house), cold and flinty on the tongue, helped to restore Kitty's spirits, and Graham's perhaps, and they smiled at each other and went up sleepily to bed and in the night made love again, and afterwards he fell asleep but she could not. In the morning, a gray, chilly November day, the street seemed even more deserted and shabby than usual. Graham slept on. Kitty left a note and went to Sixth Avenue to buy milk, rolls, and butter. Graham was still asleep, and she fell asleep herself on the couch and woke at eleven. Graham was showering.

"Good morning!" she called. "I'll put on some coffee."

"Fine."

She hadn't planned any specific sightseeing. As she had imagined it, they would just wander around on her favorite streets to her favorite places, and it wouldn't really matter where they went. Now she wondered what they would do. To begin with, get out of the apartment and off 52nd Street as quickly as possible. A long lunch somewhere. The Palm Court at the Plaza where they could watch people coming and going. No, save that for another day. Take the Fifth Avenue bus to Greenwich Village. Lunch at the Lafayette, which was very old and French—the French 'Concarneau' seemed to have pleased him—and where the people around them might be even more interesting to look at. Then stroll around the Village.

When Graham came out, freshly shaven, dressed, looking wonderful to her, she had a sudden inspiration.

"Darling, I've made up my mind," she said bravely. "I'm moving back to the Barbizon. Or if they don't happen to have any room, one of the other hotels for women, the Midston House—I have a friend who lives there—I forget the names of the others. They're all about the same, I think."

"I'd feel a lot better if you did," he said. "So where can we go today?"

She told him what she had planned.
"You're the guide," he said.

In the fin-de-siècle dining room of the Hotel Lafayette, below a window half-covered by a red velvet cafe curtain hung from a brass rod, watching a bent old waiter in a tuxedo whisking silver bells off plates of veal medaillions and mushrooms napped with madeira-flavored *demi-glace*, Graham appeared to relax a little. An aura of luminosity seemed to surround them. Indeed, it was *they* who were noticed by the distinguished older patrons—the good-looking young officer with the wings and row of ribbons on his jacket, the graceful, pretty girl in a matching wool skirt and jacket that were wonderfully becoming.

From the Lafayette on University Place they walked to Washington Square in the chill air of pale sunshine. The Washington Arch was grand but at the entrance to the square Fifth Avenue seems as narrow as a village street. Saturday afternoon and the square was a playground, a carnival. Roller skaters, balloon sellers, sidewalk artists, an old man playing a violin, strolling crowds. On Washington Square North the Greek revival houses kept their aristocratic distance.

"I love it around here," Kitty said, and clicked a twig along the wrought iron fences. Graham was noncommittal.

They had coffee in a little Italian pastry shop on Thompson Street, and when they went outside again the sky was overcast. Across the street, a little art gallery, then a bookstore.

"Why don't we look," Kitty said.

They browsed in one, then the other, Graham at once patient and restless. He covered up a yawn with a gloved fist.

"I'm not used to wine at lunch. Made me sleepy."

"When we get back you can take a nap."

They cabbed it back uptown. It was 4:30, growing darker and colder. Part of that afternoon—moving around, going somewhere, lunching at the Lafayette—Kitty had been able to put the bitter quarrel of the night before out of her mind, but she had not recovered from it and it came back to her now. That particular fight was over, but the causes of it had not gone away. They had had a lovely week on Nantucket but that was over. She wished they could have stayed there. Their last week together had started badly and as the cab drove north, uptown, and the numbers climbed, she began to think of ways she might rescue it. He would have to help, but she was the host, he was the guest, this was her town, he was the visitor. It seemed more incumbent on her to lead the way.

Back in her apartment Graham napped and Kitty sat by the window looking at 52nd Street lighting up, until it was time for her to bathe and dress for work.

Eight forty-five now. In her stylish, conservative, slightly off-the-shoulder black dress, pearl necklace, her face and hands illuminated by a pin spot, Kitty sat, ladylike, before her piano at Harry's. At a nearby table, sat Graham alone.

Soft chords backing her up, Kitty began slowly, gently to sing the verse to "I've Got the World on a String," and if any bemused listener didn't recognize that introduction the clouds parted when she began swinging the lilting title stanza.

Kitty liked to group songs together to give her performance a pattern—songs by the same composer, songs with similar themes or titles and so on—and to throw in a few words of explanation if that seemed necessary—a very few words. She did not believe patter and jokes were the business of a musician, with all due respect to the just-deceased Fats Waller whose playing and pioneer role she admired.

"Another song by Harold Arlen—new this year," said her amplified voice, and she played and sang the poignant "My Shining Hour." Followed by "Let's Take a Walk around the Block" with Yip Harburg and Ira Gershwin kidding their way through the Depression. And the lovely, neglected "This Time the Dream's on Me":

> Somewhere, some day
> We'll be close together.
> Wait and see.
> Oh by the way,
> This time the dream's on me.

As she played she was acutely conscious that as a place, Harry's was no worse than any of the other boxcars along the street, but no better either, tiny tables crammed greedily close together, a pall of cigarette smoke from waist level to the ceiling, waiters who fleeced customers and the management impartially when they thought they could get away with it, hustling bartenders, and the seemingly inevitable hard-eyed characters, at least untrustworthy and disreputable, if not actually dangerous, who drifted in and out and seemed to know the manager. The Ralphs of this world. Maybe they had gone to parochial school or done time together, who knows.

Harry Field had replaced the Rex Wilkins Quintet with a journeyman all-white quartet—vibraharp, tenor sax, piano, drums—not bad, neat, but the discerning listener learned not to expect any inspired solos from the sax or piano, no Hamptony-Norvoish flight from the vibraharp. Kitty was a better pianist than the bandsman and she charitably soft-peddled, down-played this side of her performance and emphasized her singing. In effect, now, hers was a dual rather than an intermission performance.

But now it was the quartet's turn and she broke to a round of applause to join Graham. And Harry Field who had introduced himself to Graham moments before.

"Well, Lieutenant, you got a lot to be proud of. Those ribbons and this fine girl here. I know a great talent when I hear one. In a few years you're gonna see her up there with Dinah Shore, Peggy Lee, Jo Stafford, the big names. I'll leave you two. I know you got a lot to talk about."

Harry Field walked away from the table, and at the other end of the room said to his wife, "Something is bugging that kid. He's not what I expected, not from Kitty's description. I guess fighting a war changes people. I hope they haven't had a tiff. They don't have enough time together to afford it."

"That's for sure."

"He's a nice man," Kitty said when Harry Field had left. "I think he's honest, and he and his wife have been very nice to me. They've really been my chaperones on the Street. Other people, too." Graham looked dubious. "Really darling. Nobody bothers me. Sometimes some sailor or soldier tries to get fresh, but they don't get very far. I've got friends all along the Street. Musicians help each other out and respect each other. The men aren't out to seduce all the girl vocalists. Take Coleman Hawkins. He's devoted to his family. I don't mean he's the only one, just that he's famous... But I see I'm not convincing you, so why don't we change the subject. Did you at least like my show? I know it isn't perfect."

"Kitty, I'm no judge. May I say something, though? I don't much like those torch songs. At least not you singing them."

"You mean 'Stormy Weather' and 'That Old Black Magic'? I thought you might say that. You're probably right. They're not really my kind of songs. But if I was going to do Arlen, I didn't see how I could leave them out. Maybe I should just work a few lines of them into a medley. Or just play them, not sing. You see, you're my best critic. I need you."

He smiled a little, squeezed her hand, but was obviously uncomfortable, out of place. He liked beer but was not a heavy drinker, and beer tonight wasn't relaxing him.

"Darling, you don't have to sit here the whole evening. The band isn't that interesting, and you'd have to sit through them one more time and me twice. Why don't you take a break and come back for my last show. You could go to a movie. Or read in the apartment..."

"Maybe a movie," Graham said. "These chairs aren't the most comfortable. Where should I go—Broadway or one of those places?"

"The Little Carnegie—on West 57th between Sixth and Seventh—has a good English comedy called *Jeannie*. But maybe you've seen it over there."

"No."

"It's cute. Michael Redgrave is divine and the girl—Barbara Somebody—is funny."

During her second set, Kitty played mostly instrumental things, sang only three songs. On her break, she bummed a cigarette from Frank, the bartender, who lit it for her, surprised; he had never seen her smoke before. It was only the third, possibly the fourth cigarette she had ever tried to smoke. She didn't want to get the habit, knew they wouldn't do her voice any good, didn't inhale, but was nervous enough to want one now. Awkwardly she held it and puffed at it and sat back at her table, wondering what she would do. For one thing, scuttle her original plans for the last set—

boppish sort of things she had picked up, worked out, from listening to Thelonious Monk. Something new and different. But she wasn't sure she really appreciated everything about the new music herself. (Trumpet and sax playing the same fast notes simultaneously tended to get on her nerves, for example. She liked the same notes separately.) For sure Graham wouldn't like it. Instead, she replanned a series of the kinds of things she did best, that might appeal to him the most.

If anything did.

Always since she had met him and he had asked her, out of politeness mostly, to play a request that indicated a lack of musical sophistication, she had kept her music separate from loving him. She had thought when she thought about it at all, which wasn't often, that loving her and listening to her would educate his untrained ear, but she knew now that loving her and loving her music did not necessarily follow.

As long as she was playing or singing or both, everything was all right, everything fell into place, and she believed she had the power to make people happy for a moment or two, but she knew, too, and was acutely, painfully conscious of the sad fact now, that there were those, probably the majority, who, if they could not, as they did not, appreciate Stravinsky or even Mozart, Gershwin, Goodman, Hawkins, Holiday ... the list could go on and on—Graham had been no more impressed by the names Rachmaninoff and Horowitz than he had been by Tatum—could not, did not appreciate her, could tune her out, brush aside what she was trying to do as of no importance.

Graham never minded a roomful of popular music from records or the radio or the orchestra on the bandstand, good music or schmaltz. It was all the same to him. It wasn't his fault. He was like a million others. Maybe he was born tone-deaf. He had a tin ear. As a college man he had joined the crowds before the big bands of the day, jitterbugged after a fashion, got caught up in the general enthusiasm for Krupa's drumming or loud, driving, upper-register trumpet solos, but he was just as happy or uncaring in a ballroom with Guy Lombardo or Irving Bennett.

But she loved him. If you love someone you couldn't always have everything your way; you had to make compromises. To a stranger like Graham, 52nd Street probably did look pretty slummy. But it wasn't the only place for her. There were better clubs, hotel lounges, there were recording studios, there was radio. One thing she could do now—while the war was still on—was to sign up to go on a tour with the U.S.O. Maybe she could manage to get to England on some trip! In the meantime, she'd move off the Street, get a room at the Midston House. With Danielle there too that'd be fun.

Gliding out of her second-to-last number she saw that Graham still hadn't reappeared and decided—what the hell—to conclude with a little bop after all with its dissonant chords and random, sometimes nonmelodic lines. Midway through that he came in the door and waited, standing, frowning, for her to stop making these displeasing sounds. But neither mentioned this when she got ready to go home with him.
"How did you like the flick?"
"It was amusing."
"I've got an idea for you tomorrow. When was the last time you saw an American football game?"
"Who's playing?"
"You've got a choice. The Dodgers and the Green Bay Packers at Ebbets Field or the Giants and the Chicago Cardinals at the Polo Grounds. I'm not too keen on football myself so I'd stay here, but tomorrow night I'll go to the hockey game with you at Madison Square Garden. The New York Rangers and the Toronto Maple Leafs. The Rangers haven't won a game all year, but people still like them."
"Sounds good. Right now I'm bushed."
"It's been a long day for both of us. You can sack in as late as you want."
He was asleep as soon as his head hit the pillow, and she didn't wake him to say good night or for any other reason, and was soon asleep herself.

26

When she returned from a late mass at St. Patrick's he was still asleep, but shortly thereafter he stirred and the smell of perking coffee woke him. She brought him a cup with sugar, no cream.

"Good morning!" she said. "How did you sleep?"

"S'there anything besides a top or a log?"

"Not that I know of. 'Like the dead' is a little grim. We," she segued brightly into a new topic, "are going to brunch at the Palm Court of the Plaza Hotel. Do they know about brunch in England yet? It's the big new thing around here. But we ought to go pretty soon so we won't have to stand in line too long. What game did you decide to see?"

"The Giants and the Cardinals."

"It starts at 2:30 and I don't want you to miss the kickoff. You'd better give yourself an hour to get out to the Polo Grounds and get your ticket."

He yawned and stretched his arms. "I never realized you were such an organizer."

"I just haven't had a chance to show you before. I'm the one who lives here, so I have to know my way around."

"Then I guess I'd better get dressed."

She was feeling a little sensual even though a short while before she had been in a spiritual state—or in as spiritual a state as she ever got, more of one than usual since she had formulated certain special new silent prayers that had given her hope, confidence, her present high-spirited, overflowing mood and manner, even her sensualness; the spirit and the flesh weren't always opposites, opposed, but might just as easily lead quickly one to the other in either direction. And so even though she was fully dressed and they did need to hurry a little to stay on schedule, if he had made a move, she would not have protested or resisted, and when he didn't she almost made a move herself, then decided, no, they could wait until after the hockey game, after a late supper at Jack Dempsey's that evening. Sex alone couldn't solve anything but it was necessary to them and the easiest bond to maintain while they tried to work out everything else.

"Isn't this place gorgeous?" Kitty said as they crossed the Plaza lobby toward the spacious atrium of the Palm Court, under its Tiffany ceiling, where a string orchestra played dusty waltzes and a cold-eyed maitre d', of humble origins in some mountain village or seaport of Europe and therefore now haughtier than any grand duke, stood guard behind a velvet rope. The line at twenty past noon was fairly long and didn't move for fifteen minutes or so. Then six people immediately behind the rope turned out to be a party of six who could be seated at the same table and one group of three complained of the delay, thus dooming themselves, in their odd-number vulnerability, to being refused vacant tables for four or the privilege of being squeezed around tables for two, and Kitty and Graham had the advantage of their attractiveness and his uniform, his ribbons. By twelve forty-five they were seated. The service then from wheeled steam carts was swift, and they were soon being helped to scrambled eggs, kidneys, bacon, broiled tomatoes. They had enough time, though no more than that.

"I didn't tell you," Graham said. "A friend of mine, a fellow in my squadron, is a New Yorker. Westchester County. He was on the same flight coming back. He told me to give him a ring while I'm here."

"Oh, well good!" Kitty said. "One thing we have to do is figure things for you to do at night while I'm working. You've got a million choices—plays, musicals, movies—but it'd be more fun going with someone. Maybe your friend could come in one night anyway. Westchester. I've never been out there, but I hear it's very nice."

"Do you ever hear from the Barrys?"

"Joe, Jim, and Matt. Birthday cards, Joe a couple of other times. Nothing from Mr. and Mrs. I didn't expect to. I'm going to send them cards at Christmas and see what happens."

He looked puzzled.

"Did I ask this before?"

"Right after you got to Nantucket."

He shook his head. "I was really out of it for a couple of days."

"Well, you're fine now."

Kitty thought to mention her idea to go on U.S.O. tours but decided to wait until she could check into the possibilities. She couldn't be sure what Graham's reaction would be either. It might be better to surprise him by just showing up sometime in England! The thought excited her and it seemed safe enough simply to ask the mostly rhetorical question, "Graham, are the U.S.O. shows over there any good? Do the soldiers really like them? I've seen newsreels of Bob Hope and people like that, and it sure looks as though the audiences are huge and everybody is really enjoying themselves. Especially when girls come out on stage. I think they must do a lot of good. A girl I know at one of the clubs, a singer, gets all teary when she talks about her trip. All those guys out there scared and lonely and bored and frustrated, just *seeing* an American girl even from a distance does them a world of good, and they're so *appreciative* ... I get a little fan mail from GIs and sailors, you know, kids and guys who've heard me here, and they're so sweet, really *nice* letters, nothing suggestive or dirty or anything. I haven't time to write long letters to any of them, but I've had some wallet-sized copies made of one of my publicity photos and I write a line or so on the back of those ..."

She had been so wound up she had hardly touched her brunch and noticing that now, she began to eat it rapidly even though it had gotten cold. Graham had cleaned his plate and was waiting for her. He didn't seem too interested in what she had been saying but answered her question. "I've seen parts of a couple of shows. They're all right, I guess. All depends on who's up there on stage. I don't necessarily go in for what the average GI whistles at."

He looked at his wristwatch.

"Only one o'clock," Kitty said. "You have plenty of time. But I'm finished. You can call for the check."

After Graham had taken a cab to the Polo Grounds, Kitty got another inspiration and back in her apartment telephoned Danielle.

"Danielle, would you do me a tremendous favor and ask right away if the Midston House has a room for me? Now? As early as tomorrow? If you have any pull at all, use it. I'd really appreciate it. Tell a fib if you have to. Tell them I have to leave my apartment because the owner's mother is moving in. Anything. Thanks a million."

Kitty didn't begin to get anxious until 6:30 when Graham still hadn't returned and it was dark outside and the Street was beginning to rev up for the long night ahead. At seven, the doorbell rang. His face was flushed and he was grinning, not at her but at something remembered.

"People I was sitting next to insisted I go to some Irish pub on Third Avenue with them after the game. They drove. Great bunch. Where are we going? Hockey game, right? Better shower first."

"Better eat something first, too. Thought we could just get something light at an Automat so you could see what one is like. After the game I want to take you to Dempsey's for a good steak. OK, you shower. I'm glad you're safe . . . I've got good news! I can move to the Midston House on Wednesday!"

"Good," he said, hardly overjoyed but as though he had expected at least that, nothing less, and left Kitty dangling, a little deflated, as he pulled the bathroom door closed behind him.

The Manhattan clam chowder they ordered was served across a steam-table counter and Graham didn't really pay any attention to the banks of self-service compartments like post office boxes that made the Automat different from other restaurants. From there on

Eighth Avenue they walked to Madison Square Garden. There was trash on the sidewalks, in the gutters.

"This has got to be the dirtiest city I've ever seen," Graham said. "Worse than Chicago. London is a war zone, but they try to keep it clean."

Kitty had neither the evidence nor the inclination to argue with him and this wasn't her side of town anyway.

She had gone with Danielle once before to see the Rangers lose and liked the slam-bang, never-a-dull-moment pace of professional hockey. The Rangers lost again—their ninth loss in a row, every game this season, but they held Toronto to a tie score for a while and fought skillfully all the way. The announcer's voice echoed in the rafters of the half-empty stadium.

"I forgot to ask," Kitty said on top of the crowd noises. "Who won the football game?"

"Giants. Twenty-four to thirteen."

Jack Dempsey's afterwards was crowded and lively. They were both hungry, their steaks were done as ordered, and they saw the famous owner himself. Graham drank more beer than she had seen him drink before in this short a time. She held his hand during the cab ride home and went to the bathroom to wash, to put on her nightgown. When she came out he was asleep, snoring a little. She didn't wake him and alone on her side of the bed she lay awake a while.

She could hear him in the next room telephoning his friend in Mamaroneck. Laughing. The conversation seemed to be conducted in a private language.

"Sandy's coming into town," Graham said. "We're having lunch. You don't mind?"

"No, I told you. I'm glad you have a friend here. Have fun. I need to practice this afternoon anyway, especially after a week off."

It was a long lunch. He came back to the apartment just a little after she did, at four in the afternoon. Getting over being tight as a tick.

"Good thing you're not driving, darling," she said, kidding him, kissing him afterwards.

Then she said, "Listen, I've got another brilliant idea. Tomorrow morning why don't we get up early and hightail it way out to the end of Long Island on the train. Montauk Point. I've never been out there and Danielle says it's like Cape Cod so maybe it'll be like Nantucket, too. We can take a picnic. We can take books to read on the train."

"OK, I'd like that."

While he napped she went out and brought back sandwich ingredients for their trip and for their dinner now carryout cartons from one of the Chinese restaurants on the Street. While she worked he went to Moss Hart's *Winged Victory*, the army air corps show.

He came into Harry's while the quartet was playing the final number of its second set, sat at Kitty's table and ordered a bottle of beer.

"Who are these people paying to keep them out of the draft?" he asked, indicating the members of the quartet, two of whom were in their twenties.

"They don't make enough to pay anybody. I don't know. Why don't you ask them? I walk down the Street and see a lot of guys in civilian clothes around here, office buildings all over the place full of them. What about those football and hockey players? Why don't you ask them too?"

Graham's chest filled with air. Then he let it out again. Kitty could see this very clearly, also the line of his mouth.

"You're angry with me," he said.

"You're angry with me," she said.

"I asked a simple question . . ."

"No, it wasn't a simple question. You implied musicians are draft dodgers. Maybe some of them are, I don't know. Just don't pick on my profession because musicians are out here where you can see them. Some of them are . . ."

"I know, I know, don't tell me. Out there entertaining the troops."

"Well, all right, they are, they are. So they don't fire a gun. Neither do you for that matter."

He looked so profoundly hurt by her remark, by the equation she had made, she was almost sorry she had made it—maybe she had overreacted—and upstairs in her apartment after her last set, the apartment illuminated only by street lamps and the reflections of blue and red and green nightclub lights of 52nd Street, she behaved as seductively as she knew how and made love to him to soothe his wounded vanity. In the morning as they hurried to catch the 8 A.M. train to Long Island he seemed to have forgotten the quarrel.

After checking train schedules they decided to terminate the outbound, eastward leg of their journey at the Hamptons and Sag Harbor to give themselves more time outside, on the beaches. The train was not crowded to begin with and once past the close-in commuter suburbs was three-quarters empty as it chugged its leisurely way in and out of neat little stations with English or Indian names and across farmland and sandy scrub and waterways. Graham had a detective story, Kitty had Marquand's latest, *So Little Time*. It seemed so nice to her and relaxing to sit across from him, reading, looking out the window occasionally.

My husband, she thought possessively, contentedly, *for all his faults. Well, I have them too.*

After a while Graham tired of his book and Kitty marked her place with a ticket stub when he began telling her about London, about apparently amusing incidents involving him and his friend, Sandy Cameron, and other Eighth Air Force officers and enlisted men Kitty found sometimes difficult to follow, but she enjoyed just listening to the sound of his drawling, amusing voice. She was glad she had thought to come out here—away from the city—where he was happier.

The skies were partly cloudy and the air was cold but they were warmly dressed and Kitty rediscovered her newfound preference for walking on deserted late autumn beaches over crowded summer ones, and it seemed to her her ambivalent feelings about cities and countrysides might hold the key to a solution of their problem.

On the beach at Southhampton two soldiers approached and saluted.

"Is it OK if we walk down this way?" Graham asked.

"Yes, sir," one man said. "No problem. Beach is only off-limits after dark."

Later, they passed a coastguardsman at a distance, but otherwise they were alone.

Sag Harbor, reached by a little bus, had been a whaling port. Old wooden houses and small wooden churches, water, boats, a long way and quite effectively cut off from New York City, with a separate and perhaps superior way of life, but too far from the port of Manhattan, which she needed, ever to live here, a fact that dampened a little of her optimism of an hour earlier. But she shook the thought away; she would not be daunted.

On the trip back they had a railroad car absolutely to themselves and when they weren't reading they sat at the rear of it, their arms around each other's waist. The conductor, having collected their tickets, went away. At six in the evening as they neared the city only the trains going in the opposite direction were crowded. A few people climbed aboard at suburban stations but seeing the officer and his girl so close together left them alone and took seats in adjoining cars. The conductor opened the door behind them only long enough to call out, "Pennsylvania Station!" Kitty glanced back at the closed door to the platform and assured of their isolation and under Graham's greatcoat he had taken from the overhead rack and had folded across his lap, she began lightly stroking the inside of his nearest thigh. Unexpected, it excited him quickly, powerfully—she soon determined that, and whispered, "*One new thing after the other. Let's go!*" and tongued his ear, and they hurried out of the train and the station and found a cab and trembled all the way from 34th to 52nd streets and up the outside and inside steps to her apartment and went wild, both of them, standing, kneeling, lying on the rug, bringing each other to one of the great orgasms of the year on the eastern seaboard.

"Wow," said Kitty. "That was pretty sensational."

"You see what a day in the country does for you?" Graham said.

That evening while she worked he saw Josephine Hull in *Arsenic and Old Lace* and sat in a hotel bar for a while afterwards, did not go to Harry's, and when he returned to the apartment she was asleep.

Wednesday they slept all morning and spent the better part of the afternoon packing up and moving Kitty's belongings to her new room at the Midston House. Graham was not permitted above the ground floor, but his place was taken by a sturdy chambermaid. Then they took a cab to the Waldorf where Graham had reserved a double room for his last two nights in New York. They ate at the hotel and he spent the evening at the Capitol Theater watching Humphrey Bogart in *Sahara* and Lawrence Welk on stage.

Thanksgiving was fair and warmer, in the sixties, a good day for walking in the park, for almost anything except perhaps holiday feasting. They had half planned to find a Lutheran church for both of them to attend, but they overslept and so didn't go to church at all.

They both decided it really *wasn't* Thanksgiving, at least not a traditional one, and that a turkey dinner in some restaurant would be blah. Consequently, in the afternoon they climbed to the top of the Statue of Liberty, took long walks and short cab rides from Battery Park to Chinatown, and when they had worked up an appetite ended up at Suerkens, a very old restaurant near City Hall, eating sauerbraten, red cabbage, and potato pancakes in a nineteenth-century ambiance of mahogany and stained glass. Then it was time to return to the hotel to freshen up and change clothes in time to meet Sandy Cameron and his fiancée and one of Sandy's sisters, Ann, and her beau, under the clock at the Biltmore.

Nine in the evening and the Biltmore lobby buzzed with the chatter of collegians and men in uniform, mostly officers—like Graham, Sandy, and the navy man escorting Ann.

Sandy Cameron, whose black hair somewhat belied his nickname, took both of Kitty's hands in his and looked directly into her eyes for about five seconds above a slight, close-mouthed smile, and she decided he was vain and that she really didn't like him. Ann Cameron might have been Sandy's twin, though she was four years younger, a freshman at some expensive-sounding junior college. Camel's hair coat. Her roommate and Sandy's fiancée, an ash blonde from California, gray tweed Chesterfield coat with black velvet collar and cuffs. Both girls still had traces of tan from some fashionable island summer kept partly renewed by fall sailing and tennis. Introductions to them were delayed a few moments. They had immediately spotted friends of both sexes, uttered squeals of recognition, and went off a few yards to exchange exclamations.

The ensign, who reminded Kitty a little of Tom Webster, the boy in Lake Forest, was presented to her, and by that time the girls returned and went through the motions of greeting Kitty—the

California girl said, "Hi," while Sandy's sister confined herself to a socially acceptable smile—then immediately both returned to their own animated conversation.

The plan was to go dancing at the Cotillion Room of the Pierre, then someplace afterwards. Though the Westchester group had taken the train from Mamaroneck, they didn't have to worry about catching some last return train after midnight; they were spending the night at Sandy's grandparents' house in the East 60s.

Kitty found the Cotillion Room fancy, fussy, and dull. An Irving Bennett-style orchestra played. Ann, in a red faille cocktail suit, and her roommate, sheathed in black with a short-sleeved lacy top, were still a little giggly from early evening whiskey sours and Thanksgiving dinner wine; now they were too young to be served more alcohol but sipped from Sandy's and the ensign's glasses of beer when the head waiter wasn't looking. The couples danced, exchanged partners once each, and back at the table the men talked of boats and the Army-Navy game at West Point that Saturday, and the girls talked to each other about themselves, their crowd. While Kitty accepted being left out as the natural fate of the outsider, she did not believe she would ever fit in with these people, not on their terms, not on her own, and she was reminded not only of Lake Forest but of that Lake Shore Drive apartment where she had first seen Graham and of the house in Evanston where they had met again and where she had not belonged either.

At 11:30 Sandy asked, "Where should we go now? La Martinique? 52nd Street?"

"Please, not 52nd Street," Kitty said. "This is my night off."

"You suggest then," Sandy said. "You're the expert."

"Cafe Society Uptown," Kitty said. "I think it's the best place in town. There's a midnight show."

She wanted Graham to see what a clean, spacious, well-lighted jazz club could be like.

No objections from anyone. None of them had ever been there.

A side table for six was available after a five-minute wait. Then the performance began a minute after they were seated, and Kitty knew almost immediately she had made a mistake bringing them here. Though they spoke in low voices and half-whispers, they had no intention of suspending their conversations while the show was going on. The spirituals of The Golden Gate Quartet might be an acquired taste, Kitty thought, and maybe it was possible to watch a dance team and talk at the same time, but not to listen to Teddy Wilson and Mildred Bailey and a trumpeter as good as Joe Thomas was not only a stupid waste of money but was rude and unforgivable.

They noticed things though. When the performance ended, dancing began. Among the couples on the floor appeared a black man and a white woman.

"Do you see what *I* see?" Ann Cameron asked.

"Do they *allow* that here?" asked the girl from California. "Not where I come from."

"Unfortunately...," the ensign started to say but did not complete the sentence he had in mind, evidently feeling one word was enough.

The couple on the dance floor sat down and were not replaced by any similar pair, and nothing more was said on the subject. Kitty had looked carefully at Graham, then at Sandy, but they had said nothing, and she could tell nothing from their expressions. On this she had to give Graham the benefit of the doubt, but on his attitude to the outstanding place of entertainment he was in there was no question. He was totally indifferent if not hostile to it, and most importantly, to the artists themselves, some of them *great* artists, who had performed for him. He was just one of those people who don't listen, who don't know how to listen and never will. And disheartening as that fact was it was something she would just somehow have to learn to live with. They would have to live in three worlds—his, hers, and theirs together. But now was no time to talk about it. All she wanted was for these people to go home and leave her and Graham to have their last night together, and Graham was sensitive to that. When he saw Kitty looking at him he said, "I'm going to have to call it a night. Long train ride starting early tomorrow."

"Well, I guess we've all had enough of this place anyway," said Ann Cameron.

* * *

That night in their room at the Waldorf, after she had gotten him away from his friends for a little while, they were as good for each other as two people could possibly be in this life. "Ah, sweet, sweet!" she cried, and slept beautifully. Friday morning she helped him pack and called a cab and went with him to the station, which was a mistake. Grand Central seemed as alien as the moon, as frightening, she never should have come this far, she should have let him leave her at the hotel, but here she was and it was so awful, so unromantic, so humiliating, to feel the onslaught of violent stomach cramps at a time like this, to have to excuse herself five minutes before the train was announced, and later she had no recollection of what they said before he boarded it, it must have been chitchat of no consequence, she blanked it out. There is just no way to say goodbye properly to someone you love.

27

When Kitty got word that the U.S.O. would be more than glad to have her, Harry Field agreed to find a temporary replacement and give her a leave of absence. She could sing—with a band or accompanying herself—she could also solo on the piano or fill in as a member of any size orchestra, and she was good to look at. And the European theater of operations, including England, was always a good possibility, though so was North Africa, the China-Burma-India theater, New Guinea, the Aleutians ... she'd have to be prepared to go anywhere. However, they appreciated her reason for wanting to go to England and would try to be accommodating.

"So I still can't tell Graham," Kitty told Danielle as they dined at Cavanagh's on 23rd Street December 1. "Until I really know where I'm going and when. The new schedules won't be posted until January." She sighed. "I'm not even sure he's going to approve of me going to England. But some place like *New Guinea?*"

Graham would telephone from Minneapolis on the last day of his stateside leave. The day before he had sent a telegram asking Kitty to be at the Midston House by her phone at 5 P.M. New York time. The telegram disturbed her, perhaps because it was an incomplete message, perhaps because telegrams suggested momentous events, not always pleasant ones, certainly because it left her hanging nervously for twenty-four hours, and because it came from the headquarters city of Graham's parents whom she had never met and who were the enemy. Who had been the enemy from the beginning. Graham had said he went his own way and had proved it by marrying her against their wishes. But she had never expected him to repudiate them entirely—she couldn't ask that—and they could still influence his thoughts and actions. They had never accepted her. They had without doubt reenforced or spurred on his decision not to marry her in the Catholic church, and if she couldn't hold that against them she did resent bitterly their attempt to drive a wedge between her and their son by sending him newspaper clippings aimed at blackening the name of jazz musicians in general.

So she waited by the telephone with a thumping heart and remembered waiting for him in Nelson and Bailey's drugstore in Chicago and his telephone call to tell her he wouldn't be able to see her that day after all because he had to go to a family gathering in Minneapolis, but now there was no Eileen to reassure her that she was being silly, that everything was going to be all right.

And when the telephone rang as it had rung at the Barrys' house that following week it went right up her spine as the shrill sound had done that January evening almost two years before, but this time the mere sound of his voice did not dissolve all her troubles as though they had never existed.

Why? Was she imagining things? It wasn't anything he said...

"Miss Collins—Mrs. Allen? You have a long distance call," said the Midston House operator.

"*I have a person-to-person call from Lieutenant Graham Allen in Minneapolis for Mrs. Graham Allen.*"

"This is Mrs. Allen."

"Go ahead, please."

"Kitty? Well this is it. *I leave tonight on a military flight to Boston. I have to leave for the airport in just a few minutes.*"

"I wish you could come back through New York. I miss you so."

"Well..."

"Is anyone in the room with you?"

"Not exactly."
"I said I miss you. I love you."
"*I love you too.*"
"Take care of yourself. You're sure they won't make you fly anymore?"
"*Not on missions. I'll have to keep up my flying time but just on short hops from the base. Maybe as far as Scotland but not outside the U.K. . . . I'm going to have to say goodbye . . .*"
"Do you have to?"
"Yes, I'm afraid so."
"A bientôt! darling. How's your French?"
"*Goodbye, Kitty. I'll write to you.*"
"I'll write to you. I love you."
"*Love you.*"
The line was cut off.

Kitty and Danielle ate at the Concarneau that evening before Kitty went across the street to work. Madame would let them have wine even though they weren't yet eighteen, and Kitty felt the need of it, a glass or two to calm her down.
"I'm probably imagining things—all I want is to be with him and I'm not and that depresses me, and we never talked on the phone much and neither of us is good at it with each other. But it just wasn't right. I don't know why."
"Well, he was at his parents house. Couldn't that be it?"
"Oh, for sure. But I'd hoped . . . Well, I'm not going to let it get me down. But oh I wish this goddamn war was over . . ."

A great crowd greeted the new year, 1944, in a victory spirit, the greatest revel since Pearl Harbor. By then, Kitty had not yet heard from Graham again, but that did not seem unusual; they had already exchanged Christmas gifts on Nantucket, and his letters often took two to three or more weeks to reach her. Then a V-mail letter from him arrived on January 8 with New Year's greetings and details of his new job, about as long a letter as he ever wrote, about three hundred words. And signed, "All my love, Graham." But those words gave her little pleasure or reassurance because his letter had crossed one she had just mailed telling him she'd be arriving in England with a U.S.O. troupe sometime in March. For security reasons she wouldn't be told the exact date until the day they arrived or maybe one day before. They might perform in North Africa and/or Italy before they got to England, or they might go to these other places afterwards. "The U.S.O. is always looking for professional volunteers," she had written, "and I *should* go. It's something *I* can do for the war effort. And if you're going to be gone another couple of years—as you said, if you've got a safer ground job you probably won't get another home leave so soon—this is one way—the only way!—to see you ..."

She was extremely excited by the prospect of taking her first trip out of the country, of meeting Graham—in London she supposed—but also, as she told Danielle, "because I'll get to sing, maybe play, too, with Pete Weathersby!"

"I don't know him, Kitty," Danielle said. "Sorry."

"Don't feel too bad. The public doesn't know him yet either. Musicians do, but even those of us around here haven't heard him much. He's been on the West Coast for three or four years and couldn't make any new records because of the recording ban. That's over now, but so far he hasn't cut any new discs. All we have, or all I've heard, are some old ones when he didn't have his own group and just played as a sideman. You can only hear two solos but they're powerful. Roberta and Rex have heard him in person out in L.A. and say he's sensational and so is his group."

"You haven't told me what he plays," Danielle said.

"Oh. Piano."

"But will he let you play, then?"

"I don't really know. The U.S.O. has assigned me to him as a stand-up vocalist, but if I can get near his piano when we're not doing a show and he digs my stuff I figure he might let me do a solo spot, too. But even if he doesn't—some people don't want to share the spotlight—it won't matter so much. The main thing is to be able to hear him up close and learn something, something new. He's very original."

Weathersby and his electric guitarist, O. D. Turnipseed, a kind of wild man who some said was the successor to the late master Charlie Christian, had come out of the Southwest in the late 1930s to absorb the drive of black Kansas City jazz as much or more than any other white musicians. Considered erratic, unpredictable, independent, they played when and where they felt like it, and so far where they felt like it did not include New York. Besides the Kansas City area, California was the only place they had stayed put for any length of time, and they had moved in and out of that state often enough—north as far as Canada, south to Mexico, east to Texas. In a letter Roberta had said she believed Turnipseed was a self-taught genius, but she was sure Weathersby, though he posed as self-taught, had had formal, classical training.

"Anyway, I'll be singing with the Weathersby Sextet," Kitty said. "Piano, guitar, clarinet and bass-clarinet, trombone, bass, and drums. There'll be other people going from New York—some comics, a chorus line of tap dancers, a magician, I think. Danielle, they're always looking for dancers. It'd be fun if you could come along, too, sometime."

On February 1, Graham's answer arrived and she read it in her room.

Kitty, the one positive thing about your letter of January 3 is that it forces me to come to a final decision I began to make in New York and worked on in Minneapolis. Obviously, I want to see you—anywhere. But I don't want you to come to England under these circumstances—or go anywhere else as a U.S.O. performer. I don't want my wife on a stage being ogled and whistled at and lusted after and talked about by foul-mouthed GIs. I don't blame them, and if other girls want to display themselves as entertainers that's their business and I might go to see them myself. But not my wife. That's *my* business not to want my wife to be that kind of an entertainer or any kind of an entertainer. All I want you to be is my wife and some day the mother of our children and after the war to make a home for us wherever I have to be, and that isn't any more to ask than any man asks. For a while that might have to be in a suburb outside a city or in a small town but if I have my way, eventually it would be a ranch which might be a long way from any city. Where I come from the man decides where the family has to live. Since he's earning the living it's the only way that makes any kind of sense. God knows I especially don't want you to work on 52nd Street, but I don't want you to have to work anywhere. I know you enjoy playing the piano and singing and nobody is asking you to stop, but you can do these things anywhere. You'll have a piano, the finest money can buy.

Kitty, instead of coming to England I want you to get out of New York and move to Minneapolis until the war is over. You can live with Ruth and Perry and go back to the kind of school I never should have let you leave. They have a big house and only one child and they'd love to have you. Then little by little I hope you'd get to know my mother and father. Once they met you, once they saw you and talked to you, they'd see what a wonderful girl you are, what a wonderful wife you are to me.

Ruth and Perry don't have a piano, but we'll buy one or rent one for you so that it's there waiting for you. You won't be a day without it.

You'll *like* Minneapolis, I'm convinced of that. As cities go it's one of the best in the U.S. It has a lot of attractions and you can get out to the country easily. Good symphony orchestra, so I'm told. The University of Minnesota is a great school, and it might be possible for you to start in next fall as a special student even if you didn't have a high school diploma, especially if you went to summer school. Before that we could find tutors. As smart and as well read as you are, it wouldn't take you long.

I know all of this will come as a surprise and it will take you time to get used to the idea, but we just have to do this, Kitty. It's crucial for both of us ...

Stunned and appalled, the blood drained from Kitty's face, and for a few moments she thought she might faint or become nauseated. She got that under control but could still hear the rapid beating of her heart. Staying in this room any longer would be intolerable, and she pulled her outer coat off its closet hanger and a wool scarf to tie around her head and went down to the lobby by elevator and out into her beloved Manhattan. As she walked aimlessly in the cold she was conscious that several people gave her peculiar looks, and out of the corner of her eye she could see one woman turn her head to look back at her. Kitty touched her face with one bare hand as if to feel the still clammy pallor she supposed people were staring at so concernedly.

Over and over she told herself, *I don't want to go to Minneapolis! I don't want to live with Ruth and Perry Groff! I don't want to get to know his mother and father! I won't give up my career altogether! I won't, I won't! I'm willing to compromise. He's got to be willing too, to meet me half way!*

It was three in the afternoon. That gave her about three hours to write to him and get the letter in the mail before she had to bathe and dress for work, and eat something or she might really get sick in Harry's with all that smoke and bad air on top of everything else.

Dear Graham,
I love you, I'm your wife, and I want to stay being your wife, but you're asking too much. I don't know anything about flying and I don't care anything about it, but I know it means a lot to you and I would never ask you to give it up even though it's dangerous and I would much rather always have you on the ground. Well, music means just as much to me.

I'll go to Minneapolis if you want me to so badly—but not this year, maybe next year, when you're that much closer to coming home. But I don't think it's a good idea for me to live with your sister and her husband. I did that kind of thing once before with the Barrys and there were problems. It didn't really work out, and now I'm that much older and used to living by myself in my own way. I'll get an apartment or even live in a dorm at the University. Once you talked about my living in a dorm at Northwestern. And I could still see Ruth and Perry when they wanted to have me. And try to get to know your parents, if they'll let me.

After the war I'd be willing to give up professional music to have babies and make a home for you. But not give it up forever.

I'll quit playing on 52nd Street now. The Street is probably on its way out anyway. There are other, cleaner, nicer clubs and hotel lounges, very respectable places where nice respectable people go, and there are radio and recording studios. Fifteen or twenty years from now I could teach somewhere. And right now I still want to go on this U.S.O. tour and I don't think you have any right to say I can't. It's the patriotic thing to do and I'll be singing with a distinguished group.

I'm meeting you half way. You've got to meet me half way ...

A little over two weeks later Graham sent a reply to her through a private courier, a curly haired Eighth Air Force lieutenant colonel home on leave, who hand-delivered the letter in the lobby of the Midston House after jumping up from the edge of a chair, cap in hand, when Kitty stepped off the elevator.

She took the letter and held it, still unopened, and spoke with a dry mouth in a voice whispery from lack of breath, "I guess you won't be going back to England right away."

"No, but I know someone who is. If you can get a letter to me at the Biltmore before noon tomorrow, I'll see that it's delivered to this fellow. I'll wait for it now if you'd like."

"No, thank you. It might take me a while, and I don't want to hold you up. I'll bring it over early this evening."

"If I'm out just leave it at the desk. Graham should have it in his hands within three or four days."

She *knew* what the letter would say—not because she could read Graham's mind or had X-ray eyes or because she was by nature a pessimist—she was the opposite of that—but because she was full of fear, and his first word confirmed the justification for it.

Distinguished! Oh, for the love of God, Kitty! And you claim to be such an expert on jazz musicians. Don't you know O. D. Turnipseed is a notorious alcoholic pervert and Pete Weathersby has a reputation just about as bad? That information comes from a man in my squadron who's an expert—who was in the music business as a civilian. They've been bumming together for years and you probably know what that means. Or do you? You live in a dream world, Kitty, a dangerous dream world and somehow I've got to try one more time to get you out of it. The answer is *No!* I don't want you to come to England this way, especially not singing with the Pete Weathersby sextet! Sextet is right! And I want you to go to Minneapolis *now* and No you're not going to be my wife and professional musician too! That's final. If you still can't see it my way then we'd better call it quits. Just let me know as soon as possible. More than anything in the world I hate to have to write this letter, but if I didn't love you I wouldn't need to ...

First enraged, so enraged she wanted to smash something and almost threw his glassed photograph and her alarm clock against the wall of her room; then she was grief-stricken, then stricken with guilt. Was this her punishment for not being married by a priest? "Love, honor, and obey," that was in the Catholic marriage ceremony she hadn't had. But she would *be* a wife, *be* a mother. Why did she have to choose between them and music? Music was not a bad thing, it was a beautiful, good thing. Celestial music, angels' harps and Gabriel's horn, Gregorian chants. There wouldn't be such things in paintings and the Bible and in life if there was something wrong or evil about them. Why couldn't she have both? He was wrong, not she. How could he know, when he knew nothing about music?

But the guilt, the grief, the fear, even terror, would not go away.

It did not take her long to write the note to him. She did not repeat any of her arguments, she simply said:

Graham, I *have* to see you. That's why I'm taking this U.S.O. trip, *to see you.* I have to talk to you in person, and this is the only way in wartime I can get to England ...

If Graham wrote a reply to this, she had not received it by the time she left.

28

Strapped into metal and canvas bucket seats along the inside skin of the C-46 converted cargo plane (half-filled with cargo), the eighteen members of the troupe settled themselves as best they could for the long, uncomfortable journey. Already they were airborne into the cold northeastern night. Across from Kitty sat the Pete Weathersby Sextet, outdoor and indoor West Coast types. Two beards—Weathersby and his two sun worshipers—the balding clarinetist and big, blond surfboarding bassist. Drummer with straight, stiff black hair who looked to be part American Indian. And O. D. Turnipseed, a stoop-shouldered sack of bones with hair like straw, pale blue eyes that might have been glass, skin windburned across his cheek bones and broken nose, the rest of it the color and shine of faintly pink lard. Looking at him you'd say he was a jailbird and maybe he was, possibly a killer, but the only person he would likely kill, at least from now on, would be himself—with alcohol, drugs, a speeding vehicle, crazy eating habits, lack of sleep, multiple bed partners (all female, so the stories went), or by playing music nonstop from dusk to daybreak. Kitty thought he was anywhere from twenty-five to thirty.

But Weathersby might be a modish university professor behind shell-rimmed glasses and a Van Dyke, coldly, completely self-contained, self-possessed. So far he had barely acknowledged Kitty's existence, but they had all been hurried to such an extent after they had assembled at the airport from their various separate ways that there had been little time for socializing, and some, including Kitty, were strangers to one another. Tired already and the trip just begun—she had slept poorly the night before and now had to endure the cramped tension and uncertainty of the flight. They had been told nothing, did not know their route, though they could guess part of it, did not know where they would give their first show or exactly when. Kitty had no desire to start a conversation with the chorines on either side of her, and these girls kept their own silence. She took a book from her knapsack and managed to read for a while, though the light was poor, dozed, or simply sat and tried to empty her mind.

But her mind was too full. Physically, she and Graham were well matched, and at their age that was as important as anything else, and she had enough pride in her physical self to know he would not find her match very easily in England or anywhere else, in wartime or any other time, and would look at her photographs and think of her and remember her and want her and miss her because he was deprived of her body and call that love, and it *was* love—at least it was certainly an important part of it.

Now they just had to talk over their conflict in person, in bed and out of it. They had never done that, and it was no good trying to do it in letters. All the time they had been in New York together they had edged around it, avoided confronting it. That was her fault as much as his. Once she saw how much he hated 52nd Street she had done everything possible to deflect him away from it and had succeeded all too well. That had been a mistake and now they just had to *talk* it out.

She knew his name, rank, serial number, and the number of his Group. At their first stopover in what turned out to be Labrador, the escort major flying with them said, "I can get a message through to him letting him know where you'll be."

"If we should happen to give a show at his base, will I have any way of knowing?"

The major laughed. "If it is and he's there you'll see him I should imagine. With bells on!"

"Well, thank you," Kitty said.

They talked over the sound of plane engines as Kitty, newly enveloped in an army-issue parka, walked toward a line of open-back passenger trucks with the stiff-limbed, cold, and straggly members of the troupe.

They were fed in the officer's mess, canned beef stew, freshly baked bread, canned fruit salad.

"Say, this whale meat ain't half bad," said O. D. Turnipseed.

"Where you from Mr. Turnipseed?" a warrent officer asked.

"People that found me never did say. A cave somewhere in the wilds. I'd been suckled by coyotes."

"Down Texas way?" the warrent officer said, smiling, going along with the joke.

"Texas? Now where would that be? I'm a cross between a Hittite and a Scythian myself. Them Texas people extinct, too?"

The smile that now wasn't a smile stayed on the warrent officer's face for a few moments longer, then quickly faded. He looked down at his plate and attacked his dinner.

Pete Weathersby ate calmly, obliviously, as though this was happening somewhere else.

An airplane hangar had been converted into an auditorium and a stage had been improvised from connected platforms used for other purposes plus new carpentry. There was an upright piano, its origin not explained and not important. It was somewhat out of tune, but that didn't faze Pete Weathersby. He had a tuner's kit and the skill to use it and set to work an hour before the show was scheduled to begin.

The hangar had echoes. Weathersby disconnected one of the loudspeakers and that helped a little.

There was no curtain. At 8:45 the troupe manager ordered everyone off stage into a warren of workshops adjoining the hangar that now served as temporary dressing rooms, and the American and Canadian base personnel were let in to fill up the folding chairs in under five minutes. A Canadian officer climbed up to the stage and disclaimed any intention of delaying the show with speech-making, but his speech of welcome dragged on minutes too long and the audience grew restless. Finally, the officer extended one arm to the side and one of the two comics who doubled as M.C. dashed on stage and up to the standing microphone, lowered it considerably to accommodate his diminutive size and while he was throwing out one-liners with topical references to freezing temperatures, Eskimos, dogsleds, and the like he had adapted from old jokes on the plane that day, lines that drew loud, very satisfactory laughter, the members of the Pete Weathersby Sextet came up quickly to settle themselves behind drums, bass, trombone, electric guitar, and clarinet set up at center stage rear. Weathersby sat at the piano, gave the downbeat and to the sextet's slamming, swinging "How High the Moon," the line of six, leggy, shapely chorus girls came high-kicking and tap-dancing out in one-piece, short-skirted costumes to roars of appreciation and vigorous applause. The comedian stayed on stage leering at the girls, all of whom were taller than he was, and followed them off in a comic shuffle in the manner of Willie Howard, then returned to the mike to join a fanfare from the sextet in introducing the magician, who performed several successful illusions with volunteers from the audience. Then "Pretty Kitty Collins" in an off-the-shoulder, knee-length pink party dress, white high heels, came tripping out to whistles and applause and sang a medley of "I Remember You," "Bewitched, Bothered, and Bewildered," and "Taking a Chance on Love," one fast, one slow, one at medium tempo, and felt more appreciated than she ever had at Harry's or The Ivory Tower on 52nd Street, though she realized these men were starved for any kind of entertainment. She was very conscious of the hard-driving yet tastefully subdued backup behind her, Weathersby and Tommy Osborne, his clarinetist, and Cal Clancy, the trombone man, filling in just the right, spare number of notes, beautifully placed, these inner voicings drawing even more attention to the song *she* was singing.

In deference to an audience most familiar with popular current ballads, favorite oldies, and big-band swing, the sextet did not veer far from standards and crowd-pleasers, yet, playing without Kitty, Weathersby combined the melodic instruments, including the also rhythmic electric guitar, into ensembles that seemed to her not only exciting but refreshingly original. Piano, clarinet, guitar; piano, clarinet, guitar, and muted trombone; the same, with guitar dropping out; piano, bass clarinet, trombone with open horn—swinging then going beyond swing, borrowing from bop, playing short phrases in tight unison, then free-floating into counterpoint and far more lyrical and passionate statements from older, younger times. Kenny Bell and Jerry Bowman, bass and drums, topflight, did modest, essential things, freeing Weathersby's left hand so that he could create more brilliant cascading passages, more intense harmonic-melodic interchanges. For all their wild reputation, the sextet seemed to Kitty an extraordinarily disciplined group of musicians. Soloing on an instrumental composition of Pete Weathersby, O. D. Turnipseed played with unerring flying fingers one inspired improvisation after another under the control of the most exacting musical foundation, whether formally or instinctively learned it didn't matter.

The show was divided into two forty-five-minute segments with a fifteen-minute intermission, and during the last half Kitty sang "I'll Remember April," "Someone to Watch over Me," and 1944's great ballad "Long Ago and Far Away," and for encores, audience requests—"Sentimental Journey," "Candy," and (Kitty glad Graham wasn't in the audience) "That Old Black Magic."

Kitty spent the night with the chorus line in a temporarily off-limits wing of the B.O.Q., the smaller bottom end of an L-shaped barracks, and was roused out of a deep, dream-cluttered sleep at 6 A.M. in time for a sponge bath in tepid water, a mess-hall breakfast, and a 7:30 departure. Their pilot wanted as many daylight hours as possible on the next leg of the trip to help compensate for the daylight they would lose every hour eastward.

She sat across from Weathersby and Turnipseed again and was fascinated by what appeared to be the ritual they enacted. Turnipseed pulled a fifth of bourbon whiskey (some obscure brand—Old Third Rail or something) from a canvas satchel and two shot glasses. The plane had bucked a bit at first but was now cruising smoothly though noisily. Turnipseed handed one of the shot glasses to Weathersby who held it until Turnipseed had filled it just short of the brim; then he filled his own glass. Soon enough, Turnipseed had emptied his glass and had poured himself another while Weathersby continued to hold his glass without sipping from it. Neither man looked at or spoke to each other. Over the course of the next two hours the amber level in the bottle slowly lowered as Turnipseed poured himself one shot after the other and sipped them away. Kitty took out her book but every so often looked up from it pages and saw finally that Turnipseed had passed out. Still holding his one, original shot glass full of bourbon in one hand, Weathersby retrieved the empty bottle and fallen shot glass from between Turnipseed's sprawled ankles and returned them to the satchel. Then in three or four sips he emptied his own glass and packed it away again.

"May I say something?" Kitty called across, but the noise of the engines would not allow a comfortable conversation at that distance. Osborne, the clarinetist on the other side of Weathersby, motioned for Kitty to come over. They unstrapped their safety belts and traded places.

Kitty said, "On slow numbers I thought you were getting really nifty new effects on the piano with those hesitations and interrupted runs and silences. I love those spaces you put in. You dig Debussy and Ravel, too, I noticed."

"You play a little?"

"I play a lot."

He cocked his head, rounded his lips, clicked his tongue. "I guess I got told."

"No reason you should know. I was taken on this tour as a singer. But I get paid to do both. I do an intermission routine at Harry's on 52nd Street."

"Ah, so," he said, doing a Hollywood Chinese imitation, then dropping it. "They just told me Harry's vocalist. I don't really know the New York scene."

"You should try it for a while even if you don't like New York so much. So many great people. On the Coast, too, I know. Have you ever heard Rex and Roberta Wilkins?"

"Couple of times. I'll have to go again. Every so often I need to hear that pure thirties sound live."

"I love them. They're old friends of mine."

But the plane was so noisy, even sitting next to him it was a strain to talk any more.

"Won't have any voice left if I don't shut up, " she said. "See you." She wiggled fingers at Tommy Osborne that he could have his seat back.

They gave shows at Bluie West in Greenland and Keflavik, Iceland, and Kitty hoped never to have to see such bleak and treeless places again. They then landed at Prestwick, Scotland, but stayed aboard the aircraft, and after refueling the pilot continued south and landed in England in the dark. Outside the plane they might have been anywhere—the same uniforms and American accents, the same parked and taxiing aircraft, the same ground vehicles, cement, and corrugated metal as at any air base in the world. To set foot on England's soil and still not see anything that looked like England was intensely frustrating for Kitty, but she knew even if she had the opportunity to leave the base at this late hour everything English would be closed and dark and she was too tired and a little sniffly to appreciate it anyway. She was glad enough to crawl into a lower bunk—she had flipped a coin with one of the chorines and had won the toss—to stretch one great stretch from toes to fingertips and sink fathoms, fathoms into oceanic depths of sleep.

Kitty sniffed the damp, chilly air and looked up at the gray English sky and wondered if there was anything different about either of them.
"Miss Collins?" the troupe's escort major hailed her from the back of a jeep and stepped out.
"I can tell you your husband isn't at this base. But I got word through to him to get in touch with you either here or at the Bristol or Grosvenor House hotels in London. We'll be taking you to London tomorrow morning for twenty-four hours of leave."
"Did you talk to him?" Kitty asked quickly.
"No. But he acknowledged the message."
Kitty's heart skipped a beat.
"I've delayed your breakfast and the others have gone on," the major said. "Hop in and we'll take you over."
They would be confined to the base that day and evening, the evening of the show. More frustration—in England and yet not

there at all. Some members of the troupe saw American movies in the afternoon or lay around listening to Armed Forces Radio. Kitty read awhile and after lunch wandered over to the assembly hall where the show would be given at 8 P.M. Baby grand on stage. Back in civilization. Believing herself to be alone, Kitty climbed the steps to the stage and still standing, played a few chords, slowly ran up all the keys. In tune. She began "Spring Is Here," began singing at the second chorus, and followed that vocal with a piano-only version of "Taking a Chance on Love." When she ended it, startled, she heard Pete Weathersby's voice from the auditorium: "You play too much piano behind a vocal. Roberta Wilkins' influence." He climbed up to the stage. "And when you solo why do you only play like somebody trying to play like Teddy Wilson but not articulating like Teddy Wilson?"

Kitty bridled. Her face reddened.

"Thanks a lot. You have any other compliments today? You haven't even *once* mentioned my singing since the trip started. That really must be lousy." She simply wasn't capable of preventing tears forming, but she steeled herself not to put either hand to her face, and blinked her eyes dry.

"Your singing is the best thing you do," Weathersby said very coolly. "You don't need me to tell you it's good. As for copying Wilson there's nothing wrong with that if you really work at it and if that's only a fraction of being an historical pianist. When you work at that 52nd Street club, you play less than three hours. More like two, and half the time you're singing. How much practicing do you do?"

"One or two hours."

"One or two hours is bullshit. *Five* hours, sweetheart, to get your chops in shape. Five hours every day at least five days a week *before* you go to work. And if you're going to start by being an historical pianist—which is the only way to start unless you're a genius—you can't stop with Wilson. Do what he did, go back to Waller and Hines and Tatum. Yeah, even Tatum. Nobody's expecting you to match him, you're not in a contest, but you can *listen*, you can play him at slow speed and write down some of the things he does. Then study the others and play their way too—Mary Lou Williams, Stacy, Guarnieri, Nat Cole. And if I didn't think you had talent I wouldn't waste my time giving you my fifty-dollar-an-hour advice free of charge. Now, if you don't mind, I need to take over that keyboard for a while. Go blow your nose."

By show time there was still no word from Graham, but Kitty told herself she wasn't worried. He wouldn't want to or even wouldn't be allowed to come to this base and phone calls were no good as they had both learned. She had a strong feeling he would arrange to meet her at the Grosvenor House Hotel in London which had been taken over by the Americans.

She had been feeling a little coldy ever since Iceland, and now she was getting a little hoarse. No sore throat, though, luckily. The major provided her with a supply of throat lozenges and she got through the performance in fine shape, only hacking a little during the intermission, and the extra huskiness in her voice lent it a quality of extra tenderness, of irresistible vulnerability, so that many a man who heard and watched her wanted only to hold her in his arms. The audience loved her, that was overwhelmingly obvious, and she felt in her the power to solve all problems whatever they might be.

Her coughing woke her in the night but lozenges and will power subdued it—she didn't want to wake any of the other girls—and she felt marvelous as though she could go without sleep for days, and welcomed the opportunity to lie awake with good memories and exciting prospects, for the dawn which seemed to come rapidly, and finally, finally to see England and London and Graham. She was up and dressed in warm clothes and ready to go before anyone else. In flat loafers, ready for a lot of walking. It was raining but not heavily and rain seemed so typically English she was just as glad it wasn't sunny. After breakfast the troupe piled into a camouflaged army bus, and Kitty stared intently out the window as it went through the main gate of the base onto a narrow road that ran between intensely green fields that could never be mistaken for American fields. Trees, gentle hills, a village of graying yellow stone houses with steeply pitched slate roofs that could never be in America either, a wider highway and down the left side of the road, which said England as much as anything else.

An hour later they arrived at a small railroad station at one end of a town and the major announced, "We'll be taking the train from here on into Paddington Station. It's due in a few minutes. When it comes in please try to stay together as much as possible. Each compartment seats eight passengers and they all have outside doors to the platform, so just climb aboard where there's room."

"Mind if I sit with you?" Kitty asked Pete Weathersby.

"Be my guest."

Kitty had noticed that various pairs of the sextet members took turns spelling Weathersby in keeping an eye on O. D. Turnipseed, and when the train pulled in with a cheery, very English whistle Osborne and Bowman got Turnipseed safely inside a compartment and Kitty and Weathersby, the magician and one of the chorines climbed into an adjoining compartment already occupied by three ladies and one gentleman, all elderly and dressed as people did during World War I.

"I feel I've entered a time warp," Weathersby murmured.

"Have you ever been in England before?" Kitty asked.

"Nope."

Kitty held her fist to her mouth as she coughed deeply several times and two of the ladies looked quite disapproving, though they continued to avert their glances from the strange Americans.

"That getting any better?" Weathersby asked.

"Oh probably. I get these little colds all winter and they don't last more than a couple of days. I *feel* great! . . . Pete, what I wanted to say was, about practicing, it's true, I admit it. After I started working at Harry's I cut back too much . . . I've always wanted to study harmony. Maybe that would help too."

"There's a guy at Julliard you ought to try to work with—Mortimer Sack. I'll give him a call or write to him when we get back. In the meantime—when you get back—start playing Bach two- and three-part Inventions a couple of those five hours every day."

They were both silent for a few moments, thinking. Then Weathersby said, "For a while you need to separate singing from piano work. They're getting in each other's way. That's going to mean either leaving Harry's or telling him you can only play piano. But I don't like that second idea too much because you need to keep up with your vocal work too. Let me give it some thought."

Kitty hacked again, and this time the old gentleman across from her looked at her directly for a moment.

"'Scuse me," she said to the assemblage, then to Weathersby, "Something I just can't keep to myself. I expect to meet my husband when we get to London. He's with the Eighth Air Force."

Weathersby arched his eyebrows.

"Somebody said you volunteered to go on this trip when the rest of us hoped to get Morocco this time of year. Now I can see why. Well, lucky you."

"You married, Pete?"

"As far as I know."

"Kids?"

"Four and six."

"I don't have any yet. I want them, though. Your wife a musician, or otherwise in show business?"

"She's my accountant."

"I guess she understands what it means to be a musician, though. My husband doesn't yet. That's a problem right now. Why I needed this trip, to talk it over ... Hey, looks like we're coming into a city ... Thanks for your advice, Pete. I know you're right."

"We'll talk some more," Weathersby said.

Outside Paddington, the major herded them into a green U.S. army bus for the short trip to the Grosvenor House. Through rain-streaked windows Kitty couldn't see buildings very clearly or the faces of pedestrians under black umbrellas.

The major stood at the front so everyone could hear him.

"Sorry about this rain but that's what to expect, especially this time of the year. We'll have lunch at the Grosvenor, then you're on your own until 0800 hours tomorrow. Your hotel isn't far from the Grosvenor. Close enough to walk and we can probably rustle up some umbrellas, but we can also provide transportation. Transportation to other points of interest as well. I'll show you where to ask for whatever you need."

When he sat down Kitty walked up and sat beside him.

"If my husband has left a message where would I get it?"

"Stay with me and we'll check it out right away."

The big, elegant lobby was crowded with American officers. Kitty looked quickly from face to face, but it was impossible to see everyone at a glance. She stayed beside the major until she had a sudden coughing fit and had to stop walking.

"Why don't you sit down here and I'll be right back," the major said.

He returned a few minutes later.

"Nothing so far," he said, somewhat hesitantly, then added, "It's early."

No, it isn't early, said the voice in her head. *It's noon and I've only got twenty hours left.*

"Is there any way I can phone him or you can phone him and then let me talk to him?"

The major frowned.

"We can try."

He led her to the glass door to an office off the lobby where she could see several lieutenants and a captain working behind desks. Phone booths with glass doors were ranged along one side of the corridor.

"Wait here until I can find out which booth to use."

She waited and the major came out again and said, "Number three. Wait till it rings, then pick up the receiver."

She went inside and closed the door and sat on the chair in there and began coughing and almost couldn't stop. She needed to stop to be ready to talk and held her left fist to her mouth and pounded one knee with the bottom of her right fist and then had to get a handkerchief from her bag to get rid of the thick mucus she had brought up.

The phone rang and she picked up the receiver.

"Graham?"

"It's still ringing at the other end," said an unfamiliar voice.

The ringing stopped and a more distant voice recited a string of unit numbers.

"May I please speak to Lieutenant Graham Allen?" Kitty said more loudly than she had intended, and stifled a cough.

"*I'll see if I can find him.*"

She waited thirty seconds, forty-five seconds, a minute, a minute and a half.

"*Sorry. He's not available.*"

"Is he there?"

"*He's not available, Ma'am. That's all I can tell you.*"

"May I leave a message? This is his wife. I'll be at the Bristol Hotel in London until eight o'clock tomorrow morning or he can leave a message at the Grosvenor House. Ask him to *please* get in touch with me. It's urgent, it's very urgent ..."

"Is there anything else I can do for you?" the major asked. They were in the lobby near the front entrance. She did not see Pete Weathersby or any other member of the troupe.

"No, I don't think so. You've been very helpful."

"Come and have some lunch."

"I don't really care for any. I'll get something later."

"Your luggage is at the Bristol. Would you like to go over there now?"

"I think I'd like to walk. It looks as though it's stopped raining."

"Take this umbrella in case it starts up again ... If that cough doesn't get any better soon maybe you should think about letting a doctor take a look at you. I can arrange it."

"I'm fine, really."

"In any case, here are two numbers where I can be reached any time today or you can leave word for me to call the Bristol. The third number is one you could call if I'm out and you decide you'd like to see a doctor. And this is a little map of the area, with some suggestions on the back of places to see fairly close by. Why don't we go out to the street? You can orient yourself better out there."

On the wide pavement he said, "You're in Mayfair, the poshest part of the city. Hyde Park over there, of course. We're on Park Lane. As you see on the map you walk down to the left as far as Curzon Street there and take a left. Half Moon Street, you see it's marked, too, is just one, two, three, four, five blocks or turnings further on, there on the right just beyond Shepherd Market. You'll see the Bristol in the middle of the block. Up at the other end is Picadilly with Green Park across the way and then if it stays dry you see you're not too far from the Palace and so forth."

"Thank you again. And I'll bring back your umbrella."

"Hang on to it. You may need it again."

She still felt curiously buoyant though that was fading, and a chill crossed her shoulders. She felt rather light-headed and her legs seemed at once heavy, heavy, yet almost too weak to support her weight. She walked and followed the directions and was conscious of the stately elegance of her surroundings. When she reached the little hotel she did not want to go in; she wanted to walk on and see Picadilly Circus and Bond Street and Regent Street, Pall Mall and the Palace, but she did not think she would be able to take another step. She wanted to weep. She had seen a little corner of London but almost nothing yet that people come to London for, and minutes away from it all she had to stop. Not sleeping enough last night, that was it. If she could just lie down for an hour ...

Graham wasn't going to see her. If he wasn't already in London somewhere could he even get into London in time? Maybe they wouldn't let him.

But somehow he could have left a message.

The woman at the desk said, "Your things are in the room," and handed over the key. "Up one flight and down the hall to your right ... That's a nasty cough you have, dear. Do you have anything for it?"

"Yes, I do. Thank you."

Halfway up the carpeted stairs, holding on to the banister, Kitty wondered if she would be able to climb any higher, and stopped.

"Is anything the matter?" the receptionist called.

"No. Nothing."

She made it to the top, made it to the room, got the door unlocked, found the light switch, had trouble unbuttoning her coat but got out of it, slid under the bedcovers in her street clothes, and turned on her side. Only twice before in her life had she ever felt so alone, and never in her life had she felt so exhausted.

A terrible attack of coughing woke her. It seemed an enormously difficult feat to prop herself on one elbow in order to keep from choking on the thick bitter stuff she wrenched up from her lungs. It took an agony of effort to draw the covers back and slide and drop her feet to the floor and pull herself up by holding on to the sink so that she could spit into it. There were steel bands around her chest and head and someone was turning a wheel that turned the screw that tightened them. She found her bag on the floor, the slip of paper with the telephone numbers but could barely lift the phone receiver off the hook and it slipped out of her hands and fell on the bed. She could hear the woman's voice asking, "*Hello? Yes? What is it?*"—but she simply did not have the energy to pick up the receiver and reply. She sat on the bed, slowly fell back, and began to cry, and the woman came into the room with some man and Kitty said, "Somebody, *please* help me. I am so scared."

For twelve days she was in a military hospital with lobar pneumonia. In her nightmares she was being put into the maw of some monstrous machine. Later, nurses told her she had often yelled in her comatose sleep and that they had had to use restraining sheets to keep her from climbing out of bed. She wanted to apologize for the trouble she had caused them but did not have the energy, and when she was a little stronger she no longer remembered.

She was driven one April afternoon to a convalescent home somewhere in the country, but far from feeling relieved to be discharged from the hospital she was convinced her doctors were incompetents. She had no strength at all; she wanted only to stay in that hospital bed and doze and dream and not exert herself at all. The fools put her in a second-floor room in a big house with musty, unplesant smells and no elevator, and if she came downstairs to the dreary first-floor lounge or dining room with its inedible food and discovered she had forgotten her book the thought of expending the energy needed to climb up again to get it would make her cry.

The home that was not a home reminded her in its way of St. Margaret's convent, but the convent, though she had feared it would be, had not been a prison and this was.

Gradually, over a period of three weeks, though the process most of the way seemed not only interminable but unsuccessful, she regained enough strength to be told she was ready to return to America.

The troupe had long since gone on to Italy and North Africa and back to the States, the major with them, but a captain from his office came to take her to an airfield.

"Do I have to go back through Iceland and Greenland and those places?" Kitty asked.

The captain, who was quite taken with her spectral beauty, smiled reassuringly. "No. You're going south."

As they walked toward a staff car, he offered her his elbow to hold on to. "Major Bowen sends his best regards," he said.

"He's a nice guy. Did he tell you about me?... Never mind, you either know or you don't know. Did my husband ever come to see me while I was in the hospital?"

The captain looked uncomfortable. "I understand he telephoned several times until you were off the critical list."

"But didn't see me."

"I wasn't in London then. I really couldn't say."

"No, I wasn't asking a question. I was just thinking out loud."

Settled in the rear seat of the staff car, which went into gear and moved slowly forward, the captain said, "I have something for you," and withdrew an envelope from an inside pocket of his jacket.

Pete Weathersby. A New York City address in the upper left-hand corner. She picked it open. Two lines.

"Glad you're OK. We've taken a job at The Pearly Gates in the Village. Come and see us. Let's talk."

29

Harry Field recommended a lawyer who sent a formal letter to Lieutenant Graham Allen in England. That same afternoon, Kitty went down to The Pearly Gates on Great Jones Street near Washington Square, a somewhat shabby but popular club, considered a home for the avant-garde.

To Pete Weathersby's question Kitty said, "Still a little shaky on my pins and I poop out early but I'm getting stronger. And can't wait to get back to work."

"I'd like you to start singing with us as soon as you're ready. I've guaranteed the owner three months and he'd like us to stay at least six. That may be all of New York any of us can take."

"Oh, Pete, that's a terrific compliment. You're on, man."

"I've talked to Mort Sack at Julliard. He's got room for you three days a week. Now we've got to find you a piano."

"And a place to live. I want to look for something down around here, a real apartment again."

"If you're going to do that you should consider financing a good quality spinet so you can work at home. In the meantime I'll arrange for you to use the club piano in the morning and early afternoon."

"Would you mind if I put my hands on it now? Even if I don't articulate too well? I haven't played anything for six weeks. Just for two minutes?"

"Take as many as five."

Seated before it, Kitty couldn't make up her mind.

"Something slow," Pete Weathersby said. "Anything. 'Don't Blame Me.' Key of B."

Cautiously she decided on a bass line, stuck to soft chords, only toward the end trilled a little, ran a few single notes up one octave—and got to her feet.

"Appreciate your offer of five minutes, but for now two is enough. Thanks, Pete. That did me a lot of good. I'll be talking to you soon."

"He plans to charge you with desertion," the lawyer said.

"Well that's a bunch of malarkey," Kitty said. "I went all the way to England to try to see him and he wouldn't even talk to me. Who deserted who? The bastard. But I know what you're going to tell me. I've been talking to one of Harry's bartenders who's been through this. Somebody's got to be guilty and somebody's got to be innocent. That's the game."

"In New York, yes, and just forget New York, by the way. Adultery is the only grounds here. In Illinois, yes, though there you have more possibilities, including desertion. Illinois where you were married is what he has in mind. In most states, yes. In Nevada, no. And you can do it alone on the grounds of incompatibility after establishing residence for six weeks."

"I haven't *got* six weeks now even if I could afford it. I've got a great opportunity to study and work with some of the great people in music and I'll be damned if I'm going to let him cheat me out of it. By God he can wait awhile. If he thinks he's going to claim desertion he's going to have to wait at least a year anyway. If he *can't* wait, then maybe I can get a divorce right here in New York."

"I'm afraid with him in England in wartime we'd have a hard time proving infidelity to the satisfaction of the New York courts."

"Forget it. I didn't really mean that. I don't have anything on him."

"What's your financial situation?"

"I've got about a thousand dollars in savings and twelve hundred from his allotment. As soon as I started working at Harry's I started putting his checks in the bank—to help buy us a house after the war."

"Were there any new checks when you got back?"

"Two."

"I'll see to it they keep coming in until the divorce is final."

"I don't want any alimony. I can take care of myself. I want to be free and clear of any money of his as soon as I can."

"Under Illinois law he can file suit without appearing in person—though as you point out not for quite a while. But you're not guilty of desertion and as a matter of principle I don't want to let him get away with it. I'd like to see you beat him to the punch. It's May now. What's your timetable?"

"Pete Weathersby is only going to be here six months at the most, though I hope he stays longer. I want to work with him as long as I can, and I won't be able to start until I've got the energy to work late at night. Maybe another three weeks or so."

"To be on the safe side, let's project ahead nine months. February '45. By then you should be between jobs and can take the time to go to Reno. And Allen can pay for it."

So nothing would be final for a long time, and she didn't want to talk about it to anyone anyway. She wasn't ashamed of anything, but she'd made a mistake, a very large mistake—the Barrys had been right—and isn't failure always the dullest subject imaginable, the last thing anybody wants to hear about? Time enough when she finally saw people again in person to tell it in a line when it was a past event, over and done with, final, irrevocable, not so much unworthy of comment as no longer possessing any quality to inspire it. My father or my mother died of cancer last year, two years ago. Graham and I were divorced. What more is there to say? But if she put it in a letter to anyone now she would have to say more and that would simply be an unrewarding drag for her and for anyone at the other end.

The Pete Weathersby Sextet, with Kitty Collins as its vocalist, actually stayed at The Pearly Gates through July, 1945, before returning to the West Coast. During those fourteen months Kitty played far more piano—classical and jazz—than she ever had before in that length of time, but only in April of that year did she once again play in public. As a separate feature of the evening performance, quite apart from her singing, she and Pete Weathersby began playing duo piano, and for her fingers and musical sensibility to be both her own and an extension of his, at his level—he certainly never played down, held back, to make her sound better—was a nightly challenge she met with imagination and panache. It was one of those three-month wonders that was still being talked about in music circles years later and at the time drew repeat regulars, musicians, and music lovers, from all over town. Both *Downbeat* and *Metronome* devoted columns to it and the woman who wrote the "New York Cafe Life" column for the *Sun* gave it a long paragraph. (As a vocalist, Kitty had received brief, favorable mention in the musical and daily press on earlier occasions than this.) Putting a new act together was something else again, but "You're ready," Pete Weatersby said. It would not be entirely solo. Weathersby believed she should work with a drummer and bassist, at least with a bassist, for both vocal and instrumental numbers, and she thought of Rodney Blake and Clay Mitchell, neither of whom she had seen since before Roberta and Rex had left for L.A.

But first she had a solo trip to make, though in fact she rode most of the way by train with Weathersby, his wife and two little girls, O. D. Turnipseed, and the others, the city of Reno being close to the California border.

"I don't know how to say it, Pete," Kitty said as she stood on the platform with her luggage.

"Then don't even try," he said. "Just keep up what you've been doing. That's one thing you can't ever divorce."

As Gabriel Kellerman recalled it later: "She came into Gabriel's one afternoon in September '45 just after the war ended, to audition for a spot on the bill, a lovely looking girl with long hair, a little taller than average.

"I'd heard her sing once with the Weathersby Sextet—I had always made it a point to check out the well-recommended performers at other clubs—but I hadn't heard her play. The duo piano routine she had done with Weathersby for a couple of months I had heard about, but it came at a time when I had some aggravating problems at my own club that kept my nose to the grindstone. Well, I asked her to go ahead. With the bassist from the band backing her up, she played one number without singing—Ellington's 'Prelude to a Kiss'—and it was obvious in a moment she was outstanding. She could handle flying runs and the kind of single-note filigree work in the right hand only the top people are really capable of. But there was more there than sheer technique. There was great feeling. Her improvisations were inspired, remarkable in a young girl her age, under twenty then. Mel Powell comes to mind. Marian McPartland. I'd say she played in that manner. That caliber.

"Then she sang. She started with Frank Loesser's 'Spring Will Be a Little Late This Year,' a fairly new song then, about a year old. It was a very exciting experience. I asked her to do four more songs, five or six numbers being about the length of any one performance on the bill. Each show—at nine, twelve, and two A.M.—lasted about an hour, and singers like Kitty shared the spotlight with other musicians, dancers, comedians. I remember her audition as clearly as if it was yesterday. She did Porter's 'Easy to Love,' the perfect song, and she did it simple justice, included the opening verse, too, which singers often drop, an unsophisticated mistake. Who are they to edit out Porter? Especially lines with that much charm. Then she picked up the tempo and paired two songs from 1937 by different composers and lyricists—the Gershwins on the one hand, Richard Whiting and Johnny Mercer on the other—I had never thought of in the same breath particularly, but she made you see right away why *she* had. Tenderness, buoyant good humor, all of a piece: 'They Can't Take That Away from Me' and 'Too Marvelous for Words.'

"She closed with 'Last Night When We Were Young,' which is one of the great songs of all time and difficult to sing properly, which is probably why you don't hear it too often—all that deeply felt emotion packed into just one octave—really amazing—magical. You know Arlen and Harburg originally wrote it for Lawrence Tibbett, the operatic baritone. She left me limp. I said to myself the applause will either be deafening or there'll be stunned silence. As it turned out there was some of each every time she did it—and at least one pair of moist eyes at every table.

"Well, I hired her then and there, and she and Rodney Blake, her bassist, stayed on until mid-1947. She developed what you might call a kind of cult following. People heard about her and came to her mostly through word of mouth. Back in those days singers got well known on the radio or in Hollywood or both, plus recordings, mostly with the big bands, and Kitty just wasn't interested in any of that except recordings and she hadn't made any yet. In the daily newspapers you didn't find the kind of detailed critical analysis of jazz musicians and vocalists that came along later and you see nowadays in *The New Yorker* and the *New York Times*. For that you had to read *Downbeat* or *Metronome* and they were musicians' publications most people didn't follow. So she never got famous with the public at large. And yet what quality! What equipment! A contralto voice of bells and honey with a vibrato capability worthy of the Met. There was a poignant sweetness there with a lilting sense of humor, musical comedy authority with a great jazz beat, absolute control. She could take a small, pure bell note and make it suddenly deep and big without ever letting it get away from her. Turn a delicate whisper into a gravelly little growl, bend notes in surprising, charming ways without overdoing any of that. Flawless diction and phrasing, impeccable good taste. She never screamed.

"What I appreciated as much as anything was her respect for the song, what the composer and lyricist intended. She had her own style and a unique sound, but her first instinct was to project the song, what it meant to her and how it affected her, not her own personality. She never got in the way and the song never got lost in the process. I'll leave you to make your own comparisons with the opposite of that kind of modesty and fidelity you hear so often these days.

"You know, for me, there are really nothing quite like the songs she sang, sung as thrillingly as she sang them, to bring back some of those old lost good moments we all have. At a certain level—a pretty high level, too—this is America at its best."

30   *Spring, 1946*

She lived quietly, a contemplative sort of life. She had achieved a kind of peace, but she knew the world had changed and would continue to change. No state of being was permanent and might not last out the month or the year. In the back of her mind she felt on the edge of something, the direction of her personal as distinct from her musical life no more certain now than it had ever been, while up front in the sunny bedroom of her apartment on Sullivan Street in the Village she woke—rested—at noon, and down the block in the Italian cafe, where she was greeted as a valued customer and given her favorite table in the window, she sipped juice and coffee and nibbled freshly baked pastry and read the *Herald Tribune* and watched the people passing in the street.

Letter from Roberta. Things had continued to go well. Rex was working regularly in motion-picture studio orchestras in addition to leading the quintet at night. Their contract at Melodyland had been renewed for the second straight year, and they had also been assured they would be welcome back at The Orchid Club where they had first played in '44. But they were thinking about going back to Europe. Some musicians they knew had gone already.

Scandinavia, England, France, especially, were said to be starved for American jazz.

In writing to Joe and Matt Barry about her new life after the divorce and reading over what she had written Kitty discovered she had described a life that sounded on paper considerably more carefree and sparkling than the real life she actually lived. It was all done, innocently enough, half-unconsciously, with selection, editing, compression of experience and detail, and a sprinkling of exclamation points. The importance of a new young man named Norman was exaggerated. Yes, it was true he *was* sweet, intelligent, and fun, and yes she liked him tremendously, but she recognized that adverb as female hyperbole, and the paragraphs standing alone like that ... But it was too much trouble to rewrite the letters. She mailed them off and not too long afterwards got one from Joe with more details about a girl named Lynn he had mentioned before and with whom—big news!—he was now informally engaged. Slightly out of focus snapshot included. She seemed to be quite pretty. Joe always did have good taste in girls. He wrote that under an accelerated program for service veterans he would be able to complete his remaining two years of college in one year by taking extra courses and continuing through the summer of '46. Then he would have to find a job and when he had saved enough hoped to be able to get married in 1947.

Matt wrote:

You asked how Mom feels now. I honestly don't know. I think they appreciated your Christmas letter where you said you had been wrong about Graham, but she really didn't say much. She kept your card on display as long as any of the others, I remember that, and Dad—well, both of them—sent you one—of course, you know that already.

Wish I had the money to come to New York and hear you. When are you going to make some records? Have a heart ...

Matt enclosed some photographs, some of himself. At nineteen, he had really shot up and was still the best-looking of the Barry boys. He was now a freshman in college (he had not served overseas and had lost only one year of school) and thought he wanted to become an architect.

Monday through Saturday, Kitty gave three performances nightly between 9 P.M. and 3 A.M., sharing the bill with a comedienne, a folk-singing guitarist, and a magician-puppeteer. A small swing band played for dancing. In the mornings and afternoons she practiced four or five hours, playing Chopin Etudes and other classical compositions as well as jazz, and one afternoon a week went up to 57th Street near Carnegie Hall to work with a voice teacher. On the day of that lesson she often lunched at The Russian Tea Room, sometimes with the Fields or with an acquaintance she might run into, musicians from the band at Gabriel's or from 52nd Street days. Several times she was aware of being recognized.

That winter and spring, one late morning a week, she audited a course in art history and appreciation at New York University, which was within walking distance of her apartment, and browsed when she had the time at the Metropolitan, the Museum of Modern Art, and in East Side and Village galleries where she bought several canvases. The silent art of painting calmed her. When she reached the Impressionists and Post-Impressionists, their towns and streets, coasts and countrysides attracted her powerfully to Europe and especially to France, to Provence and Paris. She had a great longing to climb into these lovely sunlit scenes.

Sunday was the only day of the week she was free to consider accepting a full-length date though most any day she could go out to lunch or an early dinner. It didn't really matter. She had been dating three young men since late 1945, but none of them could offer any more than temporary companionship, however pleasant, though one at least had more ambitious ideas. Richard, her art teacher, was gay, and the drummer in the orchestra at Gabriel's, recently divorced and lonely, was a hard-drinking wanderer who had worked everywhere and was already restless to move somewhere else. Norman, an NYU student, a child of successful parents, who gave every indication of being capable of continuing their tradition, might have been considered a promising suitor, and was serious about Kitty, but in the long run she decided he just didn't race her motor enough.

" 'A Good Man Is Hard to Find,' " said Harry Field, quoting the song title.

"But I'm not really looking for one just yet," Kitty said.

A waiter at Gabriel's delivered the note backstage after her nine o'clock performance. It was from Charlie O'Donnell.

"If you remember one summer day back in 1941 when I got you into hot water by asking you to play boogie-woogie, then you may remember me."

Kitty's was the third and last act and the orchestra was playing for dancing again, so she went out immediately, the waiter-messenger leading the way.

Charlie O'Donnell was a little stouter, a little redder in the face, and wearing the uniform of a lieutenant commander in the navy with a row of ribbons. He was at a table by himself.

"Of course I remember!" Kitty said. "What a nice surprise ... Is Sister Edmund all right? I heard from her at Christmas."

"Oh fit as a fiddle as usual. But I've been commissioned to hear you in person and bring Mary a firsthand report. I'm going out to Chicago tomorrow to see her. I was right! My Lord, I was right! You were good enough to play at the Ruban Bleu. More than good enough. That was a great performance tonight, Kitty. Absolutely shattering. When I think of some of the famous names who can't hold a candle to you I just have to shake my head. But fame is just around the corner, I'm convinced of it."

"I don't know about that but thanks for your kind words ... Tell me about yourself. Are you staying in the navy?"

"Oh, Lord no, I've been discharged, but haven't had time to buy any civilian clothes, and I hate to admit it but none of my old ones fit very well. So that's one thing I have to do in Chicago. Buy new clothes—among them a cutaway. I'm getting married in Boston a month from now. High time, I guess."

"Congratulations! Then what will you do?"

"Enjoy myself for a while. Look around ... But tell me, will you make records, go with a big band sometime?"

"As a matter of fact, as if by magic, I've just finished making my first record. On the Stardust label. Let me have your address in Boston so I can send you one as a wedding present. As for big bands, they're on the way out. Too costly. And big-band singing isn't my style anyway. I tried it once—halfway you might say. I only sang duets. But I got the picture. You're supposed to sit out there in front and look pretty most of the evening, then sing one chorus of four or five songs. Some of which you might think are awful. The band and the leader, especially if he plays an instrument, are always more important, and most of the fans know this. They're not really interested in the singer, and if the place is noisy enough and the band is loud enough they can't hear her very well anyway. I don't want to sing songs I think are no good. In a place like this I can do what I want to do. Maybe I'll never have a big audience."

"What about musical comedy?"

"I don't think I'm enough of an actress. And to have to sing the same seven or eight songs night after night ...?"

"Hollywood? Out there you wouldn't necessarily have to be an actress at all."

"Oh, no thank you."

"Well, I've always admired you and now I admire you more than ever, in more ways than one. I just hope it isn't a case of integrity having to be its own reward. In any case, you'll have to make lots of records so Mary can hear for herself. I'm sure you can guess she'd rather you were playing piano at Carnegie Hall than playing and singing popular songs in a nightclub, but she'll be enormously proud and impressed all the same."

The waiter brought Charlie another scotch and water and Kitty a glass of tonic water. Charlie sipped, paused, and said, "Mary thought she wanted a career on the concert stage. Mother scoffed at that, put every obstacle in the way, tried to push her into marriage, turned Mary into a nervous wreck. As a matter of fact there were a couple of eligible, interested suitors, and rightly or wrongly, I've always believed Mary might have accepted one in particular if left alone to make up her own mind at her own speed. Not that a good marriage was guaranteed. But pushed, she rebelled, and joined the order. Mother didn't want that either, but couldn't stop it. Perhaps the religious life had always been a vocation in reserve for Mary, a refuge. In the long run I think she finds it as fulfilling as any other. Her choir continues to have a fine, city-wide reputation, for example, and means a great deal to her. The fact she let herself be discouraged out of a concert career probably meant she wouldn't have been successful at it. But the end of a dream must have hurt all the same.

"She was twenty-five before she entered the order—with twenty years of musical training behind her. Her first years as a postulant and after, four as I recall, she had to submit to the discipline of the order and teach academic subjects. This was in Cincinnati. It wasn't until about 1935 when she arrived at St. Margaret's that she began organizing a choir and giving piano lessons, too. She took only a few very young piano pupils each year, seven-and eight-year-olds, after testing them for musical potential. Some dropped out later or moved away or went to different high schools. By the time you arrived on the scene she had, as you remember, only two other pupils with some promise, at the advanced level, and she was none too certain of them. They seemed to lack the vital fire. She had high hopes for you—to become the concert artist she had wanted to be. And you *have* fulfilled some of her hopes, I'm sure, though not exactly in the way she'd intended."

In a rather serious tone Kitty asked, "When was the last time you saw her?"

"Not since late '44. I was in Lake Forest only a few hours then, and your name didn't come up if that's what you're asking."

"Do you think she really understands about me? I mean I got married by a judge, then got divorced. I made a mistake, I admitted that when I wrote to her, but I didn't say any more than what I've just said. She didn't say anything about it when she wrote."

"And I don't think she will. It's over. She's a nun, after all—and a bit of a prude on top of that—and you have to expect her to think like one—but at bottom she's really a very warm-hearted, loving person. I wouldn't be concerned. I'm sure you're very much back in her good graces."

Kitty's recording of eight Rodgers and Hart classics received a one-paragraph review in *Downbeat*, later reproduced on the record jacket:

Kitty Collins, a new young thrush and jazz pianist, handles these standards with loving care, accompanying herself with unusual deftness on the keyboard; manages to keep the somewhat overdone 'My Funny Valentine' and 'Little Girl Blue' forever fresh. Her versions of 'A Ship Without a Sail' and 'Isn't It Romantic' are especially felicitous.

The recording had a modest initial sale in New York, Chicago, and Los Angeles. Rex and Roberta sent a four-word telegram: "LOVE IT. EXCLAMATION POINT."

Sister Edmund's telegraphic message contained the single word "BRAVO."

Kitty did not as a rule read the engagement and wedding announcements in the New York papers. It was Danielle who saw the story and clipped it out.

Mamaroneck, N.Y.—Announcement has been made by Dr. and Mrs. Alexander Cameron II of this place of the engagement of their daughter, Ann Stuart, to Graham Allen, son of Mr. and Mrs. George G. Allen of Minneapolis. Miss Cameron is an alumna of the Chestnut Hill Academy, Chestnut Hill, Pa., and of Brewster Junior College, Philadelphia. Her fiancé attended Northwestern University and plans to resume his studies at the University of Minnesota. He served as a pilot and intelligence officer with the 8th Air Force in England and was discharged with the rank of captain in December, 1945.

"Brewster!" said Danielle, the Philadelphian. "That's where dumb girls with money go to learn how to put on makeup and fry flat bacon."

PART VII

31　　　　　　　　　　　　　　*Summer, 1946*

As a correspondent for the *Times*, Ben Sinclair had covered campaigns in North Africa and Italy and the Normandy invasion to the surrender of Germany. After the war he had gone directly to Paris to work out of the *Times* bureau there. After covering the French elections of June, 1946—which, as in Italy that same week, resulted in a setback for the Communists—and the Big Five foreign ministers meeting in Paris shortly afterwards, he slept and ate his way back across the Atlantic aboard the small French liner *Fort Royal* out of Bordeaux, arriving in New York the second week of July.

It was the first time he had seen his native land in more than four long years. He was tired. He was depressed. "One World" had long since divided itself into the Communist East and the non-Communist West, and in spite of the encouraging success of middle-of-the-road parties in France and Italy, western Europe remained disrupted, disorganized, disoriented, vulnerable, before an Iron Curtain that had descended from the Baltic to the Adriatic, behind which the Communists were rapidly and ruthlessly squeezing out all opposition.

For three weeks, Ben Sinclair visited his parents in Savannah, Georgia, then went up to New York August 2 to spend the other three weeks of his leave and another month on temporary assignment before returning to Europe to work out of the London bureau.

He took a sublet on Waverly Place in the Village and intended to enjoy himself. He tried all the clubs—The Village Vanguard, Cafe Society Downtown, Nick's, Eddie Condon's ...—and one midnight at Gabriel's, was mesmerized by the pianist and singer, Kitty Collins. In the space of two weeks he returned six times, sometimes attending the 9 P.M. or midnight shows, sometimes the 2 A.M. performance. He never tired of her; indeed, his fascination and what could only be described as his ardor for her grew apace. He thought she was quite extraordinarily marvelous in every way, her voice, her pianistic skill, her face and figure, hair and clothes, the way she walked and sat and inclined her head. During the day he dreamed about her.

Princeton '38, Sinclair had the pleasant accent of a Southerner of good family educated in the North and had the cultivated Southerner's gift for conversation. Moreover, he was considered quite presentable, though somewhat rumpled and physically clumsy at times.

Not especially large, Sinclair nonetheless sometimes knocked things over as if he might be uncoordinated, or perhaps he only appeared awkward because he was often preoccupied and did not look where he was going, or look carefully enough at the physical task he might be—reluctantly—performing. He often stood up too quickly and banged his knees painfully under his desk or barked his shins on the corners of doors and tables.

As an undergraduate he had never lacked for girls, but he had been away a long time and either he had grown away from the New York-based girls he had known or they had made other plans in his absence.

How could he meet her? The notion of presenting himself as a Stage Door Johnny rather embarrassed him, though he didn't embarrass easily, and if the direct approach was the only way, he was prepared to take it, though, my Lord, he thought, it would take a genius to overcome the instinctive psychological barrier a performer like her would have long since erected against the sort of men who would try to pursue such a corny, obvious tactic.

Then, as he thought he might sometime, he saw her in the Village his fourth Sunday there emerging from a fruit and vegetable store on Bleecker Street, but he was so done in by the unexpected surprise of this encounter he was left uncharacteristically tongue-tied and unable to make a move other than to think of—and reject—the idea of following her, which would have been entirely too crude and might scare her off. But at least he had a clue he didn't have before.

She was carrying the *Herald Tribune* under one arm, a sack of something in the other, and turned left into Sullivan Street.

That week he caught her act twice again and the following Sunday showed up at Cavalieri's, the fruit and vegetable store, half an hour in advance of her previous appearance. When he had made sure she was not in the store, he sat in the window of the little coffee house across the street, feeling at once excited and rather foolish.

At one o'clock, she rounded the corner wearing a go-to-church cotton dress and heels. He saw her stop by the newsstand at the corner to buy the Sunday paper. Having thought to pay for his coffee as soon as it was served, there was nothing to delay his rapid departure. He recrossed the street and entered Cavalieri's in advance of her arrival.

At the moment he passed the cashier's counter and entered the back of the little store where he intended to make a ninety-degree turn so that he would be facing the street entrance and then could browse casually among the eggplants, red peppers, and Bartlett pears—at that moment he stubbed his toe against one crate, stumbled, off-balance, into a second crate with knee and hip, and his flying elbow demolished a perfect pyramid of lemons, scattering some two dozen of them to the wooden floor where they bounced and rolled rapidly in all directions.

"Oh, Lord, I surely am sorry about this," Sinclair said, and immediately bent over, stooped, chasing awkwardly after the fruit and trying to retrieve as many pieces as he could. "I'll pay for any that are bruised, of course." He thought to add "Scusami" in a little of the Italian he had learned during the war and after.

"Di niente," he heard as he looked up to see Cavalieri—and Kitty Collins—swiftly picking up lemons, too.

She was giving him a wide, closed-mouth grin that turned on in her eyes, too, and spread wonder, joy, and confusion through his chest.

"*You looked so stricken,*" she told him later.

"*That's the effect you have on people,*" he had said.

"Really stupid of me," he said then. "I seem to be all thumbs today. Well I'll just take a dozen of these lemons. And some of these beautiful pears and red peppers. But do wait on Miss Collins first. And thank you all for your help."

"I'm in no hurry," Kitty said. "How do you know my name?"

"From Gabriel's. I confess to being one of your devoted admirers."

"I'm very flattered. Thank you."

"Well, I've seen you eight times so far. My name's Ben Sinclair. And if you're really not in any hurry would you care to join me for a cup of coffee across the way? I think I'm going to need one to help settle my jangled nerves."

"Yes, I think that'd be nice," Kitty said with a lilt in her voice that warmed his heart. "But is coffee the thing for jangled nerves?"

"Oh, well, you know what I mean."

Cavalieri, the greengrocer, who hadn't been unduly upset by the accident to begin with, and since both Ben and Kitty selected generous amounts of his produce, and being Italian he appreciated the apparent budding of romance, especially since he seemed to have played a certain role in it, something he could tell his wife, with embellishments, later in the day, beamed at them expansively, added a complimentary bunch of grapes to each of their sacks, helped Kitty re-tuck her newspaper under one arm, held the door open for them. And shortly Ben and Kitty were ensconced on art nouveau chairs at a marble-topped table near a counter below a gleaming expresso machine.

"You really heard me *eight* times in three weeks?" Kitty asked.

"Cross my heart and hope to die. Never can get enough of a good thing. Which makes me think, you know this coffee is finite, ephemeral—transitory, evanescent, fleeting, not to mention fugitive, and when it goes that will tend to leave us high and dry—unless ... unless you let me take you out to dinner this evening. Do do me the honor, Kitty. I know I'm taking up half your one day off a week but you do inspire me."

He seemed so nice, appealing, sincere, she couldn't resist. He even showed her various official-looking identity cards with his photograph—"Since there wasn't anyone to properly introduce us. So you won't think I'm some imposter or white slaver."

"You know what I think," Kitty said. "I think you're a shameless con man, but yes, I'd love to."

They dined at The Grand Ticino, a little Swiss-Italian place on Thompson Street, which had been around since 1919.

"Tell me about Paris..."

"Slowly, slowly recovering. A lot of people still don't have enough to eat or enough heat, or the money to buy what's beginning to appear in the stores. But conditions are better than they were last year. And to look at, it's still the most beautiful city in the world."

"I'd love to see it sometime. So you're going back there to work?"

"No, to London this time. Take a vacation and let me show you around."

"I might just take you up on that sometime."

"As Elwood P. Dowd once said—'When?'"

"Not before next year, I'm afraid. I'm under contract."

"Well, in the meantime you can help make up for that by showing me around New York. I sail on September twenty-first. That's only four weeks from now and all the things I've planned to see and do would make your hair stand on end. We haven't a minute to lose. For example, have you seen *Henry V*, the new film with Olivier?"

"Not yet. It just opened. But—"

"Tuesday matinee, then. Monday, unfortunately, I'm going to be tied down to the office all day. Then Wednesday, I have matinee tickets to *Annie Get Your Gun*. Have you seen it?"

"No. I've been meaning to, but Ben, this is all very nice of you but I hardly know you and—"

"Well, don't I know that? So do we have any time to waste? But I think we're making wonderful progress, don't you?"

She didn't answer, but the answer would have been yes, and she had to laugh at him. He seemed bound and determined to sweep her off her feet in as short a time as possible, and she didn't know but what she just might let him—up to a point.

"I thought Southerners liked to move slowly," she said.
"You mean to say you've never heard about cavaliers on horseback dashing madly through the magnolia-scented moonlight?"

Afterwards, they strolled in Washington Square on one of those flawless summer evenings that represent a kind of happiness, seventy-five degrees, the air dry and still and sweet, the sky clear; trees, flowers, houses, people in harmony, in a state of beatitude.

And so Kitty and Ben took in the magnificent color and pageantry and action and sonorous cadences of *Henry V* as it unrolled on the screen of the New York City Center on West 55th Street that Tuesday afternoon. Then Wednesday Kitty added Irving Berlin's "They Say It's Wonderful" to her repertoire, and the rest of that week lunched with Ben at the sidewalk cafe of the old Brevoort Hotel on lower Fifth Avenue and dined with him at Monte's on Macdougal Street, and knew he was in the audience at Gabriel's at one show or another every night and twice on Saturday, and let him escort her home afterwards and kiss her goodnight at her door, and that Sunday they went tea dancing at the Ritz-Carlton and afterwards took in another movie, Noel Coward's *Brief Encounter*, and still imbued with its pathos and there-but-for-the-grace-of-God-go-I relief of the moviegoer who has empathized with two characters for a couple of hours but does not now have to live with their tragedy, took a walk when they returned to the Village. The weather was too fine, the late summer night too beautiful to go inside, to bring the evening to a close.

They strolled along holding hands. There were not many people in Washington Square, and one could distance oneself from them as though they might be figures in someone else's landscape. They kissed beneath the branches of a tree and Kitty tingled—surprised, disturbed—tingled for the first time in years. Years.

But everything was happening too quickly. Ten places together in one week! Where was this leading?

"You're too fast for me," she said.

"I don't figure I have any choice in the matter. Today is the first of September. I have one day less than three weeks."

"Maybe we should never have started."

"Do you really believe that?"

"No. I've had a lovely time, the best time in years."

"Then why stop?"

"Because we *have* to stop. You just said it. In one day less than three weeks."

"You don't have to stop if you come with me."

"Ben! You know I can't do that."

"Do you want to?"

"It's not a question of—it's not a question of *wanting* to! I mean, ye Gods, how do I know? I mean I know I want to keep on seeing you, but going to London? That's crazy!"

"What's crazy about it? Happens every day."

"What happens every day?"

"Falling in love. Getting married. Going to London."

"Not to me it doesn't happen every day! Not to you either! What are you *saying*? You don't know me well enough. You can't possibly. I don't know—"

He stopped her talk with a kiss. She didn't resist.

"... you well ... enough—if you keep doing that we'll never get anywhere ..."

"Sit down," he commanded gently, and they sank to a bench beneath a tree.

"Now," Ben said, "you talk about what a short time it's taken me to fall absolutely madly in love with you and decide the thing I most want to do in this world is marry you and take you to London with me. But that's only because circumstances have forced me to declare myself sooner than the case might be under more leisurely circumstances. But now, you know, even when people have conventionally long engagements—six months to a year—that's just—well, what I said—convention. Shyness. Timidity. Fear of being turned down. So it may take some fellows awhile to work up enough courage to ask. But if the answer is going to be yes they've both known it right from the start, haven't they? Now before you go saying anything, let me add—London loves singers and loves jazz and it would love you. Your career is every bit as important to me as it is to you. How would I get to hear you otherwise? You can't very well just sing to an audience of one."

All at the same time Kitty was smiling and shaking her head from side to side—not from negation alone or even at all necessarily, but from wonderment—and she took both his hands.

"Ben, I'm not saying no, do you understand me, I'm not saying no, but I just can't say yes now! And I can't before you leave either! Don't be hurt, don't be sad. I think you're pretty wonderful. But there are other things to consider. You have to give me more time!"

"Come on. Let's go to Condon's," she said, pulling him to his feet. "The more we sit here, the more we're just going to..."

"Kitty," said Ben as they walked along over to West 3rd Street, and there was a subtle alteration in the tone of his voice, a tactical backing away. "Please do relax. Of course I want you to come with me on the twenty-first. And if by some miracle you decide to, I'll be there to help with the luggage. But if you can't, I'll want to be able to look forward to a letter now and then. And the hope that 1947 will see the beginning of your European education. On any terms you choose. Sinclair's friendly and courteous travel and escort service is ever at your beck and call. Another spring and summer will surely come around no matter what, and in addition to our special tour of London and the English countryside, we offer excursions to Wales, Scotland, the land of your ancestors, too, and of course the Continent..."

Again the timbre of his voice changed, not to what it was before but to a third level of sound and meaning.

"Just don't run away."

"I won't."

Members of the Condon mob—Eddie Condon, guitar; Wild Bill Davison, trumpet; Pee Wee Russell, clarinet; George Brunies, trombone; Joe Sullivan, piano; George Wettling, drums; Sid Weiss, bass—are on stage at Eddie Condon's on West 3rd Street playing "Mandy, Make Up Your Mind," the last number of the second set of the evening. The rafters ring with two-beat jazz, the old New Orleans sound most people persist in calling Dixieland, a ghost of itself down there, brought to Chicago where it inspired a generation of the great practitioners who keep it alive these days at Condon's and such other New York outposts as Ryan's on 52nd Street and Nick's in the Village, though Brunies is a New Orleans original.

The solos done, Davison's trumpet pulls them all together from their separate, inspired ways, though each player still reaches in his own direction, too, to a rousing climax, and Ben Sinclair and Kitty Collins are on their feet applauding their palms off.

Ben's one-month assignment at the *Times* home office was extremely loose and undemanding, in effect an extra paid vacation, which both his editors and he himself felt he deserved after four arduous years as a war and postwar correspondent and with a demanding new assignment about to begin. He had to do some work for a few hours during the day and a couple of times in the evening, but during his last nineteen days he and Kitty were able to be together sixteen of them.

They took the Staten Island ferry bouncing in the wake of returning troop ships, went to Coney Island for the rides, City Island for the seafood, and Brooklyn Heights for the views of Manhattan. They went to Bleeck's, the newspaperman's saloon, Tim Costello's literary saloon on Third Avenue, and other watering holes of character and distinction, to Chinatown, Little Italy, the Lower East Side, and smaller enclaves of ethnic restaurateurs and merchants—Lebanese ... Maltese ... Ukranian ... Greek ... —strung across lower Manhatten.

He set aside any more talk about *them*. He asked about her and she told him every significant detail, though it didn't take her long, only part of one afternoon. His reaction was curious, calm and kind. He told her about himself and his family, and being a genteel Southerner was a mine of family and small-city anecdotes, a good 75 percent of them reflecting often hilarious foibles of rather eccentric, or individualistic, relatives, neighbors, friends, and townspeople. Most often they just talked about what they were looking at—things like Wall Street towers—the symbol of Manhattan—rising closer toward their approaching ferry boat, the strange and striking people on the teeming streets. In theaters and concert halls they didn't have to talk at all.

And time galloped like Ben Sinclair's horseman dashing through the romantic evening.

Kitty wrote to Joe:

I'm not asking for advice and will feel guilty if you go to the trouble of trying to give me any, though please do write again just to let me know what you've been up to, but I just wanted to let my hair down and you have one of the most comforting shoulders to lean on I know.

... I'm not sure I'm in love with him—how *can* I be after less than three weeks, for Lord's sake (or am I forgetting something?)—but I think I could be. I *believe* him. I believe *in* him, but has *he* had time to? He's thirty, a dangerous now-or-never age, and lonely—out of touch with old—American—girls he had, he's been away so long, and in Europe had to move around so much—in wartime, and right afterwards when everything was in such a mess—I gather there was a French girl he was very interested in—and that's *good*—the more you know the better it is I seem to remember somebody warning me once ...

He says he not only wants me to continue my career—which I'll never give up now, as you know—wouldn't, couldn't have it any other way, but he can't know what life would really be like—and neither can I when you come right down to it—with me performing—in London or wherever—some *good* place for me and not every city is—and he probably having to travel, move around. Where there's a will there's a way, I believe that, but—but, but, but. Things could be tough for both of us. I want a normal life but if you're a performer you can't just have a really normal life. Maybe I shouldn't even consider mixing marriage with a career. But that would be a bleak sort of half-life ...

You'd like him. He'd like you. Now there's a couple of great recommendations. Between Southerners and Chicago Irishmen, I don't know who can charm a bird out of a tree faster, so you see why I'm dizzy from this whirlwind courtship ...

To Matt she wrote:

Harry's closed last month. The building is going to be torn down to make room for a skyscraper. Harry Field is now an agent for MCA and has taken me on as one of his clients. Oh, before I forget, do you ever listen to Dave Garroway's "11:60 Club" on WMAQ? He plays good jazz and other records and will plug one of mine, so he says, next Tuesday, the 10th. DJ's in some other cities—Boston, Kansas City, San Francisco—have been playing songs from my record pretty regularly and sales have picked up there. Stardust wants me to do another. But five percent of fifty cents doesn't add up to much unless you sell a million. I'm not hurting, though. Gabriel Kellerman pays over-scale. I don't seem to spend very much except on clothes to perform in, so I can salt away the rest for my old age ...

And Matt replied:

Joe, Jim, and I joined a pickup outfit this summer (Ted was working at a Wisconsin lake resort) and played half a dozen country club dances. A few times we got to play a little jazz after the dancing was over, but mostly we had to provide ticky-ticky-tick stuff.

People remember when you sang and played with us before you got famous and don't think we aren't proud of it. We plug your records too whenever we get a chance.

Joe says to say hello for him, and he'll drop a line one of these days ...

Roberta wrote:

Baby, we're leaving California next spring. Going back to Europe! Why don't you consider coming with us?"

A British promoter the Wilkins Quartet had met in Hollywood had arranged a tentative booking in Copenhagen.

... We'd settle down somewhere sooner or later—Copenhagen, Paris— Paris has always been a good jazz town. You don't have to decide now, but think it over ...

One night, a week before Ben was due to sail, Kitty decided in her mind to go with him. By morning she had decided not to. She wasn't going to run away. But neither would he.

The evening before he sailed, Ben took her to Le Moal, a solid temple of bourgeois French gastronomy on Third Avenue below the rattling El.

"I've been good, haven't I?" Ben asked. "Haven't pushed, haven't driven you into a corner? Fishing for compliments now."

"No. You've been marvelous. You've been the best thing for me since—since they invented spring tonic in the summer.... I'm not going to say I'm sorry you have to go because with you over there I have an excuse to come visit... Should I go to Copenhagen with Roberta and Rex and Harold? Who knows what's liable to happen to my kind of music and people like me? Jazz is changing. Some of the new things are great, some I'm not so sure of, and I don't know if much of it is really for me to play. You can't sing it. If you want to know the truth I'd much rather listen to Charlie Parker playing a ballad than bop. In those ballads he does things that have never been done before, but they're still *songs.* Same with Pete Weathersby. He's never been afraid to experiment and he knows all the new stuff as well as he knows Bach. But that great sound he gets comes out of the same old fashioned harmony and melody. But it's harder now. There don't seem to be as many good new songs as there always were before . . ."

They had to dine early because it was a Friday evening and she had a nine o'clock performance.

In the cab to the Village, Ben said, "You know, I have a confession to make. That morning in the fruit store, I wasn't there by accident."

"Weren't you really? Well, fancy that."

"But knocking over the lemons was accidental."

"Accidents," said Kitty, "will happen."

His face happened to be turned her way. She gave him a quick, light kiss on his lips, creating a little epiphany he kept intact by not giving her one in return.

Kitty began her early performance swinging into Kern's "A Fine Romance," to stir things up a bit, establish a light-hearted mood, then began, without a pause through the trickle of applause, one of Ben Sinclair's favorites, "Quiet Night"—and went on to combine that wry tenderness of Rodgers and Hart with the sultrier and more dramatic "Speak Low" of Kurt Weill and Ogden Nash. She then reminded herself and Ben and everyone in the audience— including Gabriel Kellerman, who once again thanked his lucky stars for having hired her—that fall was in the air, that this was the season of change, by playing "Autumn in New York," Vernon Duke's ambivalent love song to Manhattan. She turned up the emotional level a bit more with Harry Warren's and Mack Gordon's lovely "The More I See You" of 1945, and, lowering the tempo and intensity once again, ended with Rodger's and Hart's touching "Can't You Do a Friend a Favor?"

> *. . . I'm the dish you ought to savor;*
> *Something warm and something new—*
> *I would do my friend a favor,*
> *I would fall in love with you . . .*

—And acknowledged the enthusiastic applause with a deep bow (which meant she had to toss and brush her long hair away from her forehead when she straightened up) and the modest demeanor of clasped hands and blushing schoolgirl smile.

In four weeks they had done the town, set the stage, but kept it light and laughing. He really had to sail away on schedule now. They couldn't have kept it up much longer without something breaking. They would have to get married or stop seeing each other because, in principle, Kitty would not have an affair with him or anyone. He knew this and accepted it. "All, or Nothing at All" was another song of those years. If he felt the urgent need he could always pick up a girl in some late night bar in the Village, or, in a pinch, telephone a number he had.

They strolled outside on her first break. Ben had been hit suddenly by emotional, pre-travel nervous exhaustion and Kitty could see it in his eyes, his expression and gait, hear it in his off-kilter voice.
"You are *not* going to wait up five more hours for me," she said. "You're dead on your feet as it is, and you have to get up early to finish packing. I'll be at the ship . . ."
He didn't argue and she watched him fondly, sadly, as he waved, somewhat inaccurately, and walked away down the Village street.

Ben sailed on the *Colombie* September 21, 1946. Kitty went aboard ship at the French Line's West 48th Street pier to see him off. There were others there sipping champagne, colleagues from the *Times*.
"Write to me," said Ben.
"I will!"
Tears in her eyes she embraced him, and left without looking back.

32

*Fall-winter-spring
1946–47*

Ben Sinclair did not write every day, or every week, and he did not write what could really be called love letters. During the last three months of the year and the first three months of 1947 he wrote eight long missives, composed somewhat in the manner of the "Letter from London" and "Letter from Paris" series in *The New Yorker*—polished, well-informed, often ironic or amusing accounts of public affairs in these capitals—with less emphasis, in the case of his efforts, on politics and international affairs and more on the theater and worlds of music, art, literature, and high society. He would add a paragraph or two for Kitty alone, though he kept these concluding pages oblique and witty, affectionate and nonthreatening.

He traveled all over the British Isles and covered some Continental events as well when extra hands were needed at major conferences or when the Paris or Rome men, for example, could not be in two places at once. Later, he was given semi-roving status and spent weeks in Yugoslavia, Greece, and elsewhere in the seething Balkans. Picture postcards, with a line or two at most, arrived in New York from many places. And then, once or twice weekly or less frequently, Kitty clipped his signed stories and background pieces from the *Times* and pasted them in a scrapbook.

Ben's pattern of correspondence relieved her. She was not a writer, but she was a good collector of oddities and snippets of this and that culled from publications other than the *Times*, and matching his established rate of once a month or so, invariably had assembled enough to fill an envelope plus a few obliquely affectionate lines of her own.

Every road seemed to point to Europe. Roberta wrote again and telephoned a couple of times. The Copenhagen contract was firm and clubs in London and Paris were equally interested. By now, Kitty hardly needed any time at all to decide to go along and in letters or in person told Roberta, Harry Field, Gabriel Kellerman, Joe and Matt Barry, and Ben Sinclair. Ben regretted she would not be coming directly to London but noted that the Danish capital was only a short flight from Heathrow.

On April 30, Kitty received a formal invitation to a May 31 wedding that would unite Joseph Patrick Barry to Elizabeth Lynn Halligan.

Kitty accepted directly to Joe:

Congratulations! Don't worry, I'll be there. I wouldn't miss this wedding for anything. Roberta, Rex and Harold, and their bass player whom I've never met, are going ahead around the first of May but I'd planned all along to wait until the summer to join them in Denmark. Gabriel Kellerman would like me to work through most of May, so your plans work out beautifully for me. Can't wait to see you and Matt, and everybody, Sister Edmund, Eileen, the Rosens. It's been so long...

Roberta wrote ahead from L.A.:

We're booked on the Gripsholm which sails for Goeteborg, Sweden—however you pronounce it—May 9 at noon. Train down to Copenhagen from there. Won't get into New York till the morning of the 8th. But that will give us one night to catch your act at Gabriel's and talk over plans. Can't tell you how happy Rex and Harold and me are you've decided to join us in Europe..

They had made reservations at a hotel in the Times Square area where other black musicians they knew had felt comfortable, and

Kitty was waiting in the seedy lobby when they came in, Harold Saunders, the copper-tinted sax man, melon-bellied, duck-footed, owl-beaked, and jaunty with a pork pie hat on the back of his head, leading the way with two suitcases, Roberta following with just a small vanity case, wearing a tailored black suit with two fox furs chasing each other around her neck, Rex Wilkins smiling at her side. Bringing up the rear was a bespectacled, scholarly looking young bassist introduced as Maurice Barnes.

Kitty embraced them all except Maurice, with whom she shook hands, and said, "You guys must be stiff and tired from all that time on the train. I'm going to leave you alone to get some rest. Come for drinks and a buffet supper at five."

Kitty was a little worried about the chemistry of her party, but she needn't have been; it jelled almost instantly. Roberta and Harold Saunders were at their gregarious best, while Rex was debonair and charming; they filled any gaps in the conversation of Maurice Barnes, who was rather shy at first; and all hit it off with Harry and Miriam Field, who never lacked for words, and Gabriel Kellerman, a skilled raconteur who knew how to listen, too. Charlie O'Donnell, who had just bought and moved into a farm on Long Island, came in with his wife, "a society babe," as Kitty had described her to Roberta, but who turned out to be quite knowledgeable about the work of musicians and other performers from Gabriel's and 52nd Street, and seemed quite flattered to be able to meet them. Norman, the NYU student and Richard, the art teacher, whom Kitty still dated occasionally, were there. Danielle was there. Rodney Blake had a noisy reunion with Rex, Roberta, and Harold. There were about twenty-five in all and they created a stimulating hubbub in Kitty's small apartment. Kitty had hired a caterer and bartender and could relax and enjoy her own party.

At one point, Kitty and Roberta were off to one side together.

"Roberta, am I going to *fit* with the quartet? I know you haven't heard me recently, but you know what I do. Well, you'll hear tonight."

"You'll fit if you want to fit. You're an extra dimension. I've also got some ideas for some two-piano things, also taking one composer and alternating songs, maybe even alternating lines once in a while.

More of an act. I don't mean the kind of silly duet things you had to do when you were with Irving Bennett."

"Oh, I'm going to love working with you, you don't have to worry about that."

Charlie's wife said, "So many of your guests are really quite wonderful. I've never met any jazz musicians before. Enormously talented artists from what you tell me and from what little I've heard, and they're absolutely unpretentious."

"They're good at what they do and they love doing it," Kitty said.

"More than that. That formula could just as easily produce arrogance, too. I've known some surgeons, actors, who are not quite so nice. It must be the music."

"Oh, they're not all saints and they're on their best behavior here. I made some of them promise they'd watch their language. But you're right. For every bastard there do seem to be an awful lot of really sweet guys. Their music makes them happy, I guess that's the answer."

"Gee, in three weeks, I'll see Sister Edmund again," Kitty said to Charlie O'Donnell. "I can't believe it. It's been forever."

"She's very excited about it, I can tell you," Charlie said.

"You'll come back to New York," Gabriel Kellerman said wistfully. "Musicians always do. The question is, how long will it take and will I still be around to see it?"

"Mr. Kellerman, you're ageless. You're immortal," Kitty said.

"I'm forty-eight," said Gabriel Kellerman.

Roberta's first letter from the Danish capital was encouraging. The club they were playing in was in the cellar of a very old building, as dark and cramped as clubs usually were in America, the ventilation no better, but the audience had been enthusiastic. The Danes were extremely friendly and hospitable—color bars, or even color-consciousness, seemed non-existent—and overall, Copenhagen was a clean, beautiful city with many attractions. So far, they were still living in a hotel but looking for apartments.

Kitty made a reservation at the Lake Shore Hotel, and a week after she had quietly celebrated her twenty-first birthday, she left for Chicago.

When she had looked around her furnished apartment in New York that morning, virtually nothing was left except building property. The Fields had offered to keep her spinet piano, paintings and lithographs, books and records until she could send for them. A trunk had been picked up for consignment to the steamship company. What was in suitcases would get her through the Chicago trip; what was left on shelves in the apartment would get her through until sailing time.

The train rolled on into the evening, into the past and future. She and the inside of the train itself, the lighted compartment, were reflected in the window, and she watched the towns and countryside rushing past, through the dark reflection of her own face, and thought of Ben, of Ben in New York, Ben who could show her the London she had once been denied.

Nothing needs to be decided aboard a train hurtling through the night. One decision has already been taken and is out of your hands—to set out for a destination, to go from one place to another—and for the length of the journey that is enough. In motion, there is nothing to do but lean back and let things happen, sip the drink brought from the dining car, and let memory, the faces of the past, pull thought at random, this way and that, all conclusions suspended.

33

Eleven A.M. and a warm, sunny day in Chicago, late May, platform, station, street outside, all crowded, big city, ungracious, exciting. How we stare at first at the people in different cities. Do they look like Chicagoans, New Yorkers? Is there something different about them? Have we entered another dimension, another plane of being?

A pleasant enough middle-aged cabbie wearing a cloth cap, Croatian name under his photo in the interior.

"The Lake Shore Hotel, and please go up Michigan Avenue and through Lincoln Park. Maybe you'd more or less do that anyway, I forget," Kitty said.

"Anything you like, Miss," the cabbie said. "You want to cruise around the park a little, we can do that."

"All right, and could I ask a favor? Would you turn off the radio, please?"

He did so, probably with reluctance, and the silence was a sudden blessing. The music had been dreadful, and one of those terrible announcers talking relentlessly, two or three times faster than the normal rate of human speech, had been soiling the air, peddling used cars and other unbearably dreary products.

Kitty leaned back and looked out the cab window at parks, marinas, sailboats on the lake, tall buildings on the other side.

There it was, still in the lobby of the Lake Shore Hotel, the enlarged photo of a smiling Irving Bennett. "Nightly except Sundays at The Strand." Ten years and still going strong, a triumph of mediocrity. Laurie Lee Hill was still featured—along with some baby doll named Florence Farrell. Well, you're welcome to it, dear, Kitty said to herself, and wondered when she would get a chance to see Laurie Lee and Artie Rosen. Probably not today.

Kitty had written ahead to Sister Edmund. After lunch she telephoned, and the nun who answered said excitedly, "Yes, she's expecting you. Can you come at three? She's resting now and asked me to give you that message."

Kitty took the bus, which was convenient—from a stop in front of the hotel to a stop half a block from the convent—and pleasant—along Sheridan Road, which had a certain elegance the entire way, but she regretted that the old open-top double-deckers were no more.

Sister Edmund was waiting at the opened door, and Kitty was amazed at how small she seemed. She had always thought of the nun as being much taller. The old imperiousness and the stiff carriage were still there, but her role today was to welcome the prodigal, the lost sheep. With a fervent embrace, tears, a glad cry. Kitty was escorted ceremoniously to the music room where cookies and lemonade had been laid out.

"Sister Martin died earlier this year, God rest her soul," Sister Edmund said, and made the sign of the cross. "She would have so loved to see you."

"Oh, and I her," Kitty said. "I'm so sorry."

"She was seventy-two," Sister Edmund said, and Kitty told herself, I've grown up, I've arrived, the taboo subject of nuns' ages is something that can be discussed with me in public.

"When you left you were still a child in my eyes. Now you're a woman," Sister Edmund said. "Perhaps you were a woman then, too." She frowned. "Must you go to Europe just now?"

"It's where the work is, Sister."

"Well, I can't manage your life for you. How I envy you, actually, going to Europe, England."

There was a knock at the door and Sister Edmund, skirts and beads rustling, moved swiftly to open it. Sister Clothilde and Sister Lawrence, two other nuns who had taught Kitty, came in to be presented.

Sister Edmund poured tea and passed cookies to Kitty and the other nuns, and they all sat in a circle that was stylized but not really stiff, with the focus entirely on Kitty, the admired emissary from an outside world the women in habits had in large part rejected but which still held a residual interest for them.

"It'll be awhile before I go to France," Kitty said. "First Denmark, then England. But I can hardly wait. Sister Clothilde, Sister Lawrence, I have you to thank for introducing me to the French Impressionists. I studied their paintings in a course at New York University and some of the actual paintings in museums. It's *their* France—Pissaro's and Monet's and Renoir's and the others, and the Post-Impressionists', too—I imagine. I hope I won't be disappointed!"

"France can never disappoint!" cried Sister Clothilde, and the others laughed at her chauvinism.

"Will you play something for us?" Sister Edmund asked. "The choice is yours—classical or jazz."

Kitty smiled. "Good music was the only choice there ever was, Sister. So a little of each."

For seven minutes she played the Chopin Ballade in A-flat, then for about four created new melodies from the harmonic chords of "Embraceable You."

"Bravo!" cried Sister Edmund, tears behind her glasses, and the other nuns applauded, too.

Sister Edmund went to a cupboard and from a drawer withdrew something newly bound in soft leather.

"Kitty," she said. "We have your recordings, the performance you just gave us, and now we would like you to have this—happily to welcome you back—sadly, to send you on your way again."

It was the score of Schumann's "Scenes of Childhood."

"Oh!" Kitty said in a low voice, then couldn't speak.

Sister Edmund pressed Kitty's hand, and fled.

From the convent, Kitty walked alone toward the cab stand at the Granville Avenue El station. She recognized none of the people she passed. Once she had simply taken this middle-class neighborhood for granted, noticing only the people who lived there, including herself. Now she saw how ordinary it was, undistinguished by any house or shop or apartment building that stood there. It evoked nothing like the affecting sadness of nostalgia, only empty recognition. The lot beside the building where she had lived with her mother was still choked with weeds and cinders, with here and there a rusted can or shards of broken glass, the desolate detritus of American cities.

I never forgave her because she had never asked to be forgiven. I could forgive her for being vain, lazy, greedy, a whore, but I can't forgive her for running out on me. Did it matter now? Yes, it mattered, it still mattered, it always would, but Roberta had redeemed her and that mattered more.

Where Fossbinders had been was another bar and grill called The Golden Horseshoe. Maybe Bernie and Erna had moved to Florida as they had always talked about doing some day. No entertainment was advertised in the window where Roberta Wilkins' photographs had once been displayed. Kitty didn't go in. She climbed into a taxi, and as it pulled away from the curb she sat up very straight in the middle of the back seat. As she had once carried school books, she clutched the leatherbound folio of "Kinderszenen" tightly against her chest.

34

Kitty took one look at Peg Barry and knew she was not forgiven, and never would be.

Jim had opened the door to the house; Jim, Matt, and Edward J. had kissed her in succession; Peg talked a mile a minute but held Kitty's hand only briefly, and quickly turned her over to cousins from Moline, one of whom, a farmer, said, "So you're the famous singer."

"Not really famous," Kitty said.

"Ed played us one of your records," a woman said. "Why, it was just like you were on the radio!"

Matt moved her along, got her a glass of punch and said, "If I ever get time I'd like to ask you about O. D. Turnipseed's guitar. Boy, I know he's a real screwball but to have the privilege of playing in the same group with him..."

"I didn't actually play with him, I was just singing then, but I'll—"

But Jim pulled Matt away to attend to other duties.

The house was jammed. Joe and Lynn hadn't yet arrived. There had been no mention and now was no sign of Ted, and she wondered if he was there.

If mass feeding was a necessity, Kitty supposed a buffet dinner like this was as good a way as any of dealing with the problem, but she did not enjoy them, a decent conversation with anyone was impossible, and one tended to eat too little or too much too quickly.

"There's Joe!" she said to whomever it was she was trying to talk to, and Joe appeared on the other side of the big living room, surrounded by admirers, looking somewhat like a popular politician, perhaps a victorious light-heavyweight fighter in his dressing room. Alongside him was a rather tall girl in what looked to be a brand-new and very becoming clan-plaid gingham suit with a flared peplum below the jacket, silk scarf tied at her throat, small jeweled ear clips, her dark blonde hair tied in back with a black taffeta bow. Lynn? Kitty wondered, and when Joe caught sight of Kitty, beamed, blew her a kiss, and began to fight his way through the crowd, the dark blonde girl trailed a little behind him.

"Joe! Kitty!" Huge double bear hug, back slapping, cries.

"This is terrible," Joe said. "Who are all these people? Can't talk here and we absolutely have to. What about breakfast tomorrow at the Lake Shore, about 9:30? The only time I can think of when there isn't a million damn other things that have to be done, people interrupting..."

Then he was swept away. Edward J., very red-faced by now, hove into view carrying two glasses.

"Happily, this isn't the only time we'll get to see you!" he said in passing.

Lynn had seemed very cordial, friendly, and Kitty found herself envying her. Joe really was such a great person with no meanness in him, but never dull as the good so often are, a superior man, really. But this party is getting impossible, I don't know anyone, and I would like a quiet beer and to listen to Garroway later on. At 9:30 she managed to phone for a cab and to get close enough to Peg to call, "Thank you, I didn't sleep much on the train last night. See you later!"

At the hotel, she wandered out to the Strand, just to torture herself for a minute or two with the sound of Irving Bennett's music, to enjoy not hearing it all the more at a table in the Capstan Bar. Which appeared to be exclusively patronized by dating collegians. A sea of seersucker, with pink, blue, yellow sails. To Kitty, they all seemed so young.

* * *

At 8:30 in the morning, Kitty scanned the *Tribune* left outside her door, then dressed in a white-and-blue summer frock, went to the hotel coffee shop, accepted the cup a waitress poured for her automatically, and waited for Joe.

It was 9:15. At 9:35 he came charging in in his way, somehow occupying more space than most people, more than his size would warrent.

"Joe, it's so great to see you!"

"Kitty, you're a sight for sore eyes. You look marvelous."

Kitty hadn't been sure whether he would bring Lynn along, and rather hoped that he wouldn't. Three's a crowd. He hadn't.

The waitress had juice, sweet rolls, more coffee in front of them a minute or so after they had ordered, Joe saying he had eaten eggs earlier to keep from starving, Kitty saying this was her usual breakfast.

They each had so many questions at the same time, the questions collided, overlapped, and for a few seconds produced no coherent answers. They laughed at each other.

"Let's start over again," Joe said. "I'm going to work for Lynn's father. In sales. I won't have anything to do with him directly, and I'll still have to produce, son-in-law or not."

Oh, that isn't what he wants, Kitty thought, but she was spared having to comment. He went right on without a pause—"Now tell me about Ben."

It would have been so easy to throw out some bright, optimistic generalization about Ben and her, about the future, but she had always leveled with Joe Barry, and saw no reason to stop now.

"Oh, Joe, I just don't know." She hiked up her shoulders, let them drop again. "Something's missing. I wish it wasn't but it is. Absence didn't make the heart grow fonder somehow. Maybe something's missing in me since Graham. Ben was sweet and dear and fun to be with the little while we were together. I never let it go any further than that. He's terribly interesting and he still makes me laugh. I think he'd be a devoted husband—when he was around. He has to travel a lot. He wanted me to marry him. I think he still does. But I don't know whether I can, whether I should . . . Joe, do you still play trumpet? I hope you haven't given it up. I wish I could hear you again. I wish there was time to jam a little together."

Kitty glanced around. Their booth was some distance from other customers. Even so she kept her voice very low as she scat-sang the opening bars of the Barrys' old theme song "Once upon a Time," then abruptly ceased, and said, "Joe, are you all right?"

"All right?"

"You look so ... sick or something."

"I do? Must be my hangover ... When do you sail?"

"Next Friday ... Joe, are you sure you're all right?"

"I think I'll skip the rest of this breakfast. Sorry. Sorry to waste it. Spoil our little party. Maybe we could take a walk in the fresh air."

He signaled the waitress, fished a five-dollar bill from his wallet and said, "We have to leave. This cover it?"

"Oh, yes, sir. Way more than enough."

"You keep the rest."

They went down a corridor and out through an open doorway to the Strand along the lake, past the now empty bandstand, Joe still looking pale, slowly brushing his hair with one hand as he walked, and smiling the saddest smile that touched her deeply for reasons she didn't understand.

"Joe," she said after a moment, "I really liked Lynn. I hardly talked to her but I liked her right away, and I can be pretty critical. She seems very intelligent and she's certainly pretty. I think you're doing very well."

He didn't seem to have heard her.

"Do you know that Ted and I still don't talk to each other," he said. "It's true. He hasn't spoken to me since the night of that fight way back in 1942."

"Joe! That's terrible." *Was that what he was so worried about? Just that?*

"I honestly tried to patch it up, wrote to him during the war, never got an answer, tried again in person when we came home. Nothing doing. He walked away from me and left the house. I don't know if he really still hates me or has just let this thing go on so long it's gotten impossible for him to reverse himself. The stubborn, pig-headed, unforgiving Barrys. No, not all of us. Gross exaggeration."

"Your mother, too, I'm afraid."

"Do you think so? I can't argue with you, but I'm sorry to hear it. Something said last night? It was a big crowd. Are you sure? Not just distracted, too busy?"

"Yes, I'm sure. Not something said, something un-said, un-done. Very different from your father. Look, I can't complain. I'm sorry it has to be this way, but I probably deserve it."

He stopped walking and she stopped and they stood side by side leaning on a wooden railing and looking across the wide beach to the sun sparkling lake.

"So do I, I guess," he said.

"You? Why you? Deserve what?"

"Ted was half-right that night we fought. No, of course you weren't his girl and never would be, he was too young for you and you were in love with Graham anyway, though Ted was too nuts about you to admit to himself he didn't have a chance. He was right about me. About a year before that I did take a girl away from him. She appealed to me and he was awkward and I wasn't and I did it, thoughtlessly, cruelly, unforgivably. And I cringe to this day when I think about it. I actually confessed this to a priest in the confessional, as a sin against charity, the worst kind. Got absolved, of course. Go and sin no more. But I still feel guilty. Then that night he saw me kissing you at the top of the stairs..."

"Sweetie, you were bombed, a little amorous," Kitty said, taking his hand. "So was I. I still remember."

"But Ted guessed I was in love with you, had loved you since the day you walked into our house. Even though, because of Graham, I didn't have a chance either. That night, because I was bombed, because I was going into the navy, I slipped a little, not enough for you to really notice, but enough to drive Ted crazy.

"Then by the time you and Graham got divorced there was somebody named Norman, and then Ben, and long ago I had given up hope anyway, and I was tired of being single, chasing around. If I hadn't seen you yesterday I would have married Lynn and tried to be a good husband. I would have done what three-quarters of the people in the world do. I would have settled for less, made the best of it. But seeing you again, knowing you're free, I can't possibly go through with this wedding. Kitty, let me go to Europe with you."

Kitty was absolutely thunderstruck. But not speechless.

"No! For God's sake, Joe, no!" She snapped her head from side to side. "I won't even think about it! You don't know *what* you want and I could never *do* that to this girl, to your parents, to anybody!"

"I'm still going to call it off," Joe said. "And I know what a terrible thing I'll be doing to Lynn who doesn't deserve it. All the plans, the money ... the publicity, the crowds of people waiting out there, what people are going to say, what people are liable to do, and I'm horrified at what I'm going to do—break a promise I made in good faith."

"Joe, you just like girls and you can't make up your mind about any of them!"

"No, that's not true. It was true before I met you and it was only true afterwards because you were always in love with someone else. Or I thought you were. But there's never been anyone else in my life who could really take your place."

"I'm leaving, Joe. I'm leaving right now. Today! If I can't change my train reservation I'll take a bus!"

"Will you think about it? Will you give me a chance?"

"No! How can you talk like this? How can you do this to that girl? She's a nice girl! Dear God!" She was talking with one hand clapped across her brow and walking back and forth, in little circles.

"I *know* she's a nice girl. And what I can't do to her is marry her and ruin her life when I know I don't love her. Wouldn't it be worse to do that?"

"I don't know!—I suppose so. But don't expect me to decide! Why should I?! I just came here to be a guest at a wedding, not to ..."

But Peg Barry will blame me for this to her dying day! Goddamn you, Joe!

"Will you let me see you again sometime?"

"I'll be in Europe! Oh boy, will I be in Europe! I'm not coming back here! Ever! Not even to New York for a long, long time!"

"I'll get to Europe somehow. Will you let me see you then?"

For a few moments she panicked. *Tell him you want no part of this, you'll never see him again! Oh, no, I can't say that. I can't not see him ever again.*

"I can't promise anything. Not anything! I might marry Ben after all. I might be married to someone else. I might decide I'll never marry anybody ever again! And how do you know you won't change your mind again?"

"I won't," Joe said. "I know. In five years I've never changed my mind. Only I didn't realize it."

She put her hands over her eyes. "I just wanted to go to a wedding and see some old friends and mind my own business and not hurt anybody and then take a nice peaceful trip to Europe, and look what happens! Dear God!"

"Whatever happens, it's all my doing," Joe said. "It isn't your fault or your responsibility. You're innocent. You're not part of some conspiracy, and I won't let you be blamed for what happens." Pale and shaken, he looked at his watch. "For what I have to start doing within the next hour. Nobody is going to be there tomorrow so nobody is going to notice you're not there either. Blame it all on me."

He looked at her one last time then half turned away from her.

"Now I am just going to scram the hell out of here and leave you in peace. Please do me a favor and don't say any more now, not another word."

Kitty felt an overwhelming urge to reach out and touch him, to comfort him, to say something, but she said no more and did nothing and as he walked away to his fate thought only, *Poor girl, poor Joe, poor everybody. Poor me*...

The rise and fall of Atlantic seas, great green rolling swells to the northeast horizon, between two worlds, two lives, and on into the sleepless daylight nights of a Scandinavian summer.

Was this something she had really wanted all along? She would have said "Oh, I love Joe" aloud to anyone, to Lynn, to anyone, and no one would have given it a second thought even though it was true, because it would have meant Joe's my friend, I think he's a great guy, I enjoy his company, we share the same knowledge and love of music, I can tell him my troubles, I can trust him. For starters, could any woman ask for more? And once, a long time ago, they had walked upstairs together and he had surprised her with a kiss and she had let him kiss her a second time because she had wanted him to, and then had thought there had better not be a third time if she was going to be faithful to Graham Allen. She had truly loved Graham then and faithfully, and she had thought Joe wasn't serious, that he simply liked girls, and knew in the navy he might be deprived of them occasionally or even for long stretches, and he had felt a little amorous, and she had felt a little amorous herself—Joe was not only her friend and a great guy, he was a wonderfully attractive guy, and just because you were in love with somebody else didn't mean you couldn't find other people attractive if they were. How was that for starters, too? But starters are starters, they're not enough, and maybe there isn't enough to be enough.

London autumn, still on the edge of Europe, the Channel in January, glassware and crockery sliding and crashing in the empty saloon, Maurice deathly ill, Harold, Kitty, and Rex dipping, rising, holding on, Roberta at the rail positively exulting, and on by train through rain-blurred countryside, the gloomy sides of towns, and out of the Gare du Nord into the rain blur of Paris, too much to take in, to remember; freezing cold and not enough coal yet, not enough heat, stuffy lobbies and cold hotel rooms, steamy glassed-in cafes, two of them, Harold and Kitty, knocked out by flu, up too soon, relapsing, fear of pneumonia, Rex and Roberta and Maurice carrying on at La Boule d'Or, an eighteenth-century cellar in Saint-Germain-des-Prés. *Graham never came when I was sick and now Joe isn't here because I drove him away and now he doesn't write any more the way he used to but that's the way it has to be he had never settled down and neither have I, we're always on the move. I'm an artist, a performer, that's my life. One failed marriage already and I'm not even twenty-two. Once burnt twice shy, Ben and Joe make two make twice. I caused that fight. I caused one boy to hate his brother and not to speak to him for five long years and maybe for the rest of his life. I was the cause of the terrible thing that happened to that girl that she will never forget and never forgive as long as she lives no matter how quickly she finds and keeps a better man. Bless me Father for I have sinned I don't want to be the cause of any more hatred, any more grief* ... More colds, sinus attacks, the worst winter Kitty could remember. Then one blessed day she woke and it was warm and she was well, and could meet Ben Sinclair and his new English wife.

In May, 1948, along with Coleman Hawkins and other American musicians, the quartet went to the old Marigny Theater in the gardens of the Champs Elysées off the Rond Point, to take part in the first postwar Paris jazz festival, sponsored by the Princesse de Broglie and the Duc du Brissac—great enthusiasm for traditional jazz, none for bop. And now the first big wave of postwar American tourists swept in and collegians gravitated to St.-Germain and blue jeans took over the Pont-Royal Bar on the rue du Bac and the Café de Flore on the boulevard St.-Germain, but Kitty and Maurice and Harold and Rex and Roberta had already staked out the adjoining Deux Magots and sat there at this new crossroads of the world in the sunny afternoons, watching the people and reading the *Herald Tribune*. In the mornings, walking miles, Kitty explored alone and began to take things in, and celebrated the streets, boulevards, squares, circles, quais, bridges, islands, parks, churches, palaces, stones, walls, windows, shutters, gateways, courtyards, arcades, cafes, shops, and markets of this splendid, supremely elegant, thrilling city. She was photographed with Rex and Roberta outside at Fouquet's at approximately the same table where a camera had recorded Rex and Roberta in 1935, and had eggs benedict at Weber on the rue Royale Sunday mornings after Mass at the Church of the Madeleine, and dined on boeuf bourguignon at the pre-World War I Chez Josephine on the rue du Cherche-Midi and on lobster thermidor at the historic Café de Paris, and on marmite dieppoise, braised veal kidneys, and woodcock flambé at those other wonderful survivors of La Belle Epoque—Prunier and Laperousse and Lucas-Carton. And late at night she celebrated the music of Kern, Berlin, Gershwin, Rodgers, Porter, Arlen, Youmans, Schwartz, Lane, Martin, Duke, Carmichael, Donaldson, Warren, Jones, McHugh, Ellington, Whiting, Wilder, Noble, Green, Bloom, Mercer, Loesser, Van Heusen, Blake, Young, Waller, Ronell, Swift, and a couple of dozen other American song writers, and the American lyrics of Caesar, De Sylva, Dietz, Dubin, Fields, Freed, Ira G., Hammerstein, Harbach, Harburg, Hart, Koehler, Mercer, Parish, Rose, and so many more, and the thousand-and-one memorable, uniquely American songs they had crafted and created in the first half of the twentieth century now nearing its close, and now and for a long while to come, more appreciated far from the land of their birth. And she woke and walked, and sat at the Deux Magots in the afternoon sunshine, and one fine day watched Joe Barry walking between the tables toward her ...

Coda: 198–

Generations of Sorbonne students have shortened the name boulevard St. Michel to Le Boul 'Mich'. But the name of the nightclub called The Boul 'Mich' is really a kind of play on words. The club is not named after the famed artery of the *Quartier Latin* near which it is situated, but after Michigan Boulevard in Chicago. The English-language article in the neon title is an obvious clue if anyone is looking for one, though it tends to get blurred in the bright Paris night. Even so, people find their way to this outpost of American jazz on the Left Bank whether they know the origin of the name or not—resident and visiting Americans looking for a home away from home, French lovers of *le jazz hot* also looking for something different to eat—the authentic seafood gumbo, New England clam chowder, hamburgers, caesar salad, and a few other American specialties of merit. In its fourth decade the place has become a kind of institution.

The sort of ensemble and solo jazz played at The Boul 'Mich' over the years has depended on available talent. Its policy has been to avoid high-cost transatlantic commitments and to provide instead, a haven for wandering American minstrels or indigenous European groups. It has managed to keep its prices low—low in

Paris in 198- being a relative term, of course—by paying decent, living wages to the musicians who work there, but not Hollywood or Las Vegas salaries.

The management leans toward more traditional music without closing its doors to the experimental. "Modern" jazz groups have played there, even "Free-jazz, New Thing" ensembles—if that is the word—on occasion, but it is swing and Dixieland (for lack of better one-word descriptions) that is mostly heard. The group currently in residence is a mixed sextet—trumpet, tenor sax or clarinet, vibraharp, piano, bass, and drums—played by one black American, a white American, a Frenchman, a German, and two Swedes. One of the Swedes, the vibraharpist, is a woman. An elderly black man, an American stride pianist, spells them at the breaks. The sextet plays a tasteful brand of muted swing early in the evening, that veers, somewhat coolly, cerebrally, in the direction of "modern," but in the last set, vibraharp dropping out, they switch to spirited Dixieland, echoes of the original New Orleans— Chicago ensemble jazz perennially popular with customers of all ages.

The Boul 'Mich' is not large but its barroom and main dining room have a spacious feeling simply because there are windows and because the rooms have never been crowded with too many tables. Special attractions sometimes draw a larger than usual stand-up crowd at the bar—which also has a view of the stage—but this overcrowding is inoffensive since it is a natural result of audience demand rather than management greed.

Now it is early on a June evening. Sunshine falls through the blinds, stripes the old, polished wood of the barroom floor, the floor of the main dining room. The rooms have nothing to fear from this exposure to daylight. They are clean, freshly painted, more like the rooms of the private residence this was, in the nineteenth century and the eighteenth as well.

The stride pianist is at work rippling through Waller and James P. Johnson standards, aiding early diners to digest their gumbo. There are only a few customers at the bar, among them a casually dressed American in his sixties who glances at his wristwatch, suggesting an appointment ahead. He looks up at an oil painting behind the bar, a portrait of a beautiful young girl seated at a piano, and speaks, in English, to the white-haired French barman who wears a very mournful expression.

"Even though her lips are closed she always looks to me as though she's just about to sing. Power of suggestion ..."

The barman looks up at the portrait, too, and his expression grows even sadder. His eyes fill with tears ...

Ben Sinclair, retired from the New York Times, free-lances now from his home in Gubbio, an Italian hill town, delaying year after year his permanent return to Savannah, Georgia (though he visits there from time to time), writing about travel, food, wine, music, the other arts, interviewing personalities, covering the scene from Egypt to Portugal.

Now he sits at the bar of The Boul 'Mich' commiserating with the barman with whom he has exchanged observations and philosophy on and off for over three decades.

"To leave us after so many years. Who can replace them?"

"No one," agrees Ben Sinclair.

"It simply seems time to go back," says Kitty Collins.

She stands beneath her portrait, painted by an American artist in the early 1950s, and in her sixth decade is still very much recognizable as the young girl in the painting she once was. As the artist had noted, the bone structure of her face would serve her well into middle age, old age.

Rex Wilkins and O. D. Turnipseed are dead, passed into legend, Rex of a frail constitution in his sixty-eighth year, Turnipseed a decade earlier of drugs and alcohol at forty-two. Drowned out by the louder, ruder bombardment of rock in the sixties and seventies (during those years he sought refuge on the faculty at UCLA and taught music theory to a lucky few), Pete Weathersby has enjoyed a revival in the eighties (he is in his seventies). When exhuming national treasures became fashionable, someone thought to put together a special about him and his celebrated sextet (long broken up, the others retired or playing here and there) on an educational TV channel that was repeated on a network at prime-time in the summer. The Washington Post did a feature spread on the front page of its Style section one day, and the New York Times included him in a Sunday retrospective that helped to keep the momentum going. Joe and Kitty featured him three times in the early eighties and always popular in Europe he had packed them in. Now he has formed with several younger stars a group called Two Generations—he and Rodney Blake, white-haired too, being the elder statesmen—which plays once or twice a year at the Smithsonian in Washington, and in Manhatten for a few months each year makes the rounds from Fat Tuesday's to Sweet Basil. Alone, he sometimes puts in an appearance at Hanratty's way uptown. Critics marvel at his iron chops, which he attributes to "clean living," and he is not being facetious.

Of the oldest generation, only Roberta and Sister Edmund are left. Sister Edmund is retired in England where her order originated. Roberta, remarkably, is coming out of retirement in the Virgin Islands to make a comeback in New York in her eighties. "For a limited engagement," she jokes. Harold Saunders, who married a Danish woman and lived many years in Europe, will be playing with her. Then Kitty and Joe will go on to a new career themselves.

"We've survived the rock and disco era," Kitty says, "and there seems to be a revival of jazz and my kind of theater and pop music. I have some offers, and I think I should do what I can to keep that revival going. Is it strong or is it fragile? I don't think we can take it for granted."

"Whenever I come back here," says Ben the friend, Ben the reporter, making notes, "I remember the dream you had—to have your own place—clean, not too big, not too crowded, where you and your friends could play and sing great music for the people you liked. And here it is."

"Without Joe, it would have stayed just a dream," Kitty says. "Without Joe, The Boul 'Mich' wouldn't have existed at all. That year before Joe came to Paris, from '47 to '48, he went all over Europe selling encyclopedias and mutual funds to servicemen and investing in the funds themselves, in property in Spain, to raise the rest of the money we needed to start the place, and he runs it. I have no head for business. It was his idea to offer not only the best American jazz, but also a few of the best American dishes. One thing I'll take credit for, though. I talked Joe into ending every evening by sitting in on trumpet for a couple of numbers when the band plays traditional jazz. Everybody loves that. Whatever it is, the formula works. It's worked for over thirty years in Paris. Fifty million Frenchmen can't be wrong. So we hope something like it will work in America, too..."

The elderly black stride pianist, a small man with a gentle face, is reminding himself of Earl Hines and Willie "The Lion" Smith. He plays "Rosetta," plans to go "Down Among the Sheltering Palms." Joe Barry busies himself with various tasks. Kitty and Ben sit at the bar.

"Let's see, what else?" Kitty asks herself aloud. "Billy's still with us as you can see, but he'll stay in Paris. His girl's here. Jane lives in Cambridge, Mass., with her husband, who's a microbiologist. Two kids—my only grandchildren so far. Jane plays cello in an amateur group. So we look forward to being closer to them."

"One thing I never got around to asking before," Ben says. "Sister Edmund's reaction to your marriage to Joe."

"Oh, Lord. She wouldn't speak to me for years! I had 'stolen another man's girl at the altar.' Which wasn't true but she was an old friend of Joe's mother who said that. Who never forgave me for not being a daughter. A daughter, of course, couldn't marry her son."

The stride pianist is still "Down Among the Sheltering Palms," but soon departs, and the sextet comes on stage, begins "Oh Lady Be Good," carries it through five minutes or so of collective and solo improvisation, and segues into several compositions of Billy Barry, in whose piano playing one can hear the influence of Bud Powell, Bill Evans, Jimmy Rowles, and perhaps Kitty Collins. It is an accomplished group—cool, inventive, satisfying for this hour of the evening—but Ben Sinclair waits for it to finish so that the evening star can appear.

Ben watches her walking through the tables toward the now empty, spotlit piano bench, and joins the applause when she appears suddenly in the light and begins to sing to him as she has been singing to him for forty years, her voice even richer than the last time he had heard her.

> *My journey's ended.*
> *Everything is splendid ...*

The voice of a lady, Ben Sinclair writes in his notebook. Traveled, worldly wise, but always a lady. Warmth, tenderness, a honeyed sound that gives a thrill, that causes an involuntary shiver, a secret smile, a little shake of the head ...
Joe Barry joins him.
"Ah, even after all this time, night after night, she still gets me," he says, a big, powerful man in late middle-age with a battered, Irish-American face.
"... what joys untasted ..."
... tingling in the scalp, lump in the throat, sweet pressure in the top of the chest, like falling in love ...

>... Here we are at last
>It's like a dream
>The two of us
>A perfect team ...

"That timbre that could only be hers," Joe Barry says. "A gift from God to the rest of us, to have something that sweet falling on the ear. Her pitch, her diction, her timing and phrasing and intonation and dynamics, make her as good as anyone in this business, but that timbre, that sound, is what makes her great. That and just being Kitty Collins. She came from nowhere and reinvented herself, like Wilson or Hawkins or Pete Weathersby or Rex and Roberta Wilkins reinvented songs."

Her performance over, with Ben Sinclair reluctantly preparing to leave, the sextet swinging into "That's a Plenty," Kitty says, "I love this place. What am I doing leaving it? It's just what I wanted. But it *is* time to go, and we'll set up something like it on the Cape, or maybe Newport. We have a lovely time, Joe and I, had it here, will have it there, anywhere."

"Isn't he good?" she asks, as her son solos on the piano. "Oh, I'm going to miss him. I can't seem to get away from having to miss someone wherever I am. But I've been lucky."

PROPERTY OF FRANKSTON DEPOT LIBRARY FRANKSTON TX